Accompaniment

Also by the Author

The Beyond the Tales Quartet

The Wanderers

The Storyteller and Her Sisters

The People the Fairies Forget

The Lioness and the Spellspinners

The Guardian of the Opera Trilogy

Book One: Nocturne

Book Two: Accompaniment

Book Three: Dawn Melody

Contributing Author

The Servants and the Beast

After the Sparkles Settled

Accompaniment

The Guardian of the Opera

Book Two

Cheryl Mahoney

Dedication

For Tiffany

The best cheerleader any artist could hope for.

Chapter One

I t was a long time before I stopped counting from the day Christine Daaé left the Opera Garnier, leaving both the Phantom and me behind.

It was six days after she left before I received her painfully brief farewell note, just over a week before the newspapers picked up the story of a beautiful soprano and two noblemen all disappearing at the same time. And that evening the Phantom of the Opera spoke to me for the first time in many years, when I was desperate and foolish enough to call his name in the empty auditorium.

He didn't speak graciously, not with any degree of friendliness in his tone, when he told me I might find him in Box Five after Saturday's performance, but still—he did speak to me. That hadn't happened since my first week at the Opera, six years ago when I was twelve years old, hopelessly new and lost, and he helped me find ballet practice. Five minutes that changed everything.

I didn't know yet, whether this more recent conversation with the Phantom was going to change anything.

I was looking out for him when I returned to the Opera Thursday morning for ballet practice, nine days after Christine had left. I walked up the wide stone steps facing the Avenue de l'Opera and through the enormous front doors with a thrill I hadn't felt since I was a child and everything was new. I moved easily among the streams of people, used to navigating the familiar crowd: elegant chorus members and quick-footed ballet girls, easy to distinguish by the way they walked, even if I hadn't known most of them; rough-clothed stagehands and thickly-muscled scenechangers; instructors and assistants and hurried servants, tending to the Opera's stars. Everyone had a role to play, everyone going about their own business.

The Phantom was certainly never to be seen walking amidst the crowds. Some legends said so, but I knew better. The tall, masked man I had met so few times might wear impeccable evening clothes, but he would never blend into a crowd.

I moved towards the grand staircase, the sweeping marble steps in the center of the Opera, and my gaze drifted up. Far up, roving the soaring pillars and gilded balconies encircling on three levels above. Everywhere in the Opera was covered in gilt and gold, in carvings of grinning faces or mythical figures. The Phantom was no more likely to be standing at a high balcony than to be strolling on the stairs, but somehow I still thought of him as being always overhead somewhere, always watching from some hidden spot above the rest of us. Even knowing Christine had gone to his home below the Opera, I couldn't shake the feeling.

I ascended the broad marble stairs, made my way through the richly decorated corridors towards ballet practice, and didn't spot any sign of the Phantom along the way. Which was really what I had expected.

In the high-ceilinged practice room, a handful of girls were already warming up at the long wooden barre, practicing *rond de jambs* or *grande battements* and the like. Far more were gathered together in clusters, excited chatter rising from their midst.

I hesitated in the doorway, fingering my small gold necklace. A few months ago I would have joined the circle talking easily enough, found out what the excitement was about. Today I was afraid I already knew. There had only been one favorite topic recently.

I struck a compromise, went to sit not too far from the crowd but not among them, and began unbuttoning my boots to change to my ballet slippers.

I heard the girls nearest me grow quiet, their gazes landing on me. And then Jammes said, "Good morning, Meg. Have you had any news from Christine?"

A harmless enough question, on its surface. But Jammes and I had never liked each other, and I knew this wasn't an overture of friendship. I slid one boot off, giving myself time to muster a smile before I looked up and met her gaze. "No, not yet," I said evenly. I already had a sinking feeling that I would be saying this a lot.

She assumed a dramatic pout. "Oh, what a pity—and I thought you were her closest friend."

I had thought so too. I tried to push down the doubt that kept creeping in. Christine *was* my friend. Leaving quickly, not saying good-bye—that didn't change things. Not really.

"Do you think she's *really* married to the Vicomte de Chagny?" Francesca, another ballet girl about my age, asked in eager tones. "I mean, everyone knows noblemen don't marry chorus girls."

"I think Raoul was very in love with Christine," I said, the best defense I could manage for my friend, when I knew Francesca was right. Noblemen didn't marry chorus girls. Or ballet girls.

"She probably just doesn't want to admit that she's his mistress," Jammes said in bored tones. "If he even decided to keep her after a first tumble."

I had thought I was growing less shocked by the venom unleashed against Christine since her dramatic disappearance, but now my cheeks grew hot. "Christine would not—"

"Or maybe she was the *Phantom's* mistress!" Francesca announced in a tone of delighted horror.

"Ghosts don't have mistresses," I snapped without thinking. He had been her Angel of Music, her singing instructor. And of course he had been in love with her—she had told me that, and it had been obvious enough. I had spoken with the Phantom so briefly, and it had still been obvious, when he told me not to repeat her name. But an unrequited love—that was all.

"How could she *stand* his glowing yellow eyes?" Francesca wondered aloud, as though I hadn't spoken.

And then they were all off and running on their favorite subject, the terrifying qualities and horrifying deeds of the dreadful Phantom of the Opera. I listened as I laced up my ballet slippers, with a confusion of feelings. Moments like this had always made me feel apart from the ballet girls. I knew they were nice girls, most of the time in most ways. But once they started on ghost stories, it was harder to see that. Perhaps, if I had never met the Phantom...but would I really want to tell sensational horror stories anyway? To find fun in telling dreadful tales?

And I *did* meet the Phantom. Long ago, and also just last night. That memory made me smile as I tied off the ribbons of my slipper, and gave me a feeling of separateness that, for a change, wasn't entirely unpleasant.

I skirted the edge of the crowd to take up a place at the barre, returning Adalisa's smile as I claimed the spot next to her. I began running through the positions to warm up my muscles, and just in time too. I was studiously practicing my *tendus*, working leg pointing behind me, when the voice of Madame Thibault, ballet mistress, rang through the room.

"Are you dancers or chickens? Enough clucking about and begin your work!"

I watched the room in the mirror beside me, watched the girls scatter as Madame Thibault, imposing with her long black dress and fierce eyes, strode through the midst of them. Soon the barre was crowded, and ballet practice began properly. We moved through the usual practice movements—*full plié* in first position, *grande battement* back and so on—and my thoughts drifted again.

Was the Phantom somewhere about? What was he doing? When would I manage to see him again?

And where was Christine? What wonderful new places was she exploring? Would I *ever* see her again?

I stifled a sigh, and brought my thoughts back to my dancing, though that was far less engaging.

When the lesson ended, I dressed in my blue-striped dress, donned my cloak and hat, and slipped out of the practice room too quickly for any more conversation about Christine. I descended a flight of stairs and made my way to the hall outside the first tier boxes. I glanced at Box Five, the Phantom's box—I had never walked through this hall without at least glancing at Box Five—but didn't stop. If I kept walking it was easier to resist temptation, even though I could practically feel the wood of the door against my fingertips, imagine pushing it open and…but I had to meet my mother, and he wouldn't be there now anyway.

At the far end of the hall my mother and the other boxkeepers were gathered. They'd had a business meeting, but by now it sounded like they were just discussing the news, though the snatches I heard were more about the recently crashed chandelier than about Christine.

It was only a moment before my mother detached from the group to join me.

"And how was ballet practice?" she asked, giving my hand a squeeze.

"Fine," I said, because what else could I say? Everyone's gossiping about my best friend and her scandalous disappearance?

Mother gave me a searching look suggesting that "fine" was not much of an answer, but didn't ask questions. We walked out together from the hall with the boxes and were nearly to the exit when a turn in the corridor brought us face-to-face with the managers of the Opera Garnier.

Both Monsieur Moncharmin and Monsieur Ricard promptly plastered on enormous smiles. "Madame Giry!" Ricard said with a clearly forced jollity. "And your lovely daughter. How lovely to see you both. Just…lovely."

"Monsieur Ricard. Monsieur Moncharmin," Mother said, as we both dipped into curtsies.

The managers had not generally been pleasant when they talked to us before—not when they demanded to know what Mother knew of the Phantom, just because she'd been his boxkeeper all these years, not when they fired her on the suspicion that she was involved in his pranks.

Even now, when Mother had been reinstated, I found my breath tightening. My muscles, tired from practice, went automatically taut to be in front of the management again. They were ridiculous men who held too much power in my world.

The conversation stayed almost eerily pleasant, as they offered up some remarks about the weather, and asked after Mother's health, and commented on the ballet, and finally Ricard said, "And have you any news about our, er, mysterious guest?"

Mother raised her eyebrows. "If you are referring to the Opera Ghost, I do not."

"Ah." Ricard exchanged an unhappy glance with Moncharmin. "We just thought that you might have heard from him last night."

"Why would you think that?" I asked, altogether too quickly, without thinking before I spoke.

Ricard and Moncharmin stared at me as though they had forgotten I could talk. This was about typical. Mother's gaze was distinctly searching and worried me more. I glanced away.

"It was our understanding," Moncharmin said at last, "that the Opera Ghost left letters in Box Five after performances. As his boxkeeper, naturally we thought you might have any...news."

"He did not leave a message last night," Mother said, still studying me too intently.

"And the ballet has not heard any news either?" Ricard said to me, with an attempt at a charming smile and a jovial laugh. "You ballet girls do love your dreadful stories about your Phantom."

"He's not my Phantom," I said, because he wasn't. One conversation hadn't changed that. But the managers were still looking at me, and I realized I hadn't answered the question. "And...I haven't heard any new stories."

"Ah. Well then." Ricard clasped his hands behind his back, rocked back and forth on his heels. "We were simply hoping to find out if all is...well."

"Because a new chandelier is *expensive*," Moncharmin burst out, "and if we're putting one up, we need to know he's not going to go dropping it again! Not to mention it will be very difficult to keep the police from poking about if a *second* chandelier falls. That would make it very hard to believe it was an accident!"

"But it wasn't his fault," I protested, and then quailed when their expressions both turned into searching, disapproving stares again. "Well…we don't *know* it was his fault…entirely."

I certainly wasn't going to tell them that I'd overheard the Phantom tell Philippe de Chagny that it was an accident, meaning he must have only meant it as a bluff. Saying that would mean I'd have to tell them that I saw him with Philippe, who was still missing, that I saw him carry Christine away below the Opera, that I knew more about this than I wanted anyone to know I knew.

"It *is* his fault we can't sell tickets," Moncharmin snapped, "because people think the roof might fall on them midway through Act Three. His recent actions have not been good for ticket sales! You can tell him that! And if he keeps this up, we won't be able to keep Commissaire Mifroid and his policemen from investigating and scaring people even more!"

"But of course we don't want to trouble him either," Ricard said hastily, clamping a hand around Moncharmin's arm. "You can tell him that too. We're taking care of things, nothing to get disturbed about."

"I can't tell him anything," I said faintly. I wondered if it was true. Would he really be in Box Five after Saturday's performance?

"Should he ever mention chandeliers," Mother cut in, voice so much more assured than mine, "I will certainly let you know. Good day, gentlemen." She took my arm, and off we swept down the hallway. Mother provided all the majesty. I wished I had half her regal dignity. I'd always hoped it was a trait I'd inherit as I grew up, but I was already eighteen and it hadn't appeared yet.

All the way out of the Opera, I waited. Finally, as we began the walk along the Boulevard des Capucines towards home, she asked, "When were you going to tell me what's going on?"

"I don't know what you mean." With an act of will I managed *not* to twist nervously at my skirt with my free hand.

"Why did you jump when they asked about communicating with the Phantom yesterday?"

I might have spun this out with denials. Only, I knew my mother, and that wouldn't work for long. So I gave up. "Yesterday, after I saw you in Box Five, I walked around some, then went back to the auditorium. I...said something to the Phantom. And he answered me. So he's not dead."

She had thought he was—or at least could be. That was half the reason I'd left Box Five in such a turmoil of emotions. I didn't want him to be dead, and I couldn't begin to explain why it mattered to me.

Mother ignored that remark anyway. I could feel how tense her arm had gone, still interlinked with mine. "He *answered* you. Out loud. In person."

I tried to keep my voice steady, as though all this was quite ordinary. "Yes. He stepped out of Box Five, so he must have gone there later on. He wanted to know how I knew his name, and I told him I saw it on a letter that Christine had." Should I tell her that I had told him I was lonely after Christine left, that I thought he might be lonely too? No—maybe not. I tried to brazen it through. "Anyway, he said he knew I'm friends with Christine, and—and that if I ever want to talk to him, he's usually in Box Five after Saturday performances." I didn't *quite* get it out without a stumble. It was such an extraordinary, impossible thing. And I had no expectation that Mother would think it as grand a thing as *I* did.

I had tried to make him sound friendlier, not as off-putting as he had actually been. I definitely shouldn't tell her that he had described himself as the villain in the story.

Judging from the quality of her silence, my best efforts hadn't helped.

"And I suppose," she said at last, words tightly controlled, "the idea of talking to him in Box Five on Saturday night does not strike you as the least bit dangerous?"

"*You* talk to him in Box Five," I said swiftly, an argument I had anticipated making. "You have for years."

"It is not the same thing at all."

"It's close enough. And besides, what indications do we really have that he's dangerous?" I disentangled my arm from hers, began to tick points off on my fingers. "Christine and Raoul left together and are fine."

"I would feel better if you had actually spoken to her rather than just receiving a letter."

I stopped counting, still on my first finger. "Yes, so would I, but I don't see what that has to do with it." Christine couldn't bother to visit before leaving the country, but that didn't say anything at all about the Phantom. That only said something about Christine, maybe, but really it wasn't worth dwelling on and I wasn't thinking about it anymore anyway.

"If you had actually seen her, rather than trying to interpret a brief letter—"

"Oh Mother, really!" We were in serious trouble if my practical-minded mother was going to start listening to conspiracy theories. "The ballet girls might have wild ideas, but I know Christine's handwriting and there was nothing to interpret; she *said* she was fine." I resumed counting points. "The Phantom also rescued Marie from Buquet when he attacked her backstage. He's always been polite to you while you've been his boxkeeper. He helped me get to ballet practice all those years ago when we first came here."

"He lives under an opera house and pretends to be a ghost!" Very, very rarely did my mother raise her voice.

"So he's *unusual*."

"To put it mildly," she said, voice already controlled again. She took a deep breath, gaze fixed on the distance. "I will obviously not be able to talk you out of this idea, so I am strongly suggesting that you be careful."

"And I will be." I rolled my eyes, though privately I had worried she'd raise far more objections. It was true she couldn't talk me out of this, but I hadn't expected her to accept that fact. "I'm not thinking about taking a European tour with him. I just want to talk to him in a box at the Opera, where I will be five feet from a door the entire time, with a crowded hallway beyond it."

She was still frowning deeply. "If you are going to talk to him directly after Saturday's performance, I want you to meet me in the corps de ballet's changing room no more than forty-five minutes after the closing curtain. Forty-five minutes exactly, and if you're not there I will go straight to Commissaire Mifroid and his policemen patrolling the Opera."

"Yes, Mother, fine." I sighed. "Are you going to react this way about every man I want to talk to?"

"Possibly. And certainly the *unusual* ones."

Excerpt from the Private Notebook of Jean Mifroid, Commissaire of Police

10 Mar 1881

Continuing investigation into disappearance of Comte Philippe de Chagny, Vicomte Raoul de Chagny, Christine Daaé. Second interview of de Chagny housekeeper on 9 Mar, confessed to seeing RdC and CD on morning of 2 Mar. Last known sighting of RdC and CD. Expressed plans to leave country, consistent with letter received by M. Giry. Still tracing leads re: travel, current whereabouts.

Housekeeper provided no further info re: PdC. No additional sightings after evening of 1 Mar, at Opera Garnier. If abducted, no ransom. Murder?

Suspects:

RdC - Motive: inheritance? Interference with proposed marriage to CD? Opportunity: Last seen by myself seeking PdC at Opera, emotional state extreme at time. Capability: Possible, with weapon.

CD – Motive: Same as RdC. Opportunity: Also at Opera at time of PdC disappearance. Capability: Slight physical strength, unknown ability with weapons.

Cloaked man seen with PdC on stage – so-called Opera Ghost? – Motive: Unknown. Opportunity: Likely. Capability: Unknown.

Also continuing investigation into fallen chandelier. Evidence points to sabotage. Connection between sabotage and disappearance of PdC? Connection to long-standing legend of Opera Ghost?

Chapter Two

I was desperately nervous by the time the performance curtain closed Saturday evening. I wished I could change out of my ballet outfit before going to Box Five, only I didn't dare take the time. I'd have to go to the ballet's shared changing room, which would be a madhouse right after a performance, and I'd probably get caught by someone in conversation, and then I'd have to come all the way back to the auditorium, and by then he might have vanished. Plus I only had forty-five minutes before Mother would contact the army and the navy and who knew what else.

So I just threw my blue cloak on over my white ballet skirt and tried to look at it logically. If he had been paying any attention at all, he'd already seen me in this outfit countless times. We girls ran around the Opera in our dance costumes all the time.

I separated from the other girls as we streamed out of the auditorium, and made my way to the hall outside the first-level boxes. It was busy with guests, departing or making their way to the Foyers. I glanced at one woman's long silk dress with a twinge of envy. Even if I'd had time to change into my nicest dress, it wasn't that nice.

Never mind—he knew I was a dancer, so why shouldn't I be dressed like one?

No one seemed to be watching me, but I still had to force myself not to be furtive as I opened the door to Box Five. Guests would find no significance in Box Five, and all the Company knew my mother was boxkeeper here; as long as I didn't act suspicious, no one else would be. Inside, the box was dimly lit by one low gaslight, curtains drawn, and I leaned against the closed wooden door as my eyes adjusted.

I could see a silhouette in one of the front row seats, and my heart pounded harder.

"You actually came," he remarked, nothing in his tone to indicate how he felt about it.

"So did you," I observed, and relinquished my tight grip on the door handle. I walked forward at a carefully even pace, as carefully as I might count steps on stage, trying to preserve an outward calm I didn't feel. He was actually *here*, this impossible man I'd hardly more than glimpsed in so many years. He had actually waited in Box Five to see *me*.

"I would have been here anyway," he said, and though his voice was as perfectly modulated as ever, the emotion was absolutely flat.

A sharp reminder not to build too much on this, not to hope too high. I halted at the end of the front row. "If you'd rather I left, I will."

"I didn't say that," he said, and I took that as enough of an encouragement to sit down in the seat nearest to me. That put us at opposite ends of the four-seat row. "As long as you're here you may as well stay," he continued, and looked away towards what seemed to me to be distinctly uninteresting red velvet curtains. He was wearing a full-face mask today, a cream-colored one hiding everything except his eyes, mouth and chin. That made four I'd seen, plus the skull one he'd worn at Mardi Gras—and just before carrying Christine away. A different mask every time, more masks than I had dresses. "What did you want to talk about?"

Evidently he was still going to be the unfriendly man who spoke to me in the auditorium, not the charming one who had led me to ballet practice as a child. I should have expected it, and I wasn't going to let the fact of it now flatten me—at least not enough to show. I lifted my chin and pretended to confidence I only half felt. "Should I assume you won't explain how you manage the glowing skeleton illusion?"

"Maybe it's not an illusion."

Despite the forbidding tone, I found the comment encouraging. It reminded me of our first conversation so many years ago, when he had claimed to light a candle using magic. "Very well. Then we could talk about tonight's performance."

I had to start somewhere. I couldn't just leap in with asking why he haunted the Opera, and what had happened to Christine, and where had he learned to sing, and did he have any friends, and had he been an Angel of Music for anyone else, and...no, better to start somewhere safe. "What did you think of the understudy lead ballerina? She's warmer in the role than Sorelli."

Sorelli, our longstanding lead ballerina, had taken to her bed since the Comte de Chagny's disappearance. I tried to feel sorry for her, though I couldn't imagine how anyone could be fond of the blustering, abrasive Comte de Chagny. She had been his mistress for years, though; perhaps it wasn't only a question of money for her after all.

"Mademoiselle Laurent cannot do as many *fouettés* in succession." A pause. "But she did bring more warmth to the character."

So we talked about the performance, and the ballet, and the Company. He knew all about everyone I named, seemed to have a working knowledge of ballet at least equal to my own and definitely knew more about music and singing than I did.

It wasn't a terrible conversation. It *was* stilted and strained and a great deal of effort, enough that for a good while I was sure I was going to wind up going home and crying in sheer frustration and disappointment. I played with my necklace and rethought my years of conviction that he would be fascinating if I could just talk to him. That perhaps then I'd learn some clue to the mystery of the Phantom.

But eventually, somehow, we got off on the subject of music more generally, and the relative merits of Ravel, Mozart and Debussy, though he didn't seem to want to talk about Bizet, and the conversation became easier—and more interesting, if still impersonal.

I watched him covertly as we talked, though I probably needn't have tried to hide it. He rarely looked at me, keeping his gaze on the curtains closing off the box, just as though they were open and a performance was going on. When he did look at me, it was a quick glance that slid away again at once, almost before I could glimpse the green of his eyes. What was he thinking, in those moments?

My own eyes had long since adjusted to the dim light, and I could see that his dark evening clothes were as immaculate as they had been the day I met him six years before. Whatever grief he felt about Christine leaving, he wasn't showing it in a disheveled appearance. Why did a man no one ever saw care what his clothes looked like anyway?

His mask hid so much of his face that I quickly dismissed it as a place to learn anything about his thoughts or his mood. I found myself watching his hands instead.

When I had first come in, his hands had been closed around the arms of his seat. It took some time, in the shadows, for me to realize how tightly he was gripping them.

Not so calm after all.

As we talked about music, first one hand and then the other rose, sketching points in the air. He had long fingers, the right hands for a man who played the pipe organ, as Christine had told me he did. I could almost see the notes in the air as his hand flowed through a crescendo. His voice had grown warmer too. Not enthusiastic. Barely even friendly. But at least there was a hint of interest.

Eventually we slipped off to Italian opera, by way of Verdi, and he made a remark about Rome that didn't sound like it came second-hand.

"Have you been to Rome?" I asked, without stopping to think first or I might not have chanced a personal question. I knew intellectually that he couldn't have sprung into existence the day the Opera Garnier opened, but I had never been able to picture him anywhere else. It wasn't the *most* intriguing question I could have asked, but it was the only one I'd had any opening for.

He took a long time to answer, long enough for me to regret trying even this question.

"Yes," he said at last, hands stilled on the arms of his chair again, voice not hostile but not enthused either. "Years ago."

One tiny puzzle piece in the Phantom's history. Perhaps that made me reckless enough to say, "I'd *love* to go to Rome. What did you see there?" Surely that couldn't be considered prying. But so help me, if he just said 'a lot of buildings,' I was going to scream.

The Phantom of the Opera, however, was not the Vicomte de Chagny, who circumnavigated the globe and could only tell me that he saw a lot of water. The Phantom told me about the Coliseum and the Piazza del Campidoglio, the Theatre of Marcellus and the ceiling of the Sistine Chapel, and the musical advancements of the Accademia Nazionale di Santa Cecilia. His hands drew shapes in the air, pillars and arches and towers that I could nearly see, suspended between his fingertips. Even if that did add up to mostly a lot of buildings, and even if I didn't follow all of it, enough was interesting to leave me genuinely reluctant when I realized my allotted time was up.

"I have to be going," I said, rising to my feet. "Mother will be expecting me." He didn't need to know quite how urgent that expectation was.

"I suppose they missed you in the Dance Foyer," he remarked, without looking at me.

I considered the question seriously. People would have been friendly if I'd been there, but I couldn't think of anyone who would be actively looking for me. If Christine was still here…but she was gone. For eleven days now. "No. Probably not."

He didn't comment—and didn't stand when I did, though etiquette dictated he should.

I had taken two steps when his next words snapped out, suddenly tense, "Did she ask you to talk to me?"

He was staring at the curtains, hands once more tight on the arms of his seat, and that tension told me that he could only mean Christine. Though who else could he have meant anyway? Nothing told me what answer he wanted—but I did know that this question was hard for him to ask, that he was waiting for this answer with more intense attention than he had given to any part of our conversation.

I told him the truth. "No."

I heard him exhale, saw his shoulders drop just a fraction though his fingers were still closed around his chair arms. Would it make me feel any better, if I thought Christine had told someone to watch out for me? Would I be disappointed to find out she hadn't? "I'm sorry, if you hoped—"

"I told you before," he said coldly, "I do not want your charity."

"And *I* told you, that isn't what this is." Though just at the moment, I wasn't sure what it was. For a moment or two, it had felt like friendship.

When he didn't speak again, I repeated, "I have to be going." And, I supposed, I wouldn't be coming back. I wasn't exactly sure what I was offering, but he didn't seem to want it. He didn't look at me as I made my way towards the back of the box, more slowly than I really needed to walk.

I was nearly within reach of the door when he said at last, words tantalizingly dragged out, "I suppose, if you can tear yourself away from the Foyer again...I'm usually here after the Saturday performances. If you cared to stop by again."

My throat tightened, my heartbeat quickening. So it wasn't over, whatever this strange adventure was. Not yet.

I thought of saying something equally noncommittal and unenthused. We could have gone on that way forever, though, and what was the point? "I would be delighted," I said with a smile. And then with great daring, I added, "Thank you for a very nice conversation, Erik."

It was the first time I had called him by name, discounting my one desperate call in the auditorium that had started all this. It would mean nothing with anyone else I knew. But even this quickly, I was beginning to realize that *nothing* meant nothing with this so unusual man. I slipped out of the box before I could see how he took it.

I leaned against the closed door for a moment, smile still on my face. Everything I had ever dreamed? No, not even close. Intriguing? Yes.

I hadn't learned about Christine's departure or about the Phantom's history, and I had learned a lot I never knew I wanted to know about Rome. But I had *talked* to the Phantom of the Opera. And perhaps next time...?

I walked down the hallway, now much emptier, towards the ballet's changing rooms to meet Mother. I wished I could tell Christine about this.

I rethought that at once—it would be so complicated, considering Christine's history with the Phantom. But I did want to tell *someone*, someone who was a close friend who'd be excited with me and willing to discuss all the details and all the might be's about the future. Mother wouldn't understand.

I wished I could tell my sister. But Gabrielle had died six years ago, when she was nine and I was twelve. I twisted my gold necklace, the little medallion with a G on it that had been Gabi's.

If I could really have one wish, it would be for the people I cared about most to stop departing suddenly from my life.

Baffling. The Phantom found the entire situation baffling. He leaned back in his seat in Box Five, listened absently to the distant footfalls and conversation forming the usual melody of the Opera in the hallway outside the box, and tried to make sense of the past hour.

Meg Giry wasn't afraid of him, and that was alarming. Perhaps it shouldn't have entirely surprised him—she was Madame Giry's daughter, and he had always tried to maintain cordial relations with his boxkeeper. It still unsettled him, a ballet girl who wasn't afraid of him. He had always depended on those girls to go into shrieks of terror every time he did anything; it set the right tone.

He might overlook her lack of fear—but her idea about talking to him. She had claimed it was because she was lonely, and thought he might be too.

He had thought he was used to loneliness. He had lived alone under the Opera Garnier for almost seven years, accustomed to watching, never interacting directly. He had accepted that. Until *she* came, until he gave way to the mad desire to really live, to the wild hope that perhaps love was not so impossible a dream—

He halted himself there, fingers tightening painfully on the arms of his seat. Because of course it *had* been impossible. She had left him. It had been ten days, twenty-three hours, a relentless count that would only keep growing and growing, day dragging after silent day, as he sat in his rooms that were paradoxically so empty and so filled with loneliness that space hardly remained for him.

So yes. Meg Giry was right about that.

That didn't mean that she *knew* she was right, or even that she was sincere.

That seemed extraordinarily unlikely, that she could genuinely want to talk to him out of friendly motivations. He had come to Box Five partially trying to make sense of it all. But he had come even more because, if this was an elaborate trap, it was a less direct way to kill himself than leaping from the rooftop. Surely the eternal guilt would be assigned to Commissaire Mifroid, should the police descend on him.

He couldn't bring himself to end his life directly, but this could have been an escape from the stage. Without such an escape, he might live another fifty years. He was not quite halfway through the Bible's promised three-score and ten, which seemed at the moment more like a curse than not. And what was the point of it all, now that *she* was gone? What was left to him but pain and hopeless longing?

And apparently, inexplicable conversations about Rome.

No trap, nothing suspicious and no explanations. He tapped his fingers against the arm of his seat, almost disappointed by the lack of sinister undertones. And yet it was inconceivable that Meg Giry could prefer sitting in Box Five discussing Roman architecture, when she could be in the Dance Foyer flirting with handsome subscribers. Impossible.

She couldn't possibly, since no one ever wanted to talk to him. He was a duty to the Daroga, the retired Persian police chief who had felt responsible for him ever since saving his life. Charles Garnier had been gone for years, passing out of his life once their building was complete. And *she* had left him too. Apparently without a merciful attempt to provide him with the charitable interest of her closest friend. Perhaps that was just as well though—Meg could certainly never be any substitute.

This had been nothing like that, like being with *her*—none of the passion, the fire. That had all burned itself into ashes.

She was gone and nothing was left and in the face of that, an idle conversation with a little ballet girl about Rome was scarcely important at all. And that was better. Safer. Much safer for everyone.

Chapter Three

T uesday morning, two weeks after Christine left, I slipped out directly after rehearsal to walk home alone. I didn't want to listen to any new stories about Christine. Everyone seemed to be on best behavior during Lent (perhaps even the Phantom, who had been quiet), and with no new food for the gossipers, she remained the favorite scandal. I hadn't been to the Dance Foyer Saturday night, since I had met Erik instead, and I had avoided it after Monday night's performance too. No one appeared to notice, or try to stop me when I slipped away on Tuesday.

I didn't want to bump into Commissaire Mifroid either, who was stalking around the Opera looking like a thundercloud in uniform. Rumor had it he was still investigating the Comte de Chagny's disappearance, though the stories varied wildly about what he was finding out. I didn't want to learn it first-hand.

I had made my escape, apparently unobserved, and was two blocks away from the Opera when a soft voice behind me said, "Mademoiselle Giry?"

Not Commissaire Mifroid, and not the most exciting voice it could have been—though I wouldn't have expected him out on the Boulevard de Capucines—but with its foreign tang, it still set off a ripple of interest in me as I turned around. "I've been wanting to talk to you!" I said without thinking.

The Persian cocked one eyebrow beneath his red fez, face otherwise perfectly impassive. He haunted the Opera in his own way, a much more visible, less magical but almost equally odd specter. He was always lurking about with no apparent purpose, and though the whole Company seemed convinced he possessed the Evil Eye, no one ever ordered him out. Though maybe that was why.

I had always wondered about him—and then on *the* night, the night Christine left, I had heard him call the Phantom by name. No one else ever did. One more tiny answer, raising a host of new questions about this exotic stranger.

The Persian seemed incongruous standing on the sidewalk in the bright sunlight, both of us halted outside a perfectly ordinary bakery as the streams of passersby parted to flow around us. Gaze on mine, he said, "I am not the only one you have wanted to talk to recently."

I blinked, suddenly both derailed and feeling vaguely accused. With the weight he gave the words, he could only mean one person. I didn't bother with denials or equivocations, sure he'd see through them. "True," I said, trying to pitch my voice as calm and cool as his. "How did you learn about it?" Maybe Erik had told him. The idea made me uncomfortable, although Roman architecture had hardly been a personal discussion.

The mere fact of a conversation—somehow that felt much more personal than its content.

The Persian inclined his head slightly, dark face still impassive. "I make it a habit to observe what goes on at the Opera. Especially with regard to our most mysterious Company member. Are you sure it is wise to become involved?"

I had already heard that a dozen times from Mother, and the Persian had far less right to ask the question. I folded my arms, kept my chin high. "Why don't you tell me whether it is or not? What happened the night Christine left the Opera?"

It was easier to ask the Persian than to ask Erik himself, although I still might have lost my nerve if I had tried to come at the question more slowly.

As it was, the Persian clasped his hands behind his back, rocked slightly on his heels and continued studying me solemnly. "Mistakes were made by everyone involved, threats were spoken but not carried out, and in the end Erik allowed Mademoiselle Daaé and the Vicomte de Chagny to leave together."

Well—that was more than I knew before, although it was slim on details. It contained more implications than actual facts. Threats of what kind, and if he *allowed* them to leave in the end, didn't that suggest at some point leaving hadn't been an option? My reckless courage had dissipated and now it seemed harder to ask any more questions in the face of that intent gaze. I played with the ribbons of my hat, tied beneath my chin and tried—but probably failed—to keep my uncertainty off my face.

"He is not a man to be underestimated," the Persian said slowly, "or ever to be taken lightly."

"Obviously." Surely no one who had ever met him could make that mistake. Hadn't I kept giving that same warning to Christine, back before everything had come apart? Maybe if she had listened to me, while he was still being an Angel, before she'd let him overhear her accept the vicomte's marriage proposal, things would have gone better. Maybe she would still be in Paris right now.

"And do not convince yourself that he cannot be dangerous."

I knew that too, whatever I wanted Mother to believe. I had watched Buquet die. Though I knew it was an accident, knew that Buquet had been a villain worse than most opera baritones, I had still seen a dark strain in the Phantom that night that I couldn't forget. "What are you saying?" I asked abruptly. "Are you telling me I should avoid him?"

"You probably should." His matter-of-fact tone made the words seem all the more harsh. They weren't what I had wanted or expected to hear.

"I thought you were his friend," I protested, wanting whatever reassurance that confirmation would give.

The Persian's gaze drifted into the middle distance. "It might be more accurate to say that I am the closest thing Erik has to a friend."

The words hung in the air, seeming too heavy to be sharing space with Parisian walkers and the scent of baking bread. I twisted at my necklace, searched for an appropriate response, some way to put into words my ache of sympathy, my sudden pang of loneliness. "That's very sad," I said finally, inadequately.

His gaze met mine again, and a small, mirthless smile creased his face. "I am close enough to a friend to realize that. Erik does not...form attachments easily or casually. And life has already hurt him, too many times." The tiny smile vanished. "So if you are simply seeking diversion or personal gain under a false appearance of goodwill, you are looking in the wrong place."

"That's not it at all," I said, stung by the implication that I could be that mercenary, that uncaring. I knew it wasn't like that—even if it would be much harder to explain just what I *was* looking for.

Though maybe it wasn't complicated. Maybe I just wanted a friend.

The Persian sighed faintly. "I did not really expect you were. It would have been easier in some ways. Instead—I can only say this is *probably* highly inadvisable. But..." He lifted one hand, palm up, and shrugged. "...who knows? And all I can recommend is that you be careful." Then he bowed slightly, turned, and began to walk away.

"Monsieur!" I called after him, having not the slightest idea what his name was. I had so many questions, and the one that came out might not have been the most important. "Are you worried about me—or about Erik?"

He looked back over his shoulder, eyebrow raised again, and said, "Yes." He turned, and continued his steady tread away.

The rustle of Madame Giry's skirts and the rhythm of her footsteps were as familiar as an old song as she moved about Box Five setting up for Wednesday evening's performance. The sweep of cloth removing dust from the railing, the riffle of paper and a slight thunk as she set out the program, the murmur of the heavy drapes as she pulled them closed.

The Phantom noticed that the tempo was off, a faster beat than usual. Perhaps she had somewhere else to go.

He waited for the door to open, for her to go out and leave the box to him, so that he could come out of his cramped hiding place in the back corner pillar. The sound didn't come.

"Monsieur Phantom, I need to speak with you."

Did anyone else ever call him 'Monsieur Phantom?' It was always just *the* Phantom, like he was a creature, not a man.

The tap of one foot, audible even against the plush carpet. "We both know you're here. Kindly don't waste time by pretending otherwise."

What was it about the Girys? Where did they get the idea they could just turn up and make demands on him? He swallowed a sigh. For years everyone had been perfectly satisfied leaving him alone; now they had to intrude on him, when he wanted even less to have anything to do with anyone, now that the only person he wanted to see had gone away forever. Thirteen days and nineteen hours had gone by. He had ventured out so rarely, and yet he seemed to be bothered by some Giry every time.

Perhaps he could end this now. He projected his voice to the leftmost seat in the front row, as though someone was sitting there. "What is it?"

"No, that won't do," she said, no change in the pitch of her voice to indicate she'd even turned her head. "I will not speak with a disembodied voice."

Then they would not speak, because *he* wasn't coming out.

After a silent moment, one of the front seats creaked as she sat down. That would put her back towards the pillar, deliberately or not. He had never been sure if she knew where he hid. "Very well. I can wait."

She couldn't. She wasn't exclusively his boxkeeper; she had other duties to do. If she sat here long enough she was going to get into trouble with the management. She had only recently been reinstated, and he had no desire to go through the hassle of a new boxkeeper all over again. Just at the moment, that seemed like a level of effort that was utterly insurmountable. Though just at the moment, most things seemed that way.

Sighing aloud, Erik stepped out of the pillar. Once the entrance was closed again, he walked to another seat, deliberately making his footsteps audible so she would know he was there. "You had something to say?" he said, sitting down two seats away from her.

No gasp, no other indication she was at all surprised. "You spoke with my daughter after Saturday's performance."

Of course. What else could this be about? "And you want me to stop," he said, resigned. Why should anything even faintly positive stay in his life? But really, what did it matter? "Very well, I won't bother her further and—"

"My daughter is a grown woman, and the days when I could control whom she could and could not see have passed," Madame Giry interrupted, voice stern. "I will not claim to be pleased about this, but I am not in a position to forbid you to speak with her."

That made no sense at all. "Then why did you want to talk to me?"

Her voice had a dark timbre to it, resounding, confident, not a spark of lightness to leaven its intensity. "I wanted to tell you that if you ever hurt my daughter, I will kill you."

Erik's hands tightened on the velvet of the seat arms. "Are you threatening me, Madame Giry?"

"If you have to ask the question, I have not been clear enough. If you ever, in any way, harm my daughter—"

"Do you know what happens to people who threaten me?"

"Do you know what happens to people who hurt my daughter?"

It was less the words and more the tone, the absolute, unyielding hardness backing those words up. He knew how to put steel into his voice, but this woman had diamonds in hers. He subsided. "I have no intentions of hurting her." He had no intentions of any sort, on any subject, with regard to anyone. And he still believed some lines should not be crossed.

"Good. I did not think it was probable. But I would prefer it to be as unlikely as possible. I do not know what happened with regard to Mademoiselle Daaé—"

Everything in him went cold. "I will not discuss that," he said through clenched teeth. Threats were one thing, but this was something else. If she thought she could just come in here and talk about *her*—

"Nor am I interested in discussing the matter," Madame Giry said, with no apology and an astonishing degree of dismissal. "I wish only to point out that, unlike Mademoiselle Daaé, Meg is not without a friend, relative or protector. If she ever comes home scared or bruised or worse, you will answer to me."

He believed her. He hadn't the slightest idea how she could do anything to him, but that mattered not at all. She would find a way.

Discomfort gave way to a reluctant admiration. She was magnificent, really. The intensity, the ferocity—it was primal, nature's highest imperative, the mother defending her young. What would that be like, to have someone unleash that kind of power on your behalf?

His mother had never possessed those instincts, not about him.

"I understand," he said at length.

"Excellent." Cloth rustled as she rose to her feet. "I'm glad we had this conversation, Monsieur Phantom."

That made exactly one of them. Without looking, he tracked her footsteps until she was at the door of the box, and then he said, "Madame Giry?"

The steps halted.

"Meg is fortunate in her mother."

The door handle clicked as she turned it. "Let us hope she will prove equally fortunate in her friends."

The door opened and shut, and very swiftly her steps in the hall beyond faded into the background melody of activity at the Opera. Erik sank back in his seat, not knowing whether to be impressed or irritated or just baffled by it all.

Perhaps he should be flattered. He didn't entirely believe that she was so powerless to put a stop to this if she wanted to. In a way, choosing merely to threaten him with death if he stepped out of line was probably a mark of trust.

She didn't need to worry. He had no desire to harm Little Meg Giry, and there certainly would be no repeat of the recent debacle. He had lost his head long enough to make ill-advised changes to the chandelier's structural supports, to carry *her* off below to his own realm—but that madness had burned out in her leaving. The cold ashes of grief left him no inclination towards mad, emotional impulses. He was done with that kind of passion. The only person who could inspire that in him was gone.

He could certainly see no reason he would ever want to turn the Opera Garnier upside-down about Meg.

Chapter Four

Excerpt from the Private Notebook of Jean Mifroid, Commissaire of Police

18 Apr 1881

Exhaustive inquiries, still no evidence PdC ever left Opera Garnier. Chances of finding alive dropping. Growing convinced was murdered on premises.

Opera Company full of usual Phantom superstitious nonsense—but someone broke the chandelier. Connection to PdC disappearance? Cloaked man on stage? Real man behind Phantom stories?

The weeks ticked by, counting off more and more days since Christine had left, and life settled into a new, strange kind of normal. The ballet girls were still talking about Christine, the managers were still being polite, and the Phantom hadn't yet returned to his usual letter-dropping and flickering lights—but he kept meeting me in Box Five.

Five and a half weeks after Christine left also marked the fifth Saturday since I had first met Erik in Box Five. My thoughts were already flying ahead to our planned meeting as we finished the evening's performance, as I fastened my cloak in the midst of the other girls backstage.

"Are you coming to the Dance Foyer tonight?" Adalisa asked me, sitting nearby as she unlaced her ballet slippers. "It's been *weeks*."

"No, I don't think so," I said, and shrugged when she looked disappointed. I couldn't explain my other appointment—but I had another reason that was also valid. "You know they'll all be going on about Christine. I hear it enough at practices and rehearsals."

"They don't all talk about Christine all the time," Adalisa said.

"They do when *I'm* around," I muttered. Either they wanted my opinion on the latest theory, or they wanted to ask if she'd contacted me.

I didn't want to hear the latest theory, and she hadn't contacted me.

Adalisa didn't contradict this time. But she smiled what might have been a sly smile, if she wasn't so nice. "I'm sure I saw a friend of yours there last Saturday. That subscriber who was friends with the Vicomte de Chagny—the one with those blue eyes?"

"Léon," I said, before thinking that maybe I shouldn't have been so prompt. I tried to prevaricate. "I think you probably mean Léon de Troyes."

Christine had introduced us—sometimes everything in my life seemed to link back to Christine—but I was mostly remembering the last time I'd seen Léon. The masquerade. When I had thought I might never see him again, since Mother didn't have her job back yet and we were making plans to leave Paris. I remembered the moonlit balcony where I had let him kiss me, even though I probably shouldn't have—but it was Mardi Gras.

"Yes, that's the one," Adalisa said eagerly. "*He* won't be talking about Christine."

He might. Everyone seemed to. I wasn't sure if I wanted to go and find out. "I'm sure he doesn't even remember me," I said, trying to sound casual. "I haven't seen him in weeks."

Our paths hadn't crossed. I'd been avoiding the Foyer, and he hadn't sought me out. When I hadn't been too taken up with the mystery of Christine, or excitement about the Phantom, I had thought now and then that he should have. That surely he would have, if he liked me as much as he'd seemed to at the masquerade. But he never had, and I couldn't seek him out myself. It was bad enough that I'd let him kiss me. If I went chasing after him…I knew what that would look like.

Anyway, it was irrelevant. I had an appointment with Erik in Box Five, and I wasn't going to miss that for a chance at meeting a man who hadn't bothered to look for me all these weeks.

"I really can't tonight," I concluded. "I have to go and meet Mother." Not for forty-five minutes, but I didn't need to clarify that.

"Oh, she won't mind if you come to the Foyer for a bit," Adalisa urged.

Since I was running out of ways to refuse, for just an instant it was a relief to hear a man's voice say, "Mademoiselle Giry, may I have a word?"

Then I turned, saw who it was, and stopped feeling relieved. Commissaire Mifroid, notebook out, looking serious.

As though a vacancy had been left for a local ghost, Commissaire Mifroid seemed to be haunting the Opera Garnier as thoroughly as the Phantom had ever done. The police officer was always about now, occasionally interviewing someone but mostly just watching, with a kind of fierceness in his eyes I'd never seen before. I had worked hard at avoiding him up until now.

"Commissaire," I said, curtsying slightly and inwardly regretting not leaving here sooner. Most of the other girls had already left, and I felt rather like the lone gazelle who'd lost the protection of the herd.

I glanced at Adalisa, who was hesitating nearby, ballet slippers in hand.

Mifroid looked too and added, "A private word, if you please."

I gave a half-smile to Adalisa, a signal that it was all right, and she grimaced sympathetically and slipped away. It was sort of all right. I wasn't afraid of the commissaire—but this wasn't going to be a pleasant conversation. And if it went on too long—with a jolt I remembered Erik, sitting in Box Five. What would he think? How long would he wait, if I was late?

Make this fast. "You wished to discuss something, Commissaire?" I asked quickly. "My mother is expecting me."

Mifroid looked at me over his notebook, eyes intent. He used to look at all the Opera Company as though we were slightly amusing, nothing to take seriously. I hadn't always liked that—but now I missed it. Intense interest from the police was more alarming. "You are aware, I expect, that we are continuing to investigate the disappearance of the Comte de Chagny, and the circumstances surrounding the last night he was seen?"

Of course I was aware, and why was he wasting time telling me what he assumed I knew? "Yes," I said, briefly.

"At this time," he continued, "we have not been able to locate either Mademoiselle Daaé or the Vicomte de Chagny. The letter you received from Mademoiselle Daaé is one of the few pieces of evidence suggesting they left the country voluntarily, and is one reason we are not regarding them as missing persons as well."

I *knew* all this, and it was all I could do not to tap my foot. I needed to get to Box Five! "Mm-hmm."

"Have you received any further communication from Mademoiselle Daaé?"

"No," I said flatly. The police commissaire didn't have the nasty tone Jammes would have given the question, or the voyeuristic interest many of the ballet girls would have shown—but I still didn't want to talk about the subject. It wasn't enough that my best friend couldn't be bothered to remember me with any letter after she left the country; everyone around me had to keep *reminding* me about it. I reached up to touch my necklace.

I couldn't hope to hear from Gabi, and that made it both easier and harder.

The commissaire made a note in his book, though I didn't see how a lack of a letter was of much use to him. "Did Mademoiselle Daaé or the Vicomte ever discuss an interest in traveling to anywhere specific?"

"No," I said again, and since monosyllables weren't making him go away, I took a stab at being useful. Maybe that would satisfy him. "They talked a lot about the place they met, when they were children. Trestraou, a port in Lannion." They'd talked about it so much that I'd memorized the details, without ever wanting to.

"Interesting," Mifroid said, making more notes, and I couldn't tell from his tone if he actually meant it. "It is very important to our investigation that we locate the Vicomte de Chagny. At this point, it is uncertain if he is even aware of his brother's disappearance."

Because clearly, it was all about the two noblemen, not the chorus girl mixed up with them. Though I was sick of everyone talking about Christine, this didn't feel any better. I told myself Mifroid meant well, that he was just doing his job, and tried to believe it. "Is that all then?" I asked, foot sliding just a little towards the door. I was already late—if I left right now, it wouldn't be more than a few minutes, Erik might still be there—

"I am also seeking any information about the Phantom of the Opera," Mifroid said smoothly.

I know my eyes got bigger. I clenched my hands in my skirts, heart suddenly pounding harder. It was unsettling, to be thinking of Erik and then have him mentioned—and I had so hoped the police commissaire *wasn't* interested in the Phantom, that Mifroid had decided there was no connection to Philippe's disappearance, perhaps no Phantom at all. "The Phantom?" I managed, trying to make my voice light. "What does he have to do with anything?"

He studied me—and did not explain. "Do you have any information regarding the whereabouts of the individual posing as the 'Phantom of the Opera'?"

I knew exactly where he was at this moment. Or at least, where he should have been a few minutes ago. I forced myself to laugh, tried to sound like a silly, gossiping ballet girl. "Why would I know about that? Besides, lots of people think the Phantom left when Christine did.

He hasn't given any directions at rehearsals in *ages*. I hope it's true he's gone—the Phantom is *so* terrifying."

Mifroid's face didn't change. "Your mother continues to be the boxkeeper for Box Five. Has she seen the Phantom recently?"

"She *never* sees the Phantom," I said, dramatically rolling my eyes as though this was abundantly obvious. "Because he's a *ghost*."

He ignored my second sentence so completely that I felt silly for saying it—and remembered that I probably should have objected to his phrasing earlier, about the individual posing as the Phantom. "The Phantom reportedly leaves tips and takes programs," Mifroid said with dogged patience. "Has this occurred in recent days? Has he attended any performances?"

Every Saturday. "*I* don't know, I'm not the boxkeeper," I said. "*I'm* on stage. And Mother doesn't talk to me about the Phantom. He's too disturbing."

I don't know anything, don't ask me questions, don't try to find the Phantom through me, just let me *leave*! The thoughts were so loud in my head that it was a wonder Mifroid didn't take the message.

"Is the management still paying a salary to the Phantom?" Mifroid persisted.

"Everyone says so." I shrugged. "I don't know. Ask the managers. Why do you think I know about the Phantom anyway?"

His gaze was still intent, and like every other question, he didn't answer. He closed his notebook. "You will of course inform myself or another policeman if you learn anything about the Phantom. We are seeking him in connection to the disappearance and possible murder or abduction of the Comte de Chagny. Withholding information could be considered aiding in the crime. I trust you would choose to cooperate."

A little chill ran down my spine. How much trouble would I be in, if Mifroid ever found out I knew where the Phantom was and had concealed it? Mifroid had connected the lines between a falling chandelier, a masked man on stage, and a disappeared comte. And he had connected some line to me, though it was hard to know if it was more than that I was my mother's daughter, that I was Christine's friend. If he learned more...

But to tell him that the Phantom was in Box Five—to betray Erik to the police—I didn't know what had happened to Philippe, but surely it couldn't be Erik's fault. He had left the comte on stage when he carried Christine away. If he hadn't killed Philippe then, in a towering rage over Christine, over the chandelier—no, I couldn't believe he had killed him or locked him away later either.

And somehow, I didn't think innocence was going to be much help, when I tried to imagine that cold, reclusive man in the mask, hiding a misshapen face, hiding from everyone, thrust into the light of a court trial…

I couldn't do it to him. Right or wrong, wise or foolish, I couldn't do it.

I widened my eyes, deliberately this time, and told the commissaire, "Of course I'll tell you if I learn anything—but I hope I don't! The Phantom would be an *awful* person to be mixed up with!"

Meg wasn't coming. It was ten minutes later than she had ever arrived in Box Five before and she wasn't here. The Phantom leaned back in his chair, in his little pocket of silence and solitude, the noisy clatter of the Opera Garnier going on just beyond the door as people hurried to and fro, met with friends and went off to pleasant evening plans.

Meg Giry had danced in the performance tonight so she was not ill or otherwise indisposed. But evidently she had decided not to meet him afterwards. Considering he had been faintly surprised every time she actually kept the appointment, her absence should be no shock at all. No doubt she had finally come to her senses and realized that the Dance Foyer was a much pleasanter place to spend the evening, for those who had options. And who liked crowds and silly chatter.

He certainly had no reason to be disappointed by the end of something that he had never expected would continue, and that had never made sense regardless. The trap he had half-expected the police commissaire to spring had never materialized, Meg had never pressed him for money or for information he preferred not to share, and their conversations about music and distant lands had gone on as though they were in fact the point of it all—which was patently absurd.

And now whatever little diversion she'd been having had run its course. Very well. The Daroga would be pleased. They had spoken only a week ago, and the Daroga had plainly not approved of this new social connection. But what did that matter? It wasn't as though he'd ever felt eager to leave his quiet, dark rooms behind to come here anyway. Surely it was better for him to be alone. It had never gone well, when he tried to change that fundamental fact of his life. He needed only to remind himself of *her* to have irrefutable evidence on that point. It had been made abundantly clear, thirty-eight days and twenty-two hours ago when she left him behind.

Meg was fifteen minutes late now, and he rose to his feet. It was foolish to continue sitting here as though she might still arrive. No doubt she was off with friends or some handsome nobleman and—

The door creaked as it opened and Meg entered with hurried footsteps, breath coming faster than usual, cloak rustling as it settled around her shoulders, as though she had been moving quickly an instant before.

"Sorry I'm late!" she said rapidly, inhaled and said, "You're still here."

He sank into his seat again. "I usually am. After performances." So they weren't done with…whatever this was.

"Yes, but…" He could hear the smile in her voice as she sat down in her accustomed seat, two seats away. "I'm glad you waited."

"I'm usually here," he repeated, because she didn't seem to be taking the point, to properly understand that he had certainly *not* been sitting here waiting for her. That would imply that he cared, and if he implied that—well, she might begin to get the wrong idea. Matters didn't go well, when he started caring. "Why were you late?" he asked, trying to make the question sound unconcerned.

She hesitated a long moment, and he could hear the faint sound of cloth moving as she twisted at her skirt. Finally, words slow, she said,

"Commissaire Mifroid wanted to talk to me. About the Comte de Chagny."

The comte. That wretched boy's brother. The one who had gone missing, the same night everything fell apart. "Still unaccounted for, is he?" Erik said, voice deliberately bland, palms rubbing against the legs of his trousers. He stopped when he remembered that the Daroga thought he rubbed his palms when he felt guilty. Which was nonsense.

"Yes. The commissaire is taking it very seriously. But I suppose he would, for a nobleman."

Was there the faintest hint of bitterness in her voice, or was he imagining it? "It's not surprising. The commissaire and the comte have been friendly for many years."

"They have?" Meg said, tone surprised. "I didn't think Philippe was friendly to anyone. Except Sorelli, I mean."

The comte was not a pleasant man in many ways, but he had treated the lead ballerina decently. The Phantom always checked on that sort of thing. At least, he used to, when he had still been able to bring himself to get involved. "The comte deigned to notice M. Mifroid when he was still a mere *secrétaire suppléant*. He hasn't forgotten."

Meg merely said a thoughtful, "Hmm."

Erik wondered if the information required a source. "They interacted often at the Opera Garnier. And I hear things."

"Yes, I know," Meg said, and the smile was back in her voice. "Anyway, I couldn't tell him anything about the comte, but it took a little while to convince him of it."

But why would Mifroid want to talk to *Meg* about the Comte de Chagny? And then he realized. The comte was not someone Meg would know about. But the comte was not the only person involved. "Did he want to know about *her*?" he asked abruptly, before he could think better of it.

"Yes," Meg said softly, without needing clarity about who he meant.

A very long pause, while Erik wrestled with himself. He wanted to know—and he didn't want to know—and yet… "Do you know where she is? Does she write to you?"

"No." This was even fainter. "She did once, just after she left. Just to say she was leaving the country with Raoul."

He had expected that. There was no reason to feel a new stab of anguish at this confirmation that she had gone so far away from him, that she was giving her love, her voice, her very self to a foolish boy who wouldn't value her.

He said nothing, grappling with his feelings, not trusting his voice, and Meg eventually said, "If I do hear from her—I could let you know—"

"I do not want to discuss her," he said sharply.

"All right," Meg said, and they lapsed into silence.

Everyone at the Opera kept talking about *her*. He wasn't listening and he still couldn't escape it, all the gossip, all the rumors. The endless theories about the terrible things he must have done to her. Meg had to be mad to be sitting here, when she was surely hearing all that too.

But she had said, hadn't she, that first night she called him in the auditorium, that she didn't believe the rumors. That didn't make her less mad, even though the rumors weren't true.

So taken up with his own thoughts, it didn't occur to him that Meg might be processing difficult thoughts too, until she said, voice hesitant again, "I suppose you should know—Commissaire Mifroid asked me about you too."

He was on his feet in an instant, operating on pure instinct, already backing up towards the pillar that hid his secret exit. "If the police are coming—if he thinks he can take me alive, he—"

"Erik, I didn't tell him anything!" Meg protested.

He stopped. Took a breath. He knew voices, and hers had a ring of truth, just the right blend of surprise and indignation and concern. And besides—if Meg had told Mifroid that he was here, then she wouldn't be here. And Mifroid would. Why would he waste time?

Slowly, Erik returned to his seat. "I see. Why didn't you?"

Another pause, one of the pauses that he was coming to learn meant she was weighing her words, considering what he had said and what to say in response. Her considering silence had a different texture than other silences. When she finally spoke, it wasn't illuminating. "I suppose because I didn't want to."

A sigh escaped him. "You are a very confusing woman."

She surprised him again with a laugh. "Thank you. I don't think anyone's thought I was that complex before."

Chapter Five

I went on counting the time since Christine had left, an uncomfortable habit I couldn't forsake. It began to feel that if I stopped counting, something would really be over. It would be like saying I wouldn't see her again, that she had passed out of my life for good. I counterbalanced my sad count of days since Christine by a new, happier count: Saturdays, because each Saturday was another chance to meet Erik in Box Five.

He kept meeting me. And he seemed to find me interesting. Or at least, confusing. He said I was confusing, and while it was a strange thing to take as a compliment, maybe, I liked it. I liked thinking that this complicated man with his masks and his secrets found *me* even a little bit as baffling as I so often found him.

It was silly, of course. There was nothing unusual or mysterious about me. But I liked thinking that at least one person, especially this person, believed there could be.

Sixty-seven days, nine Saturdays, brought us to early May. Another Saturday performance I was impatient to finish, so I could keep my standing appointment with the Phantom of the Opera.

As the chorus sang in Act Three, I moved with a crowd of ballet girls into place in the wings, just off the stage, ready for Madame Thibault's confirming nod that it was our moment to go on. I looked out over the auditorium, dimmer than it used to be because the management had decided not to replace the chandelier. I shifted a few inches to the right, tilted my head, trying not to be obvious but trying to see...

For just a moment I thought I must have become very confused—about the proper count of the boxes, or even about which side of the theatre I was looking at. Because where I had expected to see the thick, closed curtains of Box Five, I saw instead a wide-open box and three men sitting in it.

The thrum of excitement that had been buzzing in my stomach all afternoon turned into a more frantic hum of worry. This couldn't be right, there couldn't be people in *Box Five*...

"Meg, let's go!" Mignonette hissed next to me, and nudged me forward.

I blinked, hurriedly fell into step with the other dancers already moving onto the stage with a series of *balancés*. I took a deep breath, tried to channel my nerves into my dancing.

After what felt like an eternal round of *pirouettes* and *glissades*, the choreography finally allowed me to come to a stop, posed in First Position, blessedly on the correct side of the stage to get a closer view of Box Five. I wasn't supposed to be looking, but I did it anyway. All eyes would be on Sorelli, the lead ballerina at center stage.

Three men really were sitting in the Phantom's box, and from this closer vantage point I could even tell who they were. One was Commissaire Mifroid, so the others had to be with the police too.

This discovery only made it all worse, and perhaps it was just as well that I almost immediately had dancing to distract me again.

But underneath my careful, disciplined thoughts carrying me through the steps of Madame Thibault's choreography ran the worried refrain: why were they there? What did it mean? And, selfishly—why did it have to happen on *Saturday*?

The entire performance passed with no outcry, no alarm, no disturbance of any kind. As we took final bows at the end, I looked up at Box Five again to see Mifroid maddeningly still occupying a front seat.

Some of my worries eased, because if he was still sitting there he *wasn't* finding and arresting Erik for—I didn't even know exactly what it would be for, but something.   But if he was still sitting there, I couldn't find Erik either.

I walked slowly off through backstage in the crowd of ballet girls, following them back to the changing room because I didn't have anywhere else to go.   My legs often felt tired after an evening of dancing, but tonight my steps were especially heavy.

If it had been disrupted plans with anyone else, it wouldn't have mattered.   I'd have been disappointed, but it wouldn't have been important.   But with Erik…   He hadn't missed a Saturday evening yet, but every time, just before I opened the door, I wondered if he'd really be there.   He'd never exactly seemed excited to see me.   Now I wondered if this disruption would make a convenient excuse.   As long as we had just gone along each week meeting in the same pattern— well, we had just gone along.   But now the pattern was broken, and if he didn't want to keep talking to me, it would be easy enough to let things drop now.

In the crowded changing room I dressed without thinking about it, automatically tying up laces and fastening rows of buttons, ignoring the clamor of girls around me.   For once I was glad no one tried to talk to me.   They hadn't much, recently.

I couldn't prevent it if Erik decided to disappear.   What could I do, start lurking around Box Five at odd moments in the hope of catching him?   I could see how well that had gone for Mifroid.   I could pester the Persian, who still lurked about the Opera, but he was unlikely to help.   He'd probably be delighted to see a disruption in what he considered such a dangerous friendship.   And that left me with what, performing frequent monologues to the empty auditorium on the off-chance the Phantom might be listening?

Oh no, I wanted to be friends with him but I wasn't going to go begging after him.   If he wasn't interested, if he decided to use the police's interference as an opportunity to drop me, well then—there were other people in the world.

None quite the same, but perfectly nice other people.

Maybe it was that thought that made me go to the Dance Foyer.   A kind of anticipatory self-defense, just in case.   I wasn't going to run off home as though I had nothing else in the world to do. I'd visit the Dance Foyer instead and have a lovely time. So if that was what I ended up doing every Saturday night, well, nothing would be wrong with that.

I slipped into the mirror-lined room, looked over the crowded mass of dancers and subscribers. It felt odd to be here on a Saturday evening—and even odder that it felt odd. I used to be in the Foyer after every performance, but in recent months…even before I started seeing Erik Saturday evenings, before I started avoiding the Foyer and its stories about Christine, I had been spending the time with Christine instead. Tonight I felt strangely lost. I seemed to have misplaced my knack for wandering easily through a crowd alone.

I twisted my necklace, drifting slowly through the room, noting faces familiar and new, and tried to look as though I had somewhere I was going. I finally fetched up with a group of dancers I was more or less friendly with—more in the past, less now. They glanced my way and Adalisa smiled and the conversation went on without interruption, so I was tacitly accepted into the circle.

It was perfectly nice, chatting about the show that evening, some of the local gossip—they were finally beginning to move on from Christine—and if it was nothing terribly exciting, it was still fun.

At least until Jammes came strolling up to join us, two girls from the chorus following in her wake. She flashed a bright smile over the group, and it was only a very brief period of pleasantries before she remarked, "Why, Meg, *such* a surprise to see you here. It's been weeks and weeks, hasn't it?"

All too conscious that I didn't want to answer questions about where I'd been spending my Saturdays, all I managed in response was a stiff, "I've been busy."

Afterwards, after the conversation had turned to other topics, *then* it occurred to me what I should have said. I *should* have asked Jammes how she could know, since wasn't she usually trailing after Carlotta in the evening? She had been in Carlotta's court for years, a minor attendant to the reigning queen soprano, though I couldn't imagine a dancer had much status in that group.

I hid my clenched hands in my skirts, kept smiling and chatting, and tried my best to ignore Jammes as the conversation rolled on with innocuous topics.

I should have known better than to think it would continue that way, and it wasn't more than a few minutes before Jammes turned to me with a brilliant smile and said, "So, Meg, tell us—any new word from Christine yet?"

My fingers tightened, nails digging into my palms. No one else was fooled by her warm tone; I could tell by the way suddenly none of them were looking at me, the way feet began shuffling uncomfortably. No one spoke, but this time I was ready.

"No," I said, looked Jammes dead in the eye and smiled. "Anyone invite you to join the chorus yet?"

Everyone knew that Jammes idolized the sopranos—and that her own voice was barely passable. Her smile disappeared and her cheeks flushed pink. "So now that Christine's gone, when's the Phantom going to start promoting *your* career?" she snapped.

I must have rattled her, when she came back with a jab so easy to deflect. I merely raised an eyebrow. "Who says I need his help?"

"I bet the Phantom's gone," Adalisa said quickly, before Jammes could do more than draw in breath for another retort. "He hasn't dropped any letters at rehearsal in ages. And nothing happened to the police commissaire when he sat in Box Five tonight."

"Yes, but you *know* the hallway outside the singers' dressing room was dripping with blood just yesterday!" Francesca countered. "And that spooky Persian is still hanging around too!"

That had them off and running with the most wild of the recent Phantom stories, with an occasional Persian one thrown in, and I didn't contradict them. Even though most of the stories were ridiculous and obviously untrue. Jammes glowered for a while before abandoning the field, expressing a sudden great need to speak to someone across the room. That didn't fool anyone either.

I was already feeling pleased when I heard someone call my name, and I stayed pleased when I turned to see Léon de Troyes. He was wearing a blue waistcoat and tie that brought out his eyes, making them just as striking as on the day I met him some months before.

"Meg, I've been hoping to see you!" he said, smiling at me as he took my hand.

"Then luck must be with you tonight," I said, letting him hold it. I liked thinking he'd been looking for me—though he might have tried harder and found me. It had been many weeks since the masquerade, since we had kissed on that moonlit balcony. The memory turned my cheeks warm, and I wondered if he was thinking of it too.

Not based on his next sentence, which was, "Isn't it terrible about Christine and Raoul?"

"Oh. Yes." I took my hand back. "Terrible." Could I really not get through *any* conversation without Christine coming up, even after two months?

I glanced towards the other ballet girls, but they had, with all the best intentions I expect, already drifted discreetly away. That was usual enough, when a handsome young man came to single someone out, but just now I wouldn't have minded deflecting the conversation into introductions.

"Has she written to you?" Léon persisted. "About where they are, or what they're doing?"

Marvelous. He really wanted to stay on this topic. Although…he *was* Raoul's friend, it was reasonable if he wanted to know about him. He didn't have Jammes' undertone of nastiness. "Not really. Just a note saying they were leaving Paris together." And if he was asking, two could play at that. I wouldn't mind learning more myself. "I don't suppose you've heard from Raoul?"

"Not even a note," Léon said with a scowl. It made his blue eyes look darker. "I had to find out from the papers that they weren't dead!"

"I'm so sorry," I said, sincerely. Christine's note started to look— well, a little better.

"But never mind that," he said, reverting to a grin that seemed to sit more comfortably on his face. "I'd have to be a fool to talk to a pretty girl about another man."

"One who is out of the country, with another woman," I pointed out. I did not fail to notice that he had called me pretty, and it made me forgive him for his questions.

"It's the principle of the matter." He extended an arm. "Perhaps we might walk about the room and discuss tonight's performance?"

"We might," I agreed, taking his arm. Maybe it wasn't such a bad thing the other girls had retreated after all.

"Good! Now can you explain to me how the ballet performance fits into the storyline of the opera?"

"It doesn't," I admitted with a smile. "They just put us in because they can."

"And here I thought I was missing a crucial plot point that would explain the sudden arrival of three dozen dancers."

The conversation never grew any deeper than that—but it was a fun, light-hearted banter. Léon didn't have any stories about Rome or any opinions on composers to share, but he did make me laugh.

Erik sat in a narrow passage with his back against the hidden side of the Dance Foyer's mirrors and resented the world. After so many years of polite disinterest, how dare Mifroid decide to take up ghost-hunting. Not that it was news—Meg had told him about Mifroid's inquiries weeks ago—but this was the first time the police had actually inconvenienced him.

He should have stayed home this evening, never should have bothered to come out of his dark seclusion. He had dragged himself up into the light, and for what? To find the police commissaire sitting in his own personal box, with his officers running in and out all through the performance with reports. As if it needed that to make it sufficiently obvious that Mifroid was here on business, not for the pleasure of listening to the opera.

He should have left as soon as he realized Mifroid was here. But it was Saturday.

He had lingered in the catwalks all through the performance with a degree of regret that had surprised him. It had been sixty-six days and twenty-two hours since *she* left, which meant—he had to pause to do the math. Nine. This would have been the ninth Saturday since he had started meeting Meg in Box Five.

The conversations had been a small diversion in his otherwise empty world. Verbal conversations, a supplement to all the ones he crafted in his mind of the things he would say to *her* if she ever came back, knowing she never would.

There hadn't yet been a Saturday when he hadn't debated if meeting Meg was really worth it. He had rarely stirred out of his rooms in these past weeks—hadn't even bothered to learn more about Mifroid's poking around the Opera, or learned what had inspired the managers to permit this affront. He had attended some of the midweek performances, missed others. But every Saturday he had decided he might as well go, might as well linger afterwards.

Now the police commissaire had contrived to interfere, and he was more disappointed about it than he would have expected.

With nowhere else to go after the performance he had come here, to find out if Meg would stroll into the Dance Foyer. Which she had. And he could no more get in touch with her in that chattering crowd than he could if she was on the moon, so that was that for tonight. She'd have a pleasant evening, no doubt, no serious problem for her, while he was forced to confront all over again the utter emptiness of his life.

Or, he supposed, he could take action.

He wasn't going to walk into the Dance Foyer—that was a far more horrifying prospect than a leap from a rooftop. The stares, the comments, the hostility of the mob if they deduced who and what he was…no, venturing into that crowd would only be a less sure method of dying, with a higher chance of worse pain instead of merciful oblivion.

But he could try to do something about Commissaire Mifroid—and perhaps something less direct about Meg. The prospect was one degree more appealing than slinking off into his dark cellars, so he rose to his feet. He walked away from the light and noise of the Foyer, stalked through the network of hidden passages riddling the Opera.

What could he do to send a message to the management? He had to dredge deep, try to remember who he had been, a few months before. Back when he had derived his own kind of enjoyment, playing pranks on the Opera Company. He hadn't realized how he enjoyed that, until he stopped. Stopped doing it and stopped enjoying it.

By the time he reached the managers' office he had managed to come up with an idea, and made the detour along the way to make it possible. He used a peephole to confirm the office was empty, and stepped out through a sliding panel.

With a thunk, he set the pail of paint he had collected from the prop room down on the managers' desk. After locking the door to avoid interruptions, it was the work of a moment to yank two posters off the wall to create a suitable clear palette. He dipped a brush into the paint and wrote, "GET RID OF HIM" across the wall in flowing script and lurid red.

It was a thin paint that should drip very satisfactorily. Moncharmin was probably too sensible to believe it was blood, but it still would make the point. And it would be seen by other Company members, who would jump to the most macabre explanations. They always did.

That done, he sat down at the desk, rustled out paper, pen and ink, and wrote a note for Meg, too quickly to think better of it.

My dear Meg,

Apologies for missing our appointment this evening, which I blame on the unmitigated inconsiderateness of the local police force. Until that minor matter can be settled, it may interest you to know that I expect to be in the auditorium at seven on Tuesday morning, when it tends to be empty.

Regards,
Erik

After he was done, he had doubts about that salutation. Suppose she took it the wrong way? But no, she wouldn't. It was a perfectly reasonable form of address. He had started all his letters that way, when he still wrote letters. He had even been known to start letters to Carlotta that way (though the sarcastic overtones were rather strong in those cases). Meg would know that.

As for that early morning time, she was hardly likely to find it convenient, but the Opera Garnier was reliably deserted at very few times. And if she didn't care to come—well, that was her choice, obviously.

Excerpt from the Private Notebook of Jean Mifroid, Commissaire of Police

7 May 1881

Two months of inquiry at Opera, still little progress on finding PdC or so-called Phantom. Determined tonight to take more visible step, attended performance in Box 5, the "Phantom's box." Already extensively searched for hidden doors in box, unlikely to achieve direct effect from attending performance. But performers should appreciate the value of theater. Can only hope Phantom will take intended message. I am not going away.

Chapter Six

M onday morning I sat down at my dressing table in the ballet's changing room, reached into the top drawer for an extra hairpin, and my fingers brushed against unfamiliar paper. I pulled out a thin envelope, studied it with a puzzled frown that quickly faded. No black edges or red ink, but I recognized the curling handwriting of *M. Giry* written across the front.

A thrill ran through me and made my fingers tingle. He'd never written to *me* before.

I pulled it open, read the brief note within. I might have read into the salutation, but I knew he addressed letters to the management the same way, so it couldn't signify anything. But the rest—the rest was fairly impersonal and unexcited too, but what counted was that he wanted to meet at another time.

It was hardly an enthusiastic invitation, and I might not have received it well from anyone else. But I'd learned about Erik after these several weeks. It didn't matter how he chose to phrase it. He had gone out of his way to tell me when and where I could find him, and that was as good as receiving an engraved invitation with a firm injunction to RSVP and multiple reminders from anyone else.

I was still smiling down at the note when I heard Adalisa ask, "Is that a special letter?"

My heart jumped and my fingers tightened on the paper. "Not really," I said, voice deliberately calm. Adalisa and Francesca were both looking at me, smiling, eyes alight with interest. I carefully, slowly folded up the letter and put it back into the envelope. If I hurried to hide it away, that would only intrigue them more. "Just a note from a friend."

"A *special* friend?" Adalisa said, eyes glinting with merriment.

My heart beat harder. They couldn't suspect, could they? No one knew. Well, the Persian, and Mother of course, but no one else. "I don't know what you mean," I said, with a magnificent failure to sound casual.

"Oh come on, Meg," Francesca said with a grin. "We saw you with Léon de Troyes Saturday night!"

Oh. Léon. They thought... I dropped my eyes. "It's not from Léon, really," I said, which I knew would make them positive that it was.

Sure enough, giggles erupted and Francesca sighed dramatically. "You're so lucky. He has the most *beautiful* blue eyes."

I grinned back at her. "He does, doesn't he?" And that, at least, was sincere.

They were all abuzz with questions, and I...didn't mind answering them. I had almost forgotten how fun it could be talking to the other ballet girls, when they were on pleasanter subjects than Christine and her departure. Léon definitely qualified as pleasant.

Erik would too, in his own very different way, and I wished I had someone to talk to about him—but it definitely couldn't be Adalisa and Francesca. If anyone even suspected I was friendly with the Phantom of the Opera, I'd be shunned if not worse. It was much safer, much easier, to talk about Léon.

Ricard let out a very gratifying shriek on seeing the message scrawled on his office wall. Erik, discreetly hidden behind a panel, smiled grimly in the darkness. He didn't really need to be here—but having left the message, it was a kind of unfinished business, an incomplete task that itched at him. Hearing the reaction would complete the crescendo and let him move on.

"What is it? What's wrong?" Moncharmin demanded, footsteps suggesting he was hurrying into the room just behind Ricard. "Oh—oh, *really* now!"

Not as satisfying a reaction. Sitting cross-legged on the ground with his back to the office, Erik tipped his head back and regretted once again that M. Moncharmin was not more superstitious.

"Do you think it's blood?" Ricard asked in hushed tones.

"Don't be ridiculous," Moncharmin snapped, "where would he get that much blood? No, don't answer that. Honestly, you've been spending too much time around superstitious ballet girls lately."

Had he? Erik had no idea. A few months ago he would have known, but he had stopped paying attention. He felt a prick of guilt at that. *The* woman, the one who mattered most to him, had gone away, sixty-eight days, ten hours ago. But the other women of the Opera remained. He had been disregarding his duty if he had no idea whether a manager was taking too close an interest in the girls of the Company, possibly the wrong kind of interest.

To begin anew, to start watching and responding and getting generally involved again…he shrank tighter into himself, rubbed his palms against his coat. No, it was too much, too impossible.

But maybe he'd ask Meg, what her impression was of Monsieur Ricard.

The manager himself sounded jovial enough, which didn't prove anything about his character. "Well, Moncharmin, you can't blame me if…"

"No, don't talk to me about that either, I don't have time to hear about your paramours right now." A scrape of chair legs against floor and presumably Moncharmin was sitting down behind the desk. "We'll need someone to paint those words over."

"But what are we going to *do* about it?" Ricard asked.

"Nothing," Moncharmin said. "Do you know how much money this Phantom is costing us? If Mifroid can catch him, that's good for business."

Erik sighed, head dropping forward as his shoulders hunched. He knew, right from the beginning, that it was not a good thing to have a businessman running the Opera. It might be good for the budget, but it was bad for art and bad for ghosts. Why couldn't they just let him be? He wasn't even doing anything right now. He just wanted to sit below his Opera and be left alone to mourn for *her*.

The managers had been so cooperative after the chandelier had fallen. He had been paying even less attention then, in the immediate aftermath of her leaving, but they had left Box Five empty and paid the salary each month. He still felt guilty about the chandelier, about the damage done, but it had been effective, for a while. Apparently Moncharmin's greed had now outpaced his fear.

Ricard's fingers were tapping a nervous beat against some surface, probably the desk. "But I thought we agreed, after the chandelier fell, that the Phantom was too dangerous to—"

"Yes, yes, you convinced me about that," Moncharmin said, ignoring Ricard's indignant exclamation of denial. "But he hasn't done anything in almost two months, and I don't plan to keep draining accounts to pay a prankster dressed up as a ghost."

Erik resented the insinuation that he was running around with a sheet over his head. Moncharmin's tone managed to convey just that idea. And it also seemed rather unjust that staying quiet and not causing trouble was provoking the management into hunting him. Damned if he did, damned if he didn't, literally—but hadn't that always been his life?

Beyond the wall, Moncharmin and Ricard launched into an argument about who had been more alarmed by the falling chandelier, and he stopped listening to them.

He let his head drop into his hands, tried to think what his best course was now. Maybe he should just walk into Box Five and let Mifroid catch him. It would certainly be the easiest option, and what did he have to lose? His life? Small loss.

His freedom, though, that was of different value. A jump from a rooftop would be a swift end, while arrest, imprisonment and an eventual guillotine would not be. It was the imprisonment that made him reject the idea of giving himself up. He was never going back into a cage.

Besides, there was no style in surrendering without a fight.

If he wasn't giving in—he could run. He had run before, often enough. But this was his kingdom, his world. What was a Phantom without an Opera? Nothing but a man in a mask, a man who was different, hunted, feared, without a world of hidden passages and catwalks to hide himself in. Even with dangers within the Opera's walls, it was less terrifying than the world outside.

Not running. Not giving in. That only left fighting.

He'd have to get involved with the Opera Company again. He'd had no real interest lately in either productions or pranks, not since *she* left. He had attended performances, but not with the kind of interest he had once had, not with his mind full of ideas for ways to change and improve. After the high drama and the deep tragedy of his disastrous love affair, in the pain and loneliness left in its ashes, what weight could stage-acted dramatics or some silly pranks have? But if the result was the police commissaire poking about and the management condoning it…evidently he'd have to bestir himself enough so that they'd leave him alone again.

It wasn't as though he was heavily occupied. He hadn't realized how much time he spent composing music or baiting Carlotta until he stopped doing both. He felt a pang for the music. His music that he had spent hours and days composing, playing, filling his silent world with fancy. That was gone too, gone with *her*. He couldn't call it back if he wanted to. But he could force himself into baiting the Opera Company again.

He spent much of the day trying to decide the best options for intimidating the management. Something that would work, something that would at least be worth the effort involved. He couldn't be more dramatic than the crashed chandelier, and it was hard to know what kind of haunting would be most effective on a man who cared only about his balance sheet. Should he steal the budget book? Replace all the balances with zeroes?

Tuesday brought his sole appointment for the week. He arrived in the auditorium at seven precisely, stepping out of a secret door near the prop room backstage, and walked silently through the shadows between thick curtains in the wings. He had expected to arrive before Meg, or that she'd be sitting in one of the seats if she was here already. Instead he came to a sudden halt just before stepping out of the shadows, realizing she was sitting on the edge of the stage between the gas lights, heels tapping against the wood as her feet dangled down into the orchestra pit. Surprising, but since she was facing towards the auditorium, her back to him, it was all right. He could still manage the appearance of a sudden arrival.

He walked silently across the stage, spoke when he was a few meters behind her. "Good morning."

She turned her head and flashed him a bright smile. "Hello. You actually came."

He blinked. Hadn't he said exactly that the first time they met in Box Five? And she knew that. So it was a joke. But what was he supposed to say in response? Finally he just agreed with, "Yes," let a long pause linger awkwardly, and defensively added, "I would have been here anyway." He remembered a heartbeat too late that he had said *that* before too. It only made things worse because he was standing while she was sitting, so that he was looming above her – a useful device for haunting, but he wasn't *trying* to be threatening right now.

She laughed, a soft laugh that was friendly instead of mocking. "I don't believe you."

Perceptive, since it wasn't actually true. But what was he supposed to say to *that*? "Yes, well…" He could at least stop looming, sitting uneasily down cross-legged near the edge of the stage, a few feet from Meg.

She had him rattled today. Maybe it was the change in routine. Or maybe it was her change in clothes.

She was wearing a dress today, and it made him slightly uneasy. He had grown used to seeing her in her ballet outfit. It was the same basic outfit that all the ballet girls wore, from the eight-year-olds up to the prima donnas. It made it simple to keep thinking of her as Little Meg the ballet rat, even if neither the nickname nor the status had been appropriate for years. In this dress, she was clearly Mademoiselle Giry, adult woman. It made her look more mature—a contradiction, when the ballet outfit had hidden far less of curves and limbs. But the effect was different.

He was still hunting for some good way to finish a sentence that began with "Yes, well" when she remarked, "Isn't it awful about Mifroid sitting in Box Five?"

He seized on it. "Awful, yes. Incredibly inconvenient." But did that sound like he was putting too much emphasis on their opportunities to meet? He needed to divert this to the performances, and quickly added, "The catwalks have terrible acoustics."

They spent an agreeable several minutes abusing Mifroid generally, and he was surprised by how much she was bothered by what had seemed to be his particular problem. She really was a confusing woman. But somewhat pleasant, all the same.

Erik seemed distinctly uncomfortable when he first appeared on the stage. He was always stiff in his movements, alert and tightly controlled, and the habit was exaggerated now. Maybe it bothered him being out of Box Five. But mutual complaining about Commissaire Mifroid appeared to relax him somewhat. He was wearing his white half-mask today, and while the visible side of his face didn't reveal much, it was something. And I was getting better at reading the set of his shoulders and tone of his voice too.

We could make only so many variations on the same theme regarding the police, and soon enough we were right up against what I felt was the crucial point—what now? With anyone else, I would have just asked what he planned to do, but I tried not to ask Erik questions. I'd learned it was a nearly sure way to make him stop talking.

"So," I said, smoothing the skirts of my new dress, a pattern of tiny red flowers I thought rather pretty. I always got a new dress for the year at Easter. "I suppose Mifroid will keep sitting in Box Five. If he doesn't have a reason to stop."

We were both facing the auditorium, but now his gaze slid sideways to look at me. "You want to know if I'm going to get rid of him."

Caught. "Well. Yes." Why attempt to hide it now? I tried to look unconcerned, wrapping my hands around one drawn-up knee, resisting the urge to twist at my skirt nervously instead.

He leaned back on his hands, gaze drifting up towards where the chandelier had formerly hung. "Mifroid is irritatingly unsuperstitious. But the real problem is the management. Monsieur Moncharmin feels a ghost is costing him too much money, and is currently willing to risk a falling chandelier, or the equivalent, to balance his budget. Put a little more fear into the managers and they will get rid of the police. So I'll simply...cover a few floors with blood, or something along those lines."

I couldn't stop myself from smirking. Blood-covered floors were such a ridiculous notion, one of the legends of the Phantom that I'd always dismissed out of hand.

"I could," he said, trying and not quite succeeding in sounding stern. His voice held the barest underlying quiver, as though he might laugh, if he was anyone else. I'd never heard Erik laugh.

I forced my features to align themselves more impassively. "According to the ballet girls, you frequently do."

"Precisely." There was that sidelong glance again. "Any other ballet girl would go into shrieks of horror at the mere idea."

"Any other ballet girl wouldn't be here," I pointed out, and then out of loyalty added, "And they're not really as silly or superstitious as people think. Not all of them. They just like excitement."

"If you say so." He drummed his fingertips against the stage, each one tapping independently as though he was following a rhythm too complex for me to decipher. A piano or pipe organ—that's what it was like, like a musician's hands on keys.

So busy watching his hands, I almost missed his words, when he said, voice quiet, "Don't you think it's an awful thing, a man terrifying an Opera Company with hauntings?"

Maybe it was strange to say, but I never had thought that. I lived among the people he was frightening, and yet never disliked him for doing it. Maybe I was too used to it. Or maybe he had always drawn just the right line. "They're not actually that frightened," I said. "I think they enjoy—"

"Of course they're frightened," he said sharply, going as stiff and tense as he'd been when he first stepped out. "They have to be, that's the *point*."

Talking to Erik was like a complicated dance, one where you never knew which board in the floor was going to drop out from under you. It kept things lively. I made a tactical retreat, a *temps levé* backwards. "Yes, of course." A meaningless phrase, then a leap to a new topic. "And really, it's Monsieur Moncharmin's problem if he doesn't appreciate the valuable services of a theatre ghost."

"Perhaps," he said, and though I was distracted by my own sudden thought, I noted his fingers were tapping again. "Speaking of the managers—Monsieur Ricard seems to appreciate the value of ballet girls, and would you happen to know—that is, is he, ah, polite to the girls—"

"Everyone says he's a terrible flirt but harmless," I said without much thought. It was automatic among the girls, to classify and communicate which men were dangerous, which not, and I was still more interested in my own idea. "But your salary—all things considered, you're probably a bargain."

He turned his head to look at me this time, eyes widening in surprise. "You do know how much they're paying me, don't you?"

More each month than I was likely to earn my entire career—but that wasn't what mattered. "Yes, but don't you see, maybe that's the answer to your problem with the managers."

His visible eyebrow rose. "Convince Moncharmin I'm a bargain?"

"*Be* a bargain. Be valuable, I mean. *Save him money.* You know the Opera Garnier better than anyone, right?"

It was rhetorical, but he said "Yes" anyway.

I nodded, dashing on. "So there must be dozens, hundreds of ways a building this big, with this many people, is spending money unnecessarily. Start pointing some of them out!"

"I am an artist," he said stiffly, "not a machinist."

"Oh." My shoulders slumped. It had seemed like such a sensible idea. "I just thought…"

"Although," he said, "the Opera does spend far more money than strictly necessary on the gas lights. It's all to do with the way the lines are run. It could be managed much more efficiently…"

And while I blinked and he looked reflectively out over the gleaming theatre seats, he outlined what amounted to a multi-point plan for more efficient and cost-effective lighting of the building, involving a depth of knowledge of the building's gas lines and overall structure that was far beyond what I'd ever known.

"Well," I said when he finally wound up. "I'm sure Moncharmin would find that…helpful." And it gave me a bit of a warm feeling. Maybe I'd been helpful too, to him.

"Perhaps I'll mention it," he said, voice cool. "If the opportunity arises."

"Only then," I agreed, trying to contain a smile. "You know the Opera so well, anyone would think you had built it."

"I did," Erik said. I must have looked astonished because he added, "Not single-handedly, of course."

"Of course," I said automatically, but my astonishment had much more to do with the arithmetic I was trying to calculate. They had spent nearly fifteen years building the Opera Garnier, starting work over twenty years ago. Unless I was gravely mistaken about Erik's age, he would have been a child then. If he was around thirty-five now, at the beginning of the construction he would have been as young as I had been when I came to the Opera, only twelve years old. "You couldn't have been here when they began," I ventured, as near as I dared come to asking him about his past.

"No," he agreed. "They had been working seven, eight years before I arrived. Too late for some changes that should have been made, but early enough to have influence."

That made more sense—and now that I thought about it, it explained a lot. How secret doors got into the design to begin with, for example. That thought set off a fire of new curiosity in my mind. Somehow, every question I answered about Erik only led to dozens of new ones, ones I wasn't sure I should actually ask. I pushed my luck, just a little, and continued the line of inquiry we were already on. "You still must have been very young, when you came to the Opera."

"Fairly. Fortunately, Charles Garnier is a man of vision. He could appreciate genius when he saw it, regardless of age."

This smile was even harder to contain. "You think well of yourself."

"No, I really don't," he said simply, without looking at me. "But I am aware of my own capabilities."

I hesitated. My impulse was to pursue that first sentence, to try to tease out that tantalizing hint of just what Erik did think of himself, and how that related to the things he did and maybe even everything that had gone on with Christine or why he wore that ever-present mask to hide his distorted face...but I knew if I tried to follow that line he'd stare at me and change the subject, if he didn't actually stand up and go. I knew where *some* of the unreliable planks were in this floor we were on.

I chose the safer choreography. "So you knew Garnier."

"A brilliant man," Erik said at once, with more light in his eyes than I'd seen for any topic besides music. "Absolutely brilliant. Even if he refused to listen to me about the Emperor's Entrance."

I tried to remember where that was in the building. "...you mean that plain staircase around the back?"

"Exactly. It was intended to be Napoleon III's private entrance and the plan was to carve magnificent designs on the walls, but no— just because Napoleon III had been deposed by the time we got to that part, Garnier threw the plan out. He said it was too expensive."

"I did hear they were over budget." Moncharmin wasn't the first one to tear his hair over cost around here.

Erik shrugged. "Unfortunately, you can only funnel so many Persian jewels into a budget before someone notices the numbers are growing strange."

I blinked. "Persian jewels...?" A link to his history with the mysterious Persian who still lurked around the Opera?

But there was the stare. Apparently Persia was not a topic he wanted to discuss. I made a mental note of it as he said, firmly but not unpleasantly, "Did you know that half the gold in the Grand Foyer is only gilt? Some is just paint."

"I think I heard a rumor about that."

"Yes, but that's all right," he said with a wave of one hand, "opera houses *should* be places of illusion. The Emperor's Entrance, however..."

By the time I had to leave, my head was spinning with a multitude of information I hadn't managed to learn in six years of wandering around the Opera Garnier.

It was much more work talking to Erik than, say, to Léon, but he really was fascinating.

Commissaire Mifroid was in Box Five again at Wednesday night's performance, and early Thursday morning Erik dropped a letter on the managers' desk. Then he waited from behind the wall to listen to the response. It wasn't as though he had anything else to do; anything important in his life had ended 71 days, eight hours ago when *she* left.

The managers finally wandered in late in the morning, talking on some utterly uninteresting subject like the weather. Erik folded his arms, leaning back against the wall, and willed them to notice the letter quickly. Life would be easier if he actually had that power.

In this moment, though, they did notice quickly, Ricard breaking off mid-sentence.

"What about that storm?" Moncharmin prompted.

"There's a letter," Ricard said in heavy tones. "From the Phantom."

"Oh, what does he want *now?*" Moncharmin groaned.

A long pause followed, presumably while Ricard read. "Um...he wants us to turn the lights out in unoccupied rooms."

A growl from Moncharmin. "Of all the impertinent—"

"He says it's a waste of money to—"

"Let me see that!" A rustle of paper, then the scrape of chair legs. Erik had noted before that it was always Moncharmin who sat behind the desk. "Well," Moncharmin said at last. "Well now. This...could lead to significant savings."

"Do you mean we're actually going to implement an idea that...*madman* suggests?"

"He may be mad, but he clearly has a firm grasp of the economics of lighting a building this size and—"

"But you're always saying how much money he's *costing* us!"

"Yes, of course," Moncharmin said irritably, to more paper rustling. Waving the letter, most likely. "But that's no reason to ignore perfectly valid suggestions. Shows a willing spirit, for that matter. I wonder if he has any ideas about saving money on ballet slippers. The costs of some filmy bits of shoe, I can't understand—and I haven't heard any of your paramours suggest any saving ideas."

Erik felt a tension he had stopped noticing relax. All right, so Moncharmin wasn't marching straight to the police office to tell them not to bother anymore—but this was still a clear softening of attitude, possibly a prelude to more. That was something.

Apparently Meg knew what she was talking about. He would have to think up a few more ideas for Moncharmin's budget.

But not on how to obtain cheaper ballet slippers. He would not suggest cost savings at the expense of art. He had to have standards, after all.

Chapter Seven

Excerpt from the Private Notebook of Jean Mifroid, Commissaire of Police

11 May 1881

Breakthrough at last re: PdC. Not one hoped for, but still an answer.

I suspected Mother of deliberately not waking me up when I overslept one Thursday morning, about eleven weeks after Christine left. Mother knew perfectly well I was supposed to be meeting Erik. She didn't like our new arrangement, meeting in different parts of the building when they were likely to be empty, but she didn't raise too much argument. Just insisted I tell her each time before I went to see him. On the day I overslept, I scrambled into my blue-striped dress, ran a comb through my hair, flew out the door and made it to the Salon du Soleil only five minutes behind the time.

"Sorry I'm late," I said as I came in through the arched doorway, trying to breathe evenly, as though I hadn't rushed all the way here.

"That's all right," Erik said, contemplating the salamanders on the ceiling. He glanced at me once, looked away, and began walking through the salon out into the Grand Foyer.

I fell into step next to him, noting as I did the set of his shoulders and the way his hands were shoved into the pockets of his trousers. What was bothering him? Surely not a few minutes' tardiness. "What did you think of yesterday's performance?" I asked with determined cheerfulness. I assumed he had seen it. Commissaire Mifroid was still occupying Box Five, but although Erik didn't tell me where he was watching from, he still knew all about the performances.

Usually he had extensive opinions, and this was a nearly guaranteed safe topic to spark conversation. Today, he only said, "It could have been better."

"*Any* show could be better," I countered, and he just shrugged.

We walked the entire length of the Grand Foyer without much more contribution from him than that. By the time we got to the Salon de la Lune at the opposite end, I gave up. He could tell me what was bothering him if he wanted to, or we could just walk in silence. Asking him what was wrong—that definitely wouldn't help.

So we walked in silence, circling back into the Grand Foyer again, me sneaking looks at Erik often enough to confirm that he was steadily not looking at me. Mostly he was looking up, as though the chandeliers and the painted ceiling were simply fascinating. Not that they weren't beautiful; I just couldn't imagine he was seeing anything new in them. Anyone else, maybe they could have, in those endless gold details, the intricate carvings and hidden faces and painted murals of the muses, everything gold (or gilt or paint) except for the silver face of Charles Garnier. I still saw a new feature, once in a while—but surely Erik knew everything already.

It might have looked more natural if he had kept his gaze directed to the side instead. Mirrors lined the walls of the Salons; maybe looking into them at our reflections would have been too much like looking at me. Or maybe that wasn't it either. It suddenly occurred to me that he *never* looked in the mirrors. Mirrors were everywhere at the Opera and I had never once seen Erik look at himself. I didn't think I stared at mirrors often, but I would glance to make sure my hair looked right, or meet my reflection's eyes like I would meet another person's. Erik never—

"I didn't kill the comte."

I blinked, looked at him directly, as he went on staring fixedly at the chandeliers. "Sorry?" What was he even—did he mean the Comte de Chagny? Last I'd heard he was still missing, and presumably that was the reason Mifroid was still hanging about. Rumors had floated all along that he was dead, but—did this mean there was more definite news?

Erik turned to me at last, scrutinizing my face, and now it was me trying not to look away from that suddenly intent gaze. Whatever he saw made the corners of his eyes crinkle with embarrassment. "That is—I just thought, that you were thinking—never mind. Forget I said anything. Or—actually, well...I mean as long as I did say it...I just thought you might want to know."

I nodded slowly and said, "I see," even though I didn't see at all.

He was frowning. "You have no idea..." He groaned, head tipped back. "I should have realized. Mifroid sent the police report to the managers' office before the press got hold of it. You haven't heard yet."

"Heard what?" I prompted, when he seemed inclined to stop talking.

A heavy sigh. "They found the Comte de Chagny's body in the Seine yesterday evening." He squared his shoulders, as if nerving himself up. The words that followed came in a rapid flood. "Whether the police puts it together or not, I'm reasonably certain, to a fairly high degree, that Philippe drowned in the underground lake and washed out to the river but contrary to what the rumors will undoubtedly say, I did *not* murder him and the only reason I know what happened is I found the capsized boat later on, and I am not responsible if a clumsy comte gets into a small boat on a lake in the dark, tips himself over and drowns flailing about in—I mean, granted, he was trying to follow his brother and he wouldn't have needed to if I hadn't—but he made a choice, I had nothing to do with that and yes, I should have checked when my alarm bell went off, but I was just a little distracted at the time, and rats set that thing off on a regular basis, it's a design flaw I keep meaning to fix, and there's not much I could have done at that point anyway. So. I didn't kill him. Just so you know."

I nodded again, said, "I see" again, with greater truth this time.

So the Comte de Chagny was dead. At least half the rumors had said so already, and I'd ruled out most of the alternative theories, since I felt sure he was not with Christine and Raoul. But now I knew he was dead. Perhaps I ought to feel sad. An accidental drowning was a senseless waste. And he had been a person, so his death should be sad.

I couldn't work up much more personal regret than that. I remembered how he'd always dismissed me on the rare occasions our paths had crossed—except the time I'd accidentally heard the comte and Raoul talking about Christine, and he'd warned me not to spread the story around. And on the day he died, when I tried to stop him dragging Christine away and he'd hit me across the face.

I hadn't wanted him to die, but I decided it didn't make me a bad person to feel no personal regret that he was dead.

It would be sad for Raoul, though. I'd never had a brother, but I knew how much it hurt to lose a sister.

"You don't have any questions?" Erik said, tone abrupt. And yet, it wasn't the kind of abruptness that meant a topic was a mistake, and to pirouette clear of it. That, even more than the actual words, told me I could ask a question if I wanted to.

But I didn't. "No, I don't think so. I never thought the comte was a very pleasant topic for conversation, even when he was alive." And the questions I might have liked to ask weren't really about the comte—they were about Christine, and Raoul, and why the comte thought he should cross the underground lake, and whether he was right about that. I felt sure that Erik would have a different kind of abruptness for those questions.

We still never talked about Christine.

"No," Erik said slowly, "I suppose he isn't." Then he smiled, if only slightly. "What did you think of yesterday's performance?"

So we talked about the performance, far more easily, far less awkwardly.

My thoughts still circled around Erik's non-confession, though. The rumors had assigned Philippe's murder to him before we knew there was definitely a murder. I'd never believed those stories, and I believed them even less now. He *could* have been lying to me. Only I was pretty sure that if Erik set out to lie to me, he'd be far more articulate about it.

And nothing had forced him to say anything at all. He could have ignored the topic, let me draw my own conclusions once I heard the latest news. But since he did tell me—he must have cared, about what conclusion I would draw.

Erik cared what I thought of him. And that put a smile on my face.

On the whole, it was probably good that he had reached Meg before the gossip did. Awkward and uncomfortable, but still for the best. He likely wouldn't have even broached the subject, at least not today, if she hadn't been late. He'd spent five minutes sure she wasn't coming because she'd heard hideous rumors, and then when she arrived it hadn't occurred to him that she might not have heard them at all.

She heard them soon enough after. He followed her (discreetly) to ballet practice, because the ballet was an epicenter for gossip in the Opera, and learned that somehow word had got out. The death of the comte was the favorite new melody in the symphony of conversation. Erik paced behind the mirrors lining the practice room, listened to the ballet girls compare stories and shriek with horrified delight. No one seemed to consider it even a possibility that the Comte de Chagny had met his end in any way but murder by the Phantom. The only debate was on exactly which method the Ghost had used, with drowning and strangulation the competing favorites.

Meg gasped and exclaimed with as much horror as all the rest. He tugged on his collar and told himself that was for the best too. Obviously she was acting, and that was good. He didn't need one ballet girl convincing all the others that the Phantom was nothing to be frightened of. No telling where that would lead.

He went on pacing as Madame Thibault scolded and the girls lined up at the barre and started in on practice. This gossip was so good that it took a long time for the whispers to die away, for the girls to really turn their attention to their art.

Meg's exclamations of horror lingered longer for Erik. He told himself that it wasn't the same as when *she* had pulled his mask off, when she had recoiled in horror and fear before his misshapen face. When the fragile accord between them had been shattered and she saw the monster for the first time. Meg obviously didn't *mean* any of this.

If she had been hiding horror talking to him, why set another time to meet? And why give voice to her true feelings while still at the Opera? She understood his movements well enough to know that he'd be likely to notice the contradiction. It wasn't like when *she* had hidden her fears and pretended to still care for him—and he had been foolish enough to believe her.

He didn't want to think about that, wrenched his thoughts back to the present. The comte, the ballet, the already-growing theories. It made perfect sense that Meg would want to fit in with the rest of the ballet; those who had that option generally took it. He'd already noticed, just in passing, that she was spending more time with the other ballet girls in the past few weeks. More time in the Dance Foyer too, meeting some fellow with a penchant for bright waistcoats whose name he hadn't caught yet. And since there was no conceivable reason she should be isolated and lonely, that was good.

When he started wondering how growing popularity among the Company was going to affect her interest in meeting with the local ghost, he decided this was a pointless use of energy. He would do better to go see how the management was reacting to the report about Philippe de Chagny that was sitting on their desk. So he did.

He heard voices already in the office as he took up a position in the adjoining hidden passage, but fortunately they were still discussing the relevant news.

Moncharmin was loudly announcing his wrongs. "I don't see why Mifroid had to tell everyone that the Comte de Chagny died *here*. If they fished him out of the Seine, he could have drowned *there* just as easily."

Erik leaned back against the wall, and had to admit that the Opera Company wasn't being quite as wild, alarmist and superstitious as usual by blaming Philippe's death on him. Not if that part about location had got out of the report and into the general knowledge.

Of course, that part about location also meant that the police would be investigating at the Opera, perhaps looking for the person who sabotaged the chandelier, who spoke with Philippe on stage just before his disappearance. But it had already been clear that Mifroid had taken up ghost-hunting. Now that the police commissaire actually knew what crime he was investigating—it shouldn't change very much.

"You know what Mifroid wrote about where the comte died," Ricard told Moncharmin. "Philippe was last seen here."

"Yes, but think of the negative publicity! As if a falling chandelier wasn't bad enough, now people will start thinking they could be murdered if they come to see an opera. *That's* going to help ticket sales wonderfully."

"Perhaps Mifroid will catch the Phantom soon and—"

"What we really need," Moncharmin forged along, "is *good* publicity. Something sensational, to convince people they must come to the Opera Garnier…" A snapping of fingers. "We'll have a special performance!"

"Again?" Ricard said doubtfully. "Even though at the last one—"

"Yes, but that's the point! A successful, completely disaster-free special performance will be just what we need to make everyone forget about the mess of the last one."

Personally, Erik doubted it. No one was going to forget a crashed chandelier in a hurry, if the Opera Company's love of recounting horrors was an accurate representation of the general public's attitudes. But a special performance might at least give him some opportunities. He had been looking for other ways to convince Moncharmin a theatre ghost was a useful thing to have around, and maybe a few judicious suggestions for this special performance would do it. That couldn't require too much time or effort.

"I'll start drawing up an invitation list," Moncharmin announced, "to make sure we have the most influential people here. You talk to the Vocal Director and the Ballet Mistress about the details for the performance."

Ricard sighed loudly. "Why do *I* always have to talk to Madame Thibault?"

"You like ballet dancers so much. And how complicated can this be? Throw together a couple dance sequences, give the chorus a few songs, get Carlotta to do a solo or two—I'm sure you can handle it."

Buried in the middle of Moncharmin's absurd chatter (as if a special performance was a simple thing) was one idea that made Erik's heart sink. Carlotta. Of course they'd have Carlotta sing. And it wouldn't be a solo or two once she got a hold of the idea, it would be four, five, maybe six. They'd probably let her choose her own songs, and she had a particular genius for choosing the least appropriate roles. She always wanted to play the impossibly young ingénues, with songs that required notes impossibly far out of her range.

If he could only get rid of Carlotta—but he had sworn not to interfere with her career any more. It had been the price of getting her out of the last special performance. Back when he had been so sure that one perfect chance for *her* would be enough, the perfect gift and the perfect launching point for a career—and perhaps other dreams.

That, of course, was before everything had fallen apart. Eighty-five days, twelve hours ago.

What did any of it really matter? Who cared if Carlotta reigned over *this* special performance? It wasn't like the last one. *She* was gone.

Maybe he wouldn't bother making suggestions for the managers' show. Maybe he'd just ignore the whole business.

Except Meg was sure to bring the topic up. He probably couldn't avoid talking to her about it.

But otherwise, he'd ignore it.

After two days, I had had enough of Mother trying to ignore the subject of Philippe, his body, and who the gossipmongers thought had killed him. I waited until we were home in our kitchen, because it would be simply foolish to discuss Erik *at* the Opera Garnier, and finally said, "Will you just *say* it instead of banging cupboards around?"

Mother had been going around with a face like a thunderstorm ever since she heard the news, and though we had barely talked about it, I felt as though it was the only topic on either of our minds.

Mother banged one last cupboard shut and sat down opposite me at the table, back ramrod straight. "I don't see how you can possibly think it's a good idea to keep seeing him."

No need to specify who or why. "I told you, he didn't kill Philippe." I had managed to emphasize that, in the one brief conversation we'd had on the subject. It hadn't reassured her.

"The police believe he *did*."

I crossed my arms. "They're wrong. It was an accident."

She exhaled loudly. "I know you saw what happened to Buquet, but you don't have that evidence this time. You weren't there to see—"

"Erik told me he didn't do it." He had unnecessarily and awkwardly told me.

"That's very reassuring," she snapped.

"And I believe him," I said, firm in the face of her sarcasm.

Mother cast her eyes heavenward as though for support. "Just what do you imagine he would tell you if he *did* do it?"

I gave that a moment's real thought. "I don't think he'd tell me anything. I think he'd avoid the subject. He does that; he avoids things he doesn't want to talk about, but he doesn't seem to mind talking about Philippe." The Comte de Chagny and the police investigation into his death had been significantly less charged than any number of subjects he had firmly steered the conversation away from. Persia, for instance. Or Christine.

Mother looked at me for a long moment, searchingly, and I worked hard not to blink. "You'd tell me, wouldn't you," she said finally, "if he ever scared you?"

This was nothing new. I rolled my eyes. "*Yes*, Mother, of course I—"

"Don't just dismiss this, I'm serious," she said, voice tight. "*Would* you tell me?"

I blinked then, caught by the intensity in her gaze. "Yes," I said slowly. It hadn't come up. I didn't think it would come up. But if it did—yes, I'd tell her.

"Good," she said with a nod, stood up and went back to organizing the cupboards, with less banging.

I stared at her back, surprised that this was apparently the end of the argument.

But as I thought about it, maybe it did make sense. I could always tell when no amount of arguing would shift my mother's position, and when I'd better give in rather than prompt a possibly irreparable break. It had never occurred to me before that *she* might know when the same was true of me.

Maybe there hadn't been many things I cared about that deeply.

Chapter Eight

T hree days after the Comte de Chagny's body was found, I chanced to encounter the Persian in the halls of the Opera. I needed to get to the changing room, prepare for dance practice—but this was a rare opportunity. All the other girls were evidently more responsible and already in the changing room, because though a few people were also navigating the halls, not one was a ballet girl. No one in sight was likely to know me.

So when the Persian gave me a slight nod, I stepped into his path. "Monsieur," I said, with my own nod. "Might I have a moment?" We hadn't spoken since the day he warned me off of talking to Erik. I supposed he knew I hadn't listened, but he had taken no action I could see. We occasionally met eyes across rooms, exchanged occasional nods, and didn't speak.

"Mademoiselle," he said, voice distant, face calm and detached, but gaze meeting my own.

I always found it so hard to be direct in the face of that gaze. "I suppose you've heard about the death of Philippe de Chagny?"

His eyebrows rose slightly. "I doubt anyone in this building has not."

I glanced around, checking. No one was nearby, no one close enough to eavesdrop. And if the Phantom was hiding somewhere in earshot—I'd have to chance it. I lowered my voice. "You were there, that night. Do you know—are any of the stories true? About him?"

Someone else might have thought I meant Philippe, but I felt sure the Persian would know who I was asking about. The man we didn't name, not in this building.

This time his face didn't change at all. "If you have such doubts about him, I find it remarkable you continue to see him."

"I *don't* doubt him," I said coldly. Hadn't I told Mother I didn't, and wasn't it true? And why did every conversation with the Persian make me feel accused? "But surely you can see why I might value confirmation."

His gaze continued to study me, as though he was weighing the answer. Weighing me. At last he said, "I see. *Doveryai, no proveryai.*" When I blinked, he clarified, "An old Russian proverb. Trust, but verify. I can tell you that I myself heard the bell indicating a presence on the lake shore, and unless the Comte spent an extraordinary length of time crossing the lake, our mutual friend was otherwise occupied until well after the unfortunate nobleman must have drowned."

I exhaled slowly. Erik had mentioned an alarm bell too, so this story fit in. Not that I had had doubts, of course. "Thank you," I said, then in some kind of explanation added, "My mother was worried."

"As she should be," the Persian said.

This time my exhale was exasperated. "Are you going to warn me again?"

"No," he said. "It seems rather futile. And you are about to be late for ballet practice." Then he nodded again, and continued on down the hallway.

Somehow he always got the last word. But I really was late, so I had no time to be indignant about it. I dashed for ballet practice instead.

I told Mother about the conversation later, which predictably she found less reassuring than I did. But I hoped it might help, at least, to counterbalance the ongoing stories we both were hearing at the Opera. Although as it turned out, the finding of Philippe's body did not remain the favorite topic of conversation for as long as I would have expected—the announcement of the managers' next special performance, just a few days later, overshadowed everything else.

It was a relief. The special performance was such a harmless topic by comparison. Mostly, anyway. Except on occasions such as a break between rehearsals, when out of absolutely nowhere Francesca said, "But don't you think it's very risky of the managers to hold another gala? After what the Phantom did at the last one?"

We were all sitting on the wooden floor backstage so I couldn't look down very far, but I still turned my gaze towards my slippers, and commenced a completely unnecessary re-lacing of ribbons. Christine stories had finally been fading—it had been over twelve weeks now since she left—and I had enjoyed sitting with the girls at rehearsals and performances talking about *other* things.

"Yes, but that's because he was in love with Christine and angry that she was running about with Raoul," Lisette said in tones of perfect cheer. "Now Christine's gone, the performance will be all right."

I really had no idea how the gossipers had managed to extrapolate so much that was, probably, accurate. A few notes promoting Christine's career and they had leaped all the way to believing the Phantom was in love with her. Maybe because it was so easy to imagine any man falling in love with Christine.

"Do you *really* think she left with Raoul?" Francesca asked the group at large and then, inevitably, looked at me. "I mean, I know you had a letter from her. But maybe she wrote it under duress!"

Duress by who? Raoul? Impossible to imagine. Erik? *No.* "I don't think that's likely," I said, yanking on my slipper ribbons.

"But the Phantom was so angry—"

"*I* think Christine is a very dull topic," Adalisa interrupted, glancing once at me and then away again. "It's been weeks and weeks with nothing new. Nothing's left to *say*. Now what do you suppose Carlotta will choose to sing at the gala?"

I knew Adalisa had changed the subject trying to be nice to me. I appreciated it—except for the little part of me that resented it. Because Francesca wanted my opinion, and Adalisa thought I wouldn't want to discuss it, because they *both* thought of me as 'Christine's friend.' As though that was still one of the most important things about who I was, much more than I wanted it to be.

Especially when twelve weeks with never a word made me feel it was all too clear that I'd never mattered as much to her as she had to me.

But I didn't want to think about that, tried to tamp down that spark of resentment, and entered into the discussion of Carlotta with a good will.

It proved impossible to entirely avoid discussions of the special performance, at least without resorting to hiding under the Opera completely. Erik tried that, but found the empty rooms even more depressing, and drifted back to the upper reaches instead. He preferred listening when the topic was on Philippe's death and the Phantom's presumed hand in it—though even he could see that was rather a strange preference.

But the special performance was going to be so...far from what it could have been, if his own opera had gone differently. If *she* was still here, launched on the career only he could have given her.

Instead, Carlotta was singing six songs. *Six.* He disapproved of all of them. Each one was a painful reminder, a shadow suggestion of what might have been. Because as much as he wanted to tell Carlotta how terrible her choices were, as much as he wanted to focus on artistic outrage, it was a different thought consuming him. It was the thought of how *she* would have sung those songs.

It could have happened. If all had gone differently, if he had somehow made the right choices (though even now he didn't know what those would have been), if she was still at the Opera Garnier and pursuing a brilliant career, if she still trusted him, still believed in him, if he still had hope...

But she didn't. And he didn't. And none of that had happened. And it was foolish to think it ever could have. This ending, this tragic ending, was much more what the world had always offered him. Some operas were never meant to end happily. Though tragic heroes of opera at least got to leave the stage, weren't forced to linger on and on.

Ninety-five days, four hours. He had never thought, at the beginning, that he could live through so many days without her.

Carlotta. It was easier, hating Carlotta's song choices. He made a conscious effort to do so over the days spent preparing for the special performance.

He went back and forth repeatedly on whether or not to attend, but finally decided he would. He would be forced to listen to the Opera Company talk about it endlessly after, so he might as well see it for himself, to better judge the accuracy of their opinions afterwards. And it wasn't as if he had anything better to do that night. It would give him something to talk to Meg about too, though she had not had a great deal to say on the subject in anticipation.

He arrived in the auditorium shortly before the performance was due to begin, entering via a secret door backstage. It was the quickest, most discreet route up to the catwalks. Attendance was all much simpler when Box Five was available. The management still hadn't got rid of Mifroid's men, and he was going to have to come up with a new strategy. Some time after the performance.

By the time the managers were out in front of the curtain making a cheery little welcome speech, he was settled into an out-of-the-way corner of the catwalks. The view wasn't much but he could hear the music and the chorus. And he supposed he could put his hands over his ears during Carlotta's solos, if necessary.

Once the curtains opened, he could hear the murmur of the audience as well. They never stopped talking, more interested in their own gossip than in the performance on stage. From the noise level, it appeared Moncharmin had got the full house he'd been angling for these past few weeks. The Opera was clearly the place to be tonight, and everyone was here.

Except for *her*, of course. She hadn't been here for 105 days, eighteen hours. She should have been here, should have been starring under his careful direction, might by now have…

That familiar spiral of thought stopped abruptly when Erik's eyes focused in and stayed on the wide open, entirely empty Box Five.

He stared at it for a long, long moment, and finally shook his head, insulted. It was tempting—he was sitting on a cold metal catwalk, and Box Five had plush velvet seats and excellent acoustics, so *of course* he was tempted—but Mifroid must think he was an idiot to believe he'd fall for so obvious a trap.

The manager's new special performance was in mid-June, fifteen weeks after the previous one, fifteen weeks after Christine left the Opera. I managed to work up a credible amount of enthusiasm for the special performance, even if at first it had seemed it couldn't be remotely as interesting as the last one, with Christine gone and Erik visibly unwilling to discuss the subject. But I was enthusiastic enough to join the ballet girls' chatter backstage as we warmed up, waiting for the performance to begin…until I saw Commissaire Mifroid striding through the wings. Why couldn't the man just *go away*?

Instead here he was, with the managers and several policemen in tow. I glanced towards Madame Thibault, who was lambasting some girl on the state of her hair. I was almost sure Madame didn't *actually* have eyes in the back of her head, so I dared to rise out of my practice *plie* and drift a little closer to the commissaire.

Moncharmin was speaking as I got within earshot, in an urgent undertone. "But you *do* understand how important it is that everything goes smoothly tonight?"

"And it is also important that we bring a murderer to justice," Mifroid said coldly. "I'm sure you understand that."

"Perhaps we shouldn't interfere, Moncharmin," Ricard said, from his place hovering behind the other manager.

"Yes, yes," Moncharmin said with a flap of one hand, seeming to encompass Mifroid and Ricard both, "but do you have to bring him to justice *tonight*? And back here? Can't you try to catch him in some less occupied part of the building?"

I watched Mifroid's lips tighten and felt an odd sympathy. I could see how ridiculous the question was—but I was at the same time rather sorry that Mifroid saw it too. "This is all a careful strategy. I cannot simply rush off to a more convenient location. We are focusing on the Phantom's known areas of activity. I left Box Five empty with men stationed in the adjoining Box Seven and in the hallway outside."

Some of my sympathy vanished and my confidence returned, if Mifroid really thought Erik was going to fall for *that*.

"In addition," Mifroid continued to my regret, "we know the Phantom attended the previous gala, suggesting a likelihood he will be here tonight. We also know Joseph Buquet died falling from the catwalks."

"A suicide seems quite irrelevant," Moncharmin objected.

"Unless it was *not* suicide, and instead suggests a likelihood that the Phantom operates in the upper reaches." Mifroid's voice was growing tighter, his back straighter. "This is also suggested by the falling chandelier that I am sure you vividly remember. Therefore I have to attempt to capture him tonight, in your catwalks, not in the empty practice room on Sunday morning, which would no doubt be more convenient for you. Is that all perfectly clear?"

Moncharmin drew himself up, failing to gain much height. "I do not appreciate your tone, Commissaire!"

The rising volume of his voice was not appreciated by anyone else, as half the performers and, more importantly, Madame Thibault turned to glare at him.

That also meant Madame Thibault turned *my* direction. I got a portion of the glare and slunk unhappily back to my place, to resume my *plies* and *rond de jambs*.

I was unhappier about Mifroid than about Madame Thibault. How could he get every assumption wrong and still come to the correct conclusion? Erik had been at the last special performance because of Christine, who was very noticeably not here anymore. Buquet had come falling off of a catwalk because *he* had chosen to go up there, not because of the Phantom's habits. But none of that mattered, because Erik had mentioned he really did plan to attend tonight's gala from the catwalks. Exactly where Mifroid planned to search.

I couldn't stop myself from looking upwards, up towards the hanging ropes and unused scenery and criss-crossing labyrinth of catwalks and shadows, even though he certainly wouldn't be lurking about where a passing ballet girl could see him.

If I could somehow get him a warning…somehow get Mifroid off on the wrong track… The performance was beginning, the chorus starting their first number, making it far too late for me to go anywhere, to try to do anything. I could think of nothing to do anyway, and so I tried to convince myself that he didn't need my help. For years I had been comfortably certain that the Phantom could easily rout all enemies, but it felt different now that I had properly met him. Not that Erik didn't seem as smart as I had imagined—the contrary, in fact—but it was…different.

"What do you think is going on?" Francesca whispered beside me, and I followed her gaze to see she was watching Mifroid and his men retreat further into the shadows. Probably going to the stairs for the catwalks.

My first instinct was to say that I didn't know, because I hated feeding Francesca's love of gossip and intrigue—but perhaps that wasn't the right strategy. "I think they're looking for the Phantom," I said, loudly enough to be heard by several other girls. "The police think the Phantom is backstage right now."

"Backstage *here*?" Francesca squeaked, wobbling right out of Fourth Position. "Backstage with *us*?"

"Maybe," I said, and made a show of glancing around. "Better watch the shadows, you never know…"

Francesca gave a little yelp, craning her head wildly about and attracting the attention of another dozen girls. Whispered demands arose to know what was going on, and I quickly replied with, "It's the Phantom! He's back here somewhere. The police said so."

The squeaks and whispers and worried exclamations grew. The ballet girls were always more or less ready to go into fits about the Phantom. If I had asked any one of them individually, they all would have agreed that the opening of the special performance was a terrible time to enact any Phantom-related drama, but *en masse* no one stopped to think. They just responded with the same instinct that made them shriek and tell tales at all other, usually more convenient, times.

"Girls, be silent," Madame Thibault hissed as chaos rapidly developed among her troops. "This is inappropriate conduct."

With a timing I would have orchestrated if I could have, at that moment a tall figure came looming out between two curtains, looking positively sinister in the shadows and making even me jump. By the time the man stepped into clearer view, revealed as Samuel, the vocal director's assistant, probably sent to find out what all the hubbub was about, it was already too late.

Shrieks and screams erupted all around at the first sign of the tall silhouette, and once I caught my breath I happily joined in. I couldn't sing soprano, but I could scream. And screaming ballet girls were sure to get the attention of both the commissaire and the Phantom, with Erik far more likely to see Mifroid first.

Perhaps I should have cared about interrupting the special performance, but in that moment, flush with achievement, I truly didn't. Maybe they'd have to cancel one of Carlotta's songs to get back on schedule, and what a great loss *that* would be.

Erik was jarred quite out of his contemplation of the chorus' opening piece when a sudden calamity of screams erupted from the corps de ballet's place backstage. He rose to his feet, a frown half-worried and half-puzzled creasing his forehead. It didn't take much to set those girls off, but he hadn't done *anything* this time.

He moved carefully through the catwalks, mindful of any other activity above while monitoring what was happening at ground level. He had just reached a point above the ballet, the center of the tumult of shrieks and exclamations and shockingly ineffective orders from Madame Thibault, when the pounding of boot heels announced more arrivals on ground level.

"What is all this? What's going on?" demanded a male voice, pitched at a volume no performer would have used backstage during a performance, with the air of a man used to authority over unruly crowds.

A representative of the police. The police were backstage at the Opera tonight. Interesting.

"It's the Phantom of the Opera!" one ballet girl shrieked, and flung herself on the policeman's chest. Erik would bet money she'd taken enough time to notice he was young and handsome before she did it.

"Oh—um…" The man suddenly lost a great deal of his self-possession when confronted with an armful of hysterical ballet girl.

"Which direction?" another policeman asked. "Where did you see him?"

At once a multitude of directions were announced, mostly contradicting each other, and Erik smirked in spite of himself. No one was looking *up*. Although, he wondered if possibly…he found himself scanning for a blonde head, for the one face that might look the right direction, and stopped himself. This was silly, the one he should be looking out for was Mifroid, just to be sure he was heading the wrong direction and…and there was no sign of the police commissaire at all.

His spine prickled. Mifroid had to *be* here, it made no sense that he wouldn't be, but what was he doing that he didn't interrupt it for a lot of screaming ballet girls?

But of course there was only one thing he would be doing—ghost hunting.

Erik's head whipped around, scanning the shadows, listening for footsteps, not below this time but on his own level, on the catwalks. And far closer than he should have let them come, four men were advancing at the opposite end of his walkway. It was too dark up here to see clothing or faces clearly, but what little light there was glinted off rows of very shiny buttons.

Merde. Erik turned and ran the opposite direction, no doubt confirming all of Mifroid's suspicions, but that would have happened as soon as he got close enough to see the mask anyway. Pounding footsteps sounded behind him as Paris' finest gave chase.

"Stop! Police!" a voice that sounded like the commissaire's shouted behind him, confirming his own suspicions and certainly not inspiring him to halt.

The catwalk adjoined another a dozen yards ahead, but Erik didn't wait until he reached that point. He swerved left, got a foot up on the railing and leapt into space. A moment of flight then his hands closed around one of the innumerable ropes adorning the upper reaches and he swung for a parallel walkway. Curses sounding behind him, he landed in a crouch, back to his feet in an instant. Footsteps clanging on metal confirmed that the police were taking the long way around. That bought him a few seconds.

Two policemen were blowing their whistles now, each hitting a slightly different note, but no doubt both with the same message of summoning assistance. Probably also increasing the chaos both backstage and out in the house, if people correctly interpreted the sound. Chaos was good, reinforcements bad, and it took only a moment to flip a knife from his sleeve even as he ran down the new walkway, to reach out and slash through several ropes as he passed them.

With a groan, a heavy canvas backdrop plummeted from its place, crashing down towards the stage. The chorus was well to the front so no one would be hit, but the tumult as the canvas struck, and half the room screamed in response, made it sound as though the sky had fallen.

Not a chandelier, but still dramatic and alarming.

Erik seized another rope, helpfully in reach this time, no death-defying flights required, and ascended higher into the rafters. He checked his mental map of the Opera, thought he was in the right place, couldn't be sure until he put one hand up and felt the latch on the ceiling, invisible in the darkness. He pulled the latch, shoved the trapdoor up and open, and clambered through into the auxiliary gas control room. He had the trapdoor closed again before Mifroid and his men had reached the bottom of the rope, though probably not fast enough to keep them from realizing where he'd gone.

They might try the rope, but it wouldn't help them. He had locks on all his secret trapdoors, and it took only seconds to secure this one. Pushing from below, they'd have no leverage for breaking through.

Mifroid would try to come at him from a different direction, but it would take a few minutes. If this was a hidden chamber it wouldn't matter but this room, while unimportant enough to be unstaffed, still had a visible door. So he had very little time—but only one idea anyway.

He moved over to the rows of switches, imagining the scene below him. Half the audience would be out of their seats by now, thanks to that falling canvas and the obvious swarming of police to the scene. The performers likely had fled the stage, and if the ballet girls weren't fully hysterical before, by now they—he paused, hand stilled above the switches, thinking of the ballet girls. Of one ballet girl.

Meg wasn't the hysterical type. She'd keep her head, wasn't going to do anything stupid and, oh, fall down a flight of stairs or something. He suddenly wished he knew what she had done when the chandelier fell. He obviously hadn't noticed at the time, had certainly never brought the subject up since, but it suddenly seemed like it could be helpful history to have on hand at the moment...

He shook his head, sharply. Worrying about Meg was nonsense, just his usual paranoia turned towards a more unusual direction. He could not afford to tie his hands over sentimental paranoia.

He threw an entire row of switches, flipped a half-dozen more individually, then reached under the panel and flipped a few hidden ones besides. They'd get the gas lights relit, eventually, but in the meantime nothing increased chaos like a little unexpected darkness. Not total darkness, he didn't want people to trample each other and bleed all over the carpets, but enough darkness.

Then he drew his cloak around himself, stepped out of the room and slipped almost at once into a far more secure passageway, one quite inaccessible to anyone else.

To my great frustration, I couldn't tell what was happening with Erik. Mifroid was unfortunately not with the men who came to check on the corps de ballet, and then suddenly overhead there were police whistles and pounding feet and flurried shadows. I was still trying to work out which direction to look when a heavy canvas backdrop came crashing down onto the stage.

He did have a bit of a penchant for dropping heavy objects, didn't he?

The crash sent the whole place into a full-scale panic. An absolute herd of singers came stampeding off the stage, right into the mass of ballet girls who joined eagerly in the renewed shrieking. Some burly singer collided right into me, did not stop to apologize, and pushed on through the crowd. I dodged and twisted and finally took refuge pressed against a support pillar. With the pillar sturdy at my back, I let the crowd pour around me, pushing and shoving. I wrapped my arms tight around myself, tried to be as small as possible, and craned my neck to look up into the mysterious reaches where everything important was happening.

And then the lights flickered, flared and went out. It was never very bright backstage, but all the light from onstage, from the auditorium, went dark. I sucked in a breath as the tumult increased, pressing against my ears. It was a clever move—but I didn't like being caught in a panicked crowd in the dark.

It didn't take long, though, for my eyes to adjust, to realize that he hadn't doused *every* light. The shadows were larger, the light fainter, but we weren't in full darkness. Anyone who cared to look could avoid stepping on each other.

The worst surge of the crowd was past me by now too, everyone rushing out through the wings. And in the dim light, I caught a glimpse of figures descending a stair from the catwalks. I risked venturing away from my pillar, moving closer, and recognized Mifroid's voice when he said, "There must be another way to get up there! You two, with me, we'll find another stair. The rest of you, keep this crowd contained."

So they hadn't caught Erik. Not yet. Heart hammering, I carefully stepped through the shadows, following the dark silhouette of Commissaire Mifroid. Whatever might happen, he'd be at the center of it. What little light there was glinted off the barrel of Mifroid's drawn gun. Of course I knew he carried one, but I'd never seen it drawn before.

I followed the police through the wings, all the way to the gallery outside the boxes, better lit but also crowded with people. I knew a shorter way to get above the auditorium, but I wasn't going to tell Mifroid about it. The commissaire and his men were working towards the stairs when, over the thunder of footsteps and shouts of voices, I heard my name called.

I turned my head automatically, and a moment later Mother had got through the crush of people to reach my side. She pulled me into a hug. "Are you all right? This whole place has gone mad. Again!"

"Of course, I'm fine," I said, hugging her back but also looking over her shoulder to keep the police in sight. "Mifroid is going after Erik, I have to—"

She caught my shoulders before I had more than half slipped away. "What you *have to* do is get your cloak and we are going home. You are not getting mixed up in any police business—"

"Mother!" I twisted, but her hands stayed firmly clamped on my shoulders. "I just need to—look, the commissaire's already to the stairs, another minute and I won't be able to—"

"Just what do you think you're going to *do* if you're there?"

"I don't know, that's not the point!" I had no idea what help I could be if Mifroid cornered Erik, but I just—needed to see, needed to know.

"Commissaire Mifroid!" A voice rang out over the noise of the crowd, with a volume that would have made most artists proud. I pulled away from Mother, watched the commissaire come to a reluctant halt and turn to face Monsieur Moncharmin. All through the gallery, people were trying to hurry towards the exits or to find friends or to shove their way to a perceived safer location—many of those people slowed, stopped, and turned, instinctively drawn to the drama at hand.

I recognized any number of faces in the crowd. Half the ballet girls were still in sight, some still shrieking. I glimpsed the Persian's dark face at the far end of the hall, looking quite unruffled. Carlotta had found a strategic place halfway up a flight of nearby stairs to have a fainting spell, and the people tending her were the only ones not watching the managers.

Moncharmin stalked through the crowd towards Mifroid, Ricard hovering a step behind him as usual. Moncharmin's face was a perfect thundercloud of outrage, and for the very first time I thought I might not want to cross the manager—not because of the power he wielded, but just because of *him*.

Mifroid did not appear to share the sentiment. "M. Moncharmin, it is imperative that I continue in pursuit of—"

"You have irreparably disrupted my gala!" Moncharmin roared. "*Again!*"

This seemed slightly unfair; Mifroid wasn't to blame for the last time, though I'd happily heap guilt on him for this current mess. I was sure Erik would have attended without incident if the police hadn't got involved.

"I am going to have to refund an entire house!" Moncharmin waved an arm wildly at the crowds around him; luckily everyone was a prudent step or two away. "*Again!*"

Mifroid's lips were pressed into a thin line of distaste and frustration. "I am attempting to—"

"And special performance tickets are more expensive!"

Mifroid's voice rose slightly. "I am attempting to conduct a murder investigation and—"

"Stop throwing the word murder around in connection with my opera house!" Moncharmin was beginning to sound slightly hysterical; this was turning into a better show than the special performance would have been. Besides, the longer he delayed Mifroid, the better for Erik.

I wondered if he was watching the show too, from somewhere out of sight.

Behind Moncharmin, Ricard coughed worriedly. "*Our* opera house, Moncharmin."

Moncharmin ignored him, rushing right along on his rant. "You don't even know that a murder occurred! It's entirely possible that the wretched comte drowned himself!"

Commissaire Mifroid suddenly went very still. He took a slow, deep breath, drawing himself together, voice icy as he said, "That did not happen."

I had seen Mifroid serious before, had noticed the difference when he stopped being amused by the Opera Company. I'd never seen him look this dangerous, though. A prickle ran down my spine as I thought of Mifroid looking like *that* as he searched for Erik.

And the unexpected, unintended hero of the moment turned out to be M. Moncharmin, who pulled himself together and didn't even quail as he met Mifroid's stare. "Maybe it was an accident. Maybe someone else pushed him," he said, voice even. "Tell me what evidence you have that the Phantom killed him."

"The Phantom and the Comte de Chagny were seen onstage before—"

"That's not evidence of murder, just of an earlier conversation," Moncharmin countered. "Do you have a witness? Did anyone see a murder happen?"

This time Mifroid hesitated, and I knew before he spoke that Moncharmin had him. "We do not at this time—"

"Do you even have a *motive*?" Moncharmin demanded. "Neither one of them wanted silly Mademoiselle Daaé to run off with the silly vicomte, so if anything they should have been allies!"

Moncharmin must have been listening to the rumors about Christine too, if he believed that about the Phantom. That theory was true though, making his point reasonable evidence. I couldn't help turning to Mother, and raised my eyebrows in a 'there, you see?' expression. Her look back told me she was unimpressed.

Mifroid tried to forge onward. "The Comte de Chagny was last seen at the Opera Garnier before—"

"Last seen here *alive*," Moncharmin snapped. "You don't even know if he died here or not. You're only in this building, conducting this investigation, because I gave you permission."

Ricard coughed again. "*We* gave him permission."

"And that permission is revoked," Moncharmin barreled on. "You are no longer welcome here."

Mifroid's lips were nearly invisible, his face gone pale. "I can have a court—"

"With no evidence, witness or motive? I don't think so."

Mifroid stared at Moncharmin for a long, long moment. The manager didn't back down. I was holding my breath by the time Mifroid finally said, "Very well." His voice was low and cold and not altogether defeated. "We will go now. But this case is not closed."

"Just so you investigate it somewhere else," Moncharmin snapped.

Mifroid and his men began moving towards the exit and Mother said to me, "You needn't look so gleeful."

"You're right, people might be suspicious," I agreed, trying to arrange my face into calmer lines. "But wasn't M. Moncharmin brilliant?"

"That is not precisely what I was thinking," Mother said dryly. "And I hardly think we should condone the management's emphasizing of money over finding the Comte de Chagny's murderer."

I shook my head. "Oh honestly, they don't even have a motive for Erik to have done it! Maybe now Mifroid will go and *really* investigate. And probably it was just an accident anyway. Erik thinks so."

"Obviously that settles the question," Mother said, with just a hint of very dignified sarcasm.

"Exactly!" I agreed, and grinned at her until she gave up and smiled back.

Chapter Nine

Excerpt from the Private Notebook of Jean Mifroid, Commissaire of Police

15 June 1881

Failure at Opera's special performance. Only confirmed intruder hiding in opera house. Failed to apprehend him.

How could I have been so blind for so long? Ignored all previous stories of so-called Phantom. Now I saw for myself—he exists. No ghost, but very human criminal.

Opera's management understands nothing of importance of investigation. Must speak with the Prefect re: obtaining better backing for investigation.

The new disaster at the new gala performance was the reigning story at the Opera for days after, with much theorizing on whether the managers were actually cursed. Erik was willing enough to talk about it too, though he wouldn't explain how he had done the trick with the gas lights. I didn't tell him that I was the one who had set the ballet girls off shrieking. I could have, but somehow it felt—well, I was rather pleased with myself about it, but I didn't know that it would impress him, who could do so much more.

I expected Léon would also want to discuss the disaster in the Dance Foyer Saturday night—but when I met him, he was looking far grimmer than the situation seemed to call for.

"Sit down for a minute," he said, guiding me over to one of the green velvet banquettes. "I need to tell you something."

"All right, I'll brace myself," I said, lightly enough as it was hard to imagine Léon saying anything I needed to sit down for. We'd rarely exchanged so much as a serious word. But I didn't mind sitting, my legs tired from the evening's performance. I smoothed out the red-flowered skirts of my dress and looked up at him, waiting.

Léon took a deep breath, chest visibly expanding, then let it out audibly. "I'm leaving Paris next Friday," he announced.

"Oh. That's too bad." It was, too, and I felt heavier at the thought—although I could have taken the news standing up. I had enjoyed meeting with Léon, and I'd miss the fun he'd brought to my evenings in the Dance Foyer. "Where are you going?"

"Franzensbad, of all the godforsaken places." He groaned, dropped onto the opposite corner of the banquette and ran one hand through his blond hair. "It's all because of my mother. She wants to take the healing waters for her terrible ailments."

My thoughts flashed to my sister Gabrielle—a fever had taken her, all those years ago. But Léon's mother couldn't be that unwell, if she was planning to travel. I reached up to touch my necklace and said, "I'm sorry, I didn't know your mother was ill." He didn't talk about his family much. I had an idea he had several older brothers, but I was vague even on how many.

"She's *not*, it's only in her head." He gave a very expressive eye roll. "She'll probably outlive us all, but every six months she announces she's having sinking spells and her nerves are bad and she needs restorative something or other. Then someone in the family gets dragged around half of Europe with her. My brothers have already gone and now I'm stuck for it."

I'd like to see *all* of Europe, but I wouldn't have turned down half if it was offered. I leaned forward, hands clasped in my lap. "Isn't that rather exciting? Getting to see new places?" I'd like to go to Vienna—and Rome—and Athens—and maybe Franzensbad had never been on the list, but it was somewhere *else*, it was *different*.

Léon grimaced. "It's never worth the trouble. I always say, if it's not in Paris, it's not worth seeing."

I drew back, staring at him. He had never said that to me. I would have remembered it. "But that's not true," I protested, "there's so much to—"

"First it's off to this town in Bohemia so my mother can have magic mud put on her, and then who knows where she'll get it into her head to go from there. On her last trip she went the entire length of Italy before she finally came home." He groaned again, shaking his head. "I'm going to be exiled abroad for months."

Just at that moment I was thinking that a man who could speak so cavalierly of exploring the entire length of Italy (Venice, Rome, Milan, Florence!) was welcome to take himself off for months. And yet... I smoothed my already smooth skirts, took a deep breath to settle my mingled disappointment and irritation. Travel wasn't for everyone, and perhaps his mother wasn't a good travel companion—and the Dance Foyer was going to be dreary without Léon, with his laugh and his gorgeous blue eyes.

"Do you think it'll really be that long?" I asked. "Maybe she'll have a quick recovery."

"I couldn't be that lucky." He leaned back, glared at the entirely unoffending ceiling mural. "All because of that ridiculous special performance."

I blinked. I'd been prepared for that topic when I walked in, but it completely derailed me coming now. "The...special performance?"

"Yes, that's what set her off. She was in the audience when everything came crashing down and the police started swarming the place. She says the whole business was murder for her nerves and now she has to hare off to Bohemia for special water. As if I have nothing better to do!"

I briefly considered being angry with Erik over this. He drops some scenery, and Léon winds up whisked across Europe for unspecified months, probably long enough to forget me entirely.

I twisted at my gold necklace again, reflective. This did create a rather strange pattern of Erik dropping things and people I cared about leaving the country. Even if the chandelier had been an accident.

But that was silly, it wasn't the same thing—and who could have predicted this result from Mifroid chasing Erik through the catwalks?

"I thought you said she falls ill regularly," I pointed out. "The disaster at the performance is probably just an excuse."

"Most likely. But I don't appreciate the timing." And he looked at me with such an intensity in his eyes that I was disconcerted—but pleased too.

"Well," I said, taking a deep breath, trying not to sound as fluttered as I felt, "we will simply have to enjoy ourselves until you leave. And when you get back, I expect you to tell me all about the places you've seen."

I would have liked better to get letters while he was gone. But a girl can't suggest a thing like that to a man. Conventions could be winked at a little with Erik, who didn't seem to care, but Léon would know that a young woman didn't propose correspondence with an unmarried man. Not a respectable young woman, that is.

"I'd be delighted to do exactly that," Léon said, offered me his arm, and we rose from the banquette to take a turn around the Foyer.

As we walked and talked and laughed, I played with my necklace and wondered if he would come back. If he'd remember me, when he was off in Franzensbad in exotic Bohemia.

Erik knew he could never convince Mifroid now that there was no Phantom of the Opera, but if that was the only drawback to the evening it was a better hand than Fate usually dealt him. He'd keep dropping a few hints on savings to keep Moncharmin happy, so he'd continue barring the door for the police, and that should be satisfactory. It was ridiculous the amount of effort he had to put into being left alone, but that was nothing new.

Purely as a duty and to prevent future calamity, he kept a closer eye than he had done lately on the Opera Company over the week following the special performance. And so he could hardly fail to notice the Daroga lurking around the Opera too. More than his usual habit, and often involving loitering in empty hallways.

After two days of this, Erik waited until the Daroga had his back to a secret door, then stepped out and said, "If you wanted to talk to me, you could come knock on my door, you know."

He had never yet managed to rattle the other man by an unexpected appearance, but he kept trying. The Daroga turned now, even his footsteps steady, and quite calmly said, "Could I? I wouldn't want you to feel imposed upon."

Erik shrugged and said dryly, "Yes, because I have so many visitors. You did want to speak with me though?"

"The recent special performance…"

Naturally. "Oh, Daroga, take a positive view. Last time I dropped a chandelier. This time it was only a backdrop. An obvious improvement."

It was not surprising when the Daroga did not laugh. "Did Commissaire Mifroid see anything to identify you?"

"Are you concerned for my welfare?" Or for his pension, Erik reflected with more cynicism. It wouldn't go well if the Persian authorities ever realized he wasn't dead. "How touching. And no—I was merely a masked shadow, as usual."

"And your intentions in the future—"

"Oh, perhaps next time I'll just knock over a bit of scenery," Erik said airily. "Stop worrying, Daroga, nothing is going to disrupt your quiet life. No one is going to arrest me, and I'm not going to be violent."

"And so your life also goes on without disruption," the Daroga observed.

Considering how often and how deeply he had regretted that in the last 110 days, nine hours, this remark seemed more hostile than friendly. "Evidently," Erik said curtly. "I trust I've set your mind at ease." He turned to go.

"How is Mademoiselle Giry?" the Daroga asked softly.

Erik halted mid-stride, and turned back around more slowly. "Mademoiselle Giry is very well," he said in careful tones. Somehow he never called her that. Somehow they were friendlier than that. Curious that he'd never thought of it.

"It has been several months now, hasn't it?" the Daroga said. "That you have been spending time with this young woman."

"Has it," Erik said, permitting no emotion in his voice.

"And this continues to seem…wise?"

Of course. Of course the Daroga couldn't see good in the situation. He spread his arms to either side. "I haven't killed her yet, have I?"

A slight sigh. "I did not say that I expect—"

"But we both know you do, don't you?" Erik turned back towards the wall, hit his palm against it to trigger his secret door. "Good day, Daroga. I will try not to make your life more difficult."

"Erik, I merely—"

He stepped into the shadows, and let the door close behind him. His personal affairs were none of the Daroga's concern, and he had no intention of letting the Daroga's concern interfere with him. Just to prove the point, he would drop in on the morning's ballet practice. Discreetly from behind a wall, of course. He was trying to pay closer attention to the Opera Company, after all.

He didn't expect it to be an especially exciting morning, as he settled in behind the long mirrors lining the practice room. But as the practice went on, he realized, entirely unintentionally and only as part of his ongoing observations of the Opera Company, that something was happening to Meg.

He did not have a wide range of positions from which to eavesdrop on the ballet practice room (an oversight he had never previously noticed) but he could hear enough from the far side of the mirrors to know that a cluster of ballet girls had gathered around Meg, murmuring in sympathetic tones. He just couldn't hear enough words to know what they were being sympathetic about.

Madame Giry wasn't ill or newly fired; she came by Box Five at that evening's performance just as usual. Whatever was happening, it wasn't widespread gossip and he couldn't manage to catch any details elsewhere. Not that he was trying precisely.

When he met Meg early Thursday morning in the auditorium, he still had no idea what might be making the other ballet girls consider her in need of emotional support. She greeted him cheerfully enough when he joined her sitting on the edge of the stage, and they talked of nonessentials for a few minutes. Long enough to make it clear that, whatever it was, she wasn't going to bring it up.

Probably he ought to ease into this topic subtly and diplomatically. Unfortunately, he had no idea how to do that, and in desperation had to fall back on simply asking, rather abruptly, "Is everything all right?" And why wasn't she telling him if it wasn't? But he knew better than to voice that second question; it would surely look too demanding, too intense.

A pause, somewhat like the considering pause she often gave before her words, but this one had more of an overtone of confusion than simply thought. "...with what?"

"Well." How on earth was he supposed to say this? "With you."

She laughed a little now, but still seemed puzzled. "I'm fine. Why wouldn't I be?"

He was tempted to accept it and move on. Deeply tempted. But *something* was happening, and he wanted to know what. To be sure she was fine. He looked after the Opera Company. He had been remiss lately, but if he was going to be engaging again his own honor code meant he should be dealing with this. If a ballet girl was distressed, he should know if he needed to—threaten someone. "The corps de ballet seems to think you've had some sort of tragedy."

A pause, while he carefully didn't look at her. Finally she said, with more confusion in her voice, "How did you...?"

"I hear things," he said stiffly. Marvelous. He looked like he was poking into her business when he had never intended—anyway, it was because he was concerned, not because he was trying to pry.

"Of course you do," she said with a reassuring laugh. "Anyway it's not a tragedy. It's just that Léon has to leave for a long trip."

That *could* be a tragedy. He knew that better than anyone, that someone important going away could leave an enormous, jagged hole behind them. An emptiness that drained all the light, all the color out of life, that left only pain and loneliness to fill the silence. Though Léon couldn't be as important to Meg as *she* had been to him. And surely it was different, when you had a reasonable expectation the person was coming back. Not leaving you to linger on for 113 days, eight hours, and a possible eternity still ahead.

Distracted, he let a silence grow, which Meg apparently interpreted as having an entirely different cause. "Have I ever mentioned Léon?" she asked, and didn't seem to give any particular weight or significance to his name. "Léon de Troyes. He's a subscriber. I see him sometimes, in the Dance Foyer."

She had never mentioned Léon, but Erik had known who she meant. "The gentleman with the penchant for bright waistcoats." She blinked at that, and he just barely managed not to wince. "And...I occasionally see things too." Now he looked even more like he was poking about where he shouldn't.

"Well, you're right, that's Léon," she said, and then her voice softened, growing a touch more sentimental as she said, "Bright waistcoats and gorgeous blue eyes."

"I didn't happen to notice his eyes," Erik said dryly.

"Oh—no, of course—" She sighed, an exhale that seemed more exasperated than sad, though he wasn't sure if she was exasperated with herself or with him. "The point is, I'm *fine*."

Actually fine, or the fine where you said you were fine when you weren't remotely fine? Erik had very little social experience to draw on, but he knew everything about burying pain and hiding emotions and putting on a stoic front. He just didn't have any idea what to say when someone else was doing it. If she was doing it. He rubbed his palms, wracked his brain for something safe. "Well. I'm sorry."

"It's not your fault Léon is leaving," Meg said, tone oddly clipped of a sudden.

"No, I didn't mean…" Obviously it wasn't his fault. Unless it was. Had he done something without realizing he was—no, that was ridiculous. He took a breath, tried again. "I was just—trying to express sympathy." He had probably done it wrong. And he was almost sure that sympathy was like humor: you weren't supposed to have to explain it. Though maybe even that was wrong, he only knew that operas where they explained the jokes never got as many laughs, so—

"Oh. Thank you. But I'm fine. I think some of the ballet girls are sadder *for* me than I am. I mean, Léon is nice and he makes me laugh, but I'm not in love with him or anything." Her voice stumbled a little on the words, and her next laugh sounded forced. "And I'm sure you're not remotely interested in this—"

"I'm interested," he protested, because it seemed rude not to say so. Or should he *not* be interested in her feelings about Léon? Maybe it was bad if he appeared to be too interested. He wasn't that interested, not really. Did that faltering over the denial mean she *was* in love with Léon, or just that she felt awkward discussing the subject? "You let me ramble on about architecture and the irritations of Commissaire Mifroid, I can listen to you about—"

"I'm interested in architecture," she interrupted. "And Mifroid, but especially architecture from exotic places. I'm deeply jealous of everywhere Léon will get to see."

He seized on the topic of travel like a lifeline. He'd *much* rather talk about that than the intricacies of Meg's feelings about Léon, which was just so much more complicated and rife with the possibility of saying the wrong thing. "If you could visit one place, where would you go?"

"Vienna," she said promptly. "I've heard about it so often with so many musical connections, it seems positively mythical."

He wondered if that was genuinely her first choice, or if she just thought it would be the easiest choice to spin a conversation around. Either possibility seemed like a credit to her. "Vienna," he said with relief, "is a wonderful city. Or at least it was ten years ago."

Excerpt from the Private Notebook of Jean Mifroid, Commissaire of Police

24 June 1881

Unable to have satisfactory interview with Prefect Andrieux re: obtaining authority to continue PdC murder investigation. Prefect leaving position 16 July, can offer limited help now. Must arrange for early meeting with replacement re: support for investigation.

Chapter Ten

S aturday afternoon, I dug out all my pocket money and bought a dozen tangerines from a street vendor, a rare and lucky find this time of year when only hot house ones could be available. It cost more than I would normally spend on so frivolous a purchase, but I wanted cheering up. I went to the Opera Garnier, bag of fruit bouncing against my hip, and climbed up ten flights of stairs to the rooftop. It was empty and still, and felt like an island in the sea of bustle in the streets below.

Léon had left on Friday, and I had been all right until today's rehearsal. Then Adalisa and Francesca and all the others exerted themselves so much to sympathize with me that it made me feel far more blue over the matter. Luckily rehearsal ended early and I escaped for the few free hours before the evening performance.

I sat down on the wall bordering the edge of the Opera's roof, setting my hat and bag beside me and tucking my legs and skirt beneath me; I wasn't nervous about the drop while I was sitting down, but that didn't mean I was going to dangle my heels over the edge. Much better to look out over the rooftops, down the long Avenue de l'Opera to the Louvre and the Seine beyond, with my feet firmly this side of the void. In the quiet and the sunshine, only a few puffy clouds breaking up the blue of the sky, I tried to work out just how I did feel about Léon leaving, now when I didn't have the ballet girls telling me how awful it all was.

The prospect of the Dance Foyer tonight was a gloomy one. I had enjoyed spending time with Léon. We hadn't advanced very far in sentimental remarks, and he hadn't kissed more than my hand since Mardi Gras. But I liked him, and I liked that he appeared to like me, that he had chosen me out of the crowd to talk to and laugh with.

I slowly began taking tangerines out of my bag, piling them on the low wall beside me. On the other hand, we had always stayed on the surface of things. He was an enjoyable companion, but not an intimate one. Not someone to share secrets with, to talk over difficulties or perplexities. He wasn't, I realized as I toyed with one tangerine, the kind of friend I would talk with to sort out my feelings about a handsome subscriber leaving town.

I set the tangerine down with a faint thunk. I still wanted to talk to Christine. It had been four months since she left. She still hadn't written to me. I didn't know which country she was in, or if she was still with Raoul. It was all just a big blank, an opera stopped midway through when the heroine left the Opera Garnier.

Christine's leaving had hurt much more than Léon's did. My hand reached up to touch my necklace, to twist the gold disc on its chain. Christine's absence had put a hole in the center of my life, one that was still there. The ballet girls had been friendlier in recent weeks, and I was glad to be back in their circle—but I still missed having a best friend, a friend who looked to me first for a fun activity, a friend to chat with about news and venture into the Foyers alongside.

Léon had filled in some of the gap Christine had left, in a small way. I weighed another tangerine in my hand, thoughtfully. Perhaps I was less sad about him going than I still was about Christine.

Though of course Léon did have *some* charms Christine had not, and not only his blue eyes. Christine had always been the lead in the story; with Léon, the gazes he drew included me too, and while a friendship with Christine had turned the ballet girls away, Léon's interest drew them in. And he made me laugh, something I'd needed in recent months.

But even though all that made me wistful, I decided I wasn't really heartbroken. It was still a beautiful summer day and I could still enjoy sitting and looking out over the rooftops, eating tangerines. Surely if I was heartbroken, none of that would have mattered to me.

Léon would be back eventually, and probably he'd come back to the Opera and we'd resume seeing each other. If he didn't…well, I had fun with him, but we had no future anyway. Men like Léon didn't marry girls like me. Besides, I didn't know him nearly well enough to feel that I wanted to marry him.

I still wished I knew if Christine would ever come back. But dwelling on *that* was no way to enjoy the afternoon.

I pulled the last two tangerines out of my bag, adding them to the pyramid next to me. Where I sat was flooded with afternoon sunshine, but I knew without looking behind me that deep shadows dwelled in other parts of the roof, below the edge of the dome with the shining statue of Apollo at its top. The shadows made me wonder. About the other person who filled some of that empty hole in my life. Would it presume too much to call him a friend?

Without turning around, I remarked, "The view's much better at the edge than it is from back there."

I didn't hear footsteps, but I didn't expect to. Several seconds passed in perfect silence, and then a voice close behind me asked, "How did you know I was there?"

My heart raced, more pleased than startled. I looked back over my shoulder with a grin. "I didn't. I just guessed."

Erik was all in black as usual, even down to the long dark cloak. For an instant he looked like a bit of shadow caught incongruously in the light. I blinked, shaking that idea away, and he was just Erik again.

"Come join me," I said, and tossed him a tangerine.

He caught it with one hand, and stepped up onto the low wall. A sudden breeze ruffled my hair and caught his cloak, swirling it around him. "You're not afraid of heights?" he asked, gaze directed down at the street thirty-and-some-odd meters below.

"Not when I'm sitting down." I smoothed my blue-striped skirt over my lap, tucked a loose fold under my ankle, eyeing his feet and their position relative to the edge of the wall. "I tell myself I can't fall from this position."

"It's unlikely, at least." He walked perhaps a dozen feet away atop the wall, spinning the fruit up into the air and catching it again, back and forth from hand to hand, while I watched in horrified fascination as he stepped within an inch of the edge and never once glanced at his feet. He turned back around towards me and stopped, evidently catching sight of my expression. "Am I alarming you?"

"Slightly," I managed. I wasn't afraid of heights, but...

He walked back, more carefully on the inner edge of the wall, but I didn't really breathe easily until he sat down cross-legged beside me, the pile of tangerines between us. "I have good balance."

"So I see." I looked out again, at Paris spreading out before me, rooftops glimmering. Notre Dame's towers stood out in the distance to the east, rising from its island on the river. "Is the view any better standing?"

"Not particularly. The same things slightly higher up."

My gaze darted back to him and I wondered if that had been a joke. Unlike Léon, Erik and I didn't laugh together. In all this time I'd still never heard him laugh, not even once. But occasionally, now and then, he did betray a flash of humor.

He looked away, still tossing the tangerine from hand to hand— and then a twirl of fingers and it disappeared, a magical bit of sleight of hand. For a moment I wondered if he would pull it out of his ear—but no, not Erik, not that kind of silliness. Instead he glanced down at the tangerines piled on the wall. He picked up two, tossed them into the air. The third one returned as part of the circle as he juggled all three. They went around several times, and then suddenly a fourth one was in the air, then a fifth, and I had no idea how he'd contrived to pick the new ones up. I clapped when he got up to seven, and he bowed slightly before letting them drop back out of the circle, one at a time, until he only had one left.

"That was wonderful."

"It's only a parlor trick," he said with a slight shrug, but some warmth in his tone made me think he was pleased.

"Where did you learn to juggle?" I asked, digging my nails into one of the tangerines to peel away the rind, remembering too late that I didn't ask Erik personal questions. It was easy to relax, out here in the summer sunshine.

He looked down at the fruit still in his hand, and began to peel it in a neat spiral from the bottom. "I spent some time living with the Romani—the gypsies, as a child."

It was hard to say whether I was more delighted by the mere fact that he'd answered, or by the content of that answer. "Really? I think gypsies are *fascinating*. I mean, there's so many amazing things they can do, like juggling and reading fortunes and magic tricks." I popped an orange segment into my mouth, tasted a sharp burst of sourness, swallowed. "And they get to travel all over the place, see the whole world if they want to, always going somewhere new. Living with them must have been so exciting."

"No," he said, still looking at the tangerine in his hand, the long strip of peel. "I wouldn't say so." The words weren't harsh or even irritated, but they also offered absolutely no invitation to continue the topic.

"Oh." I pulled off another segment of fruit. Another wall, another mask, this one hiding some story from his childhood about gypsies. I mentally added it to the growing list of topics to avoid. Christine headed the list, and this one added in right after Persia. "Well." I ate the orange segment carefully, slowly.

Before I was finished, he asked, "Do you come up here often?"

I was frankly relieved. "When I can. I don't know why more people don't. I feel as if I can see the whole world from up here."

"It's actually only a few miles," he said, and if he had been someone else I would have thrown a peel at him. "But it does *feel* that way," he added, and I forgave him.

"Notre Dame looks splendid even from here," I said, picking up another tangerine and waving it in the direction of the two towers. Had Erik ever been to Notre Dame? Did he ever leave the opera house? I didn't try asking. "I go to Easter mass there, and I've climbed up in the towers a few times. You can see the Opera, and the statues on the corners shine even from there."

We both glanced up at the nearest one, a standing angel with high-reaching wings, and two seated attendants. They were gleaming in the sunlight. "They always shine," he said, "even on the cloudiest day. It's remarkable, how some things can shine even without light. And others never will."

Sometimes talking with Erik was like trying to understand a language I only half-knew. So much of what he said had several meanings to it, some hidden importance. I liked it. There was a *depth* to Erik's conversations.

"I like to think of the gargoyles and the angels nodding to each other across the rooftops," I said, half-surprising myself. It was such a silly little fancy, one I wouldn't expect most people in my world to understand. Léon would have assumed I was joking, but I wasn't precisely.

Erik only nodded. "Guardians of the temple of music and guardians of the temple of Christ. They'd have things in common. Such places need guardians."

I smiled, digging into another peel, and kept my next thought to myself. That it wasn't only the angels guarding the Opera Garnier.

She was so innocent, with her pretty imaginings about angels and gargoyles—and about gypsies. She likely didn't know their proper name, and probably pictured them in colorful clothes and lots of jewelry, traveling around Europe performing magic for awe-struck crowds. All of that was mostly wrong, of course, at least of the Romani he had known. That group had been clever and performed magic tricks, but always with an aim towards separating customers from their money, honestly or not. The clothes were colorful but they were patched, and the camps were dirty and smelled.

He didn't believe every Rom was dishonest, any more than he believed every Frenchman was dishonest. They were different, and he knew better than most how stories could distort the truth about people who were different. But his own experience still hadn't been the fairy tale Meg imagined.

It was much better to sit on the rooftop with her talking about the view, about Notre Dame, about gargoyles. He couldn't explain his past. He didn't want to talk about the recent past, about *her*, about all that had unfolded 115 days, sixteen hours ago, and he didn't want to talk about his distant past either. He couldn't tell her that his time with the Romani had been spent locked in a cage, exhibited as a freak.

No, he certainly wasn't going to tell her *that*.

How would she react? Fear? Disgust? Pity?

Maybe compassion. Even if he had been sure of that…no, it still wasn't something to talk about. He had no business bruising the fantasies of this laughing-eyed girl, casting a shadow on her light.

Such a contrast between them. He couldn't even juggle without bringing up deep-rooted horrors and exposing painful scars. But he didn't have to look at them. He could push them back into the shadows for now and sit in the afternoon light, eat tangerines and notice the way Meg's blond hair shone in the sunlight.

Excerpt from the Private Notebook of Jean Mifroid, Commissaire of Police

26 June 1881

Until able to take more direct action re: PdC investigation, have begun search into archives for detailed blueprints of Opera Garnier. Already finding indications that official plans do not match physical building.

Chapter Eleven

O nce the first wrench was over, I missed Léon less than I had expected. The ballet girls all seemed worried that I would be lonely, and made sure I wasn't. They could be very nice, when they weren't making up tales fit for gothic literature. Or when Jammes wasn't making remarks about Christine.

And Erik seemed to be around more often too.

I began spending free afternoons with the ballet girls, becoming an increasingly fixed feature in the circle. I still missed having one best friend, someone who sought me out first, but I liked having a half-dozen friends who at least included me somewhere in their list as a person to seek out. If none of them were as exciting as Christine— well, none of them asked me to carry messages to dull noblemen either, as I had done a few too many times when Christine wanted to communicate with Raoul.

On the other hand, I found myself squarely in the midst of an issue in having many casual friends one Wednesday night in July, when I wound up standing on the front steps of the Opera looking out at a dark night. I had thought I was leaving with a group of the girls to spend the night at Francesca's, but now none of them could be found.

Of course it was only an oversight, that no one had noticed I hadn't yet joined the group when they left. There was no reason to be hurt about that. Not at all. Really the concern was what to do now. I had only a hazy idea where Francesca lived so I'd have to go home—but Mother had left earlier in the evening, leaving me stranded.

The shadows were very dark out beyond the lit opera house behind me. It was already later than I liked to walk home alone, but I could hardly spend the night at the Opera, so—needs must. It wasn't far. Not very. I set off at a brisk pace, bag bouncing against my hip. I tried not to be bothered by how deserted the streets were, only an occasional passerby in the distance. The electric lights were bright down the Avenue de l'Opera, and I wished my path was that direction, instead of the much darker boulevards and side streets that actually led home. I took a deep breath against the tightness in my throat and kept walking.

I had only gone a couple of blocks when I heard footsteps behind me, and my throat got tighter. Whoever was making them was moving quickly and coming my way. I told myself it was probably nothing, scanning the street around me for any other pedestrians, perhaps someone I knew from the Opera, perhaps a very tall, very burly but friendly scenechanger… The street was deserted, except for me and whoever was walking behind me.

I had instinctively picked up my pace, but I didn't like the idea of trying to outrun someone. My legs were heavy from the day's dancing, although nerves were giving me a buzz of new energy. I'd feel so stupid running from someone harmless, and there was no telling how fast they might be too—but I did have one other option. I was probably worrying about nothing, and I reminded myself of that again as I came to a halt, bending down as though adjusting the fit of my shoe, and drew a small knife out of my boot. Just in case.

I turned to look behind me, to look for the origin of the footsteps. Perhaps it was someone I knew from the Opera, perhaps another woman, perhaps someone quite small and harmless.

Instead I saw a tall, definitely masculine figure in a dark cloak approaching directly towards me. I held the knife by my side, hidden in the folds of my skirt, and hoped the man would simply walk by.

He didn't. I had stopped walking to draw out my knife and now he stopped too, just in front of me. He was too close to pretend this had nothing to do with me, and yet not close enough for me to see anything of his face, in the black shadows beneath the hood of his cloak. My heart was loud in my chest, my fingers tightened around my knife, and I wished I had just spent the night at the Opera after all. There were couches. I could have slept somewhere.

Then he said, "Good evening," and all my coiled tension relaxed, breath exhaling in a rush.

"Oh. Hello, Erik." I felt almost silly. But it wasn't as though he owned the only black cloak in Paris, and I hadn't expected him here. Or anywhere that wasn't within the walls of the Opera Garnier, in fact. "What are you doing here?"

A very long pause followed, long enough that I didn't believe it at all when he said, "I felt like a walk."

I nodded sagely. "Of course."

"So...are you going farther that way?" he asked, with a vague gesture towards the continuing boulevard.

"No, I turn at the corner."

"Oh. Well, I don't have to stay on this street. You know, anywhere, all the same to me."

"Of course," I said again, and resumed walking. I struggled to contain a smile as he fell into step beside me. He must have seen me leave the Opera, and it was nice to think he was paying attention. And that he cared enough to come after me.

Walking next to the Phantom of the Opera, I felt confident I didn't need to worry about whoever else was out in the streets tonight. I was still holding my knife, and now I reached to my bag to put it away, easier than sliding it back into my boot.

Erik didn't miss the gesture. "What's that?"

I felt unaccountably awkward. "It's...nothing, really, just a..." Well, this was ridiculous, why shouldn't I tell him I carried a knife? He likely had a lasso in his coat, judging by the time I'd seen him with Buquet. "Bit of insurance, you might say." I held it up just long enough for him to see what it was, then tucked it away in my bag. "Just in case."

"Oh." I still couldn't see his face, but his voice sounded surprised.

"It makes me feel better on dark streets when there are footsteps behind me." A thought suddenly struck me, a realization of the other reason I hadn't expected it to be Erik approaching. "You don't usually make footsteps!" I couldn't hear him walking now.

"I was trying not to sneak up on you," he said in dry tones. "Which I will be especially careful of in the future."

I wished I could see his face—though it was even odds for whether that would give me a clue to what he was thinking. His voice didn't sound judgmental exactly, but I still felt a need to justify myself. Maybe because Christine had found the whole idea of carrying a knife "gruesome and morbid and not entirely proper." Though why a 'proper' girl shouldn't be able to protect herself... "I decided the night Buquet died, I'm not going to be a passive victim if—"

"The night Buquet died?" Erik repeated, voice suddenly warming with urgency. "You started carrying a knife after *Buquet died*?"

That may not have been the wisest subject to bring up. We'd never discussed this before, and I should have guessed it would be one of his uncomfortable topics. I might have danced away from it, but it felt like we were too far in. "Buquet's dead, but there are too many Buquets in the world, and if some man ever wants to bend me backwards over a stair railing like Marie, I want some options. Even a ghost can't be everywhere."

His head turned and I could feel him staring at me. "How do you...did Marie talk to you?"

I could have said yes. Marie wasn't even at the Opera anymore, so there'd be no one to dispute it. But I didn't want to lie to him. "No. I saw her leave during the performance that night, and I was worried about her so I followed. And then I saw what happened." I tried again to see his face through the shadows, without success. I thought he might be angry about this, though I couldn't have said why exactly.

He was looking ahead again, not at me. "Then you know I was on the catwalk with Buquet." His voice had gone flat.

I didn't understand the weight he was giving the words. Was it such a revelation? "Everyone knows that. Or thinks they do."

His words in response came slowly, heavily. "I thought…maybe you believed it was suicide, but if you saw what happened below…"

"And above," I filled in. Might as well confess it all. "I climbed the stairs too." I held up a forestalling hand. "And don't tell me it was foolish, Mother already did, at length. But I did climb up there, so…I saw what happened."

"I'm sorry." His voice was barely above a whisper.

Sorry I'd seen? Sorry for what had happened? Either way, my answer was the same. "It was an accident. It wasn't your fault." I had accepted that long ago. It had never occurred to me that Erik might not have.

"It was an accident," he agreed, voice low. He rubbed his palms against his pant legs. "That doesn't mean it wasn't my fault."

Suddenly I was out of my depth—perhaps it was better that Erik steered us away from certain topics after all. Because this conversation had turned heavier, darker, more intense than I was prepared to navigate. But I had to say *something*, respond somehow to that low thrum of guilt in his voice. I liked him. I didn't want him to feel badly. And I truly didn't blame him. I tried to sound calm, grown-up, sensible. "It seems to me it was Buquet's fault."

"I made choices," he said curtly, dismissively.

"*Buquet* made choices too," I countered, irritated that my best effort was so inadequate, that he saw how inadequate it was.

An audible exhale. "You don't understand."

"No, evidently I don't," I said in clipped tones. He probably thought I was foolish and naïve, and I hated that. And it was somehow easier to be annoyed with him for thinking it, than to try to decide if it was true.

We walked past two more buildings in heavy, charged silence, and then I stopped. "This one is me," I said, inclining my head towards the nearest doorway. "Good night." It came out ungracious and unfriendly, and did nothing to lighten the silence.

He stood still a long moment, then finally said only, "Good night."

I nodded, turned, and went up the steps to unlock the door. I glanced back from the threshold, watched him merge into the shadows, moving back down the street towards the Opera Garnier.

I felt obscurely better. I wasn't the only one bothered by how that had ended. He'd forgotten to pretend he meant to walk on farther.

I smiled, then sighed, and went in. I had a suddenly sharp missing for Christine. Not exactly Christine as she would be if she came back now—but as it might have been if our histories were different, if I could go back and talk to the girl I'd known those first few months, before she got mixed up with an Angel of Music. I could have told her about this baffling new friend I had, who was so complicated and yet who was so worth weathering the storms for, asked for advice on what I should have said and ought to do now.

I couldn't talk to Mother, who would look so disapproving about the whole business, who would be all too alert for any hint of difficulties in my friendship with Erik. And the ballet girls were utterly out of the question.

It would have been nice, to still have my best friend to talk to. She wouldn't have known what to say to Erik either, but at least she could have sympathized. Gabi would have sympathized.

I added Buquet to the mental list of topics to avoid, right after gypsies, and thought about adding personal responsibility and guilt to the list too—but that seemed too big a topic to cut off.

Not that I entirely avoided the other forbidden subjects either. I thought about them a lot. Especially gypsies. I wondered about the gypsies. Also Christine, who we still had never spoken of. Thinking about Christine hurt more, so I tried to wonder about the gypsies.

I went to the Grand Foyer for my next scheduled meeting with Erik, he appeared, and the conversation was not too awkward. We did not discuss Christine, Persia, gypsies or Joseph Buquet. But I thought. And I went on thinking as I met him in the auditorium twice, the rooftop once, back in the Grand Foyer, and again in the auditorium before I mustered the courage to turn the conversation to interesting sights and locales in Paris, with one especially in mind.

He mostly let me talk, and I couldn't discern if he'd actually visited anywhere I mentioned. Finally I seized a pause when it wouldn't be too unnatural to say, "I went to the Anthropological Gardens once too. You know, in the Bois de Boulogne."

"I'm familiar with it." His tone was guarded, the tone that meant I should drop it and add it to the forbidden list.

And yet. I had given a lot of thought to gypsies, and what someone like Erik might have been doing with them, and I had something I wanted to say. Something better than what I'd said about Buquet, that maybe would show him I wasn't altogether a silly ballet girl.

"I thought it would be fascinating," I pushed on. "They advertised all about how visitors could see people from distant lands—Zulus and Bushmen and I don't remember who else, but people from all those places I want to go see. But then when I went, it just seemed rather sad. I mean, I know what costumes and sets look like, and that's all this was, and it wasn't any more real than what we do here at the Opera. Less, even, some of the sets were dreadful. Except for the people—*they* were real. And I wondered what that must be like, to dress up in a sort of mockery of your real world, and stand around for curious Parisians to gawk at. At least on the stage, the audience knows we aren't what we're playing. There, the crowds believed it all, and I thought that must be the worst part. To have everyone believe that you were what you looked like, and never see who you *are*." I paused. "'You' in the general sense, of course. Or…who *they* are, I guess I mean."

"I knew what you meant." His eyes cut sideways to look at me. "I knew *exactly* what you meant."

And *then* we dropped the subject. But I felt a certain satisfaction that maybe, even without Christine to advise, even if it wasn't the perfect thing to say, maybe I'd managed to say something just a bit worthwhile.

Excerpt from the Private Notebook of Jean Mifroid, Commissaire of Police

17 July 1881

Had interview with new Prefect Camescasse. Useless. Laughs at notion of "Opera Ghost," believes M. Moncharmin re: claim that chandelier was accident. Wishes investigation of PdC murder to be carried on outside Opera Garnier.

I <u>know</u> this is wrong strategy. Will continue to investigate Opera Ghost, alone if necessary.

Despite my best efforts, my attention was decidedly wandering as the girls chattered on one afternoon during rehearsal about who Madame Thibault would assign to which role in our next production. I did care about assignments—but it was obvious Sorelli would dance the lead, and there were only five other girls good enough and senior enough to dance the five other principle roles. Going around and around in circles proposing names who couldn't be chosen seemed pointless.

They kept talking as we stretched, waiting for our turn in the rehearsal, and my attention drifted upwards, up towards the tangled forest of ropes and sandbags and catwalks above us. Too many shadows lurked up there for me to know if one of them was more solid than the rest. I knew he observed rehearsals sometimes, so maybe. I might ask him tomorrow—and smiled to think that I *could* ask him. It would be a more complicated but more interesting conversation than this circular discussion of assignments.

Loud laughter distracted me from my musings. Not the other girls laughing, but four scenechangers sitting on boxes nearby. They were passing a dark flask back and forth, and nothing about their unshaved faces or stained clothes inspired confidence.

I instinctively turned a little away, extended one arm to put the movement into my warming up. It wasn't really fair; they were likely honest workmen. The scenechangers had always been a rough element among the artists of the Opera Company, some more pleasant than others. I knew most of them were not like Joseph Buquet. But I did hope that Erik was around somewhere.

Another shout of laughter made Mignonette next to me sniff disdainfully as she stretched one long leg in front of her. "I don't know why the management doesn't talk to them about proper behavior. They're so unpleasant."

The other girls murmured agreement, and I glanced over at the scenechangers again. One man was tipping his head back to drink from the flask, and as the light reached below his low-pulled hat to hit his face, some feature caught my attention. The shape of his nose, or the line of his jaw beneath a smudge of grease...he wasn't as burly as the others, tall but not so stocky, though his clothes were of the same mold as the rest.

Around me the girls went back to wrangling about positions while I tried to grasp at the stir of memory the scenechanger's face had given me. This was silly, surely I'd just seen him around the Opera. And yet...

Suddenly it snapped into place, and I knew where I'd seen that face before. Commissaire Mifroid was sitting backstage in rough clothes with dirt on his face, guffawing loudly from within a group of scenechangers.

I felt my lips part, and hastily tightened my jaw, trying to keep shock off my face. There had been no sign of Mifroid since Moncharmin confronted him at the special performance, a few weeks ago now. I had hoped he had moved on, forgotten about the Phantom. I had dared to forget about the commissaire myself, though there had been no conclusion to Philippe's murder investigation in the papers. But now—hadn't I seen enough operas involving disguises? Clearly Mifroid was trying to find something out. So I'd best not let him catch me staring.

It had only been a few seconds, and now I quickly turned my head back to the other girls, lowered my gaze as I bent down to reach for my toes, extended across the wooden floor before me. All my attention, however, was for the men off to my left. They weren't so far away, if I listened hard.

First it was just snatches of phrases, then my ear seemed to catch the rhythm and the words came clear.

"No, it's not glowing eyes," one man was insisting, voice adamant. "Glowing eyes is just nonsense. Pampin said he saw a whole *head* of fire!"

My stomach did a flip. I knew who had glowing yellow eyes.

Well, not actually, but the reputation for them.

"And it must've been *horrible*," the man continued, "the way it shook Pampin. And he's a fireman! Shouldn't be afraid of fire."

"Can't blame the man," Mifroid said, voice marked with an unfamiliar slur. "Trapped on a catwalk with a flaming head coming at—"

"No, not the catwalk. The third cellar under the stage, that's where Pampin saw him."

I risked a glance at Mifroid, and saw him tapping the fingers of his right hand against his leg. Perhaps he was missing his notebook.

I locked my fingers together around my heel, to avoid beginning any nervous tapping myself. He wouldn't learn any useful information this way. People saw the Ghost all over the Opera. The story didn't *mean* anything. But the fact that he was here, talking about the Ghost—

My own name caught my ear and I hurriedly brought my attention back to the girls. I looked at Adalisa, who was looking back at me expectantly, and I had not the slightest idea what the appropriate response would be. "Sorry, what was that?"

Luckily her expression didn't turn irritated. "I said, maybe *you'll* be chosen to dance the second lead."

Still on the role conversation. "No, it won't be me," I said automatically. If Mifroid was still investigating the comte's murder and asking questions about Erik…

"Oh, don't say that," Adalisa protested, leaning in closer, "it could be you!"

"No, it *won't* be. I'm not a good enough dancer for that role." Even if Erik was up in the catwalks right now, he wouldn't recognize Mifroid from up there, so…

I realized my mistake a heartbeat too late, as an awkward silence fell and the girls all stared at me in confused consternation. I gritted my teeth, annoyed with myself. I had broken form, and I knew better than this. In the competitive world of the Opera, none of us downplayed our ability, save an occasional, presumed-insincere protest for modesty's sake. *And* I had failed to keep the cycle of complimentary suggestions going.

I formed my mouth into a smile. "Well, maybe it'll be me. But really, I think it might be you, Adalisa."

She smiled back at me, likely more sincerely, and the other girls relaxed again. "Oh, I don't know—do you really think so?"

"Yes, I really do," I said, even though I was sure it was impossible. Just as I was sure that I needed to tell Erik about Mifroid tomorrow.

Erik listened for a moment, from the far side of a secret panel in the Grand Foyer. Meg was pacing, the tap of light footsteps back and forth below the painting of Thalia, muse of comedy. Her skirt rustled as she twitched at it while she walked. Everything in the sounds suggested impatience.

He still waited until her footsteps passed his hidden door, then quickly slipped out and closed the wall behind him. "Am I keeping you from something?"

She whirled to face him, evidenced no surprise at his sudden appearance, and ignored the question. "You're late!"

"I am not. You're early," he responded automatically, but wondered—did that mean she had been impatiently waiting for *him*? How extraordinary.

"Never mind," she said, brushing past the question in quick words, "I have to tell you—I saw Mifroid at the Opera yesterday. Disguised as a scenechanger backstage."

Interesting, not altogether shocking. He had expected Mifroid to resurface eventually. Problems never went away easily for him. It was only people who did that. He hadn't guessed the commissaire would show up this way though. He thought of Mifroid's usual impeccable suits, ran one palm over his own waistcoat. "He must have hated the clothing."

"And they were talking about you," Meg said, tone suggesting this might be the shocking part.

It really wasn't. "The scenechangers often are," he agreed. They were almost as good as the ballet girls at spreading wild stories, though less creative at inventing their own. "The glowing yellow eyes?"

A quick shake of her head, her blond hair catching the morning sunlight through the nearest window. "No, the head of fire, but—"

"Ah, Pampin's apparition." That had been one of his more effective moments of haunting, a story with a gratifying refusal to die out.

"But that's not the *point*." She stared at him, her blue eyes wide and so much more anxious than he would have expected. "The Commissaire of Police is trying to find you," she said, words slow as though he was struggling to grasp them.

He shrugged with the resignation of years. This plotline was all too familiar in his opera. "Someone always is. And it's not as though the scenechangers can give him useful information."

She bit her lower lip, leaned back against a pillar with her hands pushed into the pockets of her blue-striped skirt. "I don't know. If he's so determined to stay on this, if he picks up enough stories, if he starts to put pieces together..."

He crossed his arms, studying her. "Why are you worried about this?"

She sounded exasperated now, as though he really was being slow. "Because if the commissaire starts putting the right pieces together, you are going to—"

"Yes, I know what it means," he interrupted, "but I don't see why *you* are..." Somehow, saying it out loud a second time, the question seemed to make less sense. Maybe because he could see it on her face when she realized what he was trying to ask. And something about the way her eyes softened made him feel it had been a rather stupid question after all.

"Because I don't want that to happen," she said quietly, one corner of her mouth rising in a half-smile.

He looked down at the polished floor, resisted an urge to give an awkward cough against the embarrassed tightening of his throat. "I suppose your mother would miss the tips in Box Five," he muttered, even though he didn't actually believe that was what she was thinking.

"That too," she said, voice calm and unembarrassed. "So what are you going to do about Mifroid?"

"I don't see that there's much possible," he said, relieved to move to this less charged topic. "A ghostly apparition would be counter-productive towards making him doubt my existence. Though I imagine chasing me through the catwalks at the special performance rather convinced him that I exist."

"A glowing face wouldn't scare him off either," Meg said, words slow in a thoughtful way this time. "He doesn't seem the type. But the managers banned him; if you told them he was here—"

"So they can conclude he alarms me, and maybe they ought to work with the police after all? I *don't* think so," he said, jaw tight. Seeking help from Moncharmin and Ricard sounded about as appealing as an untuned violin.

She sighed. "There must be a way to phrase a communication better than that."

"If you think it's so important for them to know, you tell them," he said shortly.

"They won't listen to me," she said, words regretful but sure of what she said. "They just think of me as Chr—a silly ballet girl. They'd think I imagined it."

As *her* friend. That's what Meg had been about to say. Her presence still lingered, 139 days, seven hours after she herself was gone, and not in his mind only. "There's no need to take action around Mifroid, because his skulking around isn't going to accomplish anything," he said firmly, trying to put a definitive close on the topic. "I would much rather discuss the next ballet production. Even if it's entirely obvious how the roles will be assigned."

He really meant it, about Mifroid. The man wasn't worth wasting time or emotion over. Mifroid could talk to as many scenechangers as he liked; stories about flaming heads wouldn't lead him back to the Phantom. And even if, as Meg seemed to think, the commissaire managed to put enough clues together to actually find him—well, Erik knew countless secret doors and passages in the Opera Garnier. He could always slip away.

And in the worst of possibilities, if his secret doors failed him—he was still sure he could avoid being taken alive, and that was the only possible eventuality that bothered him.

No, on the whole, Mifroid's presence at the Opera was far less interesting than the fact that Meg was worried about it.

Excerpt from the Private Notebook of Jean Mifroid, Commissaire of Police

23 July 1881

Early investigations into Opera Garnier providing mixed results. As expected, more stories of "Phantom" forthcoming when Company believe talking privately. Stories wildly inconsistent, many too fanciful to be useful. Investigation into building itself proves inconsistency with official plans. Possible secret passages and rooms throughout building to remarkable extent.

I didn't want to pester Erik about Commissaire Mifroid—but he had been so dismissive the first time, I couldn't stop myself mentioning the policeman again the next time we met, in the auditorium this time.

"So you're really not going to do anything about Mifroid poking around the Opera?" I asked, trying and failing to make the words sound casual.

"I told you already, there's nothing that needs doing," Erik said, leaning back on his hands as we sat on the edge of the stage. He didn't exactly sound irritated, but he was looking across the long rows of red seats instead of at me, and his tone was disinterested.

I knew I should let this go. And I knew he was wrong, that the police commissaire shouldn't be ignored. The conflict of those twin ideas frustrated me enough to say, rather shortly, "Fine, we'll just say a prayer and hope for the best then. That's a solid plan."

"No, I don't intend to do that either."

I should have heard the new coolness in his voice, a small warning bell that hadn't been there when I first brought Mifroid up. But I was both frustrated and confused. "Assuming Mifroid will go away seems to me to be simply hoping for the best, so—"

"No," he said again, and the words that followed were painfully even and precise. "I do not intend to say a prayer."

"Oh." But everyone prayed. Well, not *everyone*, I wasn't that naïve, and I knew not everyone who prayed altogether meant it—but prayer still seemed woven through life, comforting, natural and inescapable. And how lonely would it be, to live alone under an opera house, without even God or the saints to talk to?

The silence stretched between us, more uncomfortable than any silence had been for many weeks. I hadn't noticed until just now that silences were growing less frequent, and it was little comfort to realize it now. Erik was still staring out at the seats, jaw tight. Had I offended him? I had my mental list of topics to avoid, but I never would have dreamed *this* one would be a problem—at least not such a harmless comment as suggesting a prayer. And I had hardly even meant it!

I had to say something. Anything. And of course I couldn't think of any new topic at all now. "St. Antoine, he's my favorite saint," I remarked at random, because anything was better than silence. "Patron of my church in Leclair, and of lost items. The ballet girls invoke him all the time, you know, lost ribbons and things. Too bad he isn't— well, I guess you want Mifroid to become lost, sort of, but..." I trailed off, because this was not helping.

Erik sighed. "Say a prayer for me, if you must. He's far more likely to listen to you."

I wasn't sure if he meant St. Antoine or God or both. Awkward as this had already been, that put us onto more alarming theological quicksand. This was as bad as talking about Buquet, or worse. "I'm...sure He'd listen to you too..."

Erik stared up at the gold decorations on the distant boxes. "All indications have been that the Almighty is, shall we say, less than fond of me. The feeling is mutual."

That in no way fit anything I understood about God, not the kind, compassionate God they talked about at St. Antoine in Leclair, or even the slightly more distant one the priest at my Paris church liked to describe. And it was heartbreaking, for Erik, who was already so alone, to believe such a thing. "I don't think God thinks that way," I said softly.

"Yes, yes, he loves us all," Erik said with a bitter twist to his voice. "Don't quote me the Prodigal Son, I don't want to hear it. No kindly father has ever rushed out to forgive *me*. But perhaps some people don't deserve forgiveness."

"I don't believe that," I protested, instinctively reaching out to touch his arm.

He jerked away, rose to his feet in the same movement. "Keep me out of your prayers too," he growled, and stalked away into the wings.

I exhaled slowly, trying to gather my scattered wits. From an off-hand comment to all of this. I liked the complexity of conversations with Erik, but this one had me feeling all at sea. So much anger, so much self-hatred, and I felt so lost knowing how to respond.

I sat for a few minutes more, and had only just got to my feet when the curtains at the side of the stage parted and Erik reemerged, head at a sheepish tilt. He coughed, didn't quite meet my eyes. "I'm sorry." A shrug. "*Mea culpa*. My fault."

Well. At least he wasn't angry with *me*. I smiled slightly. "It's all right."

His eyes lifted momentarily, dropped again. "And…I think I'm probably beyond your St. Antoine. Better try St. Jude."

The patron saint of hopeless causes. I looked at him for a long moment. What did he see in himself that I couldn't see? What did I see that he was blind to? Finally I shook my head. "Not St. Jude. St. Pierre. He understood about being forgiven for the unforgivable."

Another moment, then Erik slowly nodded. "If you must," he said, but the sting had gone out of it.

That night, I prayed to St. Antoine, that Erik might find his lost way; to St. Pierre, who knew about keeping hope through the darkest of days; and to St. Jude, just in case. I wasn't exactly sure what any of them were going to do about Commissaire Mifroid, but weighing it all out, Erik seemed to need prayers for more important matters.

Chapter Thirteen

I didn't bring up God or saints or prayer again with Erik. I mentioned Mifroid again though. For more than a week Erik flatly refused to do anything about the policeman. I saw the police commissaire in disguise another time, and he might have been there every day without me seeing him. I was used to keeping an eye out for the Persian, who was still frequently to be seen on the edges of any crowd, and now I kept a much more worried eye out for Mifroid too. Erik still said the policeman's presence didn't matter, and I wanted to believe him—but I didn't. And I could think of no way to deal with the police commisaire myself.

I was growing desperate as July ended. Mother and I were due to visit Leclair for three weeks in August. It felt all wrong to leave when the situation with Mifroid was still unresolved. I'd spend the whole trip convinced that I would come back from my visit home to hear the Opera Company all abuzz with the capture of the Phantom.

If another friend disappeared without a trace, I didn't think I could handle it. Christine had been gone for five months now. It would be impossible for Erik to vanish more completely than Christine had, but at least I could hope she was well and happy, exploring some distant place more exciting than here. I couldn't hope that for Erik, if Mifroid took him.

Refusing to leave Paris would mean a pitched battle with Mother, and I wasn't sure I wanted to spend my energies on this fight. I couldn't articulate how it would make a difference if I was there or not, and I foresaw plenty more fights coming about Erik that could be more important.

I saw Mifroid for the third time on the first day of August. I was in rehearsal, one of a line of girls practicing on the stage, and there was Mifroid, slouching in his scenechanger garb, leaning up against a support pillar in the wings.

I lost the rhythm of my *entrechat*, landed wrong, and it took me three beats to get back into formation with the other girls. I knew I'd be in trouble with Madame Thibault, but I still couldn't help glancing too often towards the wings during the rest of our dance. Mifroid wasn't doing anything, just standing there.

"That was appalling," Madame Thibault informed us in ringing tones when we reached the close. "Mademoiselle Giry, I do not know where your mind is but do us the great courtesy of putting it back on your dancing. And the rest of you were hardly any better."

She cast her fierce hawk's gaze over us all, leaving lowered heads and murmured apologies in its wake. I kept my head down—but watched Mifroid out of the corner of my eye.

Madame Thibault clapped her hands once. "All of you off the stage while Signora Carlotta practices her aria. Then we go through it another time."

With sighs and a few muttered complaints, we all wandered off into the wings—and I made sure I went stage right, towards Mifroid. That also took me by La Carlotta as she strutted towards the stage, back straight and nose in the air, but I had little attention to spare for her. Why was Mifroid still *here*? What was he hoping to find out? And *why* didn't Erik do something about it?

I walked past Mifroid without looking directly at him and sat down with several other girls to stretch and re-lace slippers and wait until we were called again.

Carlotta was only a few lines into her song when the managers came strolling out from stage left. They liked to attend rehearsals— Moncharmin looking happily proprietary, and Ricard pretending he knew what was going on (though it was hit and miss whether he did) and flirting with the ballet.

"Ah, Signora Carlotta!" Ricard called as they approached her. "Are we in time to hear you sing? How delightful!"

Carlotta stopped singing, and around me all the Company held their breaths to see if she would be gracious or angry. I tore my glance away from Mifroid, and saw Carlotta smile and extend a hand for Ricard to kiss. No furious explosion today then—at least, not right now.

"It is always so special to have you here," Carlotta said in honeyed tones, then gestured as though pushing the managers away. "Now if you would give me room to sing?"

"Of course, of course," Ricard said happily, and he and Moncharmin completed their crossing of the stage, bringing them over near our group of ballet girls. "But I'd be delighted to see you lovely ladies dance too!" Ricard told us at large.

The girls nearest him giggled, and the managers took up positions watching at the very edge of the wings. Not far from where Mifroid was standing. And I saw him leave his position against the support pillar and move closer to the managers, standing behind them and pretending to busy himself with a stack of boxes.

First I thought that he must be hoping to learn something from them.

And then I thought that this was a golden opportunity. Too perfect to resist, even though I could be in a lot of trouble if it all went wrong.

I didn't waste time weighing the risks, but sprang up to my feet and hailed the nearest two ballet girls. "Adalisa, Therese, I can't quite get that middle part right—the *entrechat* and the two *jetés*—you know the part I mean. Go through it with me, won't you?"

Therese groaned. "We already have to do it again for Madame Thibault."

"Please?" I said, making my eyes big and soft. It wasn't hard to make my voice pleading; I *did* desperately want an agreement, if not for the reason I gave. "I want to make sure I have it clear before she's watching again."

"She's always watching," Therese muttered, but got to her feet.

The three of us got into line, and I made sure I was at the end closest to Mifroid and the oblivious managers. We went through our steps, and on the final *jeté* I deliberately leapt too far.

A few operas ago, we had danced a battle sequence involving choreographed tumbles and falls. I flung myself into one of those remembered steps now, a kind of forward plunge that I knew wouldn't hurt me if I hit the ground, but looked convincingly enough like I had simply lost my balance on a landing and fallen forward.

My palms collided straight into Mifroid's chest, as he had just started to turn towards me. I had expected him to catch me, but I must have caught him off-balance and we both went down in a tangle.

I discovered belatedly that this was closer than I wanted to be to Mifroid or his tattered brown coat, and my voice sounded very sincere as I said a hurried, "I'm so sorry!" I tried to disentangle myself, my cheeks hot.

For just a second I found myself looking straight into Mifroid's face—then he hurriedly twisted his head away. "It's all right," he muttered.

By now Adalisa and Therese were on us, helping to lift me up and providing a clamor of concern and a helpful cluster of tulle skirts and anonymity for me to disappear back into.

All of this would accomplish nothing at all, unless... To my relief, now that I was standing again, I could see the managers approaching this way.

"Some sort of problem over here?" Moncharmin asked in his usual, slightly put-out tone.

"It's nothing. It's fine," Mifroid growled, still struggling up to his feet, trying to turn away from the managers.

"Are you lovely ladies well?" Ricard asked, walking past Mifroid to approach our cluster, a warmer concern in his voice.

"Quite well, yes," I said breathlessly, wobbling a curtsy. "I just – lost my balance a bit..."

Mifroid now had a manager on either side and plainly didn't know which direction to look. He scooped his fallen cap up, tried to pull it down low enough to shade his face, attempted to sidle away from the group. "Excuse me. I'll just—"

"You really ought not to get in the way of the ballet," Moncharmin lectured him sternly, even though he himself was frequently in inconvenient places while we rehearsed. He grasped Mifroid by the arm, perhaps meaning to reiterate his point, looking up at the taller man. And I saw his face change. "Wait. Wait a minute."

I exhaled, felt a tension in my stomach start to release.

"Commissaire Mifroid!" Moncharmin roared, and I relaxed entirely with relief. "Just what do you think you're doing in my opera house?"

"Our opera house, Moncharmin," Ricard corrected mildly.

My tumble hadn't been enough to disrupt rehearsal, but Moncharmin's shout had brought Carlotta's solo to an abrupt halt. All eyes were pointed this way as Moncharmin snapped, "Well? Explain yourself!"

For a moment I thought Mifroid might try to bluff his way through. But maybe he had a sense of the dignity that would be inevitably sacrificed in the effort. Instead he straightened up, gaining several inches in height, and removed the dirty cap from his head to look Moncharmin levelly in the eye. "I am investigating the murder of Philippe de Chagny, who I have reason to believe was killed in this—"

"You are trespassing!" Moncharmin interrupted. "Do you have any warrant? Any papers? Any legal authority for being here at all?"

The barest hesitation, and then Mifroid said doggedly, "I firmly believe that—"

"Your *firm belief* is not admissible in court! And you have no evidence and no legal standing and certainly not our permission to be here. I want you gone before you disrupt any more performances or rehearsals or cost me any more money. And don't think we won't complain to the prefect about this!"

Mifroid didn't attempt to respond, merely inclined his head slightly, turned on his heel, and walked away with head held high. I clasped my hands behind my back to stifle an urge to applaud.

Moncharmin stalked out muttering to himself, with Ricard following a step behind. A buzz of excitement ran around the auditorium, in whispers and comments and exclamations.

"If everyone is done interrupting me," Carlotta said loudly, "I will attempt to begin *again*."

A new flurry arose as Carlotta's usual circle of attendants rushed to surround her with consolation, so her song was delayed further—but she seemed to approve of that interruption, so withheld a full tirade.

As I heard the girls talking around me, I could tell that lightning-fast gossip was already starting in to distort the story of Mifroid's unmasking. Within an hour, half of the Company would claim that they'd known all along, and further claim responsibility for revealing him.

I faded back into the wings, sat down again in the shadows with a thick curtain behind me, and felt satisfied with the day's work.

"I saw that," a voice behind me said.

My shoulders and stomach both tightened, but I managed not to jump in surprise. And really, I was more glad than not that he was about. "You weren't doing anything about him."

"*You* were overreacting," he countered. I saw no point in arguing that question again, and besides, I was too pleased with myself just then to be irritated. I let it go by, and after a moment he added, in a friendlier tone, "Do you feel better now?"

I grinned. "I do."

Excerpt from the Private Notebook of Jean Mifroid, Commissaire of Police

1 August, 1881

Setback at the Opera. Expected disguise would not last for extended time. Considering next steps to trace Phantom's movements throughout building.

M. Giry instrumental in revealing disguise – coincidence? Must keep closer eye on Girys. Unable to fully define their connection to Phantom, but something must be there.

Chapter Fourteen

A few days into August, Mother and I boarded a train in Gare Montparnasse to travel to Leclair. Our second-class tickets bought us seats, not a compartment, but Mother let me have the one by the window. I settled in, smoothing my blue-striped skirts and taking off my hat, and gazed out at the bustling station as we pulled away with a clack of wheels and great puffs of steam.

We were soon out into the countryside, trees rushing by and fields unrolling into the distance. It would be a long trip south to Leclair, just north of Toulouse. I leaned back in my seat, already warm. But we were lucky to be getting out of the Paris heat. Somehow the city always felt hotter than the country, and the Opera had grown quieter as the temperatures rose. No one in the Company had much energy for ghost-hunting, and I hoped that would hold true for Mifroid too, during the time we would be away. I felt better than I would have if the managers—well, Moncharmin—hadn't ordered him out.

The shadow of the train raced beside us across the landscape like a dark ghost, while my thoughts were still back at the Opera. What was Erik doing now?

I rarely baffled him, at least not enough for it to show, but I had managed it when I told him I was going away for a few weeks. I had given a perfectly clear explanation, and Erik had stared at me as though the concept was completely foreign. "You're leaving the Opera? For three weeks?"

"Yes. I always go home in January and August," I explained. We were walking in the Grand Foyer, in the early morning, two days before Mother and I left. "Home to the village I came from, I mean, not home in Paris."

He nodded absently, green eyes gone distant. His thoughtful look was familiar by now, the way his eyes shifted and one corner of his mouth creased. I wondered as always what he was thinking. This time I felt I could make a reasonable guess, that he was trying to remember my past absences.

The crease smoothed, and his green eyes focused on me properly again. "At the same time your mother goes?"

I tried not to feel slighted. "Yes, we go together," I said, reaching up to adjust my necklace. It was abundantly obvious that all he could remember was *her* absence, and that he'd never noticed mine at all.

I stifled a sigh as I sat in the train, Paris retreating behind us, and fiddled with my necklace again. If I sighed audibly, Mother would want to know what was wrong. And nothing was, not really. There was no reason Erik should have noticed if I was gone in previous years. We hadn't known each other then. I had never expected that he was paying particular attention to me. Naturally he'd be aware of his boxkeeper being gone, but why should he care where her daughter was?

At least he'd notice *this* year. He knew I was gone, of course, but I hoped he'd notice—well, a difference. Or maybe the life of the Opera would just go on without me and Erik would go on too, and he'd have no reason to think of me until I was back. Any more than Léon had any reason to think of me until he came back. Or, apparently, than Christine did.

I tried to push away the sense of loss I still felt over my absent friend. Some things were better in my life than they had been five months ago. Erik, for instance. And the ballet girls—several had expressed regret when I told them I'd be away for three weeks. They had scarcely commented on my absence when I was gone in January. I'd been so busy with Christine then that I hadn't spent much time with anyone else. And the other girls were fun.

They were fun when they weren't going on about hating the Phantom, anyway, and the gory things he'd probably done to Christine. They still told those stories with absurd regularity.

People told far fewer ghost stories and *far* fewer gory ones outside the Opera Garnier. That might be a nice change.

After a long day's ride, Mother and I arrived safely in Leclair. Uncle Jean and his family met us at the train station to bring us to their house, where I was promptly swept off upstairs with my three girl cousins, to 'unpack.'

"So, tell us everything about the Opera!" Angelique demanded, plopping onto the bed and putting her feet right on top of my trunk. At seventeen, she was my nearest-in-age cousin.

I could have asked her to move her feet so I could actually unpack—but instead I dropped down onto the bed too, sitting against the headboard and drawing my own feet up under me. "I already write you all the time about the Opera."

"It's not the same!" my two youngest cousins said in virtual unison as they piled onto the bed between us. Suzanne was twelve, Georgette fourteen.

Gabrielle used to fit in right between Georgette and Angelique in age. I could almost imagine my now fifteen-year-old sister squeezing into the empty corner of the bed, ready to tell her stories too. After six years, the picture was equal parts sad and sweet.

I wished I knew what stories she would have told.

My cousins were still eager for mine. "It's better hearing the news," Suzanne insisted.

"You don't write to us about the *really* interesting parts," Angelique said with a sly smile.

"Because Maman reads the letters too!" Georgette put in.

"Tell us about your friend Christine," Suzanne suggested, blue eyes big and eager. "The singer."

It was nice, that at least in one place in the world Christine was *my* friend, instead of the other way around. That consoled me for having to admit, "I haven't heard from her again since she left. I suppose she's busy abroad with Raoul."

Suzanne snorted in disgust. "The boring one without any stories? Why would she be busy with *him*?"

I shrugged, without an answer since I'd never understood it myself. "She likes him."

"Who cares about *him*, have you met any interesting men lately?" Angelique demanded, and all three of my cousins leaned in closer.

Interesting men. Well, a man who pretended to be a ghost and worked magic was certainly interesting. But somehow...Erik didn't seem like the subject for a gossipy, giggly chat with my cousins. "I wrote to you about Léon, of course," I said, the easier topic.

"Oh yes, your *friend*," Suzanne said, eyes batting dramatically, and clearly the word had a different meaning than when it was used to describe Christine. "Is he back from traveling?"

That pulled me up short, not having thought the topic through. It had been three months, or near enough, and he might have been swallowed up by Franzensbad's healing mud for all I'd heard from him. Of course, I didn't *expect* to hear from him. But still...it wasn't so pleasant, admitting that neither departed friend had bothered to be in touch. "No, he's not back," I said, and when that sounded rather flat and grim I quickly added, "Not yet."

Angelique reached out to squeeze my hand, and though her voice was light enough her eyes were sympathetic when she said, "Oh well, tell us about when he *was* there."

I smiled at her, squeezed her hand in return. "All right, but only if you tell me if *you've* met anyone interesting."

When Angelique's face flushed pink, and Suzanne and Georgette started giggling, I knew I had scored a hit.

"Léon first," Angelique protested. "What does he look like? Did he bring you flowers? What color are his eyes?"

"Blue," I said, and sighed with all the drama the moment seemed to call for. "A *gorgeous* blue."

We didn't only talk about men. The conversation moved on from Léon to Angelique's young man to all the latest news around Leclair and at the Opera too. Somehow, Erik never quite came up, not even when they asked if the newspaper accounts of the crashing chandelier were really all true.

It was very quiet at the Opera in August. Much of Paris fled the city's heat for the country, and the management had no interest in performing to empty houses. Erik personally felt that it could be an improvement to perform without the chattering audience who cared more about seeing each other than seeing the art. But Moncharmin did not ask for his opinion, and he did not bother forwarding one that would so obviously be ignored.

The unusual, relative emptiness of the Opera in August at least gave him the opportunity to wander the building with slightly more freedom than usual. He was still cautious, always, an ingrained habit he doubted he could break if he wished to, but the need was slighter, his wanderings wider.

Meg had been gone from the Opera for three days—not that he was counting—when he drifted through the halls near the ballet's practice rooms and found that the area was not, as it should have been, empty. He faded at once into the nearest shadow, remaining silent and growing still, noting the nearest three exits even as he studied the man farther down the hall. No outcry, so he hadn't been spotted yet. The man seemed intent on his own business, a faint tapping and scraping noise carrying through the silence as the man inspected a wall. Exactly the way someone searching for secret doors might do.

Apparently the Phantom was not the only one who thought August's emptiness presented opportunities.

So much for Moncharmin's dramatic ordering of Mifroid out. He might have guessed the commissaire would be more persistent than that, try again a different way. It wasn't as though Moncharmin could actually watch everyone coming into the building, especially now when so many of the usual gatekeepers were absent, their doors meant to be locked. He might have pointed all this out to Meg—but she'd been so pleased and relieved by the success of her strategy, he hadn't liked to.

He probably wouldn't mention this new development either, when Meg came back. No need to start her worrying again.

In the moment, he took three careful steps backward, slipped silently through a secret door he could activate almost without thinking, and was watching from hiding before Mifroid, footsteps loud in the quiet, continued down the hall towards him.

He put his hand over the mechanism that worked the door, just in case Mifroid happened to press the right spot on the wall. Though he was curious how the commissaire would have reacted, to find a secret door and a Phantom all in one single moment.

He didn't give in to the curiosity, and Mifroid remained baffled for this afternoon.

It wasn't the last time Erik saw him in the Opera. He followed him around for several days, was both irritated and impressed when Mifroid found first one secret door, and then another. They weren't the ones Erik was behind at the time so his security continued, though if Mifroid had ventured too far into the hidden passages he uncovered... Perhaps recognizing the risk, the commissaire never went far, retreating back into the light quickly and scratching notes into his little book.

Erik carefully dismantled each discovered hidden door after Mifroid had found it.

The commissaire provided his only real diversion, with the Opera Company largely scattered for these few weeks. When the commissaire failed to appear for two days—surely the man had to have something else to do for his job—Erik even missed him in a way. Well, not *him*, but the diversion of the hunt.

As August dragged on without the commissaire or the Company, the Phantom found himself with entirely too much time to think. Perhaps it was inevitable that he would soon enough end up in Box Five, listening to the silence of the empty auditorium and remembering.

Remembering *her*, of course. She had been here a mere handful of months, just a small span in the many years he had sat here observing singers and dancers and grand operas. But hers was the ghost that kept coming back, haunting him more thoroughly than he'd ever haunted the Opera.

He was wallowing and he knew it, but he couldn't seem to get himself out of it. More days ticked by, no one coming back yet to helpfully distract him with threats to his life.

He climbed all the way up to the rooftop one afternoon, 175 days and fourteen hours after she left, on the theory that sunlight was supposed to induce cheerfulness. So people claimed, anyway. That just led to him sitting by the statue of Harmony and recalling what was surely one of the five worst moments of his life, listening to *her* call him a monster.

It was one of the ten worst anyway; there was quite a bit of competition.

He shook himself, berated himself for being foolish, and wandered off to another part of the roof. Towards the edge this time, looking out over the Avenue de l'Opera. Different memories here. He sat down behind the low wall, hidden from sight, and thought about tangerines. Not remotely the emotional importance of the other memories, but more pleasant.

The sun had set and he had retreated back down below the Opera before it even crossed his mind that he had once contemplated suicide from that spot too. Memory worked in strange ways.

He shoved his hands into his pockets and strolled on through the dark passage towards home. That had been a particularly bad moment too, one he certainly would have expected to come back to him more immediately.

When he reached his apartment below the Opera, he wandered over to his bookcase. Sunlight hadn't particularly cheered him. Perhaps a little reading? If he was going to undertake any significant reading, now was the time. The Opera would begin to grow active again soon. Meg would be back from the countryside in five days. Not that he was counting; he just happened to know.

In the meantime his world was still quiet. Maybe that was why he ended up sitting with his book of Shakespearean plays at his piano instead of at the far more comfortable and really more convenient armchair nearby. But sitting there made it seem so natural when William

Shakespeare's *Hamlet* the play set him thinking about Ambrose Thomas' *Hamlet* the opera and then his hand just happened to drift over a bit to play a few bars.

Three bars, in fact, before he suddenly noticed what he was doing and stopped, staring at his fingers. He hadn't touched a musical instrument, not to play any music, for 175 days exactly. Not since *she* left. He hadn't wanted to.

But now he could feel music prodding at his mind and fingertips again, maybe only because the world had gone too silent even for him.

It had to be better than wallowing in Box Five.

So he continued playing, and the world felt less quiet. It seemed that it would help, at least for the next five days.

Chapter Fifteen

It always felt strange returning to the Opera after three weeks in Leclair. They were such utterly different worlds. My cousins viewed the Opera as a kind of mythical place, and the ballet girls had little interest in hearing about picnics, sewing circles and Sundays at Saint-Antoine-de-Padoue. I often felt like a foreigner for a day or two when I re-entered the Opera's whirl.

Though I was pulled right back in faster than usual this time, when I arrived at the ballet girls' changing room before my first rehearsal and found a black-edged envelope tucked into the top drawer of my table.

I picked it up with an odd sense of relief. I hadn't thought he'd ignore me, it was more that—well, if the Opera seemed mythical, Erik seemed positively fictional after three weeks away.

I was about to open the envelope when Adalisa pounced on me from behind with a one-armed hug. "Welcome back! Madame Thibault is on the war-path about being on time, you know how she is—better hurry!"

"Thanks, I will," I said, trying to not too obviously slide the envelope away beneath the clutter scattered over my table.

Adalisa, already in her dance outfit, leaned against the edge of my table as she tugged on her practice slippers. "So how was your trip? Did you have a nice time?"

"Yes—it was quiet, but nice," I said, gave the envelope one more push under an old program, then began on the numerous buttons I needed to unfasten in order to change.

"Oh Meg, you're back!" Francesca chirped, landing on the opposite side of my chair from Adalisa, fingers busy tying up her hair. "How was the trip?"

Before I could answer, Jammes' voice cut in from two dressing tables over. "Were you gone, Meg?" She tipped her head back, with a show of thoughtfulness. "It did seem quieter around here." Nothing in her tone suggested that was a bad thing.

I smiled grimly. "I was gone for three weeks, and I missed *some* parts of the Opera very much."

"Is that so," Jammes said, eyes hard and smile insincere. "And where did you go? Did Christine finally remember that you're her friend, and invite you to visit?"

Always with Christine. I was so sick of having Christine thrown at me. I held onto my smile, though that was growing harder. "But surely you remember I always visit family in August. Or are you too busy paying attention to Carlotta's every move to notice anyone else?"

"I have no interest in noticing—"

"Meg, we've been making plans to go out to the Tuileries after tomorrow's practice," Adalisa cut in, voice with a forced brightness. "Would you like to come?"

"I'd be delighted to," I said firmly, turning my gaze away from Jammes.

Adalisa, Francesca and I carried on a pleasant conversation while we finished changing, Jammes flounced off to practice, and I was feeling good—except that it took me entirely too long to get ready. After three weeks I couldn't seem to recall where I kept my things anymore and I had lost the habits that normally made this easy. So of course I was the last one out the door.

I only got four steps down the empty hallway before a shadow detached from the wall to say with unusual speed, "Hello, did you get my letter?"

If he had appeared any closer we would have collided; as it was, momentum carried me two steps closer than I usually got to Erik. I backed up a hurried pace, breath catching as I tried to recover. "Oh—no—well, yes, but—the ballet girls were around and—"

"Of course, black edges, not very discreet," he said with a nod. "I should have thought of that, apologies."

"Yes, well…" I tried not to bounce from foot to foot and look too obviously over his shoulder towards ballet practice. I probably failed. It wasn't that I wouldn't *rather* talk to Erik, but if Madame Thibault was on a particular tear about punctuality…

"I suggested a meeting tomorrow afternoon," Erik said, and if I was a nervous bundle of energy, I suddenly realized that he was too. He was more subtle, of course, but the way he was standing, the way he didn't seem to know what to do with his hands—he was agitated, maybe, but he didn't seem unhappy. He was…excited? What was causing that?

"Yes, all right, tomorrow is—oh no, I can't," I corrected myself. "I just made plans with the girls…" It might have been different if I'd read his letter first.

"Ah. Of course. Well." And all that unusual energy abruptly dissipated. It wasn't exactly as though he looked actively dejected, or disappointed, but there was a change to the line of his shoulders, a slight flattening of his mouth.

Without thinking too much about it, and still more occupied with the idea that I should be at ballet practice, *now*, I quickly said, "I don't have any plans this afternoon."

To which Erik smiled and said, "Excellent, the auditorium is empty today too," which for him was a remarkably enthusiastic response.

I blinked, assimilating that unexpected smile. "All right. Good. After ballet practice then?"

"Very well," he said, and glanced over his shoulder towards ballet practice. "You had better hurry," he remarked casually, "Madame Thibault is on a rampage about punctuality."

"Yes, I *know*." I darted around him and dashed for practice, tossing "See you later" behind me.

I was two minutes late to practice—but just as I stepped across the threshold all the lights went out. Perfect blackness reigned for a few seconds, then the lights flickered madly on and off and by the time they settled into normal lighting again all the girls had gone off on shrieks about the Ghost. By the time Madame Thibault had order restored, she didn't remember that I had come in late—and no one else noticed my only half-stifled fit of giggles either.

I liked Leclair, but the Opera had its advantages too.

I tried to thank Erik, when I joined him sitting on the edge of the stage of the auditorium some two hours later. He just blinked once and said he had no idea what I was talking about. He was wearing his half-mask today, and what I could see of his face remained perfectly smooth and impassive. But his green eyes were smiling.

"How was your trip home?" he asked, and I wondered if he really wanted to know or if he was just changing the subject.

"Nice. I like my cousins. And it's quieter than Paris."

"It was quiet enough here," he said, glancing away. His eyes had stopped smiling.

I should think a man who lived alone under an opera house had to *like* the quiet. Maybe. The Opera Garnier itself wasn't often quiet, so perhaps he was here for the bustle and noise after all. "They'll be planning the fall season soon," I ventured, to see if that would strike him more cheerfully.

It did, as he straightened immediately, eyes lighting. "They're already discussing which operas to put on. Moncharmin has this perfectly awful idea about performing Gounod's *Faust* followed directly by Mozart's *Don Giovanni*. We can't do two operas in a row about men going to Hell."

"I don't know," I mused. "*Don Giovanni* is so much more comical. They're not that similar."

"But on a thematic level—"

"So present it as a deliberate theme and promote the similarity," I suggested.

"A very grim deliberate theme," he countered, perfectly animated and engaged—and then suddenly his eyes shadowed again. "Though life is grim, so perhaps it fits."

"Life isn't *always* grim," I said swiftly, because how could I not with that expression in his eyes?

He didn't exactly agree, but he did move on to remark, "Besides that ridiculous notion, Moncharmin also thinks he can use the same jewelry from the masquerade in *Romeo and Juliet* in *Faust*'s jewel song, even though it's not at all the right style for the time period *Faust*'s costumes suggest. The man has no eye for art."

"Doesn't *Faust* have its own set of jewelry anyway?"

Erik's mouth immediately pulled into an expression of long-suffering exasperation, much less charged than his bleakness of a moment ago. "They can't *find* it in the prop room. Perfectly absurd, but they went and re-arranged things so it would be better organized, and they haven't been able to find anything for a week. Come on, I'll show you."

And with that he was rising to his feet and striding across the stage and what could I do but scramble up and follow him? I was taken slightly by surprise, but it wasn't as though I didn't want to.

"What if someone's in the prop room?" I ventured.

"They aren't," he said, descending a flight of stairs off the stage, without explaining how he knew this. But ghosts know things.

The prop room was an enormous vault below ground level, and while I wouldn't have said so to Erik, I could easily see how someone could lose something in there. Or lose themselves. Endless rows of costumes jostled for space with shelves of jewelry and swords and vases and fake fruit and everything else that might turn up on a stage. A stack of chandeliers sat in one corner, vastly smaller than any real ones hanging from the Opera's ceilings. One corner was entirely taken up by half of a galleon hanging from the ceiling, while an elephant loomed from another.

A whole stretch of wall was covered in masks, laughing and hideous, tiny and all-concealing; my gaze ran over them, wondering if this could be where Erik's masks had come from. Somehow I didn't think so. He inhabited his masks, the shape fitting to his face with perfection—and there was something *real* about his masks that stage props didn't share.

As promised, no one was present, and Erik forged through the clutter with perfect confidence. "You see, the place had been arranged by type of prop, which seems reasonable enough though an argument could be made for organizing by time period, or by geographical origin. But someone got it into his head to organize by production, which really only works in a limited sort of way because it doesn't allow for overlap. And then they came in and *moved* things," he concluded, with a sweep of his arm as though I was likely to observe at once how things were different than formerly, and understand why this was a catastrophe.

"I see," I said, even though I didn't, and smiled at his enthusiasm. I wondered if anyone else in the Company cared as much as Erik did. And I noticed again that unusual energy he had today, the way the words flowed so much more swiftly than typical. If he could bring all that interest and effort to the conversation, I ought to give a better response. "I haven't been down here much," I offered. "I don't usually get below ground level."

He nodded to that. "Wise policy, on the whole, though belowground has its own fascinations."

He had told me not to go below, that day when I was twelve. Suddenly I was dwelling on that and didn't want to—it was too complicated a memory—so without thinking I said, "You live somewhere farther down, don't you?" and *then* remembered that I didn't ask Erik personal questions.

"Yes." Just that one word, and he was looking the wrong direction for me to see if that shadow was back in his eyes, if that had been a truly stupid remark or not. Just when everything was going so well— and now silence stretched out instead of cheerful words.

I stared hard at the prop swords in front of me. It *was* stupid, I never should have said—should I explain that Christine had told me? No, he must be assuming that anyway and bringing her up was worse than a personal question. She still topped the list of things to not discuss with Erik. Better to change the subject entirely, if I could only think of absolutely anything else to—

"I could show it to you some time."

I looked up from the swords, blinked at him while he stared at the galleon looming above us. This was utterly unexpected and my automatic assumption was that he couldn't really mean it. "You don't have to," I said, twisting at a fold of my skirt.

Gaze away from the galleon, a darting glance at my face, then down to his shoes. "Oh. I just thought—I mean, of course if you'd rather not…"

I was worried that he didn't mean it—and based on the way he was avoiding eye contact, the way he was shifting his weight, he was even more worried that I wouldn't want to go. "No, I'd love to see where you live," I said quickly, then couldn't help adding, "if you don't mind."

"I don't," he said, just as quickly. He was finally looking at me, intently now, as though studying me for clues. "Are you sure?"

"Yes." And I was, excitement rising up inside of me like champagne bubbles. I was desperately curious to see where he lived. I had never been able to get satisfactory details out of Christine, and asking the Persian was obviously hopeless. Now I worried I had hesitated too much, that he was going to take the invitation back. "I have time now. If it's not far."

"It's not. If you know the way." A pause, until finally he shook himself and turned towards the racks of masks. "So there's a secret door over here…"

"Very appropriate location," I commented, watching as he tapped a half-dozen pegs holding masks in what seemed to be a random order, then pushed against the wall. A portion swung inwards, forming a narrow door.

"It did somewhat amuse me." He stepped onto the threshold, turned back and extended a hand towards me.

Suddenly I was twelve years old again, the Phantom of the Opera beckoning. I wasn't afraid of this Ghost anymore, but the ghost of the memory was momentarily so strong as to be paralyzing. He was even wearing the same mask he'd worn on that long ago day.

"There are uneven places," Erik said, voice unusually diffident. "And it's dark even with a candle, so it's probably better…"

His hand was starting to move back, in another instant he'd be saying it was fine if I'd rather not, and we could do that dance all day. I reached out and closed my fingers around his. "Of course," I said, voice calm and heart hammering.

Then I followed him into the shadows.

Chapter Sixteen

T his was probably a terrible idea. Last time he had invited…
someone below—well, to say it had ended badly was like saying
that Napoleon had had an unpleasant day at Waterloo. 180 days,
fifteen hours. That was how long it had been, since the last time he had
brought someone below the Opera. When he had carried *her* off, in the
wake of the fallen chandelier, as she had pretended to be in a faint and he
had let her pretend.

Obviously this was entirely different.

He had no *plans* this time, no delusions. It had been an impulse to
invite Meg, because he had been feeling so pleased to see her back at the
Opera, because it had been so pleasant to have someone to talk to instead
of his own thoughts filling up his mind with no outlet, because these past
few weeks had been so very quiet. The opening had come for an
invitation and he had impulsively taken it. After all, it was perfectly
socially acceptable to invite a friend for a visit. Wasn't it? Would the
Daroga think it was? Anyway, Meg had agreed. That must mean it was all
right.

Socially all right, and also…safe. Safe enough. It was obviously
mere paranoia to imagine he could be in any danger from Meg, from
letting her enter his world. If she wanted to snatch his mask off, it would
have happened by now. And if she wanted to memorize the way to his
apartment across the lake and tell Commissaire Mifroid about it? There
were far simpler ways to hand him over to the authorities, and a plan this
elaborate—no, the idea was absurd. He resisted the impulse to take a
route with a few extra turns, just in case.

He tried not to look at Meg as they walked through the cellars and tunnels. If all the dark corridors, punctuated occasionally by reddish light from the furnaces and boilers, were making her nervous, he didn't want to know. He was used to this world, but it seemed suddenly strange with this girl walking beside him. She was a creature of the sunlight, the upper world, out of place in this cold, damp realm. Here silence reigned, broken only by the skittering of rats, the dripping of water or the moan of wind caught by crevices and shafts and pulled from the free air above. Meg belonged in the Opera, full of life and voices and music. And yet, here she was.

Her hand was warm, fingers wrapped around his with every sign of trust and confidence. He had never touched her before. Not her hand, not her shoulder, not even grazing fingertips when they passed tangerines back and forth. He had nearly forgotten, how warm another person's hand could feel, even through gloves.

He tried again to tell himself that this was not a significant event, that in the world above friends visited each other quite routinely, quite casually, and that this was nothing more than that. He tried telling himself this wasn't important, but he knew that was never going to be true.

He hesitated for just a beat at a branching of two corridors, then turned left. Not the way he had gone with *her*. This was a short cut, a convenient one that wouldn't give Meg a simpler route. Just supposing she did want to memorize the way.

This passage ended abruptly, at an open doorway with a sheer drop down a dozen meters, air cold beyond. Before them, the great black reaches of the vault over the underground lake, the only sound the soft murmur of water lapping against the ledge below.

"Are you sure this is the right way?" Meg asked, a light humor in her tone.

"I don't get lost," he said, though Meg's laughter never bothered him; there was no edge to it.

He released her hand to reach around the open doorway, to press a spot on the outer wall. He snapped the fingers of his other hand just as there was the faintest of clicks. A series of steps slid silently out from the formerly smooth wall, leading down to the ledge below.

He heard Meg's inhale behind him. "That's amazing."

"Just a parlor trick," he said automatically, turned to take her hand again and didn't realize he was smiling until she smiled back. He always had liked showing off, and it was nice to have an appreciative audience.

At first, the places we walked were mostly real, working parts of the Opera. The furnaces, full of glowing coals, or store rooms, or half-forgotten work spaces. But even there, Erik always seemed to know just how to avoid anywhere that was occupied, knew side-cuts through hidden passages and secret doors. And we went lower, and lower, and soon we were in a stretch that might have belonged to Paris' catacombs, all stone walls and dark branching corridors, dusty, cobwebbed, clearly rarely used. And that was *before* he produced a magical staircase.

I knew long before we reached the staircase that I couldn't find my way back to the surface without help. I had a decent enough memory for directions, but this world was too strange, too dark, punctuated with too many near-invisible doors and near-identical passages.

I supposed I ought to be frightened. When I was twelve I had feared becoming lost forever and dying unfound below the Opera, and that had only been a level or two down. I knew now I wouldn't really have stayed lost there, even if the Phantom hadn't stepped out of a wall to help me. All the way down here, it seemed like a more real possibility.

But I had a Phantom to help me. I had Erik, his hand wrapped around mine, moving with confidence through every turn.

That wouldn't reassure my mother. As though arguing with her voice in my head, I reminded myself—both of us—that if Erik wasn't well-intentioned, he could have harmed me long ago. He never had.

That probably wouldn't reassure my mother either, but it seemed like a reasonable point to me.

And how could I be frightened when I was finally *here*? When I had finally been invited into the near-mythical world of the Phantom of the Opera. Christine had come here, all those months ago, but that had never given me any chance, or even much information. Now Erik had asked *me* to visit him, and I was here seeing it all for myself.

We descended the magic stairs to a narrow walkway alongside the underground lake, and the sense of entering a fabled realm only increased. I had heard of the lake for all the years I had been at the Opera. An offshoot of the Seine, perhaps, but it was spoken of as though it was an offshoot of fairyland, with a castle and demon princes on the other side. No one went down as far as the lake—almost. The very few men whose jobs infrequently required them to be down here never went in a group of less than four.

Supposedly many men had drowned in the lake (though one had to wonder, since no one had ever come down alone), lured by a Siren's unearthly singing. Most stories said the Siren was another manifestation of the Phantom, despite Sirens being traditionally female, and it was one of the most popular theories about how Philippe de Chagny had died.

I glanced up at Erik as we walked beside the lake. The stories were at least right in that he was a possible, obvious source for unearthly singing. A source for drowning people too? No, I didn't believe that, but a source for the stories probably.

I looked back out towards the lake, dark waters stretching into the distance beneath a cavernous stone roof. I possibly stared for too long, when Erik suddenly asked, "Are you thinking of the Siren?"

I jumped, and lied. "No."

"No truth to that anyway," he said, voice dismissive. "A very effective story to keep people off the lake, but merely a story. After all, a creature who can sing while under water…that's impossible."

I hadn't been worrying, I had assumed this anyway—but I still felt a touch better. "Says the man who just created a magical stair by snapping his fingers," I said amiably.

A pause. "Yes, well. Some things are impossible, and other things are *impossible*."

We walked beside the lake for perhaps half its length, though it was hard to see the far edges in the dim shadows. Then it was into a break in the wall almost too narrow to be called a passage, the full skirts of my blue-striped dress brushing the nearest side as we walked next to each other. We made three more turns, and finally reached a hallway that ended in an imposing wooden door, two stone creatures with outstretched wings and fanged grins crouching before it.

"Gargoyles!" I said in genuine delight.

"They're deeply misunderstood creatures," Erik said, expression going dark again as he released my hand.

"I know." I reached up to stroke the carved stone wing of the nearest with one fingertip. "They're supposed to keep demons out of churches, but since they look so strange, they end up being labeled as demons themselves, which seems very unfair. It's not their fault they look different."

I realized Erik had stopped walking and was staring at me.

I shoved cold fingers into the pockets of my cloak. "I like Notre Dame," I said by way of explanation, though he already knew that from earlier conversations. "I've read about gargoyles."

"Interesting," Erik said, and crossed the last few steps to the door. He didn't produce a key, but neither did he simply turn the handle. He did something much more complicated, pressing different portions of the carving just around the handle until a click sounded. Then he pushed the door open, revealing only shadows until he snapped his fingers once and a warm glow lit the space beyond. He held the door wide with a nod to gallantry and let me precede him into the room.

"So…here it is," he said as the door closed behind us.

My immediate impression was of a surprisingly spacious parlor. The gray stone that lined the tunnels was repeated here, but the room stretched long before us and a vaulted ceiling dispelled any sense of oppression from being so deep underground. Racks of candles on stands and in nooks shone pleasantly, and warm colors glowed throughout from paintings and rugs.

The brightest point was the far wall, covered by an enormous pipe organ, with ranks of ivory keys and hundreds of shining metal pipes reflecting the candlelight. I couldn't imagine how it had got here—and yet, it was exactly the kind of extravagant musical instrument I would expect the Phantom of the Opera to possess. What a sound it must make, an incongruous, unearthly music far beneath the ground.

Erik shifted his weight beside me and I realized he was watching me for a reaction. I had only begun to take in the details, but I flashed a smile and said, "It's very nice" because I had to say something. And it was all rather less strange than I might have imagined.

"Thank you." His response sounded just as automatic as my comment. He rubbed one hand along the back of his neck. "Do you...want some coffee?"

"That would be lovely," I said with a distinctly surreal feeling, this imitation of an ordinary social call in such an extraordinary moment.

"Right. I'll just...be right back."

I would not have been shocked at this point to see him walk through a wall. In actual fact, he crossed the room to a normal wooden door on the left-hand wall. Only then did it occur to me that he must have a kitchen. I had never thought of that; it was too prosaic a detail for the mythical Phantom. But of course Erik had to eat.

Where did he get coffee? Or food? I never pictured him outside the Opera either, but if he ate he had to get food somewhere...

The door closed behind him with a click and a tightness in my chest relaxed as I let out a slow breath. I felt as though I had been left alone in a royal treasury. I had been so curious about this place for so long. Now I looked eagerly about, wanting to look at everything and yet breathing lightly lest I break the spell. I walked slowly forward, almost on my toes, and stepped onto a round red and gold rug. The pattern was intricate and the rug sank beneath my feet, soft and plush and luxurious.

I stepped carefully, moving between a high-backed armchair and an upright wooden piano. The chair was padded, the seat deep, and I tried to imagine Erik lounging in it. I had to smile and shake my head. The picture was impossible. I'd never seen him that relaxed.

It was much easier to imagine him at the piano, seated on the low bench, hands flying across the keys. I'd seen his hands move just that way, idly, unthinkingly, as he spoke, though I'd never seen him touch a musical instrument. Unlike the too comfortable chair, the piano matched his elegance, all dark wood with carvings of flowers and serene faces on the back. I reached out one hand towards the glossy ivory keys, caught myself just before depressing the nearest. Maybe I shouldn't touch things.

I drew both hands to my sides, closed them into fists among my skirts, and looked away from the tempting keys. My eyes went to the painting on the wall above the piano.

Ballet dancers, pale in wide skirts, a few dancing on the stage but the group in the foreground stretching or resting on a low bench. It was a scene I had witnessed, been part of, a thousand times, and the stage, even the girls, looked familiar. The lines were too soft, the details too sparse for me to identify faces, and yet I felt sure I knew those dancers. This had to be a painting by Monsieur Degas. I had seen him sketching around the Opera Garnier for years and everyone said he was a great artist, but I had never seen any of his paintings before. Ballet girls might be artist's models, but we're not invited into the places where fine art is hung.

The painting distracted me for a few moments—but not longer than that, not with the rest of the Phantom's parlor to explore.

I ventured deeper into the room, stepping on more soft rugs with elaborate designs in glowing colors, and stopping to look at the fireplace cut into the wall beyond the painting. The mantle was full of curious things. At one end stood glass roses in a small vase, vivid red and exquisitely detailed. Next to the roses stood a stone bust of a frowning man who looked like a Roman, if I could judge by the operas we put on, with the name Vitruvius carved into the base. I did not remember any Vitruvius in any operas, and my gaze wandered on to the copper pot next to the bust, inlaid with glowing turquoise. Next to that sat a pistol with an intricate hilt, and an octagon-shaped box, made of a dark wood. At the end sat a wooden metronome; I recognized the pyramid shape from seeing others around the Opera, though this one looked worn with age, and the shine of the wood made it seem more art than tool.

I wanted to know the story behind each item, the reason Erik put *these* things on his mantle and not something else, to know where they had come from and what they meant to him. I knew I wouldn't dare to ask.

Two maroon couches sat opposite the fireplace, at right angles to each other so that one faced the fire and the other the pipe organ, a low table between them. It was a little easier to imagine Erik sitting there, with their high backs and carved wooden frames. I had seen him sit on the banquettes in the Dance Foyer, when we met there while it was empty.

I could see couches anywhere, rendering them much less interesting and unusual than an object on its own small table next to the fireplace. It might have been a musical instrument, with a horn that looked like it could come from the orchestra's brass section, but I'd never seen an instrument attached to a box like this one, with some sort of mechanics connecting them. Maybe I'd risk asking Erik about that.

The painting of Apollo and the muses on the wall above it was much easier to understand. Those characters were everywhere in the decorations in the Opera Garnier.

By now I'd walked all the way across the room, all the way to the pipe organ. It seemed even bigger, even grander, up close, and I also noticed a violin resting atop the back, behind the keys. I let my gaze wander up, ran it over the multitude of metal pipes. What music had they played?

Had he played music for Christine, when she was here?

I took a deep breath, clasped my hands behind me, and turned my back on the organ. I noticed then that two more gargoyles flanked the door inside. These two were still grotesque but grinning, more mischievous than ominous. I grinned back at them. I'd never been able to learn any details worth knowing about this place from Christine, but now *I* was here. Me, Little Meg Giry, Christine's friend, finally got to see all this myself. Maybe I didn't know what all of it meant, maybe I still had questions. But at least I was here.

I walked back to look at the painting hanging over one couch, and even without knowing art I could tell this was a very different style from Degas. This one was like looking through a window it was so realistic, the light shining on the figures of the Madonna and Child, the baby asleep while three angels played music for him.

So the man who claimed he didn't get on with God had a painting of Mary, Jesus and the angels on his wall. The man known for hiding in darkness had chosen a scene flooded with light.

I wondered too what the Opera Company, what all those ballet girls with their horror stories of the Phantom's depravities, would think if they knew he had a religious painting on his wall. It made me smile.

Back near the armchair, there was an inset bookcase, reaching from floor to ceiling and entirely filled with dozens, perhaps hundreds, of books. I wandered that way. Erik would surely be back soon, and this seemed like a harmless place to be found examining. I hadn't touched anything else, but I let my fingertips run along the spines of Erik's books. That was surely harmless too.

It was a mix of elegant leather-bound volumes and worn, cheap copies, as though he had picked them up at different times in different places. Adding to the confusion, the books themselves were a disorganized muddle of novels, history and philosophy, mostly French but with at least seven languages in view; I could only assume he had everything in the original, though I could manage a rough translation of most titles, recognize a handful of authors.

The Count of Monte Cristo. Faust. Paradise Lost. General History and Specific Abnormalities of the Organization in Humans and Animals. Volumes by Rousseau, Verne, Poe. *Mr. William Shakespeare's Comedies, Histories and Tragedies. The New Paris Opera* by Charles Garnier. *Frankenstein. The Hunchback of Notre Dame.*

Maybe because I had gargoyles on my mind, or because it was the only one I'd read, I pulled that last one off the shelf. It was a heavy volume with thick, creamy pages. I flipped a few of those pages before the book fell open, as books will, to what was evidently an oft-read page.

My eye went automatically to the neatly underlined sentences: "From his very first steps among men, Quasimodo had felt himself spewed out, blasted, rejected. Human words were, for him, always a raillery or a malediction. As he grew up, he had found nothing but hatred around him. After all, he turned his face towards men only with reluctance; his cathedral was sufficient for him." I turned a page and found another underlined sentence: "Egypt would have taken him for the god of this temple; the Middle Ages believed him to be its demon: he was in fact its soul."

I drew a breath and closed the book. I carefully put it back on the shelf and went to sit properly down in one corner of a couch, hands in my lap. I was *not* prying. I couldn't help it if Erik had invited me into a place that inevitably gave glimpses of his soul.

He returned very soon after that, carrying a tray holding a silver coffeepot and two cups. My earlier surreal feelings redoubled. He put the tray on the low table between the couches, and sat down on the opposite one, all the while watching me furtively.

"Does it seem dark in here to you?" he asked as he poured coffee. "If it does, I could find more candles, I have more—"

"It's fine." Christine had described his rooms as dark, but they weren't. The rich colors of the couches, the rugs, the paintings—they all glowed in the candlelight.

He set down the coffeepot, picked up a spoon and stirred the sugar cubes in their bowl. Somehow the gesture seemed more born of nervous energy than actual necessity, and I tried to swallow a smile. I was alone in the Phantom's rooms below the Opera Garnier, and maybe that should have frightened me. But I still wasn't afraid, and it was hard to even feel worried when he was clearly more nervous than I was.

In fact, I felt daring—at least enough to suggest, "You could try to relax, you know."

His glance darted to me, then back to the cup in his hand. "I'm relaxed. I'm fine." He dropped six lumps of sugar into the coffee.

"Mm-hmm. Do you always take that much sugar?"

This time when he looked up, he just looked perplexed. "...yes."

"Oh. Never mind, then." I sipped my black coffee—not bad—while I hunted for a different topic. "What's that thing with the horn over there?"

It was a good instinct. Erik smiled, his grip on his coffee cup tightening. "It's a phonograph. In a few years, everyone will have one. It's the most revolutionary invention since the segmented arch."

I had only the vaguest idea what that was, so I just nodded.

"Well, since the printing press, anyway," he amended, as if I had argued. "What the printing press did for literature, the phonograph is going to do for music."

I knew about the printing press, but that didn't explain much. "What does it *do?*"

"It plays music. I mean, without a musician. You can record sound and then play it back. They've been able to record music for a while, but reproducing the sound was the hard part. Edison, an American inventor, he finally solved it a few years ago. It almost makes me want to forgive him for his work on electric lights."

Why anyone would need forgiveness for advancing electricity I didn't know, but I nodded, leaned back on the couch, sipped my coffee and let Erik talk. He demonstrated the phonograph, which sounded rather scratchy and not much like the music the orchestra produced upstairs, but I didn't care. It was part of the magic of the moment, and I had no complaints. I only wanted to savor it all, every detail. I'd spent years remembering a few brief minutes when he'd guided me through secret passages to get to ballet practice, long ago when I was so much younger and newer to the Opera. I wanted to remember *this* moment too.

Chapter Seventeen

How could I not stay longer than I meant to in Erik's apartments? When I finally mentioned leaving, he was perfectly courteous about guiding me back up into the daylight—though if it hadn't been August, with its long days, there would have been scant daylight left.

I was late getting home. Mother was in the kitchen, preparing supper, which was better than if she had met me at the door. But she did say almost immediately, "I expected you sooner than this. Something come up at the Opera?"

"No, not really," I said, and tried to brush past her to my room.

Maybe I spoke too fast, or my eyes were too bright or my cheeks too pink. *Something* made her turn away from the stove, and study me more closely, with eyes narrowed and expression thoughtful. "Are you sure nothing happened?"

How did she always *know*? "Of course," I said, trying to seem cheerful but not *too* cheerful. "I mean, first day back, it's exciting. And the girls were so nice about it. Even Madame Thibault smiled, just a little."

"Mm-hmm," Mother said, with no change in her expression. "Is there some new word from Léon?"

This came at me completely unexpectedly, with no counterfeiting of surprise required. "What? No, nothing about...Léon." Too late it occurred to me that that could have been a perfectly good excuse for being just a little too happy today.

"Mm-hmm," she said again, and turned back to her cooking. I managed three steps towards my room before she said, "And how is the Phantom?"

I gave up. I'd have to tell her eventually, and maybe this way I'd at least get points for honesty. "Erik's good. I think he was glad to see me." I took a breath, flung myself into the fray. "And he let me see his home."

At twelve, I would have shared this news with some naïve expectation that she'd think it was exciting too. I was older now. Though my tone tried to make it sound as good as *I* thought it was, I was not surprised when she turned around much faster and stared at me with an expression rapidly approaching horror.

"He did *what?*"

I refused to quail as though something dreadful had happened. Friends invited each other for social calls. That was all this had been. There had even been coffee, all very proper. "He invited me to see his home. Under the Opera, you know." That didn't sound quite as proper as it might have. "It was really very lovely," I forged ahead, "he has this beautiful Degas painting, and Persian rugs. Oh, and a phonograph, that's a—"

"He invited you to his home, and you *went?*"

I still wasn't shrinking, but it was getting harder. "It would have been rude to refuse."

"Meg!"

"Oh honestly, Mother! It's been six months. If he was going to kill me, he would have done it by now." I didn't even hope for a retreat anymore, just dropped into a nearby kitchen chair, crossed my arms, and stared back as hard as she was staring at me.

"You went alone to God knows where underground—"

"Just the other side of the underground lake."

"—with the Phantom of the Opera—"

"He *has* a name."

"—who might have done God knows what to you—"

"Just because the ballet girls tell stories, that doesn't mean they're true."

"—and I wouldn't even know where to look for you if you were lying dead somewhere—"

"I *trust* him!"

And Mother fell almost alarmingly silent. She was still staring at me, but it was a more measuring stare, an assessing stare. Somehow it was harder to hold that gaze than her angry one.

"Well, I do," I said. "I trust him." I waved one hand, as if I could wave off some of the sudden weight of those words. "Anyway, if he wanted to kill me he could have done it in Box Five. What difference does it make if I'm alone with him there, or under the Opera?"

She sighed. "When you first started meeting him in Box Five, you argued that it was perfectly safe because it was just a few feet from a door with people all around."

"Did I?" I said vaguely. I'd been hoping she'd forgotten that. "But really, Mother, it's fine. It's not like people talk about, some lurid, misty lair full of skeletons. It's really very charming."

"Yes, it was the room I was worrying about," Mother said, with a level of sarcasm that was unusual for her. But then she sighed again, pressed the back of one hand against her forehead and said, "You will tell me before you go down there? Whenever you have plans?"

"Yes, of course, Mother," I said, rolling my eyes but privately relieved. If she was asking this—that was just the same old thing, and that meant this was going to be all right.

"And you'll be careful?" she pressed.

Also the familiar script. "Yes, Mother, if he ever scares me—"

"No, I don't mean—well, yes, that too, but I meant..." She sat down across from me at the table, reached out for my hand. "You know he's not like other men. Not like the subscribers in the Dance Foyer, not like the people we know in Leclair. He may not have the same plans, or the same intentions for his life."

I stared at her, genuinely confused, because obviously Erik was different, that was why he was so interesting, but why bring it up like it was some kind of warning? "I don't understand."

Now it was Mother who wasn't meeting my gaze. "Just…be careful. How close you get to him. How much you expect him to be able to offer."

"I don't expect him to offer *anything*," I protested. Aside from stories about distant places and insights on music and, perhaps, the occasional pot of coffee.

"We joke sometimes about him being your Phantom, but we both know—"

"He's not my Phantom, Mother," I said with a groan. If he was anyone's Phantom, if that distant, shadowy man belonged to anyone, he was obviously Christine's Phantom.

Maybe, if he hadn't been so obviously Christine's, I might have felt he was just a little, tiny bit mine. In a different way, of course.

"All right, good," she said, and then rose to her feet again, voice brisk once more as she said, "And make very certain no one else learns about this. It is not good for a girl's reputation to be alone in a man's apartment and—"

"Oh Mother, *really!*" I said, dismissive but relieved to at least recognize this ground to fight over. As if spending time with the Phantom anywhere wouldn't ruin me at the Opera anyway, if word got out. I'd known that from the beginning, accepted it long ago.

I didn't want her to bring it up though, or give her the chance to keep talking and change her mind about tacitly accepting this whole situation, so I jumped to my feet and made for my room.

Mother turned to her cooking again, shaking her head. "May you someday have a daughter who dreams of adventures."

I couldn't stop myself from leaning back into the room to say, "If life is supposed to be boring, we never should have come to the Opera!"

Excerpt from the Private Notebook of Jean Mifroid, Commissaire of Police

2 September, 1881

Forced to curtail investigations into Opera with return of Opera Company from August break. Efforts sufficient to prove Opera floorplan not showing full picture. Located five hidden doors, two disabled on second visit. Phantom must be aware of investigation, but has taken no overt move. If he would only show himself—

Investigation into hidden passages uncovered little proof of Phantom's present activities or current whereabouts. Still suspect belowground more important to pursue, but also more difficult to access.

Note also, M. Giry returned from August travel. Have yet to definitively link to Phantom, but will continue to monitor.

Erik was not entirely sure how it became a habit, inviting Meg to visit his home. He wasn't entirely sure how it had happened the first time, a sudden impulse that had seemed like a good idea at the time and then, astonishingly...continued seeming like a good idea. It was just so much easier, so much less risky than remaining aboveground where the wrong person, such as the police commissaire, could come stumbling in at any moment.

Though he never would have guessed that he'd describe letting someone else into his private refuge as 'less risky.' But after all, Meg was…well, she was…well, she wasn't going to go haring off to Mifroid, he felt confident enough about that. And she didn't know the route, or how to maneuver the secret doors anyway.

So he went on meeting her aboveground and then traveling belowground with her, and it was all quite simple and pleasant and he could almost pretend there was nothing unusual in the situation at all, that he might be any other member of Parisian society, inviting a friend for coffee.

Except for the reminders inevitably arising that he was, in fact, nothing like the rest of Parisian society. Big things could remind him, like the dark labyrinth itself, or the necessity of always meeting in an empty part of the Opera. Or reminders could come in something small, like the crucial snapping of a string.

It was unfortunately the string holding the Phantom's black mask in place, and unfortunately it broke while he was in the catwalks as ballet rehearsal ended, and unfortunately the mask went tumbling down out of sight below before he could catch it, landing somewhere in the shadows and clutter of backstage.

Erik clapped one hand over the side of his face, the distorted side, the side he never, ever went aboveground without covering, and stared down into the darkness below, heart suddenly pounding to a faster tempo. His mask could have settled into any crevice between boxes and props and spare furniture down there, and too many people were backstage to risk a search.

And he was due to meet Meg in just a few minutes. The ballet girls were already leaving the stage. She'd be heading to the prop room shortly, and—

The prop room. Maybe…?

He descended from the catwalks at a possibly unsafe speed, but made it to the ground unseen, with no further disaster. A slip through a secret passageway to the empty prop room, where he hurried between rows of clothing until he came to the wall holding masks. It was not a complete collection, many more were archived elsewhere, and with a quick glance he could see that this was a problem.

Most of the masks were narrow dominos, completely useless for hiding any meaningful portion of his face. There was a row of Venetian-style masks from a recent Italian opera, but while those would cover his forehead, they'd do nothing about his cheek. He hesitated briefly over one that would be concealing, but…the upper half was a man's sculpted eyes and nose, rather bulbous, and a veil covered the mouth. It would hide everything, at the cost of looking completely ridiculous. He could see nothing useful at all on the wall, and turned to the table nearby. He moved aside a few stacks of additional masks, searching with increasing alarm for *anything* he could use. He picked up an elaborate metal helm— was it meant to be a hawk, maybe? Still no good, it didn't extend far enough. Why did so many masks end at the cheekbones?

Footsteps two rows of costumes away. "Erik?"

It was a rare moment when someone *other* than Meg would have been preferable, someone he could simply avoid. He could retreat, only that would mean embarrassing explanations later. In desperation he snatched up a mask that was evidently still in progress, a gray-brown oval of cloth with a squared-off top and just one eyehole. Utterly lacking in elegance, but concealing. It would have to serve.

"Oh, there you are." Footsteps behind him. "This place is a maze and—oh!" She fell back a step in surprise when he turned around, and Erik sighed.

"Just don't say anything, all right?"

The fingers over her mouth didn't hide her growing smile. "It's not quite your…usual style, is it?"

He grimaced, an expression covered by brown cloth. "I had a…mask problem, and had to improvise."

"That's the best you could find?"

"Yes. Now if you're done being amused, can we go?"

She gave up trying to repress the smile. "We can go, but I'm going to be amused for a while."

As he triggered the secret door behind the masks and retrieved the lantern beyond it, Erik realized that Meg was on his left side, his blind side thanks to this one-eyed mask. He nearly objected, then reconsidered. Though it gave him an instinctive uneasiness, he knew that wasn't grounded in any genuine concern. *Meg* wasn't going to attack him, and better to have her watching the side he couldn't see.

Almost uncannily, her thoughts seemed to be going the same direction. "You can't see on this side at all, can you?"

He turned his head in time to catch her waving one hand. "It's fine," he said, and began walking through the tunnel.

He could hear her footsteps as she fell into stride with him. "If you say so. But if I were you, I'd just drop the mask entirely. It can't be comfortable."

"You're not me, and the mask always stays on." The words came out harsh and set off echoes of memory in his mind. He had told *her* that too. See how that had turned out.

"All right, just don't blame me if you crash into a wall because you can't judge distances," Meg said, voice light. "I don't know what dreadful thing you think is going to happen if you take that mask off, anyway. I'm not going to run screaming away."

Erik came to an abrupt halt, turned again to stare at her. "Why would you assume that I'm assuming that?"

Her forehead creased, eyes crinkling. "I just thought—I only meant…"

Her inability to explain was the clue itself. A casual comment with nothing behind it would have been dismissed as such. This had a basis. "You know," he said, stomach like lead. "About my face."

Her eyes widened now. "You didn't know that I know."

He glowered at the dark shadows ahead. How he could have been so stupid—to delude himself all this time into believing she simply wasn't curious about the mask—but how else could he explain her willingness to be friendly? "That accounts for why you never asked," he said shortly. "I suppose *she* must have told you."

"Yes," Meg said, voice faint.

He thought of how she had described him to that stupid vicomte— face distorted, misshapen. A monster. He winced. "That must have been a *wonderful* conversation."

"She exaggerated."

The words were too flat, too sure, too knowing. And they made no sense at all. "How can you possibly know that?" he asked, turning to look at her again for whatever clue her face might give in the lantern light.

Her mouth twisted into a rather sad smile. "You really weren't paying attention, when the chandelier fell."

This seemed like a complete non sequitur. Though, he had taken his mask off when he confronted Philippe de Chagny, in a moment of madness and fury.

"I was trying to help—her, and the comte had just knocked me back into a prop table," Meg filled in. "It gave me a very good view."

"I see," he said, and resumed walking. "I'm sorry."

They walked on a few paces in silence before Meg said, "What was that an apology *for*? For letting me see your face, or for not paying attention?"

"Because I—that is—well..." He had meant the first, but he suddenly suspected that wasn't the right answer.

"Never mind," she said quietly.

There didn't seem to be any more to say. So she knew. She knew what he looked like, knew that he was not like other men, could never be like other men.

And yet—she was *still here*. She had known all along. It had been 192 days, fourteen hours since *she* had left, so Meg must have known all that time. And she had still decided to become friends with him. It was almost as if she...didn't care?

Maybe she hadn't really had a proper view. Or maybe that moment, when the chandelier fell and he tore his mask off, had been too emotionally-charged for an adequate assessment, so—something she had said suddenly came back to him, came clear for the first time.

"The comte knocked you back into a prop table?"

Meg made a faint murmur of assent, then remarked, "I had a bruise for a week."

Her tone was unconcerned, but Erik found his hand curling into a fist. "I should have hit him harder."

This surprised a laugh from her, then, "Oh, I shouldn't laugh at that..." He glanced over in time to see her shake her head. "My mother would agree though. Right after the comte disappeared, I almost wondered if she was behind it. Though I suppose that sounds ridiculous."

"Not at all," Erik said, with feeling. He hadn't forgotten Madame Giry's warning to him, when he first began talking to Meg. They hadn't spoken on the subject since, but he had no doubt she was still on watch.

They lapsed into a more comfortable silence, then resumed a much less fraught conversation about music and composers once they reached Erik's apartments and he had replaced his ridiculous substitute mask for his half-face white one.

They were soon deep into discussing the distinction between Mozart and Wagner, when Erik quite naturally went up to his pipe organ and played a brief portion of Mozart's concerto for two pianos, possibly playing slightly more than was usually done by only one person in that duet.

"There, you see, Wagner would have given this a completely different tone," he concluded, turning away from the keys only to realize her eyes had gone wide. He shifted, tugged at his collar with one finger, and she still hadn't spoken. "Is something wrong?"

She started, blinked, said, "No... I just—that was very good."

"I know," he said automatically, realized a half-second too late that wasn't etiquette, and quickly added, "I mean, thank you."

She half-shrugged, raising just one shoulder. "I haven't heard you play before. I mean, and I'm not a musician, but that was...that really was *very* good."

"Thank you," he said again, and because he couldn't think of anything else to say he turned back towards the keys and said, "But take this piece from Wagner's Ring Cycle, it's not at all the same..."

And the curious thing was, he didn't feel at all the same by the time he finished it. What started as awkwardness gave way to an odd sort of pleased feeling. She wasn't a musician and she was hardly a meaningful critic and he already knew he was very good. But it had been a long, long time since anyone had said so.

Chapter Eighteen

M eeting Erik below the Opera wasn't the same as meeting in Box Five, or the Grand Foyer. I had never so clearly noticed the underlying air of wariness in Erik until it disappeared. Aboveground, he was always listening, always alert for a threat. Belowground, he relaxed. I mean, he hardly sprawled across a couch and put his feet up, but some tension went out of his shoulders, out of the way he watched the world. Which, it occurred to me, meant he didn't consider me a threat. I liked that.

And I liked the music too.

I had always been sure he was a musician. He had to be, the way he gave directions and advice to the Opera Company, and then Christine had confirmed it. It was one of the few details she had managed to give me about him.

Assuming he was a musician was merely abstract; hearing him play was real. I had listened to a lot of music in my time at the Opera, and I'd never heard anyone play like Erik did. The most impossibly intricate melodies, and he'd just casually play them off, note perfect, with never a musical score in front of him.

I'd been coming below the Opera for just over three weeks (my sixth visit, not that I was counting) and was quite comfortable by then sitting in the corner of Erik's maroon couch, sipping coffee and discussing Opera gossip and operas, with occasional musical accompaniment.

Erik was sitting at his pipe organ, playing some piece rather idly, Charles Gounod, I think, when he either reached the end of the piece or just stopped playing it. For a moment he sat silently, fingers resting on the keys, and I wondered if I ought to say something. But he wasn't looking at me, staring at his hands, apparently deep in thought.

Then he started playing a new piece, one I was sure I'd never heard before because I would have remembered it. It was haunting and slow and sweet, like moonlight, or mist on a river, or like being outside as dawn was breaking, not in Paris but in Leclair where the world is silent and all the edges are softer and everything seems to be holding its breath in wonder. Minor notes wove hints of sadness into the picture, and yet it was the kind of sadness that makes beauty more intense, that makes every lovely thing all the more precious for its fragility.

I was holding my breath in wonder. I might have asked as he began what it was; I had done that with other pieces, but not this one. I couldn't have interrupted this one, even if I'd been able to find the words.

The melody slipped away more than it ended, and it took me a few seconds to realize it was done. I exhaled a long, slow breath in the silence that followed, blinked as I suddenly discovered my eyes were wet. I was still without any words until Erik turned his head, just far enough to look at me out of the corner of his eyes with an odd caution in his gaze, and I realized I had to say something.

"That was…beautiful." An easy word, an inadequate word. "Magical and lovely and…what composer was that?"

"Me," he said softly, looking at his hands again but with a very faint smile on his lips. "That was me."

I exhaled in a gust. "Why on earth aren't we playing your music upstairs? Or are we? You're not secretly Hector Berlioz, are you?" I asked, naming the first composer to come to mind.

"Berlioz is dead," he pointed out.

"According to the stories, so are you," I countered.

"Hmm, true. But no, I am not the ghost of Berlioz or anyone else. And the Opera Company does not have any of my music. They wouldn't appreciate it."

Not appreciate *that*? "Did you ever give them a chance to?"

"Moncharmin would say it's not marketable," he said, which appeared to me to be completely without foundation—but the words had the firm tone I recognized as meaning I should let the subject drop.

Another personal subject, another topic Erik was sensitive on. And I really should have known that, because the music was so obviously personal, so obviously reflecting and evoking emotions Erik was never going to put into words. The more I thought about it, the more honored I felt that he had played his own music for me.

But I couldn't quite let go of the idea that he ought to be sharing this beyond me. Music that sounded like that had to have a piece of the composer's soul in it, and something so beautiful ought to be heard.

Excerpt from the Private Notebook of Jean Mifroid, Commissaire of Police

21 October, 1881

Still no support from Prefect for investigation into Phantom in Opera Garnier. Management of Opera remain uncooperative. Have examined records of sewers and catacombs, and believe have found access route to area below Opera. Have no faith in accuracy of records re: tunnels below the building – must investigate personally. I cannot give up. I will not be stopped.

Erik came perilously close to not noticing his warning bell. He was playing a symphony with crashing chords, and if the timing had been a fraction different or the bell a note less discordant he might not even have noticed. As it was he stopped, a jarring stop midway through a crescendo, and cocked his head to listen to the bell ringing on one wall, telling him about an intruder.

It might be nothing. It was the bell indicating movement by the lake, and it could be set off accidentally. A large rat might have triggered it. He'd always meant to fix that problem, but somehow, he'd never been able to bring himself to do it.

It had rung 234 days, two hours ago. The night she left.

Philippe de Chagny had drowned in the underground lake that night. Erik had ignored the warning then. Would Philippe be alive, if he hadn't?

He grimaced, rubbed his palms against his trouser legs, and rose to his feet. He'd check on it. It was probably nothing. Not the Daroga; he took a different route that didn't trip this signal. Not a routine inspection crew, not this late at night, but it could be merely a rat.

Just in case it wasn't, he donned a long dark cloak and a black mask.

He made his silent way down the passage to the near shore of the lake, all quiet and calm. But as he reached the lake, he halted. Normally the far side, the side closest to the opera house, was lost in darkness.

Tonight a light stabbed through the shadows, piercing the black veil that lay over his world.

Rats didn't carry lanterns. At least, the four-legged kind didn't.

With a frown, Erik pulled his hood farther forward and set off for the shortest route to the other side of the lake. It was impossible to walk all the way along the shore—in places there was no shore—but he knew the way through the labyrinth of tunnels and cross-passages.

Even the fastest route meant losing sight of the lantern for several minutes, and when he neared the light's last location only shadows greeted him. Whoever it was could have retreated to the surface, but he hoped not. He wanted to know who was here, and why.

He dropped down to his hands and knees, wiped the dust away from a small patch of stone floor, and pressed one ear against the ground. There—faint, but unmistakable. Footsteps. Somewhere down the passage he was in, running parallel to the underground lake, moving the opposite direction Erik had come from.

He rose again, automatically brushing off his knees and palms, and moved silently in the direction of the footsteps. He passed the bottom of the stairs that led up to the Opera Garnier, the most conventional way to come down to the lake, and kept walking.

He was looking for a glow up ahead, confident that a man carrying a lantern was blinding himself with his own light. A Ghost who stayed in the shadows wouldn't be seen.

There—a faint lightening of the darkness. Erik moved against the wall, a friendlier habitation for shadows, and cautiously advanced closer. He could hear the footsteps now too, the tap of boots. And another noise—faint, very faint, a scritching, squeaking sound, but not like rats would make. This was continuous, punctuated with an occasional tap...

And then he noticed what was on the wall beside him, just below eye level. A thin white line.

Chalk. The man in the boots with the lantern was marking his path, drawing a line of chalk as he advanced.

Someone was clever. And determined.

Erik lifted one fist, pressed the side of his hand against the line, and rubbed it out as he continued to follow. He'd probably never get the chalk dust out of his black glove, but he had a drawer full of others.

The man up ahead was only a silhouette in the lantern light, unidentifiable—until the skittering of a proper rat somewhere in the tunnel made him stop and turn around.

Erik froze, a black shadow among shadows, close to the wall where shadows belonged.

"Who's there?" a voice demanded, more assertive than afraid.

The police commissaire. Mifroid himself.

Well, he might have known. In these past few quiet months, part of him had been waiting for Mifroid to resurface all along. A man who disguised himself as a scenechanger to spy at the Opera wasn't going to simply give up.

And life had never been that easy for him anyway.

After a long moment, Mifroid turned again and resumed his slow progress forward. Erik waited a few breaths, then resumed following.

It was strange that Mifroid was alone. Generally the commissaire had come to the Opera with a few of his officers to support him. But now he was acting alone again, and unlike his earlier espionage, there was no reason this mission wouldn't be supported by more men. Just what was the commissaire doing here all by himself? Why conduct a secret investigation?

They soon reached a branch in the tunnel. Mifroid hesitated a long time, then turned left, the direction that continued to parallel the lake. Regrettable, as the right hand side would have led him out into the catacombs that riddled the ground beneath Paris, a labyrinth the Phantom had found readily available for him on arrival. From that turning on, the only paths would have taken him well away from the neighborhood of the Opera.

But Mifroid had gone left. And that meant, in about a hundred meters...

He heard the click a bare second before Mifroid's sharp inhale, the clunk of the dropped lantern, the slither of cloth over stone.

Erik smiled in the darkness. He liked trapdoors. Such useful things, for stage productions, for escape routes, and for traps.

But wait. The thud was missing. There had been no thud as Mifroid hit the bottom of the tunnel beneath him, depositing him neatly into the catacombs. Instead, the echo of harsh breathing, scratching and scraping of cloth against stone. Mifroid had managed to catch hold of the edge, was pulling himself back up.

It was so inconvenient when his pursuers turned out to be competent.

Within minutes Mifroid had got himself out of the trap, lit the candles he had evidently stocked in his coat in case of losing his lantern, and discovered that he could continue forward on the narrow strip of ground remaining to the left of the trapdoor.

Determined man, to keep going. And to keep going alone. The commissaire wasn't stupid. If he hadn't known it before, he certainly knew now that it would be better and safer to have others with him on this search. So he had to have a compelling reason to do this alone. Perhaps it was an unofficial investigation?

Erik followed him to another branching of the tunnel. Mifroid went right this time. Had he gone left, closer to the lake, Erik would have triggered a flood and swamped the passage. The right hand branch was more dramatic.

Erik slipped through a hidden door into a parallel side passage. From there he moved ahead of Mifroid a dozen meters. He listened, counted footsteps to track the commissaire's progress, and at the most dramatic moment hit the mechanism to send flames shooting up in a line, blocking the passage with a wall of fire.

Mifroid jumped back from the flames with a curse. The fire had been far enough away to leave him unharmed, but close enough to warn him that it might easily *not* have been that way.

Surely he had to be discouraged now. There was no way to keep going forward—the flames would burn as long as the Phantom kept the gas on, and left no convenient gap to slip through.

The commissaire still paced in front of the fire for an absurd length of time, with the heavy steps of a man searching for an answer and frustrated to find none. He had to believe he had found the path to the Phantom's secret chambers, and now was blocked from pursuing it.

He hadn't actually. He should have turned the other direction back at the underground lake, gone around on the south instead of the north. Erik had lain traps in a half-dozen passages under the Opera, because if only one route had obstacles, that would be a bit of a give-away, wouldn't it?

The actual route had two hidden doors posing as dead-ends, and the hidden staircase besides. Erik didn't like uninvited visitors.

The commissaire finally gave up, turning around and commencing a slow trudge back the way he had come. After a few minutes he stopped suddenly. Erik, in his parallel passage, stopped too. This was about the point where he had left the commissaire's passage before. He couldn't have noticed the secret door—but the chalk line was rubbed out beyond here.

"Where are you?" Mifroid growled. "I know you're here. Show yourself!"

It was remarkable how otherwise intelligent people believed that he'd come out of hiding just because they told him to.

"I am Commissaire Mifroid of the Paris police. I know you were involved in the murder of Philippe de Chagny, and I know you are hiding down here. Your tricks will not work. I will keep looking and I *will* find you."

It was also remarkable that Mifroid didn't appear to realize that he'd just given him every reason in the world to kill him. Quietly, neatly, down here where no one ever came and no one would ever know.

Erik sighed inaudibly. But he would know. He had too many dark deeds and darker memories to contend with already. He'd let the commissaire live.

Commissaire Mifroid finally gave up for the day and found his way back to the surface, even without the aid of his chalked line. Erik was too much a pessimist not to believe that he'd be returning.

He'd be careful, keep an eye out, perhaps do a check of his traps and his secret doors to make sure he wasn't missing anything. He'd have to keep a watch on things above ground too, make sure the managers weren't helping Mifroid, see if he could pick up any hint of why the commissaire was undertaking this investigation in such an unconventional, unprofessional way.

He thought he wouldn't mention this to Meg, though. She'd worry. And while it was rather nice to think that she *would* worry, he didn't want her to actually *be* worried. So he'd keep this quiet, for now.

Excerpt from the Private Notebook of Jean Mifroid, Commissaire of Police

22 October, 1881

Completed first investigation under Opera Garnier. Must explore alone to maintain secrecy until gaining enough proof to merit official investigation. No conclusive success yet. Encountered traps and

evidence of presence of so-called Phantom—not substantial enough to convince Prefect. Must find rumored home underground, evidence to tie to Philippe's murder.

I ignored prankster's existence for too long. I will fix that mistake. Too late for Philippe, but I will see justice.

Chapter Nineteen

I n October the opera we were performing presented me with a rare opportunity. Along with a number of other dancers, I was only needed in the first act, and Madame Thibault had told us all we might leave when our parts were finished. What she actually said was that there was no need for us to sit around and be tripped over when it wasn't strictly necessary, which I think was an attempt to not look as though she was trying to do us a favor.

I might have gone to the Dance Foyer early, as most of the girls intended, but instead I separated from the group, heading in the direction of the first tier boxes. Should anyone notice, it was a perfectly logical place to find my mother. But it was also where I might find someone else.

I lingered in the hall until no one was in sight, then stepped carefully up to the door of Box Five. I hesitated on the threshold. It was possible this was a mad thing to do. I had imagined this throughout my childhood, finding an opportunity to burst into Box Five during a performance and catch the Phantom there.

I'd never done it, of course. It was one of the absolute rules, that you never disturb the Phantom in Box Five.

But things had to be different now. I visited the Phantom's home on a regular basis. We were friends. Surely Erik wouldn't mind.

I took a deep breath and decided to risk it. But I still knocked first. I waited a moment, then opened the door and stepped inside. Closed curtains, low gaslights, empty seats.

"Erik?" I said softly. "Are you here?"

He might not be. Or he might not choose to answer. If he didn't, I'd have to slip back out and hope he wasn't upset and—

"Not the Giry I was expecting," a calm voice remarked.

I turned my head to the left and there he was, standing against the corner pillar, arms crossed, as unruffled as though he'd been there all along—but I was fairly certain he hadn't been.

"Good evening," I said, trying not to betray any surprise or nervousness. His tone hadn't sounded annoyed, and at least he hadn't led with any angry reprimand for my uninvited presence.

"Good evening," he returned, and walked over to sit down in his customary seat in the front row. "Madame Thibault let you go after you finished dancing in Act One?"

I had been expecting to explain this—but wasn't surprised that Erik knew the order of the evening's production. "Yes," I said, and went to sit in my own customary seat, two away from him, just as though this was quite ordinary. "I thought I'd like to see the rest of the performance. And ballet girls don't generally get into boxes."

"And you assumed I'd just let you into mine?" That might have been worrying—but I could hear the trace of humor in his voice. I might not have recognized it a few months ago, but I could identify it now. That fact was as encouraging as the humor itself.

So I just grinned at him. "Exactly."

"Well, that's true enough," he agreed with a slight smile. "But did you forget that I keep the curtains closed?"

I blinked, looked at the thick, closed curtain. "Yes, I did, actually." Or rather, two truths of the world had blocked me from thinking of this particular problem. I knew the Phantom kept the curtains closed. I knew the Phantom watched every performance. The contradiction in the two, if it had ever occurred to me at all, had been dismissed years ago as some trick of the Phantom.

"Come sit over here," Erik said, indicating the seat directly next to him with one hand. "You'll probably be able to see most of the stage."

I had stopped noticing those two seats between us. Now they seemed charged with significance again. Erik had invisible walls, and for all the times we talked or walked or sat together, there was always a careful distance between us. But now he had invited me. I took a breath, switched seats, sank into the new one next to him. It was exactly the same as all the others, and yet...

"How's the view?" Erik asked.

I realized he had the curtain open, just a few centimeters, but the angle was right to see nearly all the stage. Paradox resolved. "Better than it is from backstage," I said with a smile.

"You could have gone to the Dance Foyer early instead," he pointed out.

"Yes, but the only people there right now are the ones who don't care about art at all," I said, because it was true, and because I guessed it would make him smile—and it did.

"To that point," he said, settling back in his seat, "Act Three is just beginning."

Watching the performance from a box seat made me feel like quite a grand lady. I'd never be able to afford to rent a box like this. Watching it with the Phantom of the Opera made it all feel magical. I didn't think anyone else in the entire Company had ever watched a performance from Box Five.

I thought that at first—and then I got caught up in the story, silly though the plotline was. It felt different, watching from the audience, watching a performance instead of a rehearsal. More exciting, more real. Or at least, I could pretend a bit, even when there was nothing very realistic about how the opera's events unfolded.

When the final curtain closed, I leaned back in my seat with a satisfied sigh, then remarked, "Operas get it all wrong, you know."

Erik shifted in the seat next to me. "What?"

"Love," I said, gesturing towards the stage. I should have thought before I launched on this topic, but all I was thinking at the time was that the last solo the tenor had sung was distinctly cloying, and did nothing to help the realism of an absurd plot. "Or at least, they don't get it very right."

Erik looked back towards the stage. "How so?"

"Nine times out of ten they tell the same story, and it's not at all reasonable." I straightened, warming to my topic. "It's always the same—a tenor sees a soprano and falls madly, passionately, hopelessly in love at that very moment. He pursues; she refuses; he persists, while she keeps refusing. Sometimes a baritone comes in and spoils things for a while, and in the end the girl suddenly capitulates without warning, usually vowing that she was really in love all along. Life just doesn't happen that way. I mean, he falls in love with her just by seeing her? He doesn't even know anything about her, so what's he actually in love *with*?"

"You don't believe two souls can form an immediate connection?"

I waved a hand. "Perhaps it's possible, but I think it's a very risky thing to count on. He doesn't know if she's nice or a shrew, if she wants to get married and have twelve children or if she's obsessed with her singing career, maybe she has an annoying laugh or is cruel to anyone she doesn't like. He doesn't *know*, yet he keeps pursuing this girl who insists she doesn't want him. People can change their minds about things, but when she refuses a dozen times? When someone keeps saying no, it's because she's not interested and she's never going to be, and continuing to push is just going to scare her. Yet the heroes of operas are constantly doing all sorts of extravagant things in the name of love, like...oh, I don't know..."

"Dropping a chandelier, perhaps." His voice was very quiet, almost without inflection, and he wasn't looking at me.

I came to an abrupt halt, frantically reviewing what I had been saying, and with a sinking feeling I realized just whose love story I had been describing. "Well," I managed after a moment. "Yes. Speaking hypothetically, of course."

"Of course."

I clasped my hands in front of me, stared out at the stage. Should I talk about something else? Should I make some sort of apology? Should I ask another question? This was the closest we had ever come to talking about Christine, about Erik and Christine… "I just mean—that is, I thought…oh, I don't know why I think I know anything about it anyway, I've never even been in love."

"I don't recommend it. A painful business all around."

I slid a look sideways at him, and though his gaze was still on the stage, the set of his shoulders was thoughtful, not guarded. "I hear it's better when it's requited," I ventured.

He glanced at me then. "Well, that's always been my problem, hasn't it?" The words were mild, but his eyes were sad.

For just a moment I caught a glimpse of something, a tiny peek behind the mask, a hint at answers behind the whole mad Christine love story and I wanted to ask…why her, and why did you keep pursuing, and why didn't you just realize it wasn't right when she started up with Raoul and what did you even hope to have happen and…just, why? All the questions we'd never talked about, that I'd given up even thinking of asking a long time ago, in the face of Erik's walls and forbidden topics and silent, looming grief.

I wasn't sure why I didn't ask—if I didn't want to cause him more pain or if I was afraid he'd be angry or if I wasn't so sure anymore, somehow, that I really wanted to know.After a moment he blinked and looked back at the stage and said, "I've always found that last song rather overly sentimental." With that, the mask was back and it was too late.

We talked of other things, but I kept thinking about that conversation, about what I thought I'd seen behind the mask. It made a sad kind of sense, that a man who had never fit into society but who loved music and theatre would try to take his cues from what he saw playing out on the stage. But the stage wasn't life, so of course it went horribly wrong.

Erik knew so much about the world, and yet he knew so little at the same time.

Excerpt from the Private Notebook of Jean Mifroid, Commissaire of Police

27 October, 1881

Tunnels under Opera Garnier labyrinth riddled with dead-ends and death traps. No success on additional explorations. Unsure if OG knew of subsequent investigations. No direct encounter with him.

Clearly something strange under Opera, but not enough evidence for official route for investigation into Philippe's death. Attempted to present report to Prefect, no success. Still told to investigate elsewhere. Prefect suggested I am too intense, too focused on this one angle. <u>Because it is right.</u>

Need Opera Company support. Cannot convince management. Must seek other avenues for information.

Where are Raoul de Chagny and Christine Daaé? Their evidence growing increasingly vital. Could verify existence of OG, involvement with PdC's death. RdC as noble next of kin could put money and pressure behind investigation. Alternative: what information does Charles Garnier know re: secret routes in and below Opera?

Chapter Twenty

E arly in November, Moncharmin had what seemed at first like a perfectly terrible idea. This was not unusual. Erik had fallen back into the habit of paying attention to the Opera Company, occasionally nudging them into a direction more convenient for himself or better for art, and he was not impressed by the management.

He barely waited until he and Meg had stepped behind the masks in the prop room before he brought the newest problem up. "Have you heard Moncharmin's latest?"

"I don't think so," Meg said, picking up the lantern Erik had begun leaving here.

"He wants to find *new talent*." He snapped his fingers and the lantern Meg held up flared into burning life, reflecting golden on the pale stripes of her dress. "New pieces to perform, by new people we haven't performed before."

Meg cocked her head slightly to one side, considering. "That doesn't sound particularly awful. The way you said it I thought—"

"No, but wait—he's not just looking for new musical pieces, in a perfectly reasonable, research sort of way. He wants to have a *contest*. He wants everyone in Paris to submit music!"

Meg raised the lantern a little higher and started along the passage. "Well, it doesn't really matter what kind of trash is submitted, as long as they make a good choice for winner."

Erik's eyebrows rose, though it was possible she couldn't even see that in the dim light. "With Moncharmin and Ricard doing the selection? You find them reliable?"

"Oh. Yes, I see the point."

"As long as they work with the masters they can't go too far astray— I mean, astray, certainly, but not *too* far—but this? This is simply hopeless."

"Hmm," Meg said noncommittally, with the even more noncommittal, "Maybe."

He shoved his hands into his pockets and brought his feet down harder than usual as he walked. Silent steps were a habit for self-preservation, but sometimes good solid thumping was more satisfying. "And they probably won't listen to me about what to choose."

"Probably not," she agreed, and then was rather quiet all the way through the cellars, past the magic staircase and alongside the underground lake.

It was long enough to worry him. She was not usually quiet. Maybe he should ask if something was wrong. Maybe that would make things more uncomfortable. Maybe it was rude not to ask. Maybe it was rude to ask if she didn't want to talk about whatever it was. Maybe—

"I was just thinking," Meg said finally, looking out across the misty reaches of the lake, face more thoughtful than upset. "Maybe this idea of Monsieur Moncharmin's isn't *all* bad. Maybe it's an opportunity."

"For someone," he said, relieved that she had begun the conversation again, "but the trouble is it will probably be the wrong someone, knowing Moncharmin's taste—"

"No, an opportunity for *you*."

He should have seen this coming. He turned now to frown at her, as they entered the passage leading off from the lake. "What on earth are you talking about?" he asked, which was a perfect lie because he knew exactly what she meant. But maybe she wouldn't have the nerve to pursue it if he pretended he didn't.

Which was foolish and really, he knew Meg better than that. Of course she pushed on to say, "Why don't you submit to the contest? Someone besides me ought to be hearing that music you're writing."

"Not writing," he said crisply. "Have written. I don't compose. Not anymore."

He took two more steps before he realized she had stopped walking. When he halted and looked, she was staring at him with a rather alarming expression.

"You *what?*" she demanded.

He had the strangest feeling of guilt. He rubbed one palm against his jacket front. "Did I never mention it?" But of course he hadn't. He knew he hadn't, because it skirted too close to topics he didn't want to talk about.

"You don't *write music* anymore?"

"No," he said, trying to rally, straightening his back and lifting his chin. "I don't."

She waved the hand not holding the lantern rather wildly. "Why don't you just—go smash a Stradivarius! Or go around defacing Da Vinci paintings! Or—or—it's like burning the Library of Alexandria!"

Even the lantern was beginning to swing. He carefully reached out and took it from her grasp. "It's no one's business but mine whether I write music anymore, and I do not—"

"How *dare* you deprive the world of all the music you could write! Not that they're hearing it anyway, if you just hide it all away down—"

"I haven't written anything since *she* left!"

Silence, and for a horrible moment he was afraid he would have to explain who *she* was. But no, Meg apparently understood that perfectly well. At least, she didn't ask for clarification.

She pulled her cloak around her and strode off down the corridor again, so abruptly he had to hurry to fall into step.

How long had he been not writing? 246 days, fourteen hours…and a bit. He couldn't actually remember just when he'd last written something, the last composition before she left. He hadn't been counting from that.

"Fine," Meg said after two more turns, head down and not looking his direction. "*Don't* write music anymore. Let her take that away too."

"I didn't let her do anything," he said hollowly, automatically. Though he had let her leave, hadn't he? But he'd had no choice. Like he had no choice about this.

"Fine," Meg repeated flatly, and did not speak again for the rest of the way to his apartments.

Inside, she dropped into her usual spot (strange how quickly she'd developed a "usual spot") on his couch without looking at him once, while he tossed his cloak onto his armchair and then stood there awkwardly. He did not want to talk about writing music, he did not want to think about why he wasn't doing it anymore, he did not care what she thought about any of this and it was none of her concern.

"Even if I submitted," he said into the silence, "Moncharmin and Ricard won't choose mine."

She straightened up in her corner of the couch, turned to look over the high back at him. "They won't if you don't give them the chance."

He spread his hands. "What would I even send?"

She quirked an eyebrow at him. "What do you have available?"

Quite a lot. Before he stopped composing, before that part of his life came to an abrupt end, he had written...quite a lot. He crossed the room to the wall beyond his piano, pressed one of the stones, and a drawer just below it slid open with a faint hiss. He reached in, lifted out a stack of musical scores, and dropped them with a whump on top of the piano. "There's these." He went over to the fireplace; another stone, another drawer, another stack dropped, this time onto the coffee table, a few pages slithering off the pile in a rustle of paper. "And these." Another hidden drawer above the phonograph, and when he slid a panel back near the pipe organ where he'd stored an entire long shelf of papers, Meg finally interrupted him.

"All right, so, clearly there are choices," she said, staring down at the pile on the table in front of her. She reached out for a sheet that had slipped off and slid her direction, then stopped just before her hand touched it. "Do you mind if I...?"

"I dropped it in front of you, didn't I?" he said, sitting down on the bench of the organ, back to the keys, facing her.

If she thought that comment ungracious, she didn't mention it, just lifted the page to read the musical notes. He watched her face for a moment, watched her blue eyes moving as she scanned the page. "Which one is it?" he asked finally.

"Um...Sonata #112."

"Ah." He turned towards the keys, played the first few bars. "That one?"

A long pause, and he could hear the faint rustle as she slowly put the paper down again. "…yes. That one. Do you have all of them memorized?"

"I wrote them," he said, turning to look at her again.

He caught a glimpse of surprise in her expression, before it changed into the one she always wore when she was trying not to laugh. "I see."

He didn't, but he liked that expression better than the 'defacing da Vincis' expression she had been wearing, so he didn't dispute the question.

Meg poked through the pile, picking up the stray sheet here and there, until she landed on one with lyrics. "I can't quite see how this part is supposed to go—if you'd sing a few—"

"I don't sing," he said flatly. Just when things had calmed a little.

Her eyes did that widening thing again and he braced himself for another accusation of artistic massacre. Instead her lips just got tight and she merely said, "I see," again, set the page down and picked up the one she had been reading previously. "I like this one. You should submit this one."

"I still think it's a ridiculous idea," he hastened to say.

"Yes, I know, but that's not really the point, is it?"

Perhaps it wasn't. He wondered if she knew what the point was. He felt he had rather lost track.

Of course Erik won the managers' musical contest. I knew he would. Even Moncharmin and Ricard weren't *that* dumb. Though Monsieur Montagne the vocal director and Madame Thibault the ballet mistress also weighed in, so that might have helped.

I waited for Erik to bring it up, and he waited until we were all the way under the Opera, already sitting, already drinking coffee before he finally said, "I suppose you heard the latest about the musical contest."

"Didn't I *tell* you?" I said, bubbling up with the excitement I'd been holding down, waiting for my opportunity.

"Yes, well, there was probably very little meaningful competition," he said with a dismissive gesture of one hand. But he was smiling faintly too, and Erik only smiled when he was pleased. He dropped another lump of sugar into his coffee, watching the ripples as he stirred, while he said, "They've also asked if there would be a possibility of any more music."

It was lucky I'd already drunk some of my coffee, or I would have spilled then, liquid sloshing as I tightened my grip. "They did? That's wonderful! Not surprising. But wonderful." Then I frowned with a sudden thought. "Wait, how did they ask you that?" He obviously couldn't have sat down for a proper business meeting in the managers' office. Moncharmin and Ricard didn't know what the Phantom looked like, but a man in black wearing a mask was bound to raise some questions.

"They wrote. I got a post office box." He was looking down at his coffee again. "Just in case, you know. And they could hardly address a letter to 'across the underground lake.' "

I grinned at him. "You thought you'd win too." And this also proved he left the Opera, at least sometimes. He couldn't get a post office box without venturing outside. I filed the detail away.

He hesitated. "I thought…it was not an impossibility. But more importantly, I need to find another piece to send to them."

Most of the stacks of musical scores he had brought out before were still sitting around, and we spent a pleasant hour or two sifting through them in search of what to send the management next. Once he had selected a piece, Erik wrote a letter to accompany it, signing it with a flourish as Erik Rouen.

I may have stared slightly at the signature. A last name. *Finally*, after all this time, a second name.

Somehow he realized I was noticing the name, because he commented, "I was born near Rouen." He wasn't looking at me, fiddling with his pen, making it appear and disappear in his hand.

"Oh. So it's…sort of like a stage name?" I hazarded. Not a last name after all, not a new piece in the puzzle. Although—he was born near Rouen. I filed that detail away too. I had been nearly sure that he was French, despite his un-French first name and the multiplicity of languages he spoke, and now I had confirmation.

"I haven't used the family name I was born with in over twenty years, so—this will do." His expression did not invite questions.

I just nodded. I knew nothing about his childhood, and now evidently I needed to put it on the avoidance list. Christine, Persia, Joseph Buquet, gypsies…I didn't have to avoid so many subjects with anyone else I knew, and yet somehow I still felt Erik was better to talk to than anyone else.

And for all the things that weren't said, every detail that did come out *mattered*. If he hadn't used his birth name in over twenty years— he must have been a child, possibly a young teenager. What had caused the break? What was in his childhood that made him reject that identity so completely? How had a man with a facial deformity been treated as a child, and how had he wound up with gypsies? There were clues there, and I could make some guesses. After all, a man who chose to hide alone under an opera house was probably not comfortable out in the world, and that must have started somewhere.

It felt very strange the first time the Opera Company performed Erik's music. He sat in Box Five, uncomfortable through the whole evening. It was a selection of pieces, rather than a full opera, and his own came at the end. Moncharmin made a little speech about the contest, rambling on about how delighted they were, and Erik shifted position and drummed his fingers on the arm of his seat and waited.

Finally the music began. It was not a deeply emotional piece, one written more with artistic intent than anything else. But still—hearing notes he had put together, a melody he had designed, played on the stage of the Opera Garnier... He reached out and twitched the curtains closed, feeling suddenly that the usual two inch gap was altogether too open and exposing.

He had listened to rehearsals, of course, but the energy was so different at a performance. The music sounded good. He could hardly achieve the effect of a full orchestra alone under the opera house, though he wasn't sure the musical talent was the same among the Opera's musicians. Still, it sounded good. Mostly. Aside from a half-dozen changes he felt perhaps he ought to have made, a half-dozen choices that maybe weren't as right as he had believed.

But it was—well, acceptable. He found it acceptable.

He was rather astonished by the thunderous applause that followed the close of the piece. But then, what did the viewing public know about art anyway?

Meg would be pleased. The whole business had been her idea, after all.

Sure enough, soon after the final curtain, Meg came bursting into Box Five with flushed cheeks and a brilliant smile. "Wasn't that *wonderful?*"

"I don't know," Erik said, not rising from his seat, "I think I prefer the operas to these medley evenings."

"Oh stop it," she said amiably, dropping into the seat next to him. "Your piece, wasn't it wonderful?"

"I don't think the first violinist quite captured—"

"*Erik!*"

He surrendered. Conditionally. "Yes, it was rather nice."

She grinned at him. "I'll accept that."

He did not expect to discuss the subject with anyone else, and he did not expect the knock on his door that came early the following morning.

He was already in his parlor, and the sheer unexpectedness of a knock had him rising to his feet and taking a step towards the door before he could conjecture what it meant. Or who.

Not Mifroid. He wouldn't knock. He was the sort to pound, and shout about opening for the Paris police, and then probably break the door down.

Not Meg. She didn't know the tricks of his secret doors to get here, and besides, ballet practice had started just a few minutes ago.

Not...her. She didn't know the way either, supposing she wanted to come, which obviously she did not and never would. It had been 267 days, nine hours and she was never going to come through that door.

So that only left…

He swung the door open. "Good morning, Daroga. To what do I owe this honor?"

"Good morning, Erik," the Daroga said, strolling in with his usual quiet tread. His voice was mild, so evidently this wasn't the kind of call where he was outraged. How refreshing. Things had been…delicate for some time though, so it was difficult to believe this was a purely social call.

A kind of coolness had grown up between them in recent months. The obvious, blatant betrayal of bringing Raoul below the Opera at just the wrong moment had been something they could get past. The Daroga's ongoing caution that maybe it wasn't the wisest idea in the world to carry on a friendship with Meg Giry had created a more serious awkwardness. Not an actual hostility. Half the time Erik agreed with him—more at the beginning, less recently, but still, he could see his point. And that might have made it worse, because it wasn't a point he wanted reminding of.

So they had spoken only occasionally recently, both keeping rather more to themselves, though Erik still saw the Daroga about the Opera now and again, usually the single dark face somewhere in the back of the crowd. But now, here he was striding through the door.

"Do come in and tell me your business," Erik said dryly, letting the door click shut.

"I attended yesterday evening's performance," the Daroga said, the sofa cushions shifting with a faint squeak as he sat on one couch.

"Ah." Erik sat on the opposite couch. "And?" The Daroga never had been willing to simply get to the point. Unless he was angry, so maybe this was a good sign.

"The new composer seemed to quite impress the audience." A weighted pause. "Erik Rouen, I believe?"

Erik leaned back on the couch, locked his hands behind his head. "Are you here to congratulate me?" He might have known the Daroga would work it out. For someone who knew his first name and his musical style, it was no great trick.

"Congratulations," the Daroga said, and even sounded sincere. "I enjoyed hearing your music again. It reminded me of the…more pleasant parts of those long ago days in Mazandaran."

The parts that didn't involve death, presumably. There were few things Erik liked to remember about those days. "How very nice," he said blandly. "And how kind of you to drop in to tell me."

Then the Daroga hesitated, and Erik felt something inside him sink a little. Not a purely social call, not if he was reading the Daroga's pauses correctly. But he hadn't expected that it was, so that was no reason to be disappointed.

"I did wonder," the Daroga said at last. "Why? You've never given your music to the Opera Company before. Why now?"

Because surely he must have some kind of devious motive. For all the Daroga's comparative friendliness, he always expected the worst. "The contest provided an opportunity, and Meg thought it was a good idea to enter," Erik said airily, refusing to be intimidated out of using her name casually.

Another pause. "And how is Mademoiselle Giry?" the Daroga asked evenly.

"Don't you know?" Erik asked. "Surely you pay attention."

"She seems well," the Daroga acknowledged, and then suddenly his voice grew warmer, less impersonal. "And how are you, Erik? Are *you* well?"

This question was unexpected and the answer didn't come ready to hand. It wasn't a question Erik often asked himself. "I am…better than I have been at other times," he said slowly, somewhat surprised that it felt true. "I'm well enough." Well enough to continue, and that was all that really mattered, wasn't it?

"Good. I'm glad," the Daroga said, which sounded fine, but was also accompanied by the sound of his fingertips tapping against his knee, which meant there was something else. "And it was because of Mademoiselle Giry? That you've begun selling music?"

"I just told you that," Erik pointed out.

"Yes. I only thought—if the music begins being played outside these walls. If it ventures out into the world beyond, as sheet music or played by others, there could be consequences."

That was a strange idea, his music leaving this place that had always been his refuge. It would almost be like a part of himself leaving, and that was unthinkable. But perhaps this idea did point to the Daroga's true concern here. "No one is going to recognize my music. No one is going to trace it back to me here, or connect it to that prisoner you supposedly executed long ago in Persia. Your pension will be fine."

"That was not my concern. But someone might recognize it. Mademoiselle Daaé might—"

"Don't say her name," Erik snapped out, an automatic response before he even caught up to the rest of the Daroga's words. *She* might hear his music, recognize it, think of him. Did she think of him, ever? Did he want to know how she thought of him? Perhaps not.

The Daroga was still on his inexorable questioning. "Tell me the truth, Erik. Was that why you sold the music? Are you hoping it will lure her back?"

"Lure her...?" Erik almost wanted to laugh. Except that he never laughed, not anymore. "Daroga, she isn't coming back. I know she isn't coming back. She is *never coming back*. Are you satisfied that I am not deluding myself about that?"

"Yes," the Daroga said simply. "I am glad to know that you are not attempting some mad plan to—"

"Oh Daroga," Erik said with a sigh, "why do you always think that I'm plotting something terrible? I'm really not, most of the time." He felt too weary by the whole business to be angry. It was all just so—pointless. What difference did it make if he had a plan or not, if she heard his music or not? He was never going to see her, ever again.

"I don't think you're plotting, I merely...fear that you might be," the Daroga said, a nuance which seemed equally meaningless. "And you are of course not plotting anything with regard to Mademoiselle Giry—"

"Of course not," Erik said, with the tiniest spark of anger after all. "And besides, if I ever did anything terrible to her, which I will not, her mother would kill me, and you could stop worrying about me. Would you feel better then?"

"No," the Daroga said in reflective tones, "I don't think I would." Which was almost a nice thing to say. "And…you are not plotting anything else regarding Mademoiselle Giry?   Anything that is not terrible?"

Erik didn't even know what that was supposed to mean. "No, Daroga, I have no plots, no plans about Meg. Possibly a Christmas gift. Nothing more alarming than that."

"Good," the Daroga said, and seemed to mean it. And then in a softer tone said, "In fact, Erik, I am almost certain I would not feel better, if I did not have you to worry about."

"Well, that's fine then," Erik said gruffly, suddenly awkward at this near approach to sentiment. And yet… "I suppose I might do any mad thing if I didn't have to think about whether you'd get upset over it. And I suppose that's…just as well, really."

Chapter Twenty-One

O nce we began performing Erik's music, the whole Opera Garnier was soon abuzz about this new composer. Despite that, it took me by surprise the first time one of the ballet girls gave a loud sigh and said, "I bet he's wonderfully *romantic*" and I realized she meant Erik. Erik the composer, not Erik the ghost, but still.

We were sitting around the ballet's practice room, lessons done for the day, undecided about what to do with the remainder of the afternoon. The conversation about plans had turned quite easily into one about the latest doings at the Opera. Plenty of girls were present to chime in agreement regarding the new composer, but it surprised me how many did.

"His music sounds so *passionate*," Celine said with her own dreamy sigh. "I'd love to meet him."

I hid a smile as I finished lacing up my boot, sitting on the practice room floor. No, she probably wouldn't.

"Doesn't anyone else think it's odd that no one *has* met him?" That discordant note could only be coming from Jammes. "We're performing his music but no one in the Company has ever seen him."

"None of us have seen Berlioz," I pointed out, stretching my legs and smoothing my red-flowered skirts. Or many of the composers we performed.

Jammes gave me a withering stare. "Berlioz is dead. This Rouen is alive, *and* has a Paris postal box."

"How did you know that?" Celine asked eagerly, leaning forward and staring at Jammes as though she was some kind of marvel.

Jammes gave an airy shrug, head in the air, and said smugly, "I hear things."

She snooped around; that was the truth of it.

"Maybe he'll come to a performance!" Celine buzzed in delight. "Maybe he'll come to the Dance Foyer after! Everyone knows it's much better than the Singers Foyer." This comment prompted a murmur of satisfied agreement.

He was sure to be at the performance—at every performance—but I couldn't imagine Erik strolling through the Dance Foyer with the subscribers, flirting with ballerinas. He belonged to a different world.

Besides, he plainly had no interest in flirting with anyone. We had still never talked about Christine directly, but I had seen how bleak his eyes grew whenever even the faintest allusion to her came up. A man who cared that much wasn't going to move on easily.

"I think there must be a reason he's not coming," Jammes announced, snapping my wandering thoughts back to the conversation. "Or why hasn't he come before?"

I didn't like the direction she was going. I tried to look bored and said, "Oh honestly, now you're imagining things. So what if he doesn't like crowds?"

"Maybe he's afraid of the Phantom!" Francesca said, clasping her hands over her knee. "Maybe he doesn't want a chandelier to fall on his head."

That was greeted with a moment of considering silence.

"Ooh, did you hear about the blood dripping in Sorelli's dressing room?" Mignonette asked, eyes alight with at least as much excitement as Celine had shown over the mysterious new composer.

Mignonette didn't get much response; blood dripping was an old and regular story. Francesca did better when she followed it up with a claim that she had actually *seen* the Ghost in the Salon de la Lune just yesterday.

"What did he look like?" I asked, newly alert, wondering if she might have actually seen Erik.

"Oh, he came lunging out of the mirror right at me!" she exclaimed, hands pressed dramatically to her chest.

Still not impossible, if he had stepped through a secret door. "Yes, but what did he *look* like?" I persisted.

"Like a death's head," she happily embroidered, "with flames in his eye sockets!"

Not Erik, unless it was a deliberate illusion. I subsided, while around me the girls squeaked delightedly. That took them right off the subject of Erik Rouen and onto the Opera Ghost. At first I was pleased—not the least because Jammes looked distinctly put out.

But then they kept talking. About bloody handprints and mysterious voices, about disembodied heads frightening the storyteller into hysterics. About how vicious the Phantom must be, about how he marked out certain Company members to be the victims of disaster. About all the people—never people we knew by name, always mysterious other people somewhere in the Company—who had disappeared in the Opera and never been seen again, victims of the Phantom's appetite for blood.

It was all more or less the usual thing, but maybe it was the contrast between praising Erik's music and then promptly turning around to discuss the horrifying nature of the Phantom of the Opera. It got my skin prickling, more than it usually did, until finally I broke in when they brought up a scathing letter he'd dropped during chorus practice. That was relatively harmless, but at least I was sure it was a real incident.

"He had a point though," I said flatly. "The chorus really was being lazy at that last rehearsal. We all saw it."

The girls stared at me for a moment, then Celine resumed, "He was so frightfully *angry* in the letter—I wouldn't want to be a member of the chorus right now!"

I'd heard the letter's contents in an earlier round of gossip, and it wasn't that angry. Why did everyone always assume he was angry? "But he was giving good advice," I pointed out. "Maybe he was trying to help—"

"Oh *honestly*, Meg," Jammes purred, "don't tell us you could possibly think well of the Opera Ghost?   After what he did to Christine?"

I could have thrown my ballet slipper at her head.   Why did anyone have to bring up Christine after all this time?   It had been nearly nine months now!   "Christine wrote me that she was fine, but no one ever thinks about that.   You just run along with your horrible theories instead."

"Yes, but she only wrote the once, didn't she?" Jammes said, voice oh so sweet.   "Unless you've heard from her again...?"

I swallowed, hard.   Why didn't it ever get easier to say this? Instead the passing months had only made it worse.   "No," I muttered.

"Well, *that* seems suspicious," Jammes concluded with too much triumph in her voice.   "If Christine can't even write to her *good friend*, something must be wrong.   The Phantom must have done something to her."

"And what about the specter leaping out of the mirror at me?" Francesca put in quickly, plainly eager to get her story back into the conversation.

"And the blood dripping in Sorelli's room?"   And this, and that, until I was avalanched under wild stories about the horrors of the Phantom and finally had to concede the point.   But I didn't like it, and when the conversation at last moved on and they elected to go out to a nearby bakery for a snack, I decided I didn't want to spend more time with the ballet girls.   Tomorrow, probably, I'd want to again, but not now.

So they all departed and I was walking through a deserted corridor thinking I'd just go home when a specter stepped right out of a wall and said to me, "Don't do that."

I backed up a pace, automatically, and looked up at him.   "Do what, jump out of walls at people?"

He frowned, looking affronted.   "I didn't jump at you, I merely stepped into the hallway.   But don't do *that*, with the ballet girls.   Don't try to convince them that I mean well."

I was not in the mood to be lectured, especially not by him. "Oh, so you'd prefer they just go on telling dreadful, ridiculous stories about you?"

He blinked in evident surprise. "Yes."

I threw up my hands in half despair and half disgust. "Of course, naturally, because you *want* them to hate you!"

"I want them to *fear* me," he snapped out, and then his gaze shifted away. "I can't stop them hating me," he said in a lower voice.

Caught up in my own self-righteous frustration, I'd stopped paying attention to the choreography. I'd grown better at dancing through the intricate, sometimes fraught conversations I had with Erik, but today I'd stumbled—and deserved it. Anyone could have guessed that Erik's feelings towards the Opera Company, about what they felt towards him, would be complicated. How could it *not* be complicated when a man chooses to hide under an opera house pretending to be a ghost?

A month ago I would have pirouetted away from the topic. But today—his tone, when he insisted he wanted to be feared, spoke more of pain than of anger or domination. I didn't want to sidestep and tried going forward instead, a careful *balancé an avant*, and ventured, "They love your music."

"My music, yes, but not me." He sighed, rubbed a hand along the back of his neck. "I know you meant well, but just…don't, all right? It won't help."

His tone had gone softer, almost conciliatory, and though I wasn't sure he was right, that it wasn't possible to choreograph a path that didn't involve either fear or hatred, I didn't carry on the argument. "Fine."

We were silent for a moment and I stared down at my boots, toying with my skirts.

Finally Erik said, "So…are you busy this evening?"

It wasn't easy to let go of the previous idea. Part of me was still hunting for the right argument to convince him that there had to be a better way, that starting by telling the ballet girls he wasn't all bad wasn't, in fact, a bad idea. All I said aloud was, "No, I'm not busy."

He nodded, after a moment ventured, "It's a nice day outside."

I almost asked how he knew, but that seemed harsh. I was still frustrated with him, that he was so obviously unwilling to hear any new idea, but I wasn't frustrated enough to be nasty. Maybe too frustrated to make this easy though. "Yes," I said, "I expect it is."

"The view should be good from the roof."

"Yes," I said again, then relented enough to smile and say, "Should we go see it?"

We did, sitting in the shadows near the front of the rooftop, looking out towards the Seine and talking of everything and nothing in particular as the last portion of the afternoon wore away.

We watched together as the sun dipped below the horizon and the shadows deepened. For a little while, the city was bathed in a soft twilight, the air painted in shimmers of gold and in velvet shadows. Then the electric lights down the length of the Avenue de l'Opera flared into bright, vivid life, a line of light unrolling at our feet, stretching out towards the Seine. Electric lights had been shining on the Avenue for three years now, since the Paris Exposition in 1878, but they still seemed magical.

I smiled, clasping my hands around my knees. "It's beautiful, isn't it?"

"If you like that sort of thing." Erik's voice wasn't irritated exactly, but it was cold. I snuck a glance at him, couldn't read anything from his face in the shadows. He must have seen the query on my face though, because he shrugged and said, "I like candles. Gas lamps are all right too. Electric lights are so…harsh. An attack on the darkness."

I considered the stretch of light from that angle. "Perhaps they are. 'Attack' is a negative way to put it, but perhaps they are humanity's defiance against the night. Against the fear of the dark."

"I have never understood that. Why do people fear the dark?"

From someone else I might have taken it as an idle inquiry or even a joke. But I could tell now when Erik's words were weighted with significance, and his tone didn't sound idle. "You don't fear the dark, do you?" I said slowly, mind connecting new ideas about shadows and hiding and how Erik lived that I had never put together before. "I bet you never did, even as a child."

He shook his head. "It's like saying that you're afraid of clouds, or of stars, or...I don't know, the color green. It doesn't make any sense. Darkness is intangible; it can't hurt anyone."

He really didn't understand. One more thing to make Erik different. He had never been a child huddling beneath blankets against the terrors of the night. I had never thought before, how basic a part of life I had always assumed that history to be. Surely everyone was afraid of the dark, some time. "I suppose it's...it's the not being able to see," I said, groping to explain a concept I had imagined to be universal. "The fear of the horrors that could be lurking just out of sight."

He made an impatient sound. "But that still doesn't make sense. Horrible things happen just as often in light as in darkness, and if it's the surprise, they can always come up behind you or sneak around a corner. People aren't afraid of closed doors, or of blindfolds. And if it's the fear of ghosts and demons and things like that, fine, but why should the sun setting or a candle going out make any monster more likely to appear? Nothing is in the dark that wasn't there in the light."

"And that is a perfectly reasonable point," I agreed with a slight laugh, "but it never seems to weigh much *in the dark*." I shook my head. "It's not just what might be in the dark, it's...there really is something about the darkness. I don't know. It doesn't make sense, it's some deep-down instinct, I guess. Things that are frightening just seem *more* frightening in darkness than they do in light. But you know that. You exploit it all the time." How often had the Phantom put out the Opera's lights, or loomed up from the shadows? The ballet girls' stories frequently took place in mysteriously dark corridors.

"Yes," he agreed. "I know that it works to enhance a haunting. But I don't understand *why* it works." He ran a hand over his hair, looked out over the lit Avenue and the dark city beyond it. His voice went softer. "I see darkness differently. Darkness is a refuge. Everything feels *less* dangerous in the dark. The dangers of the daytime lose their power. No one can see me, no one can find me. And darkness...there's so much beauty in darkness. It distills the world, stripping all the extraneous away and you can only see what you really want to look at..." His voice trailed away, and when he spoke again his tone had changed, more aloof than that momentary vulnerability. "But I don't imagine that makes any sense."

"No, it does," I protested, even though most of it was ideas I'd never thought of, virtually a different world view from the one I knew, the one where dark streets were dangerous and sunlight banished ghosts.

"Are you afraid?" he asked. "Of the dark?"

Was it a challenge to my claim to understand, or did he really want to know? Either way, I answered, "No. I was, when I was small. Not now, though, not for a long time." I smiled slightly. "Unless I've just heard a really dreadful ghost story. But not usually."

He might have asked for clarification, might have tried to puzzle out why a ghost story should make shadows seem any more dangerous. I suspected that didn't make any sense to him either. But he didn't ask, just nodded, and without an invitation I couldn't quite bring myself to break the silence that descended for the next few minutes.

I thought the topic was closed until, very quietly, without looking at me, Erik said, "It scared me, the first time they turned the lights on, on the Avenue. It felt as though they were trying to destroy all the darkness, bring the world into an eternal daylight, and then where are the creatures of shadows supposed to hide? But then I realized...every light they put up, it just makes the shadows that remain that much darker. And you can never banish every shadow."

I had never imagined the Phantom admitting he was afraid of anything. I had never imagined the Phantom *being* afraid. He was someone other people feared. But Erik was a man, not a myth. He was clever, powerful, incredibly talented, but he could also be lonely, sad and, yes, afraid. I could believe that.

And then suddenly something connected in my mind, I made the *grand jeté* between two ideas. Of course he wanted the Opera Company to fear him. Because he was afraid of them. Of course a man hiding a deformity behind a mask, a man who had been so stiff and uncomfortable when he first started talking even to harmless, insignificant me, *of course* he was afraid of the laughing, chattering Opera Company.

It gave a sudden weight to my response. I had to say something, after he'd just told me he was afraid, even if he hadn't painted in the full picture. I had to tell him it was all right somehow, even though my first instinct, *saying* that it was all right, would clearly make him deny the whole business.

After what felt like already too long a pause, I said, "We all need shadows, even people who like the light. We all need magic."

Excerpt from the Private Notebook of Jean Mifroid, Commissaire of Police

18 November, 1881

Inquiries into whereabouts of RdC and Daaé remain inconclusive. Best evidence suggests Rome, but hints only. Sources in Italy cannot reach definite answer.

Have obtained address of C. Garnier in Monte Carlo, to write to him with questions re: his opera house.

Chapter Twenty-Two

T he end of the year flowed by in a rush, November turning into
December, the opera house busy with holiday plans and
performances. There was no Christine to spend Christmas with this
year, as we had last year, but Mother and I spent the day with
neighbors. I didn't try to invite Erik, though I was half-tempted to do
it.

I saw Erik the day after Christmas instead. The green scarf I gave
him matched his eyes, and he gave me a beautiful copy of *Around the
World in 80 Days* by Jules Verne. I was as much touched to think that
he must have gone out to get it as I was by the book itself.

Somehow, and I didn't exactly plan it, I spent a lot of the days just
after Christmas with Erik. The ballet girls had scattered, the Opera was
quiet, and he needed help deciding what music Erik Rouen was going
to send to the Company in the new year. And I liked spending the time
with him. It was magical, sitting deep below the Opera, listening to the
Phantom play whatever music was wandering through his head.

Usually he was casual about it, intricate melodies spilling out from
his fingertips as easily as words might come from anyone else's mouth.
Those were coming more easily from Erik in recent weeks, but still
seemed to require more thought than musical notes did.

On the Saturday after Christmas, he seemed oddly fidgety at the
piano.

"Is something wrong?" I finally asked, even though I expected exactly the answer I received.

"No." He frowned down at his hands, sighed and said, "I want you to listen to this piece."

"I listen to every piece," I said swiftly. It was true.

He only shrugged, flexed his fingers once, and began this new melody. It was light, airy, a little faster than he often played, still with the haunting magic that told me it was his own composition, and yet...*something* was different. Sunlight, instead of his usual moonlight, perhaps.

The melody reached a flourish of an ending, and he looked at me expectantly.

"It was...different," I said, still trying to define the difference. Besides, I'd said 'beautiful' so many times it was losing any meaning.

"It's simpering, isn't it?" he said with a grimace. "And simplistic."

"No, it isn't either. There was nothing simplistic about—what is it called, that part where it gradually got faster?"

"Accelerando. But it was sort of, I don't know, it was..."

"I liked it," I said firmly, before he could come up with another disparaging adjective. I was surprised; it wasn't like Erik to criticize his own music. To downplay its extraordinary quality, yes, but not like this. "It was different, but I liked it."

"Hmm. Well." He looked down again, fiddled with a few papers on top of the piano. "It was new."

I may have squeaked.

His head came up again, quickly, and he added, "It's not important, so there's no need to—fuss."

"I do not *fuss*," I said, clasping my hands together tightly. "I may, on occasion, get excited."

"Oh, one melody more or less, that's nothing," he said, waving a hand at the stacks of musical scores still lying about.

"Nothing at all," I agreed, but I was grinning.

That *had* to be good, if he was writing music again. Maybe he was starting to see that it hadn't really been the end of all that was good in the world, when Christine left. I knew that perfectly well, and maybe Erik was starting to realize it too. Maybe some of that sadness that lurked behind his green eyes was going to fade away.

Maybe, eventually, I'd get to hear him sing too.

Meg's opinion aside, he was not at all sure that this new musical piece wasn't absolute drivel. But still, it had been a long time since he'd felt any desire to write anything, since any new arrangement of notes and chords had arrived in his head. Not for 304 days, sixteen hours. And a bit. However long it was, between the last piece he wrote and when *she* left. He had thought he perfectly accepted that composing was over for him and yet—this had been surprisingly refreshing.

A pleasant afternoon was followed by a pleasant evening watching the Saturday performance, even if the chorus was still exhibiting some post-Christmas laziness. The ballet, on the other hand, was excellent; Madame Thibault did not permit laziness, so this was no surprise.

He thought he'd like to mention his compliments to the ballet to Meg. Perhaps he'd be able to catch her before she went into the Dance Foyer. Consequently, he waited in a hidden passage adjoining the corridor between the ballet's changing room and the Foyer. Meg did come along eventually, but three other people were in the hall and that wouldn't do. He could see her clearly enough; the hall was lined with mirrors and every one of them was transparent from his side, so he paced along parallel to Meg, hoping for a secluded moment.

Instead, he was on hand when a fellow in an offensively garish red waistcoat hailed Meg. "*There* you are!" He came galloping over to her in the hallway, footsteps loud and discordant. "I've been looking for you; I was afraid you weren't coming to the Foyer tonight."

Who was *this*? And why did he seem to think he had any business expecting Meg?

Memory stirred—bright waistcoats. A remark from Meg about gorgeous blue eyes. Erik squinted, couldn't get a good view of the eyes, but that was certainly a brilliantly colored waistcoat. What had that young man's name been? Leopold?

Meg had halted, staring at this new arrival. "Léon?"

Léon, that was it, Léon who had gone abroad, months and months ago. The ballet girls had been heartbroken on Meg's behalf and she had been fine. That was how he remembered this story.

"You're back from traveling," Meg said, smiling up at the brightly-dressed young man.

"Yes, of course, Mother wanted to be back with the family for Christmas," Léon said, reaching out to thread Meg's arm through his and steer her towards the Foyer. "I couldn't wait to see you—this is the first chance I've had to get to the Opera."

Were her cheeks turning pink or was he imagining it? Maybe he was imagining it. Her voice was quite composed as she said, "Did you enjoy your travels?"

"Not a bit, you wouldn't believe the ghastly places Mother dragged me off to. But now that I'm back we'll have such a good time. I'm blocking my calendar for the upcoming performances, and we should plan a carriage ride, and—"

"Wait a minute, don't make too many plans," Meg said with a laugh. "It's silly, but I'm about to leave town myself."

Léon footsteps stopped short, which was fine since Erik did too. "You're what?"

She was what?

"Leaving town," Meg repeated. "Not to go anywhere very exciting, but Mother and I will be visiting our family in Leclair for three weeks. We leave at the end of this week."

She was leaving *again*? She had just gone in August. Erik shoved his hands into his pockets. Why were people always feeling they had to go gallivanting around the country? He never went anywhere.

"But I just got back," Léon protested, "that's terrible timing."

Meg laughed again. "I can't help that. It's not as though I knew you were coming."

Léon heaved a sigh. "So much for surprises. But you'll be back in a few weeks?"

"Yes," Meg said, smile widening. "So we can have fun then. And tonight."

Tonight. So she wasn't going to be available for a Phantom to step out of a wall with friendly comments about the evening's performance.

Erik didn't hear Léon's response, because they crossed the threshold into the much busier Foyer, with all its intertwining conversations, and left him standing alongside the corridor feeling rather nonplussed.

Well. He didn't *need* to talk to Meg tonight. He could talk to her...perhaps tomorrow. Monday, anyway. And he could write a letter to Madame Thibault, complimenting the ballet's performance. Yes. That was what he would do tonight.

The Monday after Christmas (which might also have been described as the Monday after Erik started writing music again, or the Monday after Léon came back to the Opera), Erik appeared in an empty corridor and announced, "You didn't tell me you were leaving town."

"Yes, I did," I countered, "I told you last August that I visit Leclair every August and January." Erik had developed a habit of stepping out of walls and talking to me as though we had already been in conversation. Mostly it amused me, and felt rather natural—maybe because I spent so much time thinking about talking to him. You had to think about talking to Erik, even now when it was easier than it had once been.

A frown creased his face. "Oh. Yes, so you did. But you could have reminded me."

"I was going to mention it today but then you—" A new thought made me break the sentence off. "Wait a minute, since I *didn't* remind you, how did you remember I was traveling?"

Erik immediately failed to meet my gaze, studying the ornate detailing on a nearby pillar lining the wall. "I…hear things. I don't mean to, you know, it just happens. I was going to talk to you Saturday night and then instead…"

"You heard me talking to Léon," I finished. Well, it hadn't been a private conversation. We hadn't been alone at any point in the evening, even discounting a ghostly presence.

"Was that Léon?" Erik asked blandly. "The gentleman with the appallingly red waistcoat?"

"It was not appalling!" I protested. "It was just—red."

"It was an appallingly bright red."

"This from the man who came as Red Death to the last masquerade?" I parried, and too late realized that I had no idea if he had known that I had known he was Red Death.

If it was a surprise he didn't show it, just said, "That was different. That was artistic."

"It was also very bright."

He abandoned that line of argument and said, "So how is Léon?"

"Léon's…well." I found I was smiling in spite of myself. "Léon's very well." He was watching me now, more closely, and I wasn't sure what was evident on my face. "You know, he's really very nice," I said quickly.

"I never said he wasn't," Erik said, just as quickly, just as though I'd accused him of that. "I just said his waistcoat wasn't nice. But—it makes you happy? That he's back?"

I hadn't thought of it in quite those words, but… "Yes. I guess it does." Happy and oddly relieved. "I'm happy he didn't forget about me."

Erik's eyebrow rose and he said, as though it was the most unlikely thing in the world, "Why would he have done that?"

Which really was wonderful of him to say. I didn't entirely appreciate how wonderful it was until I thought about it later, because in that moment I was caught in a different cross-current of thought, and I perhaps unwisely said, "It wouldn't be the first time." Unwisely because I meant Christine, but if he asked for any clarification he was not going to like the sudden new topic—and I didn't want to talk about Christine anyway. "So aren't you going to wish me a pleasant trip?" I said before he could say anything else.

"Have a pleasant trip," he said amiably enough. "Any exciting plans?"

I laughed a little. "Leclair isn't exactly exciting. I mean, I love it, but I wouldn't call it exciting. It's more like—visiting a friend you've known for your whole life. It's comfortable and reassuring and you can be perfectly relaxed, but there probably won't be anything unexpected in the conversation."

"That has advantages," Erik said softly. "Or so I would imagine."

"Of course, but sometimes a girl wants something *exciting* too." I grinned at him. "You know, ghosts and thrills and things like that."

Excerpt from the Private Notebook of Jean Mifroid, Commissaire of Police

6 January, 1881

Have sent repeated inquiries to C. Garnier. Still awaiting response.

Would like to visit Monte Carlo to interview myself, but not feasible to leave Paris at this time.

Still no definitive lead on RdC and Daaé, but network continues to search.

Chapter Twenty-Three

I t was so strange. For years Meg had been absent from the Opera Garnier for weeks at a time and he had never even noticed. Erik couldn't understand how he had missed it. Even during her trip in the summer, the Opera had merely seemed a bit quiet, and there had been ample other reasons for that, in the lull of August heat. And the police commissaire had been around to distract him too.

Now, in January, he couldn't seem to shake a constant awareness of Meg's absence, constantly noticing her *not* being there. An empty space where she should have been moving and dancing and talking. He was distinctly aware of a note missing in the ballet girls' conversations. Life at the Opera was like an enormous symphony, one he knew in every detail, only now the first violinist had gone missing. The symphony went on, but he kept getting caught on that one strain that should have been there, but wasn't.

He had not expected the note that arrived three days after Meg departed. A very brief note, bordering on impersonal, merely a "safely arrived from traveling" note, but all the same it was thoughtful. Despite writing many letters to many people, he had received none.

She had been gone for 312 days, ten hours, and she had certainly never—but he had never expected her to, of course. It was an entirely different situation.

This letter from Meg, though, it did present a dilemma. Was he supposed to write back? *Could* he write back? He'd quite like to write back, but surely there were rules about these things, and he had no idea what the etiquette was on letter-writing, any more than he had known it about Christmas. Could he write immediately? Maybe that would be the polite thing to do. Or would it be alarmingly eager, even shading into disturbing?

He did know that he couldn't send black-edged envelopes outside of the Opera—people would get the wrong idea—so he slipped out one evening and bought less distinctive stationary from a stall near the Seine. The old man raised an eyebrow, gaze lingering on the right side of Erik's face, the masked side—but he accepted his money.

The paper sat on Erik's desk for days. Finally, when Meg had been gone for a week precisely, he sat down and picked up his pen, intending to write a short, simple letter.

It ran to fifteen pages, and when he finally affixed a flourish of a signature, sat back and drew the scattered pages into a stack, he was somewhat appalled. He hadn't *meant* to write that much. It was only…there were such a lot of things he'd been meaning to say, things he would have said in a conversation if she had been here, and one thing had led quite naturally into another, and…

Maybe it was too much. How long were letters supposed to be? Maybe she'd find that extensive a correspondence to be strange, even alarming. She was probably busy, probably wouldn't have time to sit down and read a whole tome of a letter. Maybe he should just send half, or pull out a few pages or…but everything did flow quite naturally into each other, and it was all things he wanted to say, and anyway maybe she would be interested to hear the news at the Opera, after all…

Erik finally sighed and gave up. He added a hasty apology for the length of the letter in a note at the bottom, then bundled the whole thing into an envelope. It was dusk by now, so he set off to drop it into the nearest post box.

It had been exciting to realize that Erik's post office box meant I could actually write to the Phantom of the Opera. I hadn't written to Léon. He would have known it wasn't proper, and might have taken the wrong idea from it. Erik likely knew it wasn't proper, but he wouldn't make anything of it. So I had dashed off a quick note.

After ten days, I had all but given up the idea that I would hear back from him. I wished I dared write to him again, a proper letter this time, but I didn't quite.

When my uncle came in with the day's mail shortly before supper, I didn't even look up from my knitting (it was the kind of thing one did in the evening in Leclair; quiet but nice) until he said he had a letter for me. And then I only said, "Really? From who?" I could think of few options, but Erik still didn't seem the likeliest.

"It appears to be from an E. Rouen," he answered, inspecting the envelope. "Whoever that is, they use a lot of flourishes."

I dropped my knitting and stood up so quickly that my ball of yarn fell off my lap and rolled across the floor. "Oh bother," I muttered, caught up the yarn and tossed it back on the couch, and snatched the envelope from Uncle Jean's hand.

No black edges—which would have been hard to explain—but unquestionably the flowing script of Erik's handwriting.

"Someone special?" my cousin Angelique asked, teasing and curious.

"No," I said, too quickly. "I mean, a friend. I'll just take this up to the bedroom to read." I knew this would only fuel speculation, but I couldn't help that. Envelope in hand, I fled.

Once I was alone, I sat down on the edge of the narrow bed and ran my fingertips over the black ink of the address, noted the delicious thickness of the envelope.

Erik had begun to seem imaginary. When you're in a perfectly ordinary village, full of prosaic farmers and shopkeepers, it's hard to believe in the existence of a masked man who lives beneath an Opera and controls a flaming skeleton. Maybe that was why I still hadn't mentioned Erik here. How could I begin to explain him?

The letter was wonderful, just like a conversation, full of all the latest Opera news and what he thought of it. He offered details on planned productions, assessments of current set design and the somewhat startling news that the managers were seriously considering installing electric lights in the Opera; Erik seemed to be taking that news better than I might have guessed, perhaps thinking how much darker the shadows would be when some parts of the building blazed with electricity.

The letter filled up an emptiness I hadn't previously been able to define, a blank spot in the past twelve days where conversations with Erik should have been. I sat down at once to write back, commenting on his letter and sharing any news that seemed sufficiently interesting. A girl can't start a correspondence, but *responding* is different.

I was only in Leclair another week and a half, so only a couple letters flew back and forth. Still, I reveled in that thin thread of connection back to my other life. I liked Leclair's quiet homeness, but it was even better with a Ghost to add zest.

My cousins, of course, teased me endlessly about my "letter-writing paramour." I refused to explain because they couldn't possibly have believed me, citing it only to a (very non-romantic, thank you very much) friend. They mostly persisted in believing it was really Léon, using a false name, despite my consistent and truthful denials.

Mother, who must have known exactly who was writing to me, neither commented nor told our relatives anything. I knew she wasn't enthusiastic about Erik, making me appreciate her silent loyalty even more.

Erik's last letter arrived the day before we were due to leave Leclair, and suggested a time to meet the day after I returned to Paris. Knowing how long the train ride was from Leclair, I wouldn't have got up early the next morning for just anyone—but I hated to miss the opportunity. Besides, there was no time for a letter from me to reach him, and I didn't like to think of him waiting for me, and me never arriving.

So I went to the auditorium at the appointed time—and he was perfectly punctual about being there too. I didn't have a great deal of time before ballet practice so we stayed in the auditorium, sitting at the edge of the stage.

"How was your trip?" Erik asked, the conventional phrase and something about how he said it made me think he knew that too, was trying to follow the proper forms.

"Nice," I said automatically. "Quiet, but nice."

He half-smiled, looking at me out of the corner of his eye as he sat next to me. "You say that to everyone, don't you?"

True. "It *was* nice," I protested with a laugh. "And quiet. And I always like seeing my family, even though—" I broke off abruptly. That was two words more than I had meant to say.

"Even though?" he prompted.

I reached up, fingered my gold necklace. Then I finished the thought. "Even though it always makes me miss Gabrielle. And I don't say that to everyone."

I saw his brow crease, knew the question before he voiced it. "Who is Gabrielle?"

I had never found an easy way to introduce the topic of a dead sister into a conversation, and I didn't bring her up very often anymore. Mother still didn't like to talk about her. So in all these months of talking to Erik, I had never mentioned her. Though it was probably only more recently that I might have wanted to.

"Gabrielle is my sister," I said, looking at the seats, twisting my necklace. "She died before we came to Paris. Almost seven years ago. I miss her—often, but especially in Leclair."

"I'm sorry," Erik said softly, and I just nodded. After another moment he said, "It's not actually G for Giry, is it? On your necklace?"

I hadn't known he ever noticed that. "No. It was hers first. Mother still has an M one somewhere, mine, but I've been wearing Gabi's ever since…" I let the words trail off, and shrugged. "Ever since."

Erik rubbed one palm against his pant leg, drummed his fingers. "You don't have to talk about her—if you don't want to—"

"I *like* talking about Gabi," I said, because it was true, I did. I liked remembering her; I liked other people knowing about her.

"Mother doesn't, and most people get uncomfortable, so I don't usually—and we don't have to, if you don't—"

"Tell me a Gabrielle story," he suggested, and it felt like the nicest thing anyone had said to me in a long time.

I smiled, let go of my necklace. "Gabi loved to dance. She was much better at it than me too. I remember once, when I was nine and she was six, my uncle held a big party..." And I told him all about that long ago night, when the grown-ups were dancing downstairs and we were supposed to be asleep with our cousins, but Gabi and I had snuck out of bed. It had been my idea to go out to the landing of the stairs and watch the dancing, but it was Gabi who started dancing there in the shadows, and pulled me into joining her. We spun and twirled together for what felt like hours even though it probably wasn't, and we never did get caught. I'd never told anyone about it, not even Mother. Or Christine.

Sometimes, when I was dancing with the ballet now, when the music lifted me up and it all felt magical, I still thought about that night. It had never yet been quite as magical as it was then, dancing with my sister.

Erik didn't laugh at the story. Of course, he never laughed. But he didn't make me feel it was silly or unimportant either. It didn't take any of the magic off the memory, to share it.

That was the best kind of friend—someone who listened, and understood.

The rest of the hour before dance practice passed swiftly. We didn't talk about Gabi the entire time, we moved on to other news from the Opera and from my trip, things not covered by our letters. And even though the conversation turned ordinary, I felt just a little more comfortable then I ever had before. Eventually, though, I had to make some noise about getting to ballet practice.

"Hmm, I suppose," Erik said, and then was silent for a moment, a hesitating silence. So I waited, not saying anything, and finally he reached into his jacket pocket and drew out a folded sheet of paper. I had watched him make papers and other objects materialize in his hands often enough that this visible production lent a sort of gravity to the moment. "Here," he said, passing me the paper. "I thought you might…find a use for this."

I unfolded the paper, scanned across the lines of words, distinctive in Erik's handwriting. Not a letter or even paragraphs but bullet points. *Third mask from left, fourth row…second passage on the right…immediate left and then right again…* "These are directions," I said, half-expecting to be contradicted.

"Yes," he agreed, gaze on the rows of seats in front of us.

"Directions…to your apartments." I had been through the route often enough that I might have been able to find the way—though in the dark and the turns, I wouldn't have felt confident. But I could recognize enough details to know what this was.

"Yes." He rubbed the back of his neck, still not looking at me. "I thought—well, if you have some spare time and I don't happen to step out of a wall—I mean, if you ever wanted to…"

It was awkwardly put and the sentence never quite finished, but I was still reasonably sure that the Phantom of the Opera had just invited me to drop by any time. "But what if you don't want to see me?" I blurted without thinking.

He finally looked at me then, smiling slightly. "Then I suppose I won't answer the door. But I don't really imagine that will come up."

He expected to want to see me. The Phantom—no, *Erik* expected to want to see me; in fact, wanted to see me enough that he was willing to tell me how to find him. The man no one could ever find, the man who guarded his privacy as though it was under constant siege—and who was probably right about that most of the time, but was likely still paranoid beyond even what was reasonable. "Thank you," I said, and it was for many things.

"Yes, well." Back to looking at rows of seats. "You'd better hurry or you'll be late for practice."

I almost leaned over and hugged him. The impulse, the instinct, was there. But you couldn't do that with Erik. We never touched each other. The only times we had were when he took my hand to guide me on the trip below the Opera, and once he had lanterns in place and I knew the way better, we'd stopped that too.

So I just got to my feet with a "see you later, then," tucked the paper with directions away deep in my bag, and went to ballet practice.

I may not have been *entirely* focused during practice. Madame Thibault scolded and Jammes smirked, but what did I care? If I could go find Erik any time I wanted to—if he really trusted me enough to let me do that...

I wouldn't be using the directions that afternoon. I might not have dared anyway, since he had just seen me, but as it turned out, Léon appeared outside the practice room just as we were finishing. With a bouquet of flowers, no less.

"Welcome back," he said with a sunny smile, handing me the roses and taking my free hand to thread through his arm.

I closed my fingers around his arm, bent my head to sniff the flowers and hide the surprise on my face until I could replace it with a smile. "You remembered I would be back today." I hadn't expected him to remember, but I didn't want him to know that. And it wasn't hard to smile, since it was such a pleasant surprise.

"Of course!" Léon said, with a boyish enthusiasm that fleetingly reminded me of Raoul. But not in a bad way. "And now let's celebrate. We can go anywhere in Paris. There's so much to do."

"There's a bakery near here I like," I suggested.

"Oh, we can do better than a bakery," he said, with a dismissive wave of his free hand. "Perhaps the Anthropological Gardens—"

"No," I said at once, fingers tightening on the stems of the roses.

He blinked at me, brow furrowed. "No? But it's so much pleasanter than going to the hassle of traveling to foreign places—"

"I've been and I didn't like it. All those people on display—it's so sad." I knew most of Paris thought it was a charming way to spend the afternoon, an education even, to see examples of foreign races. Once I'd seen it myself, seen actual *people* on display like they were somehow less human because they were different—I couldn't understand it.

If Léon caught any of the depth behind my words, he didn't show it, merely shrugging. "Very well. Then perhaps the Café de la Paix. You can't object to that."

He was wrong about the Gardens but he was right about the Café—I couldn't object, and I couldn't resist. I had walked past the Café de la Paix nearly every day for the seven years I'd danced at the Opera, set as it was just across the square, but I'd never been inside.

So off we went. I'd have to tell the ballet girls all about it later. None of us could afford to eat there.

Excerpt from the Private Notebook of Jean Mifroid, Commissaire of Police

28 January, 1882

After weeks of waiting, finally a reply from Garnier. Brief in the extreme, most relevant passage quoted as follows:

I regret that I cannot assist you re: your inquiries into supposed secret passages in or below the opera house. Such things were certainly not part of my design. I recognize that the labyrinthine quality of some sections and the complex substructure of the building itself may give the mistaken impression of intentional hidden areas. I cannot speak to what you may have encountered. As regards a supposed ghost at the Opera, I can only tell you that we had no hauntings during the construction. If anyone took up residence in the building, it must date from a later time.

I do not believe he knows so little, but have no power to compel him to give up answers. Garnier too well-connected.

Every direction I try, Phantom has a trick to block me.

Chapter Twenty-Four

I nevitably Erik began seeing Meg more often after she knew how to find his home. He still dropped in on her at about the same rate, but now there was a new option too. He had wondered if she'd really take advantage of the knowledge—not to tell Mifroid or anything ridiculous like that, he wasn't worried about that—but to actually visit. Perhaps she wouldn't want to venture through all those dark passages alone. But she did, and he grew used to it far more quickly than he had expected, having Meg suddenly turn up on his doorstep. More than used to it. She always politely knocked. And it was pleasant, having her drift in like a stray bit of sunshine somehow reaching deep below the ground.

Sunshine with interesting opinions about music and all the latest Opera Company news. Like about the fast-approaching Mardi Gras. She mentioned it, and then turned thoughtful. So he waited, dropping another lump of sugar into his coffee, as they sat on opposite couches.

When she spoke again, it was the relatively innocuous and not very enlightening comment, "You know, the wonderful thing about a masquerade, everyone wears a mask."

True enough, they did. "Yes." And?

"I was just wondering…are you planning to go this year?"

Ah. "No," he said shortly, stirring his coffee with slightly more vigor than necessary.

He was sure that a few months ago that would have made her drop the idea, but now she ventured on with, "I mean, you went last year and—"

"That was unusual and it was a mistake." What a horrible evening it had turned out to be. The beginning of the end, the first stanza of the tragic last act that had ended 351 days, fourteen hours ago.

"Well, the 'don't touch me' sign was," she agreed, with a smile that invited him to join into the joke.

Last year's masquerade was hardly something he wanted to joke about. He had started with such hopes, such dreams of seeing *her*, and instead—even in a world where everyone wore masks, still no place existed for him. He could still find himself betrayed, rejected, cast-out. "The entire evening was an ill-conceived idea and—"

"But it's so *perfect*," she bubbled up, "we can go together and you can mingle with everyone and they won't even know it's you!"

"Why on earth would I want to *mingle*?" Were they even discussing the same world? He sipped his coffee, found it only fitting that it was too hot. "I don't like them, they don't like me—"

"They don't like the *Phantom*. That doesn't mean they wouldn't like *you*."

That caught him up short a bit. He hadn't realized she understood that nuance. It didn't stop him from saying, "It's the same thing."

"Not quite," she countered, accurately. "So if you don't want to mingle, just come and don't talk and watch all the costumes and the inevitable mayhem."

"I can do that from behind a wall."

"Not as well."

"But safer."

She sighed. "All right, fine, *don't* come. But it's too bad really, because it's always a good party. One of the highlights of February. And February is my favorite month."

Seeing a glimmer of a topic change opportunity, without thinking Erik said, "No one's favorite month is February." He realized a beat too late that this might have been too severe.

"It's mine," she responded with an impudent smile.

Well, if she wasn't going to be off-put by an argument, and was willing to pursue this less fraught topic… He settled back on the couch, coffee cup warm in his hand. "February is cold and dark—"

"I should think that would appeal to you," she murmured, studying her fingernails.

"Not to most people—and it's long past Christmas and still weeks away from spring and it has essentially no redeeming characteristics," he concluded and started to sip his coffee again, feeling this was the irrefutable end of the debate. He remembered at the last moment that the liquid was still too hot.

Meg just smiled. "Except the daffodils."

"The...daffodils?" he repeated, with no idea what flowers had to do with anything.

"Daffodils start blooming in February." She sat back on the couch, hands wrapped around one knee, eyes alight. "I watch for them every year, and suddenly from one day to the next they spring up in the most unlikely places all over Paris. Like little pieces of sunshine in window boxes and street corners. They were planted months earlier and waited all through the winter to suddenly spring up in February. They stay in flower for days and days when they finally do bloom, and when they fade, by then it's spring. They're like the heralds of spring, and since they come *before* the nicer season, there's still all the anticipation."

"But it's still a cold, miserable month." A few flowers did not change any of the other characteristics of the month.

"Yes, I *know*. But there are daffodils, and daffodils are my favorite flowers."

"Oh, well, in that case," Erik said, lifting his cup in acknowledgment and surrendering the argument. That should have been the end of it, but she was looking at him with a certain intensity. After a moment he rubbed the back of his neck and said, "What is it?"

Meg sighed, looked down and smoothed her skirt over her lap. "I know you think I'm silly and naïve, but I'm not really."

"I don't think that," he protested, because it was obviously the thing to say. Even though he did think she was naïve, and maybe a little silly at times—though it was a nice silliness. That wasn't quite the word anyway...light-hearted, rather. The kind who enjoyed masquerades without dark undercurrents.

"I know that February is cold and dark and all the rest that you said. But there *are* daffodils," she continued. "I know there are bad things in the world, plenty of them, but it doesn't make me naïve because I believe there are good things too, or that I'd rather focus on those. Bad things aren't somehow more real because they're bad. I'd rather think of February as the month when the daffodils bloom, not the cold middle of winter."

Had he ever been hopeful enough to see the world that way? He couldn't remember a time. "Not everyone finds it that easy to think about the good things."

She half-smiled, a lopsided smile. "What makes you think it's always easy for me?"

The idea that she might work at it, that she might not be just naturally sunny, had never occurred to him. And it should have, he realized; he knew about her father, her sister. He had supposed she just had a pleasant nature that rose above life's tragedies.

He looked away, rubbing his palm against his leg and suddenly wishing he was sitting at his piano because it was easy to launch a melody as a distraction but much harder when you had to stand up and walk across the room to do it. Maybe there was some trick to it, some skill she had that he lacked, to look at February and see daffodils and a masquerade party, instead of cold winds and long nights.

"Also," Meg said after a moment, "my birthday is in February."

Erik's attention was thoroughly diverted from flowers and parties. "What? It is? When?"

Her smile looked slightly guilty, and she reached down to pick up her coffee without meeting his eyes. "…two weeks ago."

He fumbled his own coffee, narrowly avoided spilling the steaming liquid. "You didn't *tell* me!"

She shrugged. "I didn't want you to think you needed to, I don't know, do something."

He should have done something. What was he supposed to do? "Do you like chocolates?" he asked in reckless desperation, because at least he knew that was something people gave each other. It felt impersonal, but he had used his one personal-but-not-too-personal idea up at Christmas already.

She grinned over her cup. "I love chocolate."

Fine. Maybe chocolate would do for a birthday. That idea settled, he felt a little better. And a sudden, quite inconsequential question occurred to him. "Did you mention your birthday to Léon?" he asked impulsively.

Her brow creased. "No. It didn't seem...no."

He still didn't altogether understand the etiquette of who was informed of matters like birthdays, or exactly why she hadn't told Léon either. But somehow, knowing she hadn't, made him feel better too. And his coffee was finally cool enough to drink.

So he'd have to go buy a good box of chocolates. And there might be something else he could do. If he decided it wasn't an entirely mad idea. "You know, maybe I'll think about it," he said, looking into the depths of his cup. "The Mardi Gras, I mean. I might come. Maybe."

He snuck a glance at her, and if she thought this was an odd topic change, she didn't show it. Her smile just broadened, as though she had already won the debate. Which, really, he supposed she had.

Excerpt from the Private Notebook of Jean Mifroid, Commissaire of Police

16 February, 1882

After series of dead-ends, finally a new lead. Received letter as follows:

If you are still interested in locating the Phantom of the Opera, you would do well to investigate the upcoming Company masquerade. The Phantom attended last year in a Red Death costume, and is likely to take advantage of the masks to attend again this year. If you can incite the crowd to remove their masks, look for a man who refuses to take his off. Or a man with a twisted face.

Signed "Raoul de Chagny." Attempting to trace letter, of course, though so far inquiries unsuccessful. At least this gives proof RdC is still alive. Aristocratic name has overcome Prefect's reservations for an attempt to infiltrate masquerade with trusted officers.

Must find appropriate masks.

Chapter Twenty-Five

E rik was determined not to repeat the clothing mistakes of the last masquerade. This time he wore black. All black. Black suit, black gloves, black cloak. Black mask, all-encompassing, leaving only his eyes, his mouth and his chin showing. He was shadows, he was darkness, he was—he hoped—no one anyone would want to talk to.

He wandered through the crowds at the party, trying to look for Meg and to avoid meeting anyone else's eyes at the same time. The rooms were filled with a crushing swirl of humanity that made him feel claustrophobic in a way tunnels never had. At least most people had stayed a few feet away from Red Death. Finally he took up a position at the top of one of the sweeping wings of the Grand Stair, in the niche between a pillar and the stair railing. It was no less crowded, but it gave him something solid at his back.

He had a good view of the entire length of the stair and the antechamber beyond it, the balcony areas and even the Grand Foyer through the open doorways. The rooms echoed and re-echoed with footsteps and voices, laughter and cries. Somewhere behind that he could hear faint strains of music, but they were nearly lost behind the noise of unbridled humanity.

Though he had balked before telling Meg he would come, he had always liked the *idea* of Mardi Gras, the theoretical concept of it. In some ways, it was the most honest day of the year, the one day when everyone's mask became as visible as his own. All the other days people wore masks too, whether it was self-interest behind kindness, vulnerability behind anger, condemnation behind a smile. Mardi Gras stripped away one layer, the layer where everyone pretended to be showing their true selves when no one really was.

Confronted by, not the idea but the reality, it was impossible to ignore other things that Mardi Gras stripped away: inhibitions, moderation, restraint. How did they do it? How did they all cast themselves so effortlessly into the frenzy, cast away all second-thoughts, all doubts and control? How did a man and a woman meet in the throng, smile and nod and slip into an alcove to kiss and perhaps more, then part ways again within the hour and go on untroubled and unattached? How did they achieve such easy understanding, such an easy letting go? How did anyone know what to do or say in this madness, or was the real trick to not know and not care about not knowing? To not think, and to not even think about not thinking.

He would have liked to account it all to liberal doses of champagne, but couldn't convince himself that was the entirety of it. These people, young and old, rich and poor, wise and stupid, all possessed a confidence he did not, a surety and an ease in themselves and their place in the world that he had never been able to claim. He could write symphonies, walk on roof edges and perform feats of illusion anyone would call magic, but this particular trick eluded him.

The thought was a cold stone in the pit of his stomach. This was ridiculous, did he even *want* to be a part of the mad dance? No.

And yes.

It was Quasimodo and the Festival of Fools. The Hunchback would have been happier if he had stayed in his bell tower, and the Phantom should have known to stay in his vaults.

He felt a homesick yearning for darkness and silence. This cacophony of colors and lights and chattering voices was overwhelming, it was—his gaze locked on one white figure amidst the rainbow throng.

Meg. Despite the distance and the white lace mask over the upper half of her face, almost certainly Meg. She had just come in on the lower level and was still standing near the doorway, looking around as though searching for someone—for him?

He had worked halfway down the stairs before it occurred to him to wonder what he would do if he had the wrong girl. He dodged left around a man with an inconveniently large hat and looked for the girl in the white dress again. No, she still looked like Meg. Her blond hair, of course, but also the tilt of her head, the way she was standing as if she might go up on her toes at any moment. Besides, he was getting closer and that lace mask wasn't very concealing.

Looking at the mask, he almost didn't notice the direction of her gaze. She looked directly towards him, smiled (recognizably Meg's smile) and started moving his way. New worry—she did know it was *him*, right? His mask was very concealing, or so he had thought. And if it wasn't, could anyone else realize…? He shoved the thought down as lower priority than the most immediate problem (the man with the large hat also had sharp elbows and waving arms) or the second most pressing issue (trying to find a path to meet Meg in the bedlam) or even the third (the possibility that the sheer crush of humanity was going to drive him to desperate action, like dropping a chandelier on their heads—though he hadn't been driven to that for 355 days, twenty-one hours). Being recognized could take fourth behind all that.

His path met Meg's at the bottom of the staircase, near the feet of the candle-bearing statues marking the end of the banister. He could see a tiny crinkle between Meg's brows, visible behind the lace mask, as she looked up at him. Then her face cleared, blossoming into a smile. "Oh good, it is you," she said. "Hello, Erik."

"Good evening," he responded, and meant to ask how she had recognized him. Distraction arrived in the form of a drunken reveler swaying backwards altogether too close to Meg. Erik put out an arm to block him, and the man bounced cheerfully off and plunged away into the throng.

Meg moved a side-step closer and raised her voice to remark, "It is a bit mad here tonight, isn't it?"

"A bit." And yet—his worry about losing control in the face of the chaos was quietly receding. The throng had in no way lightened, but Meg was like an island in a thrashing sea. A familiar face, a friendly voice, a focus in the tossing ocean. And while her eyes might be brighter than usual, smile wider, it was a recognizable and unthreatening excitement, not the unfathomable madness that seemed to infect the crowd at large.

"It's not quite so crowded in the Grand Foyer," she said, smoothing her full white skirts, fingers lingering to twist at a bit of lace decoration. "There's dancing…"

Not a subtle hint, that. "Would you care to dance?" he asked, executing the very shallow bow that was all the space available permitted.

"I'd be delighted," she said, flashing that smile again. "There's nothing I'd rather do."

Technically she took his arm, but he knew full well that she was the one leading the way through the crowd.

They found a space among the dancers and began a waltz, and at the beginning Erik felt sure that there were a great number of things *he* would rather do. Yet somehow, as the evening went on, dancing began to rise in the list.

It was three dances before it occurred to me to wonder how Erik had learned to dance. I had seen him with Christine at the last masquerade, so he knew something—but that had not been a long dance and I hadn't been paying attention to whether he was any good. By the time I thought to wonder, it was obvious he knew enough, though I couldn't imagine where dance lessons would have been in his past. Maybe he'd learned just by observation; with anyone else I would call that impossible, but I didn't put anything past Erik.

He didn't move like a natural dancer, though he'd always walked gracefully; he *was* always perfectly in time with the music. He was a good partner too, leading without dominating, his hand on my waist or in mine guiding me through the steps with just the right amount of pressure. I had danced with partners who weren't paying enough attention, and Erik was just the opposite, focused and careful—and that despite the amount of tension I could also feel in him.

He had looked as uncomfortable as a cat with its fur up when I found him on the stairs. That had led me to guess it was him as much as the all-black clothes; he was the only one who didn't appear to be having a good time. That worried me. I had convinced him to come, after all.

Erik was so *confusing*. He wanted to belong, he didn't want to belong, he complained about coming to the Mardi Gras but he did agree to come when he didn't have to...

Despite the worries, I was selfishly glad he had come. I'd never had trouble finding dance partners before, but it was nice to attend *with* someone. Also for someone to talk to between dances, to discuss funny or elaborate or deeply unfortunate costumes, to bulwark a bit against the crushing crowd.

The first year I came to Mardi Gras, it had been in a circle of wide-eyed, giggling girls. By the following year, some of them had left, and none of the remaining ones wanted to spend Mardi Gras with other girls—and I don't suppose I did either, really. I'd had high hopes for last year, and it had turned out...different than I had expected. It was almost exactly a year, since the last Mardi Gras—and since Christine had left. The Mardi Gras hadn't been what I thought I wanted, a chance to enjoy a party with my best friend. I wasn't sure whether to lay the blame for that on myself, for hoping too high, or Christine, for not meeting my hopes. Maybe I should blame Raoul.

And then I had spent the evening with Léon instead—and wondered for a time if that had been a mistake, if he was going to assume the wrong things after I let him kiss me once. But he didn't give any sign he even remembered it, which—did not really make me feel happier about the memory. Though he had kept coming around, so perhaps it meant something after all, even if we'd never spoken of it.

I could have come to Mardi Gras with Léon this year. He hadn't ever suggested it, but I had been steering us off the topic once I thought Erik might attend. I would have had fun with Léon, but this was such a...unique opportunity for Erik. Only once in the year when he could blend into the crowd. I could wander in a crowd with Léon any time, if I wanted to.

Come to think of it, Mardi Gras wasn't a bad metaphor for life. A kind of microcosm. One could walk through the party, or through life, alone or with friends or with a partner…

"You look very deep in thought," Erik said, leaning closer than the step called for so I could hear him over the music and the crowd.

"Not *very* deep." Though it probably was good that my body knew how to dance without my thinking about it much.

"Anything interesting?"

I shrugged slightly. "Just…life. People. Connections. Walking alone through a crowd."

He tilted his head, and I guessed his eyebrows were rising somewhere behind his black mask. "What do you know about walking alone through a crowd?"

I could have been offended, but I knew he probably meant it as a compliment, that he couldn't imagine any reason I should be alone. "You might be surprised," I said, just as the music came to an end for another set.

I dipped into a curtsy, in unison with most of the women around me. Not all, as some had clearly already been at the champagne. Though I wouldn't mind one glass myself.

"Perhaps we could get a drink?" I suggested, as the music began for the next set.

"Of course," Erik agreed, though I wondered if he'd agree to anything at this moment. He seemed willing to let me navigate the party for both of us, which was all right by me.

We pushed through the crowd to the buffet tables, and secured two glasses of champagne. I'd just taken the first fizzing sip when my glance, roving the crowd, met the gaze of the Persian, just a little distant. Like last year he wore ordinary evening clothes and a small mask that did nothing to disguise him. I gave him a slight nod, as I'd been doing for months now.

He stepped closer, nodded in return. "Mademoiselle Giry." He glanced at Erik next to me, and nodded again with no sign of recognition.

I watched as Erik's mouth quirked into a smile. "Good evening, Daroga. Having a pleasant Mardi Gras?"

The Persian's eyes widened. Evidently he knew the Phantom's voice too. "Yes. And a surprising one."

Erik had mentioned the Persian to me rarely, and only described him as someone he had known from long ago. He had told me that "daroga" meant "police chief," which raised more questions than it answered. I looked between the two men now, wondering if I was about to learn more.

I wasn't. The Persian merely said, "Enjoy the evening. And try to stay out of trouble."

"I always try," Erik said, then with a slight shrug amended, "Or at least, I usually do."

The Persian just smiled, and faded into the crowd again. Evidently Erik knew how to get the last word with him.

I let out a breath and took another sip of champagne. The Mardi Gras was no place for revelations anyway.

I had just finished my drink when I recognized another face, a man dressed in gold on the other side of the buffet table. He wasn't looking my way and I could see his profile, mask removed and dangling by a ribbon from his wrist.

At any other time I would have been perfectly happy to see Léon. If I hadn't been looking for Erik at this masquerade, I likely would have been looking for Léon instead. But Erik *was* here, and I couldn't abandon him to the crowd after I had convinced him to come, and yet if Léon saw me he would certainly expect me to spend time with him and—my mind stuttered to an absolute halt trying to picture choreographing a conversation between Erik and Léon in the middle of the Mardi Gras.

The whole thing was impossible and I should have thought to wear a more concealing mask.

"It's rather warm in here," I said, which wasn't a lie. "Perhaps we should step outside for a minute?" I nodded towards the doors, leading to the balconies at the front of the Opera, and hoped he would continue to go along with my suggestions.

Erik bowed slightly. "Your obedient servant."

I laughed, took his arm, carefully did not look in Léon's direction, and we proceeded towards the outside balcony.

We passed Carlotta, laughing riotously as she danced with a man in a dark blue costume who I didn't recognize, and Ricard standing along the wall, wearing a bright red coat and a rooster mask; it wasn't likely to help his flirtation with a ballet girl I knew only slightly, but with that girl, it probably wouldn't matter. I saw Jammes amidst a cluster of singers and carefully didn't turn her direction either; Jammes and her curiosity would be almost as bad as talking to Léon right now. Half of my awareness was listening, just in case I suddenly heard Léon or Jammes calling me, but no name came my way as we moved through the doorway to the balcony.

We stepped out into the coolness of February, and back into Erik's world. Even with the lights of the Opera directly behind us, the balcony was full of shadows and darkness. It was far less full of people, though not deserted. We found an empty corner looking out on the Avenue de l'Opera, and I let go of Erik's arm. Amidst the crowd, taking his arm or catching his hand in the dance had seemed like only normal custom, utterly inconsequential. Alone (relatively) in the darkness, it seemed…different, and I remembered that we never touched.

"The view is better from the roof," Erik remarked, leaning on the railing.

"Yes, but there's all those stairs." I took up a similar position beside him. "I suppose we could—" I suddenly remembered the previous Mardi Gras, and the significance of the roof. Of the conversation Christine had told me about, that I was (nearly) sure Erik must have eavesdropped on. I snuck a look sideways at Erik, and from the tensing of his shoulders, I thought he must have remembered too. "Maybe not tonight."

"No." He turned around, leaning with his back to the railing, blocking out all views. "How did you recognize me on the stairs inside? I meant to ask."

"You were the only one all in black," I said, accepting the topic change and not mentioning my cat-with-its-fur-up metaphor.

"Am I? I didn't think about that." He sighed, rubbed the back of his neck. "I'm really not very good at this blending-in concept."

"Some people aren't meant to blend in," I said softly, and because that felt too significant, too intimate somehow, I hastened to add, "Anyway, this one stands out less than Red Death did."

"I suppose that's something." He looked back towards the swirl of the crowd behind the glass doors, and his shoulders, momentarily relaxed, rose again. "And I suppose if anyone was going to suspect me, they would have by now."

"No one even knows what you look like," I pointed out. Any time he was seen, he'd been wearing a skull mask or something else equally concealing. At least, as far as I knew. "Besides, with that mask—even knowing what you look like, the Persian didn't know until you spoke, and I had to make sure when I got close too."

He frowned. "But that's the point, how could you make sure?"

"Oh—I looked at your eyes." It had seemed perfectly natural at the time; it hadn't occurred to me that there would be anything awkward about saying it out loud. "No one else has eyes the same shade of green as you." That clarification didn't make the moment less uncomfortable. My cheeks felt hot, and I hoped the shadows were thick enough to hide any redness.

Erik tipped his head to one side, stance going thoughtful, apparently not observing any awkwardness. "Hmm. I never noticed."

That surprised me right out of my embarrassment. His eyes were so striking. "Don't you ever look in a mirror?" I had never seen him look in one, but still.

"Not if it can be avoided," Erik said with a shrug. "And I don't look at other people's eyes very often either."

That statement, and especially the off-hand way he said it, seemed unbearably sad on too many levels for me to deal with in the middle of Mardi Gras.

I grasped desperately at the first distraction that came to mind. "Did you see Carlotta's costume? Do you think she's supposed to be something in particular?"

He rolled amiably enough with the new topic change. "I hope she's something, or I don't know how she can justify the enormous shoulders on that dress. Maybe she's the Church of the Madalon."

I giggled, and the evening righted itself to be enjoyable again. We talked, we danced, we ate from the buffet and I only ever saw Léon across large crowds which, while not what I would have wanted another night, was all for the best tonight. At three minutes to midnight, I would have said it was the best masquerade I'd ever attended.

Chapter Twenty-Six

A t three minutes to midnight, Erik and I were standing on the marble stairs, next to the right-hand statue flanking the entrance to the auditorium, and at that precise moment Carlotta appeared on the upper balcony opposite us and began calling for attention.

It wouldn't have worked an hour earlier. People don't quiet down at the masquerade easily. But by now the crowd was growing tired enough, had drunk enough and danced enough, to be ready for a new diversion. That, and Carlotta's devotees throughout the party began shushing the people around them.

"What fresh nonsense do you suppose this is?" Erik murmured, standing just behind me with one shoulder leaning up against the base of the statue.

"Maybe she's going to sing," I suggested.

"Heaven help us," he muttered.

"Or heaven help her voice."

"Lost cause. The champagne won't have helped it either."

By now the room was growing quiet, as quiet as a packed crowd of slightly tipsy Opera Company members can be—which is not *very* quiet, but quiet enough to clearly hear Carlotta when she called out, "It has been a *marvelous* Mardi Gras, and now that it is midnight, I wish to make it even more..." A pause as she searched for a word, swaying slightly as she leaned on the balcony. Erik was right—champagne.

"...marvelous!" she chose at last. "I wish to institute a brand new tradition!"

"It's not a tradition until it stops being new," Erik murmured behind me. "It can't be both."

I tried to stifle a laugh, even as a chorus girl near us loudly shushed him. I glanced back over my shoulder to see Erik glare at her, though I didn't think it was a particularly intense glare. She just shrugged and looked away, which had its own comical aspect considering I'd seen that particular chorus girl go into shrieks over the merest hint of a Phantom sighting.

Meanwhile, Carlotta was meandering to her point. "A new tradition, which I hope we will always continue! A tradition—at midnight, at right now—there will be—a grand unmasking!"

My stomach dropped. A grand *what*? I looked back again at Erik, who said nothing. What I could see of his face was perfectly expressionless, gaze locked on Carlotta with a much more intense glint than there had been in his glare a moment before.

"Find out if your guesses were right!" Carlotta went on. "Do you know who you were dancing with?"

The crowd was murmuring now, thoughtful, interested. Only a few masks were coming down though, a few girls who were always particularly eager to please Carlotta. Jammes and her friends were unmasked now, predictably, but maybe no one else would go along with the idea. Maybe this was just a tipsy bit of nonsense because *no one* wants to reveal themselves at a masquerade.

I looked up at Carlotta again, and noticed the man in blue I'd seen her dance with before was next to her. Right next to her, leaning over in fact, to whisper in her ear. I didn't recognize him, but at a distance and wearing a mask over the upper half of his face that didn't mean much. All the same—who was he, hanging about Carlotta? A subscriber? He wasn't built like a dancer, but could have been from the chorus. I noticed Jammes was standing on his other side, and the idea that they might know each other was not reassuring.

He finished whatever he was whispering and Carlotta returned to her proclamation. "It is midnight! Let the unmasking begin!" And then she pulled away her silvery mask, disordering her hair in the process, and flung it out into the crowd.

This was met with laughter, a scattered applause—and more masks coming down.   And once enough started, more followed. Monsieur Ricard was one of the first, flinging away his rooster-beak mask. More and more joined in.

"It has been a charming evening," Erik said in flat tones, brushing past me. "Pardon me if I leave early."

My heart was pounding in my throat and I caught his arm as he went by, because I needed him to know— "Erik, I swear, I never expected—"

"Of course not," he said, which might have meant anything, but he gave me the faintest ghost of a smile and a slight tip of the head, and that helped.

I let go of his arm but took a step after him as he moved towards the nearest stair. "I could come too."

"Nonsense," he said, curt enough again, gaze scanning around the crowd. "You can take off your mask."

I winced, but I don't think he saw, and there wasn't time to discuss it.   Fewer and fewer masks were still being worn, and Erik started pushing through the crowd in earnest, ascending up the marble stairs.

I reached to take off my own white mask. It would do me no good to be the odd one out here either.

Erik was halfway up the stairs, half a staircase of people between us, the same amount still between him and the top and whatever escape he was aiming for. My gaze flicked upward, to the head of the stair— and I noticed another man in dark blue there, in the same mask the man by Carlotta had been wearing. He couldn't have got over there so quickly—and no, that man was still next to the soprano, still wearing his mask too. His attitude had changed though, no longer carousing with Carlotta, instead leaning over the balcony and looking hard at the crowd below. Likewise the man in blue at the head of the stairs was standing quite still in place. And he too was watching the crowd.

My heart started pounding harder. I turned my head, looking around, looking for men in blue and they were there, still masked, another at the top of the opposite stair, one by the exit out to the street. All of them, watching.

A trap. It was a trap.

I tried to push through the crowd myself, tried to reach Erik to warn him. They were like a solid wall, a bulwark of bodies and brightly colored clothes. Erik had got through them, but he was tall and broad-shouldered and dressed all in black. They didn't want to move for a little ballet girl in white.

I squeezed past a large man with a feathered hat, skirted an amorous couple, came up against a knot of laughing chorus members who weren't moving for anyone, and Erik was getting farther up the stairs all the while, closer to that man in blue. Could I call to him? Was it worth the risk? He wouldn't even hear me, the noise level had gone up again and one voice in the crowd—

I could see it, when Erik realized on his own. Suddenly his head rose and his shoulders, already tense, went tighter. He was looking directly at the man in blue, and that man was looking right back.

I risked a hurried glance around. There were virtually no masks on anymore, no crowd of disguised people for Erik to disappear into. His black outfit, always marking him out, now seemed doubly ominous and odd with his all-encompassing mask still on in a sea of bare faces.

The man in blue was starting to move down the stairs, the one by Carlotta was looking this way, I tried again to get past that wall of singers and Erik shoved sideways on the stairs. He was more forceful about it than I was, moving the people who wouldn't move themselves, reaching the banister, but what good would that do when there was only empty space beyond it?

Erik leaped onto the wide banister and then, impossibly, ran up the slick marble slope. Shrieks and calls rose from the crowd as people noticed and my hand was over my mouth trying to keep back my own scream. He swung past the candelabra at the top of the stair, around to the pillar behind it and went straight up the pillar. He got just high enough to reach to the carved molding at the top. I may have screamed then, when he held onto the molding with one hand, turning out to face the crowd, other arm free.

"Happy Mardi Gras," he called over the increased cries, and swung his free arm sharply down.

A plume of red smoke blossomed up, covering the entire pillar, reaching in wisps for the ceiling. It faded out again in seconds, long before the screams faded. Erik, of course, was gone.

I dared to inhale, concentrated on breathing again while all around me the crowd began their inevitable murmur. The Phantom. It was the Phantom.

Of course it was the Phantom. No one in the Company would ever believe it wasn't the Phantom, with a stunt like that. All right, so they knew he was here, that wasn't important—who were the men in blue, that's what I wanted to know. Were they working for the managers? Or was it Commissaire Mifroid and his men, trying a new trick?

I didn't have long to catch my breath, only a few heartbeats it seemed before someone caught my arm. "Meg, did you see him?" Francesca asked, breathless herself. "The Phantom! It really was!"

"Yes, of course," I said, watching the man at the head of the stairs, who was peering up at the top of the column as though he still might find Erik there.

"And you were *dancing* with him!"

That brought my attention sharply back to Francesca, to Adalisa and Celine and Bridgette clustered alongside her (how had *they* managed to get through the crowd to reach me? Strength of numbers, maybe). "Me?" I said shakily. "Dancing with the Phantom? No, of course not."

"But you were," Francesca insisted, "the man in black. I saw you earlier—and then he came from this direction just now."

"You must have seen some other girl in white dancing with him," I said firmly, profoundly grateful for my mask, for the scattered dots of white dresses and blond hair throughout the crowd, for the way Erik and I had avoided any conversations with Company members that would have definitely tied me to him. Because if they knew *that*—how could I ever explain? How could I ever maintain my place in the society of a Company deeply devoted to hating the Phantom? How could I even keep my job?

Francesca frowned, troubled, perplexed. "No…I thought…I was almost sure…"

"Oh, Francesca, maybe you were wrong," Adalisa said briskly. "There's lots of girls in white, and if Meg says she wasn't dancing with him—"

"But I *saw*," Francesca maintained, and I got more worried when Bridgette chimed in, "I saw too, I'm sure it was you."

I almost tried to shrug it off, realized just in time that was the wrong strategy. "Do you really think so?" I said in my best horrified tones. "I can't remember everyone I danced with—maybe one dance was with the man in black—and if he was really the Phantom…" I tried to fake a shudder, and after all the terrors of the last five minutes, it wasn't hard. "Oh, how awful!"

"What was it like?" Francesca demanded eagerly.

Lovely, actually, he was a very good dancer. "I don't know, I didn't even know it was him! If I even did dance with him."

"Meg, *there* you are!"

With a distinct feeling of relief, I turned to see Léon shouldering his way through the crowd to arrive in front of me. "Léon, I've been looking for you all evening." Well, looking out for him, anyway.

This seemed to set him off stride, the frown that had been forming on his face smoothing out again. "Oh—that's strange, I've been looking for you too…"

"She was dancing with the *Phantom*!" Francesca reported.

"What, that story that flies around the Company?" Léon said, puzzled frown returning.

"Yes!" three girls clamored together, Francesca adding, "The Phantom just disappeared up the column."

"Oh," Léon said, without much appearance of interest. "What was that, some sort of planned midnight entertainment?"

"No, no, it was the Phantom!" Francesca said, as though this should explain everything.

"Never mind, I don't want to think about it anymore," I broke in. "Léon, let's go dance, before the musicians get sleepy."

In actual fact, the party would probably last another two hours at least, but I had to say something to get away from the ballet girls and their suspicions. I glanced around, looking for the easiest path through the crowd—and noticed with a new stab of alarm that a man in blue was working his way down the stairs, headed towards me. He wasn't wearing his mask anymore and he wasn't Mifroid, but I was certain he was the man who had been standing at the top of the stairs. Who must have seen me with a man in black too, and now was coming this way.

I stepped closer to Léon, took his arm. "Let's go dance," I repeated.

"All right with me," he said agreeably, and we started to move down the stairs.

I glanced back, trying not to be obvious, and saw that the man in blue had stopped, a frown creasing his face. He was still looking my direction, but now he seemed to be focusing on Léon, as though he was the cause of this new hesitation.

Apparently there were some advantages to knowing a young nobleman. They were harder to accost in the middle of a crowd than a ballet girl.

"So where have you been all evening?" Léon asked, bringing my attention back to him. "I couldn't find you anywhere."

"Here and there," I said, waving a hand. "We must have just been in opposite places all night." And because he didn't look convinced, I leaned in and kissed his cheek, just a quick brush that meant little, and said, "I'm glad you found me now."

Now, not earlier. Now, I really could have a nice time with him, especially as the comment, or maybe the kiss, cheered him up too. I tried not to feel guilty about Erik. It wasn't my fault he had to leave early, and so what was wrong with spending the rest of the party with Léon? It was probably even necessary—what would Mifroid's men think, if I left directly after the Phantom did?

Léon was both a better and worse dancer than Erik—more skilled but less careful. He didn't step on my feet but he did sometimes swing me around a little too much, grip my hand a little too tight. But it was late in the night on Mardi Gras and that all seemed inconsequential, as I threw myself into enjoying this second portion of the night, and pushed away regretful thoughts about Erik.

An unmasking. What had put an *unmasking* into Carlotta's head? Or rather, who?

That was the question, that was what Erik wanted to know as he paced in the ceiling above the Grand Staircase. It had almost certainly been Mifroid who suggested the idea directly, wearing his own mask and whispering to the lead soprano. But how had the idea come to Mifroid? Who told him that would be a way to catch the Phantom?

How many people even knew the Phantom wore a mask, or that he might be at the masquerade? Well, Meg. But that was ridiculous on the very face of it. And there would be far easier ways for her to betray him to Mifroid, for her to help with his capture. If she had wanted to do it.

The Daroga, he would know and he was here. But this wasn't his style and besides, Erik hadn't done anything recently to provoke an effort to capture him. No, the time that might have happened was 356 days ago, and even then, the Daroga would have shown up at his door with the police. He wouldn't have orchestrated this farce at the masquerade.

She knew. She knew about the mask, knew he had attended last year's Mardi Gras, knew how deeply, deeply unlikely it was that he would ever take his mask off with an audience around him. But she was gone.

Raoul? He had seen the truth on that fatal night and besides, she had told him even earlier. The night of the last masquerade, in fact. But he was gone too. And what would his motivation be? He had won.

It made no *sense* and Erik didn't like it. Maybe he could learn more from Mifroid, if he could find him in the crowd again.

He descended down a level, less dramatically and entirely more secretly than he had ascended, and prowled about to various hidden vantage points in the walls to look for the police commissaire.

Mifroid had been with Carlotta, so he looked for Carlotta. She was always an easy figure to find, with her loud voice and the crowd she liked to gather around her. He was still maneuvering to a position close enough to eavesdrop, when the goal became suddenly easier.

"But you! I know you!" Carlotta exclaimed, voice piercing. "That police officer!

Apparently someone had managed to get Mifroid's mask off. Had the commissaire calculated for that in his plans, when he'd arranged for an unmasking?

Erik was close enough by now to hear Mifroid say, "I was attempting to be discreet, madam..."

And that was no longer achievable, as a new voice joined in, "Commissaire Mifroid!" Unquestionably Moncharmin. "Causing more disturbances? I thought I told you we wanted no more of that!" The man's tone was blustering, but less furious than it had been the last time they'd had a conversation like this. Perhaps Moncharmin had been at the champagne too.

"He didn't do any harm." Ricard's voice now. The managers hadn't been together earlier; it seemed Ricard hadn't had any success with that ballet girl he'd been flirting with.

"But there could have been," Moncharmin countered. "He went and provoked the Phantom again, obviously, and it's only good luck that another chandelier didn't come down on our heads. And if you're going to cause all this trouble, you might at least have caught him."

Erik winced at this. He had never considered Moncharmin a supporter, but at least the man had been championing leaving the Phantom strictly alone for some while now.

The strained note in Mifroid's voice was clear—and new. "If you had given me any cooperation whatsoever, perhaps I would have by now. Instead you have interfered every step of the way—"

"I am merely trying to protect my opera house—"

"*Our* opera house, Moncharmin," Ricard interrupted. "You are always forgetting that."

Carlotta apparently felt she had been ignored too long. "I think someone *ought* to catch the Phantom. He has been meddling and insulting and probably murdering people for years, and now we can't even have a party without him showing up to terrorize us!"

This remark, on the other hand, was only what Erik might have anticipated from her. What followed was equally to be expected: Ricard tried to reassure Carlotta, Moncharmin complained about Mifroid's presence, Mifroid made only very terse statements about pursuing his duty in response. Erik leaned back against the wall with a sigh.

He had had every intention of attending the masquerade without bothering anyone. But of course the story that would go around the opera house was that he had come with the express intent of frightening everyone, of ruining their party. Never mind that the party was still going on, never mind that he'd probably provided the most interesting entertainment of the evening. Carlotta would tell the story that he'd been there with evil intent, and that was no doubt the story the gossip-mongers would prefer to spread. Even if Meg wouldn't believe it, Erik had no illusions about the Opera Company's preferences in Phantom stories.

Mifroid eventually took his leave, if less dramatically than the last time Moncharmin had ordered him out, Carlotta's fans spent a long time trying to sooth her, and the managers wandered off through the crowd, arguing with each other.

The Phantom went on lurking in the walls, listening to the party he could no longer participate in. Not that he wanted to. Though it hadn't been a *bad* evening. Up until the end.

As he wandered around the edges of the masquerade, he saw Meg in the Grand Foyer again. She had joined Léon, and the two of them appeared to be having a grand time dancing. Well, that was good. No reason to ruin her evening.

He watched for a while, as Léon leaned in close to Meg to speak, as she lifted her face in a laugh, eyes sparkling. Probably—he was too far away to really see, but they usually sparkled when she laughed. He watched as they danced together, rather close, though that was likely necessary in such a crowded room. She was a good dancer. That is, of course she was, she was in the ballet, but she had been easy to dance with. And somehow it hadn't felt strange, being so close to another person. It was just dancing. It hadn't meant anything then, just as it likely didn't mean anything now, now that it was Léon instead of him.

Perhaps he'd best start keeping an eye on Léon, if he was going to be around so much. Just out of friendly concern, just to make sure he was an appropriate companion for Meg.

And it appeared he'd have to be more wary of Mifroid too. The man was turning into his own personal Javert. Not that he was any Jean Valjean himself.

Excerpt from the Private Notebook of Jean Mifroid, Commissaire of Police

22 February, 1882

Failure—complete failure! I had the madman in sight, and still he vanished—publically, dramatically, absurdly, by climbing a column in a puff of smoke! If I believed in demons—but I am a rational man. *He* is a man, this so-called Opera Ghost. But very, very clever.

I must be more clever too.

If that was not unpleasant enough, my identity was uncovered by Opera's managers, who complained to Prefect. Unlikely to get further support for investigation.

Two useful observations: 1, suspect M. Giry was with OG during Mardi Gras. Blond woman seen dancing with man in black throughout evening. 2, Carlotta, unlike managers, wishes to capture OG.

Have considered confronting Giry directly, but may be better to move more cautiously. Intend to seek meeting with Carlotta re: obtaining more information from inside Opera Company. Information on OG and on Giry will give me stronger position.

Chapter Twenty-Seven

D espite the late hour at the masquerade, I dragged myself out of bed reasonably early, intent on going to see Erik. I was waylaid by my mother and wound up at an Ash Wednesday service instead, where the reflections on death and ashes did not do a great deal for my mood. I had always liked Easter so much better than Ash Wednesday.

After *that* I went to the Opera. It was closed, of course, but that's not the sort of place that's ever really *closed*. I slipped in by a side door, into what felt like an entirely different place than where I had laughed and danced only a few hours before. Empty like this, even the aboveground portions seemed magical, full of echoes and shadows. It might have been spooky, if I hadn't been friends with the resident ghost.

Well, if he wasn't upset with me about the night before.

I stopped in the ballet's changing room, a place I'd almost never seen empty before, to get my directions to Erik's apartment. I'd hidden them at the back of the locked drawer in my dressing table, to be sure I'd have them whenever I needed them. I almost had the route memorized, but today I felt anxious enough to want the security of directions to follow. Then I made my way belowground, to reach Erik's door, and knocked with more trepidation than I'd felt since the first time I did this. I was already assuring myself that he might not even be here, or might still be asleep, as a kind of anticipatory emotional protection in case he didn't answer. It didn't *have* to mean he blamed me for the Mardi Gras debacle.

But as soon as I knocked, I heard an answering, "Come in," from within, and the click that meant he'd just unlocked the door. That didn't mean that he was anywhere near the door. Sure enough, when I went in he was sitting on one of his couches, papers spread on the ivory table in front of him. Papers had been spread around for weeks, but he seemed to actually be engaging with these.

I crossed the room, sat down in my usual seat, spreading my skirts around me, fingers lingering among the folds. "Good morning," I said a little cautiously.

"Good morning," he said, and his gaze drifted above my eyeline. "Been to mass already?"

I remembered the smudge of ash on my forehead. The one day in the year when mass attendance was visible afterwards. "Yes." I took a deep breath and rushed into saying, "I'm so sorry about last night."

His eyebrow quirked higher. "If that was sympathy, thank you. If it was an apology, it wasn't your fault."

It was…both, really, but it was the second one making me anxious. "But I convinced you to come, and you said—and I didn't listen and—"

"And it was still not your fault," he said, with a reassuring firmness. "I entirely blame Mifroid."

I relaxed a little at that. "Did you hear the managers found him with Carlotta? I thought he was the one talking to her—and he had his men in the crowd too, in blue masks." I'd much rather talk about how it was the commissaire's fault than how it was mine.

He smiled slightly. "Ah, you noticed that too. I wondered."

"About a minute too late," I muttered.

"It turned out well enough in the end. Now it simply remains to be seen what Mifroid will do next."

I slumped back in my seat. "He's not going away, is he? I thought he had gone away. And it just—it isn't *fair*." A heartbeat too late I realized that that statement was not going to support my case that I was not in fact young and naïve.

"I don't know about that," Erik said mildly. "I have been extorting them for years."

"You give good service," I countered. "The advice for the productions—that helps so much, when they listen."

He tipped his head. "It is kind of you to say so. But I'm afraid I'm a pessimist about this. I can't be too upset about Mifroid because it's hardly new. Inevitable, really."

Inevitable? Inevitable, that someone was going to be chasing him down for a murder he didn't commit? Unthinking, I asked, "How do you live like that?"

"Long practice, I suppose." Erik shrugged. "And it's like Napoleon said. 'Oh well, no matter what happens, there's always death.' "

"That's *awful*," I protested.

"Is it?" he asked, making it sound like a genuine question. "I never thought so. It's a bit nice to think that there is ultimately an end to any of the troubles of life. To the heartache and the thousand natural shocks that flesh is heir to." His eyes cut sideways to me and he added, "That last part was Hamlet, of course."

"Of course," I said, just as though I had known that. "But that makes it sound as though we all ought to just kill ourselves to avoid any more trouble!"

"No, Hamlet thought of that too. Because, after all, 'in that sleep of death, what dreams may come?' Who would keep living 'but that the dread of something after death, the undiscovered country from whose bourn no traveler returns, puzzles the will.' "

It wasn't a funny comment at all, but I found myself smiling. I didn't know anyone else who would calmly drop Shakespearean quotations into conversation. And if he'd rather talk about Hamlet than Mifroid, even though part of me thought we ought to talk about the police, about what he was going to do, about why this wasn't all right—part of me would rather talk about Hamlet too.

"I've never seen *Hamlet*." I only knew about it vaguely. "Doesn't he kill his uncle or something?"

"He spends the entire play trying to," Erik said, rising to his feet and crossing over to his bookcase. "I can't honestly say that the plot is one of my preferred ones, but Shakespeare does have a knack for quotations which is rarely so well displayed as in *Hamlet*." He reached out, pulled an enormous book off the shelf and brought it back to the couch. He paged through, running a finger down the creamy paper. "An argument could be made for *King Lear* as a superior play, but I find myself leaning to *Hamlet* regardless."

Me, I leaned over to look at the page. I could recognize 'Hamlet' at the top, but all the rest was indecipherable to me. Evidently he had it in the original English. "Was it ever made into an opera?"

And so we passed right off of the probably more significant discussion about Mifroid to the less charged topic of operas and music. And while I knew it wasn't really that important, I kept thinking about *Hamlet*.

It was easier somehow, this time, to not worry so much about Mifroid. Maybe because it had all been all right for so long so far. Or I was just busier, dancing and seeing Erik and spending time with Léon.

Léon and I had still been meeting in the Dance Foyer every Saturday night, and he had begun suggesting Sunday afternoon expeditions too. We went out for a luncheon on the Sunday after Mardi Gras, the first Sunday in Lent, and I convinced him to go for a walk afterwards.

"My carriage would have got us anywhere faster," he pointed out, as we strolled beside the Seine.

"You can't peruse interesting stalls from a carriage," I countered, pausing at one of the many that lined the wall, with the river behind them. This one sold little statues and knick-knacks, nothing that particularly caught my fancy, and I walked on.

"You won't find much of quality out here," Léon said dismissively.

I glanced around quick to make sure none of the stall-owners were listening, but we were between stalls at the moment and it seemed to be all right. "Sometimes you get surprised. You never know where treasure might be hidden." I supposed Léon, with his wealthy family, had never had much need or opportunity to go looking for treasure.

The next stall we came to sold old books, soft and worn around the edges. I ran one fingertip along the row of spines laid out in a line on the shelf.

"What do you think you're going to find *here*?" he asked, tone still disinterested. "Some book with good pictures?"

"Well—maybe," I said, because I didn't know quite what else to say, because the comment didn't make sense to me—and then I stopped thinking about it, my finger stopping on one faded leather volume, dull gold leaf picking out the single word, *Hamlet*.

I wiggled the book out of its tight pack between the others, flipped it open and found French words within. A translation, then.

I wasn't sure why *Hamlet* had stuck in my head so much. Erik and I had only talked about it briefly; I still didn't know much about that plot he had said wasn't so wonderful (but the quotations were good). It was just something about the way he had said those quotes from it, the way he had so easily flipped open to the appropriate section in his enormous volume of Shakespearean plays.

Maybe I was wrong and it wasn't important to him. But something about that play seemed to matter to him.

Léon's voice broke right into my thoughts. "No pictures at all in that one."

And that mattered why? Out loud I just said, "I've been wanting to read *Hamlet*. I wasn't sure I'd be able to find a translation."

Léon was looking at me very oddly suddenly, in a way that made me feel as though my hat was sitting askew or I had something on my face. Looking as though he wasn't sure what he was seeing but it surprised him. "You can read?"

Oh. Well, that explained the comments about pictures. "Yes, of course," I said, a little nettled, even though really there wasn't any 'of course' about it. Most of the ballet girls couldn't, or could only pick out their name and not much else. Mother had sent Gabi and me to the school in Leclair before we came here. I was surprised to realize the subject had never come up with Léon, but evidently it hadn't.

He was smiling slightly now. "Are you sure you want to read *Hamlet*?"

"Yes. Of course." I turned to the stallowner, to ask the price of the book.

"Fifty centime, mademoiselle," he said with a polite inclining of his head.

High for a diversion, but my pocket money would stretch that far, this once. You don't spend as much when your chief social activity becomes sitting under an Opera discussing music. I reached into the pocket of my skirt for the money.

"I'll cover that," Léon said, producing a wallet from within his coat.

"You don't have to do that," I said, nettled again—or maybe still.

"I know," he responded with what should have been a charming grin. But it felt wrong. He had paid for the meal we just ate, but this was different.

"I *have* the money," I said, and put the required coins into the stallowner's hand before Léon could.

"*Merci*, mademoiselle," the stallowner said, tucked the money away and then backed away himself. Maybe he thought we were about to have an argument.

We didn't. Léon just kept smiling, I tucked the book under my arm and continued along the riverbank, and he followed. After two more stalls I started talking to him again, and we passed the rest of the afternoon amiably enough.

He had meant well, after all. It was just—I wasn't sure I wanted him to start buying me things. A book was one of the things a man *could* buy a woman without any impropriety, but still. It felt better, safer somehow, simply buying it myself.

In between dancing, afternoons with Léon and conversations with Erik, it took me a month to read *Hamlet*. It wasn't nearly as long or dense as Victor Hugo, with significantly less architecture. Instead there was love and sword fights and betrayal and conspiracy. And Erik was right, the plot meandered as Hamlet tried to bring himself to kill his uncle (or decide definitely not to), but they said wonderful things along the way. There were a few perfectly ordinary phrases I'd been using my whole life without knowing they'd come by way of *Hamlet*.

I thought it was delightful. Right up until the final Act. And that sent me marching off to Erik's apartments in a state of righteous outrage.

I knocked first (I wasn't *that* outraged) and once he invited me to enter I strode in and demanded, "Why didn't you *tell* me Hamlet died?"

Sitting at his pipe organ across the room, Erik stared at me as though at a complete loss. "Why did I—what?"

"Hamlet! I read *Hamlet* and he has that whole speech about killing himself and he decides not to and then he dies *anyway* so what was the point of it all?" I flung myself on a maroon couch, crossed my arms, and awaited an explanation.

Erik sat down more slowly on the opposite couch. "You read *Hamlet*?"

Not again, not from *him*! "A French translation, yes. You were quoting Hamlet so I read it. Just because I'm a ballet dancer and not a genius composer and architect doesn't mean I can't read Shakespeare, thank you very—"

"No, that's not what I was thinking," he said with a shake of his head. "It's just...I quoted Hamlet so you read it." He shook his head again, more of a wondering shake. "Did you like it?"

"Until everyone *died*."

"It's a Shakespearean tragedy," he said with a ghost of a smile. "Everyone always dies."

"I hate stories where everyone dies at the end, especially when a bit of common sense would have prevented the whole thing."

"You'd better try a Shakespearean comedy instead. Everyone gets married at the end. Less realistic, but happier."

"Dead bodies all over the stage is not realistic."

A beat. "If you say so."

I shook my head. "It's just—it's like so many operas that have tragic endings. If the people involved had just *talked* to each other it all could have ended happily."

"I don't think Hamlet having an amiable conversation with his uncle would have solved very much."

"No, maybe not, but if he had talked to Ophelia or his mother..." I shook my head again. "Well. What else should I read?"

"With a happy ending?"

I considered. "Not necessarily. I don't mind tragedies, it's just unnecessary ones that bother me. I like dark stories sometimes. Like Mr. Poe's."

"That's fortunate, since I have few happy endings on my bookshelves."

At that comment, I rose to my feet, to go look at his shelves myself. He hadn't exactly told me I could—but he hadn't said not to, and he didn't stop me either. Not even when I ran my fingertip along the spines of the books, stopping when a title caught my eye. "What's this? *Frankenstein*?" Sounded German.

"Rather dark," Erik said, and glanced down at the papers in front of him. "The story of a misshapen creature rejected by both his creator and the world."

"Oh." I stared at the silver lettering on the spine, wondered if this was possibly a very bad story for Erik to be reading, and whether that meant I should or shouldn't read it.

I was just starting to move my fingertip down the line again when Erik said, "That's the original English, but I have a French translation somewhere. I could hunt it out for you. If you want."

I did. I just hadn't been sure if he'd want me to. But if he offered—so I smiled and said, "Yes, I'd like that."

He presented a copy to me a few days later. It looked remarkably new. But maybe he really had had it tucked away somewhere.

Excerpt from the Private Notebook of Jean Mifroid, Commissaire of Police

30 March, 1882

With aid of Carlotta, have successfully established solid informer within Opera. Information so far has been of minor value, but will continue to press to produce more. Many rumors about OG, but little of tangible use. Hope to learn more about Giry too, if she does not grow suspicious.

There must be answers. Someone must know more about OG.

Chapter Twenty-Eight

E rik sprawled on a maroon couch, one arm behind his head, and stared at the stones of his ceiling. Life was flat, empty and dull.

The Opera Garnier had been closed and quiet since the conclusion of Wednesday night's performance. This was Saturday, and it felt like years. The building wouldn't wake up again until Tuesday morning, eons away. Why did Easter holidays have to be so *long*? Had they really done this every year? It had never before felt like such an endless stretch of days. He'd even enjoyed the quiet most years, and taken advantage of the opportunity to wander the halls more freely. Last Easter *she* had been gone less than seven weeks and he had stayed under the Opera the entire time, doing nothing and not caring.

She had been gone 403 days, 12 hours now. But what was the good of dwelling on that?

Easter holidays. They happened every year. There had to be some way he could fill the time. Two years ago he'd done a thorough check on all his hidden doors and spyholes. He could do that again. Only somehow he couldn't work up the slightest interest in the project.

Erik heaved up to his feet and wandered over to sit at his pipe organ, tap a few idle keys. There was plenty he could do. He could break into the managers' office, steal the notes for the next round of performances, make some judicious comments in the margins. He could finish that half-done sonata he'd been poking at since Thursday. He could try to bring some order to the stacks of papers all over the room, the way Meg kept saying he ought to.

He sighed, rubbing a hand over his face. He could pretend that he didn't know why this year was different than last Easter, or any Easter before, but that was just lying to himself. He hadn't seen Meg since Wednesday, and all the light had gone with her.

Though that was a serious confusion of metaphors, since he *liked* darkness, he was comfortable in darkness, he didn't even like light.

No, that wasn't true, the problem had never been that he didn't like light; it was that light worried him, exposed him, created a risk. Meg's light was different, though, not the electric light that attacked the darkness, but the light of a summer afternoon. Not the summer afternoons he'd actually experienced either, but the ones he'd imagined in his more sanguine moments, ones that were welcoming and friendly.

This was not helping.

Saturday afternoon to Tuesday morning—that was *lifetimes*.

He slammed a hand on the keys, then winced at the resulting clang of notes. He retreated back to the couch, away from the delicate musical instrument. Back to ceiling-staring.

Maybe he could visit her. He knew where she lived, and that was allowed, right? Friends visited each other, right?

Sure, she wouldn't find a masked man showing up unexpectedly on her doorstep to be at all strange. That wouldn't be alarming in the least. Her mother wouldn't find that the tiniest bit problematic.

Madame Giry would probably be the one to open the door, and then what would he say? That he just happened to be in the neighborhood, and…maybe there was something urgent he needed to discuss, so… It was no good, no excuse would be anything more than completely transparent, would fail entirely to hide the truth. Which was that he just missed Meg.

Hopeless. He couldn't say that. That was sure to look obsessive, dangerous, heading towards chandelier-dropping territory. Which was ridiculous, but it's how it would look. He couldn't risk that.

Saturday, Sunday, Monday, Tuesday…

Wait. Sunday. Erik straightened up. *Sunday*. Meg had told him— she and her mother both went to an Easter Vigil mass Saturday night, but then Meg went alone to a Sunday morning mass too. Easter mass at Notre Dame. And why shouldn't a musically-inclined Phantom decide to go hear Notre Dame's music on Easter morning? That was perfectly reasonable, wasn't it?

He pushed off of the couch, began pacing the length of the room, trying to look at this rationally. Could he? Should he?

There were hundreds of reasons this was a bad idea—all those hundreds of people who would be filling Notre Dame Cathedral. On the other hand, plenty of shadows lurked in a big old church like that. And didn't he have just as much right to be there as anyone else?

Besides…it would be Easter morning. Surely if ever a time existed when there was enough sunlight in the world to give even the Phantom a share, that would be the day.

When I stepped out of Notre Dame Cathedral after Easter mass, fumbling to tie the ribbons of my hat beneath my chin, my head and my heart were still caught up in the soaring strains of music. The brilliant light made me blink after the dim interior, but even the bright sunlight and the jostling crowd seemed less real than the melodies still echoing in my mind. It had been a lovely mass.

A tug on my sleeve pulled me back down to earth. "Mad'moiselle?"

I looked down to see that a grimy-faced urchin had attached himself to me. He looked shabby, but had a wide grin that kept him from being too alarming. "Yes?" I said, automatically reaching for my purse for a coin. I was sure "spare a sous?" would be his next sentence.

Instead, he said, "Message f'you," and held out a folded triangle of paper.

"For me?" I repeated, half confused and half suspicious.

"Yes'm." The grin threatened to split his face in two. "A gen'leman gave me two francs to hand it to you!"

I took the note, and the boy bobbed a bow and disappeared off across the square. I unfolded the thick paper, and one mystery cleared as soon as I saw the handwriting.

Alcove on the right side of the cathedral

- E

So much for who, leaving just how and *why*. I refolded the note and tucked it away, then turned right, threading through the milling churchgoers to get around the corner of the cathedral. People had spread out mostly across the front square, and there was less activity on the avenue beside the cathedral. I scanned along the stone walls, and was nearly to the back of the church before I saw an alcove with an unusually solid shadow, one that touched his hat when I approached.

"Happy Easter."

"Good morning," I answered, smiling despite how odd it felt to see him outside the Opera. Odd, incongruous—but still *good* to see him. I wondered inconsequently if he'd notice my yellow dress, new for Easter. He was dressed just as usual in his cloak, with a black felt hat. A full-face mask today, the cream-colored one that just showed his eyes and a squared-off space around his mouth and chin. "What are you doing here?"

Erik shrugged, setting his cloak rippling. "I came to hear the music. You were right when you said they're very good." From him, this was the highest magnitude of praise. "Different from the Opera Company's productions, of course."

"Of course," I agreed, "but it's like sonatas and rondos, you can't really compare them."

He blinked, seeming faintly taken aback, though I didn't see anything surprising in the statement. And he certainly knew the difference between a sonata and a rondo. "Quite," he said after a beat. "Apples and oranges, too." He then made a show of looking up at the sky. "Clear day today—there must be an excellent view from the towers."

I felt wary...but excited too. What plot was behind that so deliberate comment? "Yes, but with all the crowds for Easter, they have the towers closed."

A smile spread below his mask. "To most people." There was a door behind him, and now he reached back and pushed it open a few inches, far enough to reveal a stair within.

My thrill of excitement grew, though I tried to keep it out of my voice, tried to remain practical. "How did you find an unlocked door?"

"What makes you think it was unlocked when I found it?" he asked, a new glint in his green eyes.

I looked quickly around; no one seemed to be noticing us. "You can't break into *Notre Dame*," I hissed, torn between genuine unease and that teasing thrill of delight.

"Of course I can. Big old church like this, not even a challenge. Their security measures are 600 years old." He turned towards the door, swinging it open farther.

"That's not the point!"

"If you say so." He looked back over his shoulder, one foot across the threshold. "Are you coming?"

"Yes," I said, already stepping forward. Vague moral outrage was no competition for the lure of an adventure. And I had never been able to resist following Erik. Not even when I was twelve years old.

We didn't enter by the usual visitors' entrance to the towers, but Erik seemed to know where he was going. We encountered no one, and within a few flights of stairs we were in the main stairwell leading up into the towers. I recognized it from previous, properly sanctioned, expeditions.

We ascended hundreds of steps in the narrow circular stair. It was vaguely mesmerizing, going around and around, up and up. Climbing the stone steps behind the Phantom of the Opera did not make the situation seem less dream-like.

Finally Erik reached the top, opening the wooden door and letting a new flood of light into the stairwell. A few steps more and I stepped out of the stairs onto the narrow walkway. I lifted my face to the sunlight, adjusted my hat a little farther back, and wrapped my fingers around the rough stone of the waist-high wall. I closed my eyes and let the wind play over my cheeks. It felt different all the way up here, and a relief after the tight curl of the stairway.

"You're missing the view," Erik said, and I opened my eyes and hurried along the walk to join him around the corner of Notre Dame's tower.

I drew in a breath as I gazed out over the city. "Oh, that's wonderful. It never stops being wonderful. I see something new every time."

"An excellent view is like an excellent symphony," Erik said, "always the same and yet always different." He gestured with one gloved hand. "There's the Opera."

"Mm, of course." I leaned on the stone wall, as if the extra few inches would make a difference. There was the Opera Garnier, with its gleaming copper dome and white pillared front, an entire world all contained in one single view. "It's beautiful, even from here."

"Some things can't be shrunk by distance. They stay important even from afar."

"The statue of Apollo on the dome does look just as sure of himself from here as he does up close." I leaned on one elbow and half-turned towards Erik beside me. "You know, I told someone once that I liked the view of the Opera from the top of Notre Dame, and she couldn't understand why I would walk across half of Paris and climb hundreds of steps, to look at the place I had just left."

"Clearly a girl who hears a symphony the same every time," Erik said with obvious disdain. "Who was it?"

I looked back towards the Opera Garnier, the dome glinting in the sunlight, angels shining on the corners of the roof. I twisted at the skirt of my dress. "I forget." I remembered, but it had been Christine. That conversation had been a long time ago now. She'd been gone for over a year. Somehow, we still didn't talk about her.

I pulled my attention back to the present moment. "It's worth climbing the stairs just for the gargoyles," I said, reaching out to pat the head of the nearest. He was an old friend, the horned fellow with his chin in his hands, sticking his tongue out at Paris below.

"That's very familiar of you," a gravelly voice remarked. "Have we been introduced?"

I snatched my hand back, staring at the stone figure.

"I don't really mind," the voice continued, and this time I was sure it was coming from—well, at least from the *direction* of the gargoyle. "Always pleased to meet a pretty girl."

"Don't waste time with him," a new voice behind me said, very low-pitched but with a squeak somehow too. "He's very rude, pointing his tongue at people for centuries. I'm much nicer."

I turned to stare at a bird-headed gargoyle around the corner.

"Ignore him," the gravelly voice advised, coming from the horned gargoyle again. "Featherbrained."

I realized my mouth was open, and closed it. Notre Dame's gargoyles could *not* be talking to me. I didn't believe that sort of thing could happen. Yes, I'd spent parts of my childhood half-believing in a ghost but—and at that thought, it all became clear.

As the bird gargoyle protested, "I have not got feather brains," my gaze darted to Erik. He was leaning back against the tower wall, arms crossed and face perfectly impassive. I stared at him, willing that nonchalance to crack. He held it for a few moments longer, and then very slowly, one corner of his mouth curved up in a smile.

"Aww, she worked it out," the gravelly voice complained, and even knowing it was a trick of ventriloquism, I could still almost believe the gargoyle was talking.

"That's *amazing*."

Erik shrugged, and tugged the brim of his hat. "Just a—"

"—parlor trick, I know." I grinned, and shook my head. "It's never boring with you, Erik."

"Remind me to show you my card tricks some time."

"You don't need card tricks to be interesting," I said, still smiling at him.

"Yes, well..." He looked away, shoulders hunching awkwardly. He was good at so many things, but not at taking a compliment. "So," he said after a moment, with obviously forced heartiness, "have you been coming to Notre Dame for long?"

He wasn't looking at me, but I still tried to smother down my smirk. I was certain he was unaware of the flirtatious undertone lurking in that innocently-meant question. "Since I came to Paris," I answered. "Not often week to week, there's a church closer to our house, but every Easter. I always like it...though of course it's not Saint-Antoine-de-Padoue."

His mask covered his forehead but I could see his eyes crinkle in confusion. "Where?"

"Our church in Leclair. It's hardly bigger than one of Notre Dame's side altars, but it's home." And there was something to be said for a church where you knew the name of every person in the pews.

"What's the choir like?"

I should have known that would be his first question—and now I was conflicted between honesty and loyalty. "...enthusiastic."

"Ah. So it's bad," he said, too matter-of-factly to offend.

"*Enthusiastic*," I repeated stubbornly. "Although, it's not Notre Dame. And the bell tower doesn't have this view," I added, turning my gaze back towards the sweep of rooftops and the ribbon of the Seine far below.

I leaned against the wall, risked a glance directly downward, and quickly turned my gaze out again. I didn't mind the long view, especially with a chest-high wall between me and it, but straight down was still dizzying. "Ever walk on these walls?" I asked, remembering Erik skirting the very edge of the Opera Garnier's roof.

"No," he said, and eyed the wall in front of us speculatively. "But I could."

He shifted his weight as though he was about to attempt it, and I instinctively caught his arm. "No, don't!" The roof of the Opera was bad enough—this wall was half the width of that other one, and twice as far from the ground. "Honestly, Erik, do you *try* to scare me?"

"No." He looked down at my hand on his arm. "Never."

I was suddenly acutely aware of the soft fabric under my fingertips, of the warmth of his arm beneath the sleeve. Somehow the moment seemed far more intimate than similar poses had during the Mardi Gras, with its prescribed dances and crowded rooms, or even than holding his gloved hand on our first walks through the tunnels. Had we ever touched, any other time, when there wasn't an etiquette-dictated or a practical reason for it? I didn't think so.

I relaxed my fingers and drew my hand away. "If you don't want to scare me, kindly stay off of ridiculously high walls."

He subsided backwards and to all appearances relaxed. Yet the moment had shifted, just a little, in some way I couldn't define. It wasn't long before I found myself remembering that Mother was going to be expecting me back soon, if not already, and it was a lot of steps back to the street.

It was much faster, going down the stairs than up, and soon we were back on the ground, back to the little hidden alcove along the side of the cathedral.

"I'd better get back home," I said, straightening my hat and hoping my hair wasn't too wind-blown. Erik, of course, was still perfectly neat. I smiled up at him, and impulsively said, "I'm glad you came today. I missed you."

His eyes widened. "You did?" he said, as though the idea was a complete surprise.

"Of course," I said, feeling shy suddenly. When he said nothing more, I concluded, "Well, see you next week," and turned to go.

I had gone several steps when I heard his voice just beside my ear whisper, "I missed you too."

I looked back over my shoulder at Erik still standing in the doorway, flashed a smile and gave a small wave, which he acknowledged with a slight lifting of his head. Then I turned again and continued down the avenue.

All in all, I was reasonably sure I had not shown the realization that had struck me as I heard that whisper, the sudden knowledge that was vibrating through every part of me, sweet and aching at once.

Was this how it happened to people? You go along day by day, never thinking, never paying attention, and somehow someone becomes more and more important and then one day, for absolutely no good reason, suddenly on that day, you *know*.

I loved him.

Chapter Twenty-Nine

I thought I was perfectly calm and in control—externally at least—by the time I got home. Yet it was only a few minutes before Mother looked up from the chicken she was preparing for Easter supper and asked if everything was all right.

"Of course," I said. "I'm a little tired." It was sort of true. I was feeling dazed, certainly.

She frowned, studying me with too intent scrutiny. "I knew you shouldn't go to vigil and then get up for morning mass."

If I hadn't gone, would I never have realized how I felt? But no— I wouldn't have realized today, but it would have hit me tomorrow or next week. Already my feelings for Erik seemed so much a part of me that I couldn't believe they would have stayed hidden for much longer, whatever the circumstances. "Perhaps," was all I said out loud.

Her frown faded, though she still looked altogether too thoughtful. "How was the mass?"

"Very beautiful." I was torn—part of me wanted to tell her everything, and part of me wanted to hug the secret tight. I settled for a compromise and said, "I saw Erik there." No need to tell the rest.

Just that was surprising enough, as her eyebrows shot up. "Really?"

"He wanted to hear the music." And he missed me, I finished silently, remembering that whisper, his voice beside me. Remembering his smile as he played tricks with the gargoyles, remembering he had, indirectly, said that I was pretty, remembering the warmth of his arm beneath my hand...

"I wouldn't have imagined him at Notre Dame," Mother remarked, gaze returning to her chicken. "Quite the surprising person, your Phantom."

"He's not *my* Phantom," I snapped out. "Why do you always have to say that? It's not true and it's not funny and it's been *years* and— and it's never been true!"

Mother was looking at me again, eyebrows raised again, and why couldn't I have just kept my mouth shut? "Meg..."

"Sorry!" I said hastily, trying to get the apology, the explanation in before any questions. "I'm tired. I'll just go put my bag away." I hurried away upstairs.

My thoughts whirled around and around in circles for the rest of the day, making very little progress by the time I was going to sleep— which really meant lying on my back in bed, one hand closed around my gold necklace, staring up at the ceiling and circling in those same thought whirls.

I wished I had someone I could tell. I loved Mother dearly, but— she wasn't going to like or understand this. I longed fiercely for my sister. I could have told Gabi. We could have talked about this. But Gabi wasn't here, hadn't been for so many years, and I didn't have someone else like her. I might have told Christine, if Christine had been different, if everything had turned out differently—as it was, even if she was here, she'd be the last person in the world I'd want to tell about this.

Possibly the second to last person.

That, maybe, was the heart of the problem. I *had* a friend I could talk to, about so many things. But I couldn't tell my closest friend all about falling in love, when the person I had fallen in love with was *him*.

Could I? I didn't know. That was why I needed to talk to someone, why I needed someone who could help me figure out my confused tangle of feelings. Help me figure out what I was going to do now.

How was I going to go on seeing him practically every day (how had it even become that frequent?) while feeling everything that I was feeling? The uncomplicated enjoyment I'd had in being his friend was suddenly so much more confused, shadowed by this realization that I felt something I had never meant to feel. That I wanted something I didn't intend to want. And that I couldn't have.

Maybe I should stop seeing him. But how would I even do that? Leave the Opera—and go where? Stay at the Opera, but tell him I couldn't talk to him anymore? I couldn't even begin to imagine having that conversation. How could he take it as anything but a rejection?

Unless I told him the truth. But how could I? He was surprised that I missed him; how could I possibly tell him that I *loved* him?

I understood now. I understood Erik's masks. I understood about needing a mask to hide away the part of yourself so personal, so important, that you can't stand someone else seeing it. Can't stand having them mock or shrink away or maybe worst of all…just not understand. Or have them feel nothing but pity.

He would be kind, and awkward, and probably baffled, and I could not imagine anything more painful than hearing Erik's stumbling attempts to explain why he didn't feel that way about me, couldn't feel that way about me, was never going to feel that way—not about me. About Christine, yes, of course about Christine. About beautiful Christine who was so much more than pretty, about talented, charming Christine who drew every eye, who attracted everyone's attention, who everyone, absolutely everyone, felt strongly about, one way or another. And who the Phantom loved so very much.

But he was never going to feel that way about me.

So, telling him—not an option.

Ending our friendship—the mere thought made my gut clench and my heart ache. Not an option either.

Go on as we had been, try to pretend nothing had changed? A terrible option. But the only one even faintly possible.

The last few days of the Easter holiday passed (interminably, but they did pass) and finally Tuesday morning dawned. For a man who disliked crowds and preferred solitude, Erik was remarkably pleased when the Opera Garnier returned to its customary bustle. He had hardly observed the difference last year. But by now, *she* had been gone for 406 days, seven hours, and he was glad to see the rest of the inhabitants of his world return. The managers came striding into their office, the scenechangers resumed their usual seats backstage, the chorus' practice room filled with the sounds of warming-up, flocks of ballet girls flew chattering through the halls, and the Phantom wandered about in the midst of it all—hidden, of course, in secret passages and behind mirrors, listening.

He observed the ballet's morning practice, sitting cross-legged behind one of the mirrors. Madame Thibault was particularly scathing, but he was almost sure that was her way of saying she had missed everyone over the intervening week. She was like that.

He followed the corps de ballet back to their changing rooms, then paced around in a hidden passage alongside the hallway—because really, he had to have standards about just what he would spy on, or what would that make him?

Meg finally emerged in a pack of girls and he briefly despaired of separating her out of the group. *Léon* no doubt would just go plunge into the crowd if he was here—which he wasn't—but that was obviously not an option for him.

Then Meg remembered she had forgotten a scarf, went back into the room and emerged again just when the corridor was empty—enabling Erik to step 'through' a mirror and offer a cheerful, "Good morning."

She jumped more than usual—she had begun to take his sudden arrivals without so much as a blink, in fact—and responded with, "Oh. Good morning."

"Did you have a pleasant holiday?" he asked, because surely that was what one asked. He'd heard the question tossed about by other people at least a dozen times this morning.

"Yes…yes, it was very nice," she said, which sounded fine but there was something about the way she was standing—and her gaze was flicking over his shoulder. Not like she saw someone there, she'd warn him about that, but just like she was looking around to find someone else.

Maybe she wanted to go off with the ballet girls, and if she did—well, he wasn't going to stop her, if she'd prefer—but he could at least get a bid in. "With everyone back the managers will be wanting new music. I thought I should send a piece in—maybe you could help me choose? If you're not busy."

"I—well. The girls were talking about…we didn't exactly have plans though…" She was twisting at one fold of her skirt and not quite meeting his eyes which was not normal and he didn't understand why.

He rubbed one palm against the front of his jacket, uneasy. Maybe he shouldn't have ambushed her at Easter mass. Was that how she saw it, an ambush? It wasn't supposed to be, it was a friendly, semi-chance (not very) meeting and she had seemed perfectly pleased on Sunday. "Of course, if you have plans…" Foolish, she had just said she didn't have plans. "I mean, something else you'd rather…"

"No," she said with a sudden lifting of her chin and almost disconcertingly direct gaze. "No, I'd be glad to help you choose music for the Company."

"Ah. Excellent." He was not quite sure why he'd just won this discussion, but he wouldn't argue about it.

He ushered her ahead of him through the hidden door and they began the walk down below. Meg was uncharacteristically quiet, enough so that finally, in desperation, he asked, "Is everything all right?"

She jumped again and said, "Yes, of course. Madame Thibault was especially severe today but other than that."

Maybe that was it. He didn't think Madame Thibault had singled Meg out especially, but maybe she felt that way. "I think it's how she shows she cares."

That might have deserved a laugh, but she did at least smile. "I guess people can be funny about that."

This was not going to be easy. I had half-thought that maybe I ought not to see Erik Tuesday, maybe I should take some time—I had not considered that it isn't so easy to avoid someone who steps out of walls.

And it was all confusing anyway, because even as I was thinking I shouldn't see him, I was so *happy* to see him, the same lifting happiness I had been feeling every time he did that appearing trick, only suddenly I was seeing it in a new light, was realizing all it meant to me—and not to him.

I thought I should make an excuse and leave. But with him right in front of me, it was much harder to do the logical thing. And besides, if I was going to carry on as his friend, what kind of precedent would that set? Better to confront this face-on, right in the eyes. Or at least, only slightly to the left of his brilliant green eyes.

Once we got down to his apartments, I promised myself I was going to think about *music*. That's why I was here. To help choose music for the Opera Company.

I looked at musical scores and discussed songs and it was…somewhat distracting. We couldn't seem to settle on anything, and I'm not sure which of us was being too particular. Usually it was him, but today, it could have been me.

"I don't know, I think we've looked at everything here," Erik said, leaning back on one of the couches.

"Have you got any others? Or do you want to write a new piece?" I was pacing near the fireplace, still considering the score in my hand. It didn't feel *quite* right.

Erik rubbed the back of his neck. "I do have more scores; there's another drawer—right next to you, that pale gray stone above the fireplace, the one with the crack. Just tap it twice."

I complied, and the stone emerged a half-inch, revealing a narrow gap. I got my fingertips into it, pulled...and found myself looking at more money than I had ever seen in my life. An untidy mound of banknotes, banknotes with enormous numbers on them, nearly filled the drawer.

I couldn't help reaching in. "Erik..." I turned to him, holding up a sheaf of bills in mute query.

He glanced over. "Oh. Wrong stone."

I stared at him, at that calm expression. "Wrong stone? I stumble onto a fortune and you say *wrong stone?*"

"Well, it is," Erik said in reasonable tones. "You were looking for music. That drawer must be behind the stone two to the left. I always mix those up."

I felt breathless. "You always—you have a fortune in money sitting around and you forget which drawer you—where did it even come—oh, your salary, that's where that's going?"

"Yes, exactly," he said, just as though I wasn't babbling.

"Yes," I echoed. "Exactly." I looked into the drawer again, as though I had been mistaken about the sheer amount of money in there. I wasn't. Just the small fraction in my hand was more money than I'd earned in the last five years. And he had it all just...sitting here. It was baffling, and I tried to find some sort of explanation. Maybe...he was saving for something? "You know," I said carefully, "I always wondered about that salary. I wondered what a ghost could spend money on."

Erik shrugged. "Even a ghost has to eat. This one does, anyway. And sometimes I need a new shirt." He raised the stack of paper he was holding. "I go through a lot of paper too."

"But no one spends 20,000 francs a month on paper." I looked again at the stack of bills in my hand. "And obviously most of it is still sitting here."

"I save a lot of money not paying rent."

I couldn't help feeling that he was missing the point. If I wanted an answer to my question, I was going to have to actually *ask* it. "But if you don't *spend* 20,000 francs a month…why do you ask the Opera Company to pay it?" Why did he provoke the management and outrage the Company and bring a whole lot of trouble on himself for money he wasn't going to *use*?

His gaze shifted away and he straightened a stack of papers, squaring the corners. I thought he wasn't going to answer, but after a long moment he said, "People take seriously something that costs a lot of money. A free or inexpensive ghost…that's just a joke. One who demands a large salary—and gets it—that builds the mystique. And," he added, tone lightening, "I suppose there's a certain element of doing it because I can."

"Naturally." Erik the prankster. A very expensive prank. I put the money back into the drawer and closed it again, watching the stone fit seamlessly back into the wall. "So you must leave the opera house sometimes. Besides special excursions for Easter music. It must be fairly regular, if you go buy shirts and paper."

"Now and then. On dark evenings, with a low hat and a dark cloak."

Naturally. "Does that actually hide the mask from anyone?" I asked, genuinely curious.

"Sometimes," he said in defensive tones. Then he sighed. "No. Never. But I don't have a lot of options."

Maybe not, but this didn't seem like a good option to choose. "Did you ever consider just walking into a shop on a sunny Sunday afternoon? If you didn't make a big production out of it, who would even blink?"

"You must live in a very pleasant world," Erik said dryly.

"Don't patronize me," I said, mostly automatically. I was too interested in my own idea to really be annoyed. "I'm serious. If you didn't try to hide, no one would think anything was being hidden."

"That's circular."

"*Yes*, it is, that's the point. It doesn't *have* to be this way." Somehow, suddenly, this seemed very important, vital that he understood this. That he see that things could be different, that there could be…all sorts of possibilities for his life.

"It does," Erik said simply. Not angrily, not defensively. He just…said it. "It does have to be this way."

That deflated me more than an argument might have done. Especially because I was afraid to examine why I suddenly wanted him to understand all this. I had been trying hard not to think about…that. "Two stones to the right, you said? For more music?"

"To the left," he corrected.

"Of course."

I found the other drawer without incident—I was growing accustomed to hidden drawers by now—and lifted out an untidy stack of musical scores. Erik may have immediately begun critically examining these new options. I scanned through at least three without taking in anything at all. This might have gone on, but with the fourth score I turned over, I found a song.

I began to read the lyrics, only half paying attention at first, then realized they were exceedingly apropos to what I'd already been thinking about. It was a song about hiding in shadows, watching behind walls. For a verse, it was what I might have expected, about safety in darkness and solitude.

Then the song took a turn, began to tell about sunlight on the river, about laughter in the crowds. It became a celebration of light and life and camaraderie, about the effortless, unthinking way people went about their ordinary lives. It became a song of longing for the warmth of sunlight, for a welcoming glance, for the opportunity to belong, so completely and easily that you don't notice it anymore.

I don't ask for love. I don't dream of glory. But just to walk down the street without stares—to be just one man in the crowd—is a gift beyond my grasp.

In the final verse, the song ended where it had begun, in darkness.

"Did you find something?"

My head jerked up and I struggled to refocus my eyes away from the words and onto Erik across the room, looking at me with a quizzical expression. "Did I—what?"

He gestured towards the paper in my hand. "You've been looking at that for a couple of minutes. Do you think—"

"No. I did think for a minute—but no, it's not right." Before he could ask to see what it was, I slipped the score into the middle of the stack in front of me. There was so much longing, so much vulnerability—I wasn't sure he'd like me reading this song. I was sure he wouldn't want to share it with the Opera Company.

But I couldn't stop thinking about it. I had always guessed, supposed, imagined…it had never seemed to me that this life could be what Erik wanted. If he truly just wanted to be left alone, why involve himself with the Opera Company at all? For the sake of a good seat at the performances?

And all these musical scores, these ones he never, ever used when he was actually playing…they didn't make sense either.

I kept my gaze on my hands as I straightened up yet another stack of papers, tried to think of the most careful way to ask this. "I was just thinking, if you have everything memorized…and you don't organize the scores anyway…why even write the music down?"

There was a long pause, and the quality of Erik's silence made me think that he was genuinely searching for an answer, not trying to come up with a way to dodge the question. "Habit, I suppose," he said finally, which was not much of an answer after all and made me wonder if he knew the reason himself.

I didn't say more, but it seemed to me that a man who didn't need music in front of him to play it could only have one reason for writing it down—so that someone else could read it. As far as I knew, until he started selling music to the Opera Company, he had not been showing his music to anyone, except me. He probably would have denied wanting to. But I wondered. Because all around me were stacks and stacks of written music.

Erik was such a mass of paradoxes. He said he didn't want to share his music, yet he wrote it down. He said he didn't get on with religion, but he had angels on his wall. He claimed he didn't like the light, but his paintings were full of sunshine.

I didn't think he was lying to me. He was just…complicated.

Erik was not having a good period with regard to information-gathering. He could find no sign that Mifroid was at the Opera again. With no idea of Mifroid's plans, he could make no counter-plans, which was distinctly frustrating.

He could not manage to find out much at all about Léon either. Or rather, nothing very interesting. He was exactly what he seemed to be, a handsome, wealthy young man with no pressing need to do anything besides attend elegant soirees and run after ballet girls. He was a type who ought to have been done away with several revolutions ago, and yet they never disappeared. Erik found his sort intensely irritating, young men who had had absolutely everything handed to them from the moment of their birth, who did nothing with it and didn't even appreciate it.

Those were not, however, reasons that he could present to Meg as sufficient rationale for cutting ties with Léon. Besides the fact that they likely wouldn't carry sufficient weight, he'd have to explain why and how he had been investigating Léon. That was an explanation he was only prepared to attempt if he had something very serious to convey as a result of said investigation, serious enough to warrant it—and to distract Meg from the way he'd obtained the information.

And Meg. He could not work out what was happening with Meg. She seemed both oddly distracted and intent, sometimes at intervals, sometimes even at the same time. She scarcely ever turned down an invitation, and yet she often hesitated about it first. He'd catch her studying him, but then she'd look away and have nothing much to volunteer when he asked what she was thinking about. She didn't seem unhappy, but she did seem to have something on her mind that she wasn't sharing with him.

It was all so…complicated.

In some ways it had been less complicated with *her*. But that simple, straightforward tragedy that could only end in disaster had ended in the predicted disaster 409 days, seventeen hours ago, and now he had much more confusing, complicated business to be dealt with. The heroes of operas never seemed to have to deal with new complications after their stories ended.

Chapter Thirty

E rik didn't seem to suspect how I felt about him. Mother, on the other hand, was harder to fool. It was my own fault; I was walking around distracted, spending more time in my room thinking, of course she was going to notice something was happening.

I kept telling myself to pay attention when I was around Mother, to be *normal*. But I couldn't help retreating into my own thoughts, when those thoughts were so loud, so confusing, so deeply absorbing.

I was lying on my bed, toying with my necklace and gazing up at the ceiling Sunday morning after mass when Mother came knocking at my half-open door.

I started to sit up. "Is it time to eat already? Do you need me to help cook?" That was good, wasn't it? Nice and normal, offering to be useful.

"No, I wanted to talk to you," Mother said, sitting down on the foot of my bed.

That wasn't normal. I drew my feet up out of her way, tucking them beneath me as I sat against the headboard. "What about?" I asked, trying to make my voice bright, unconcerned, relaxed.

She was gazing at me with a searching expression and I knew I wasn't fooling her. "I'm not sure. But something is upsetting you."

I looked away. "No. Not really." I drew my knees up tighter, wrapped my arms around my ankles. It wasn't *upsetting* me, exactly.

It was…confusing me. It was filling me up with all sorts of conflicting feelings.

"You can tell me anything," Mother said, voice soft. "Any trouble you're in, any problem you're having. If anyone is—"

"No one's hurting me, Mother, I'm fine," I interrupted. Of course she'd go to that, of course she'd think I was under threat or something.

Her lips tightened slightly. "I wasn't thinking that precisely. Only that something is on your mind."

I said nothing. I felt as though if I said anything at all, she'd guess everything.

"Well." She rose to her feet. "Perhaps you'll feel you want to tell me another day. I'll always be willing to listen."

I held on until she was within a step of the doorway, her back to me, and then suddenly it spilled out of me. "I'm in love with Erik."

Mother stopped, standing still for at least a full breath, if I hadn't been holding mine, her face hidden. When she turned back around her expression was quite impassive. "I thought it might be something like that," she said, sitting down again.

I stared at her, incredulous. "You thought it might be *something like that*?" How could she have thought that, when it had been such a shock to me?

She inclined her head slightly. "You go around smiling at odd moments, then at others you look as sad as though you'd lost your dearest friend, and all the time your thoughts are clearly not on whatever is front of you." A pause, then she added, "I did think it might be Léon."

"Léon," I said blankly. Léon was fun, and I was very fond of him really, and he was probably the sort of person I should have fallen in love with, but…but there was no *magic*. "No. No, it's…it's Erik." I looked down at my hands again. "Are you angry?" I whispered. She had been angry over everything else relating to Erik, it seemed, and surely this was worst of all.

It felt like a long, long pause before she answered, words very careful. "I am concerned. About where this might lead you. What you might do."

That felt more like a stable ground to fight on. "Oh Mother, really, I'm not going to lose my head." I turned pink suddenly. "Or...or anything else." I barreled on. "I mean, I couldn't even if I wanted to. And I don't. But I couldn't because he certainly doesn't—I mean, I don't think he would—but anyway, it's impossible."

It seemed virtually incomprehensible too, but somehow Mother emerged from all that with the conclusion, "You haven't told him."

I squeezed my eyes shut for a moment. "No."

She let out a slow breath, as though relieved for all she had seemed so calm. "Well. That is very sensible. Obviously there is no future in this, considering how entirely unsuitable he is and I'm glad you realize it."

I stared at her, taking those words in. It wasn't that I didn't realize it. I *knew* he was about as far from a conventional romantic prospect as I could get. And yet...I felt a hot bubble of resentment forming in the pit of my stomach. "Why, exactly? Why is he so unsuitable?"

It was a rare time when I took my mother by surprise. "Meg...he's the Phantom of the Opera."

"No. He's Erik."

"They're the same person."

"No," I insisted, shaking my head. "They're not." Even though I couldn't begin to articulate what I could only feel.

"Meg..."

"You don't understand," I said helplessly, knowing that I was falling back on the last defense of rebellious children the world over. "You don't know him like I do."

"I daresay I know him well enough. Well enough to know that you have not chosen an easy man to fall in love with."

"I didn't *choose* to fall in love with him," I protested, stomach tight and eyes burning. "I didn't plan this!"

Her lips pressed tightly together. "That's as may be. But surely you can see there are certain...drawbacks."

"His face isn't nearly as bad as Christine said."

"I didn't mean his face. If that doesn't bother you—then I don't suppose that's really anyone else's business. But I assume you want a life with family, friends…*sunlight*."

That seemed like an unfair jab. "What makes you think Erik doesn't want all that too?" I demanded.

"I don't know what he wants; all I know is what kind of life he's currently living, underneath an opera house, alone. If you were to join his life—surely you don't intend—"

"No, of course not!" I loved it below the Opera. I loved Erik. But limit my world to a few rooms underground? No. "I'm not planning to live underground, I'm—" I broke off. I closed my eyes, inhaled slowly. "I'm not planning anything. You want to know what I would imagine my life with Erik to be like. But you must see—it's all irrelevant. It doesn't matter what life with Erik would be, whether it could be made to work somehow, whether it would be hell or heaven. He *doesn't love me*. He's never going to. There's no point worrying about how I could spend my life with a man who doesn't want to spend his with me."

It was no good imagining a *pax de deux* for a partner who doesn't want to dance with you.

"Are you so sure?" Mother asked, voice gentle. "Are you so sure he could never—"

"He loves *Christine*."

"Christine is gone."

"No." I shook my head. "No, she isn't. Not for Erik."

"It's been more than a year, hasn't it? He must have begun to—"

"What, move on?" I could hear the bitterness in my words, felt a kind of wild ache in my chest. "No. Not at all. Know how I know?"

"Meg…" she said, a soothing tone in her voice. Maybe she heard the rising hysteria in mine.

"I've thought about this a lot, you see. I *know*. Three things." I held up my fingers, for emphasis. "He never laughs. We have conversations that should make him laugh but he doesn't, ever. He never sings. He's finally writing music again, but singing? No. And he never says Christine's name. Not once, not in all this time."

"Meg, he knows that Christine is gone."

"No, he doesn't," I said, rubbed my eyes. "And besides…after falling in love with beautiful, talented Christine, why should he ever be interested in me?"

"That is ridiculous," Mother said sharply. "There is absolutely no reason why he shouldn't fall in love with you."

"You don't want him to!"

Mother hesitated, then said, "I don't want you to make a choice which you will later regret. But I also do not want you to ever believe that you are not just as good as anyone else. Christine Daaé included."

I sighed and said, "Yes, Mother." But I didn't believe it.

She was biased. No one else at the Opera, Erik included, would have agreed. Oh, maybe they wouldn't have *said* that Christine was more beautiful, more vital, more talented, but it was all perfectly clear. People I had known for years very comfortably referred to me as 'Christine's friend,' even after she had been gone for a year.

This seemed doubly terrible, as the more time that passed, the more clear it became that she'd never considered me as close a friend as I had. I would have written to her, long ago, if I'd been the one to leave Paris.

From the way Mother's brow furrowed, I don't think she believed me any more than I believed her. But what she said was, "And what are you going to do about Erik?"

"Nothing," I said in a low voice. "There's nothing to do. I'm his friend, and that—is enough."

I don't think she believed that either. And I can't blame her. It wasn't true.

Chapter Thirty-One

In the days after Easter, life somehow, as it always does, went on. I kept seeing Léon, because—well, why not? He still made me laugh. And there was little chance that he was going to fall in love with me either; we both knew exactly what kind of future was available to a couple like us, and what kind wasn't.

I kept seeing Erik, and tried to grow accustomed to the happy ache I felt around him.

And of course life for the Opera went on too, quite as usual for a week or so. Until the day it wasn't. It began innocuously enough, with a Tuesday afternoon rehearsal that saw all the ballet girls grouped backstage, stretching to warm up. Or most of us.

Madame Thibault cast a sharp eye over the crowd, but didn't focus on anyone. The reason became apparent when she sighed and said, "Has anyone the slightest idea where Mademoiselle Jammes has betaken herself? We are due to rehearse in a mere ten minutes."

"She's probably with La Carlotta," I remarked, barely glancing up from the book I had propped open in front of me as I rolled my shoulders. It was where Jammes could most often be found.

"Very likely," Madame Thibault agreed. "Go and fetch her, Mademoiselle Giry. Quickly."

I managed not to sigh audibly, but I heartily wished I'd kept my mouth shut. Any girl here could have said the same thing, and been handed this same thankless task. I rose to my feet, tucking my book under one arm. Adalisa cast me a sympathetic glance as I passed her.

I hurried through the corridors to Carlotta's dressing room. The door was half-open, revealing the diva holding court within. Carlotta sat at her vanity table, with three singers plus Jammes clustered around her. I halted in the doorway, hoping I could catch Jammes' attention without needing to interrupt whatever Carlotta was holding forth on.

Jammes, of course, could not be so cooperative as to meet my eye, and finally I rapped my knuckles against the open door.

Carlotta turned very slowly, stared at me, and paused just slightly too long before saying, "Yes, what is it, little Mademoiselle Giry?"

My fingers clenched on my book but I kept my voice even. "Madame Thibault is looking for Jammes. We're due on stage shortly."

"I *know* the schedule, Meg," Jammes said with an elaborate roll of her eyes and no move to rise from her low seat near Carlotta. "I'll be there."

Madame Thibault might not be happy with me if I came back without Jammes, but she'd be even less happy with Jammes—so I'd risk it. "Very well." I turned to go. If I walked quickly back to my place, maybe I'd be able to finish this chapter before we went on after all. I only had another page.

"Why, Mademoiselle Giry," Carlotta said loudly, "are you reading a book? Is it interesting?"

I hesitated, said, "Yes," and should have just kept walking, but politeness is a hard habit to break. And maybe, just possibly, it could be a friendly overture? I half-turned back, held up my book. "*Frankenstein* by Mary Shelley. A French translation, I mean."

One of the singers, whose name I couldn't place, exclaimed, "But isn't that a terribly macabre tale? All about dead bodies and nastiness like that?"

"It's actually very good," I said, protective of my book. "And no darker than Monsieur Poe."

Carlotta let out a peal of laughter that was as grating as her singing. "Why, Mademoiselle Giry, I had no idea you were such a scholar! You had best be careful. Men find that a *very* unattractive quality."

A man had loaned it to me, the only one who mattered, so this was hardly an effective jab. "Not all of them," I said coolly.

Carlotta's eyes narrowed. "Yes," she said, voice silky, "but what does that charming young Monsieur de Troyes think about such habits?"

The heat on my cheeks suggested I hadn't been quite accurate about no one else mattering. Léon didn't matter *as much*, but I still felt suddenly defenseless when I had him flung at me. Maybe because he had given every indication of viewing my ability to read as a rather odd trick. "That's hardly—"

The singer who had called *Frankenstein* macabre interrupted me with a shriek, pointing towards Carlotta's table. A big spider was squatting there, presumably having just scurried out from somewhere.

I should have taken advantage of the distraction to walk away. Instead I took two steps forward, leaned over the table to look at the spider. I had had an amateur interest in spiders for years. This one's body was a good half-centimeter long with legs extending well beyond that, but I could tell from the shape and markings that it wasn't a type carrying dangerous venom.

"I think it's harmless," I announced, reaching for a handkerchief tucked into my cloak pocket. There was a window just down the corridor, easy enough to drop a spider out onto the ledge. "Just give me a moment and I'll—"

Carlotta reached out, snatched my heavy copy of *Frankenstein*, and dropped it right on top of the spider with a thud.

She might have jabbed the book into my gut for the way I felt.

"Better safe than sorry," Carlotta said, voice altogether too warm and sweet for someone who'd just murdered a creature that had never hurt her. "And one can't be too careful. Now I believe we're all due onstage soon, no?"

Carlotta, Jammes and all the rest swept out while I was still staring at the gilt writing on the leather-bound *Frankenstein*. I had been thinking of it quite easily as my book, the book I was reading, but now it was suddenly, clearly, *Erik's book* again. And how was I going to explain this?

Biting my lower lip, I lifted the book up with careful fingers on two corners, and peered at the underside. For such a small creature, the spider had had a surprising amount of guts. Not to mention crumpled legs. I winced and looked away—and my gaze landed on Carlotta's water glass, a cut-crystal affair half full of clear water, left sitting on her table.

I looked back at the dead spider, speculatively this time. I shouldn't...but it was her own fault, really. And maybe it made a difference that I'd just been thinking how much I'd like something awful to happen to smug, unfeeling, self-absorbed Victor Frankenstein.

Gritting my teeth and trying not to look too closely, I used my handkerchief to brush the remains of the spider right into Carlotta's water glass. Drink well, Signora.

I got back to the rest of the ballet girls before we were due to rehearse, if not by much. Madame Thibault gave me a sharp look but nothing more. Jammes was already among the girls; I carefully did not look at her.

Our dancing went well enough, and then we all wound up backstage again while Carlotta sailed out to sing an aria. I should have been stretching like the girls around me, but instead I picked up my book again, scrubbed at the smeared place on the back with my handkerchief. I didn't accomplish much.

I wasn't paying attention to Carlotta, until she stopped mid-aria, coughed dramatically, and ordered one of her ever-present maids to go fetch her water glass.

My head snapped up at that, and I watched Carlotta at center stage, heart suddenly beating harder. She could have waited until she got back to her dressing room. Even now her maid might fetch her a different glass. Or the maid might notice the spider before bringing the glass out. Anything might happen to prevent a public spectacle.

But nothing did. The maid came rushing back, hurried and anxious-looking and I just knew she hadn't looked closely at the glass.

She handed it to Carlotta, who swept it up towards her lips…and let out an almighty shriek.

I ducked my head, fighting the urge to laugh, and watched through my bangs as Carlotta went on shrieking. She flung the glass down, where it shattered on the plank stage.

She started out in Italian. By the time a herd of people had converged around her, she switched to French. "A *spider*! There was a *spider* in my water!"

At least half of the solicitous people clustered around suddenly went pushing backwards again, as though they expected the spider to rise up out of the shattered glass and puddle of water to leap at them.

It was all so utterly ridiculous that I couldn't contain the fit of giggles creeping up my throat. Luckily the crowd around me was reacting as much with laughter as with horror, so I blended in well enough. I wasn't the only one who wasn't fond of La Carlotta.

Those who were went on clustering around her, waving their hands or proffering handkerchiefs or doing other equally pointless things. Even the managers came rushing up from their seats in the front row. Carlotta was back to screeching in Italian.

"If we've had enough disturbance," Moncharmin said, raising his voice to be heard, "can't we get back to the rehearsal? I'm not paying overtime if this goes long."

Carlotta cast a fiery gaze at him, visibly inhaling deeply for what would no doubt be a renewed tirade.

Before she could begin, Ricard stepped into the fray, glaring quite fiercely at his business partner. "How can you think of money all the time? It is clear that Signora Carlotta cannot go on after an emotional shock like this!"

An audible sigh rose around me, while I bit back another laugh. Signora Carlotta couldn't go on if the weather was bad, if her shoes hurt, if anyone looked at her crossly—and sometimes, just because it was Tuesday.

Moncharmin was turning red. "What do you want to do, cancel tonight's performance because of a *spider*?"

"No," Carlotta snapped before Ricard could speak again, "we will cancel because *I* am being targeted for vicious attacks! A dead spider did not crawl into my glass by itself!"

Moncharmin threw up his hands. "Fine! We'll mount a great investigation into your attack by spider and root out the guilty party!"

Carlotta drew herself up, nose haughtily in the air. "That will not be necessary. I know who is responsible."

My bubble of laughter popped. But it was all right, really it was. I'd just open my eyes wide and swear I had *no idea* what could have happened and after all, anyone might have gone into Carlotta's room after I left it...

"Everyone knows who is responsible," Ricard said, brows pulled low over his eyes. "The Phantom of the Opera, of course!"

Carlotta turned her head to look at him, eyes widening for an instant in what I guessed was surprise—and then she smiled. "Yes. Quite obviously the Phantom is behind this."

And I just felt silly. Of course they'd blame Erik. Carlotta would probably find a way to get me back later, but she wouldn't miss a chance to get the Phantom now. But that was all right too. Everything was blamed on the Phantom, so what was one more thing?

Moncharmin tugged on his collar. "Yes, well—I'm sure it was simply a harmless prank..."

"A harmless prank?" Carlotta said in her tones of greatest outrage. "To put a venomous spider into my drink? I might have been poisoned! I might have been *killed*!"

I was nearly certain the spider hadn't been dangerously venomous, and also suspected that you couldn't actually poison someone that way. That didn't seem to matter to Carlotta.

It didn't seem to matter to Ricard either. "Signora Carlotta is right—we cannot simply ignore this," he fired at Moncharmin with surprising force. "I have had enough of you sacrificing artistry to a madman skulking in the basement, just because he gave you a few ideas for how to save money!"

"I still say that shows a very willing spirit," Moncharmin countered, but not convincingly. Perhaps he was as surprised as anyone by the sudden spirit Ricard was showing. "And he offers so much artistic advice too, you know…"

"And we do not need artistic direction from a crazed murderer! I've stood by and let it all pass, but I will not do it anymore. If you won't take steps to stop the Phantom, I will." Ricard nodded once, decisively, then turned to Carlotta and extended one arm. "Signora, may I see you to your dressing room? Obviously you cannot continue rehearsal after this."

"But tonight's show—!" Moncharmin said in a strained voice.

They both ignored him. Carlotta took Ricard's arm and they proceeded off the stage, Carlotta's devotees following in a wave behind them.

"I suppose that will be all for rehearsal today," Madame Thibault announced in resigned tones. "You may go early."

There were exclamations of delight all around me as the girls scrambled to their feet to rush off to the changing room.

I got up slowly from my place and walked away from the auditorium with heavy steps. I took a back corridor, a service one, not the one most of the girls took. I needed a few moments without distractions from their laughter and chatter.

I had given in to a stupid impulse to bait Carlotta, and the result was worse than if I had been caught myself. The things they might do to Erik were much worse than what they might do to me.

For all that he loomed very large in my thoughts just then, I was still taken by surprise when he stepped out of a shadow just ahead of me, between two of the crates lining the wall. If he felt the sense of impending dread I did, it wasn't on his face or in his voice when he said, "That was brilliant, wasn't it?"

"What was?" I asked, keeping my voice calm despite my suddenly racing heart. Which, if I was honest with myself, wasn't beating fast purely from surprise.

I was also acutely conscious that I was still wearing my dance costume, the short skirt and sleeveless top that showed so much more than my proper dresses. I had stopped being self-conscious about it in general years ago, had stopped worrying about Erik seeing me in it after our first few meetings. Until recently.

"Ricard was brilliant," Erik said, with no sign of noticing my unease, waving a hand in the general direction of the auditorium. "He finally stood up to Moncharmin. He's been trying a little harder lately, but I was beginning to think he'd never find the nerve to really do something."

I stared at him, trying to fathom how an event filling me with guilt and dread and amorphous worries could be making him look pleased and amused. "He stood up to him for the purpose of hunting for *you*."

"Yes, well, it's not like he'll find me," Erik said with another wave, dismissive this time as he wiped that possibility out of the script. "He doesn't have *that* much nerve. Or capability."

"Yes, but...I mean..." I wanted to believe him. I wanted to believe that he really was that good, and that I shouldn't worry, and that everything was fine. I certainly believed he was much smarter than Ricard. But I did worry.

"And Carlotta, that was fairly brilliant too," Erik went on, all worry ignored. "I haven't seen her that upset in months. Must've been a big spider."

He was smiling, while guilt was making my throat tight. If Ricard *did* accomplish anything, if this really did make trouble... "It's my fault," I said in a low voice, even though I didn't have to, even though he probably never would have known. But I knew, and I didn't want to keep thinking of it when I looked at him.

His eyebrow quirked up. "What is?"

I waved a hand vaguely. "This. All of this." I groaned, sat down on a nearby crate lining the corridor. "I dumped the spider in Carlotta's water."

"Did you really?" He sounded positively delighted by the idea.

"It's not a good thing!"

He nodded wisely, visibly trying to smooth the amusement off his face. "Yes, of course, not at all. It's possible I've been a bad influence on you." The amusement did fade then. "Maybe you shouldn't mention this to your mother. She probably wouldn't—"

"But if everything goes horribly, awfully wrong, it's going to be my fault!"

He just shrugged. "Can't we say it's Carlotta's fault? I assume she provoked you." He sat on an opposite crate, one knee drawn up, and looked at me as though he expected to hear a story.

I stared at him, not sure whether to be relieved or profoundly irritated. "You're really not going to be angry with me about this, are you?"

"No," he agreed. "So what did Carlotta do?"

I gave up. "She smashed the spider." I held up the stained copy of *Frankenstein*. "Using your book."

He winced, took it from me to look at the smear. "So, clearly she deserved it."

I smiled a little wanly. "I thought so."

"What do you think of it?"

"The stain?"

"No, the book."

"Oh." I had been full of opinions before all of this occupied my mind, and now I scrambled to come up with them again. "I hate Victor."

"Oh, definitely," Erik said with a nod. "Plainly a man who would smash a spider without a second thought."

"No," I countered, "he'd smash it, and then spend pages detailing what a painful ordeal it was for *him*."

Erik positively grinned, green eyes lighting up. "You're right, that's exactly what he'd do!"

I smiled back, relieved and happy and aching a little bit too. I couldn't help being pleased when he smiled at me like that. Even though my life would surely be easier if he made it harder to love him.

Excerpt from the Private Notebook of Jean Mifroid, Commissaire of Police

24 April, 1882

Support at last. Those bunglers at the Opera have finally come seeking help to catch OG. Should have been here months ago. Prefect refuses to even hear of pursuing case at the Opera now. Claims I am too narrow-focused. Still, with manager approval I can finally search openly, if unofficially. And it does free my hands in some ways, to act as is necessary. I will find this Opera Ghost and see justice.

Erik wasn't sure how to feel about it when Commissaire Mifroid came striding boldly into the Opera Garnier. It was like watching a lion come in the front door of his home—but at least that meant he knew where the lion was.

And evidently they still hadn't learned that discussing plans to capture the Phantom while at the Opera was decidedly foolish.

Ever since Moncharmin and Ricard had come here they'd been doing that. They ought to have learned better the night of their first gala performance, the night the chandelier came down and *she* left. 415 days, eleven hours ago.

Erik settled down behind the wall as Moncharmin and Ricard welcomed Mifroid into their office, and listened to the scraping of chairs as they took their places. It was all unpleasantly familiar. He had spent so much time in the past eavesdropping on the management. Things had been so peaceful lately, he hadn't felt the same need.

"The problem is as it has always been, gentlemen," Mifroid began. "How to locate the Phantom."

"You've tried watching Box Five," Moncharmin pointed out. "That's never worked."

Erik smirked. No, it really hadn't.

"That was more a demonstration of intent than an actual trap. We need to think larger," Mifroid said. "He goes to Box Five during performances, yes, but where is he the rest of the time? He appears at random times and places all over this opera house. But what is his base of operations? That is what we need to find."

"But…what does that mean?" Ricard said, sounding as confused as the words suggested. "So he comes to the Opera at different times, that doesn't mean…"

"Not comes," Mifroid interrupted. "I believe he *stays*. I have reason to believe he does not engage the world outside of this Opera. This is where he is. This is where he remains. This is where we find him."

What reason to believe? What information did Mifroid have? Erik would have given quite a bit to know that—and where it had come from. Mardi Gras had demonstrated that Mifroid suspected something about his face. Had he surmised the rest from that, or did he have solid sources? Just like at the party, none of the possible sources made sense. *She* was gone, this wasn't how the Daroga would handle things, and Meg was— well, obviously out of the question.

"But how do you expect to find him here?" Moncharmin demanded. "He climbs about inside the walls and has secret doors all over the place. How do you find a man under those circumstances?"

"We need to learn more of what he knows. Have you had any conversation with the architect, Garnier?" Mifroid asked, voice betraying a new level of tension. More, possibly, than the so-professional commissaire had shown before. "He has to know there are secret passages all over the building. It's his design, after all."

Ricard sighed deeply. "We contacted him, practically when we first arrived. Both previous managers contacted him. Monsieur Garnier's unchanging statement is that there are no secret passages and no hidden doors."

"The man is very consistent," Mifroid said, almost a growl. "He sent me the same message in response to my inquiries. Even though we know that isn't true, and that Garnier *must* know it isn't true."

"He told us that he will swear under oath that he has no knowledge of any such things in his design," Ricard said. "If they exist, he doesn't know about them."

Erik smiled in the darkness, and touched a hand to his forehead in salute to the absent Garnier. It was likely true enough that he didn't *know* about any secret passages, or about a Ghost who might be walking them. But Erik hadn't been as careful as he might have been, back in the days of the Opera's construction, and Garnier would have to be an idiot to not have suspicions. And he knew for a fact that Charles Garnier was not an idiot.

It was almost certainly very definite suspicions. Erik had tried to put a cover together, near the end of the Opera's construction, making some noise about plans to go abroad again. It hadn't meant much, though. That was clear enough from the last conversation he'd had with Garnier, the night they'd shared a bottle of champagne sitting on the edge of the darkened stage. Erik thought of that as the real dedication of the Opera, more meaningful than the public display and official inauguration the next night.

They'd talked about the difficulties of the construction, had one last, now-meaningless wrangle over the Emperor's Entrance, and finally he'd made some remark about a few buildings he planned to visit once he left Paris.

Garnier had been silent in response, and Erik knew that *he* knew that there were no actual plans to go anywhere.

Finally, looking at the champagne bubbles and not at Garnier's shadowed face, he had said, "Please don't tell them about me."

"Of course not."

That was all. No more than that. It was enough, because unspoken between the words and filling the empty auditorium was the tacit understanding that had always existed between them. There had never been anyone else who understood their mutual obsession for this building, no one else who loved it as they did. He had liked to think of it as similar to two men in love with the same woman, each uniquely able to understand the feelings of the other.

Of course, when that situation actually came about, it had been utterly different. No special understanding had ever existed between himself and the Vicomte de Chagny. So much for metaphor.

Garnier had a career, a family, a public face, and had gone on to design other buildings, explore other landscapes. Erik was the shadow he left behind to watch over his masterpiece.

"So what do we *do*?" Moncharmin demanded, voice loudly breaking into Erik's thoughts.

"We gather more information," Mifroid said firmly. "We interview the Company, we map the building, a true map, and we find out where the Phantom is hiding himself. I am not without resources for learning more about our mysterious adversary. This is a hunt, gentlemen, and you win a hunt when you can track the beast to its lair."

Erik smiled grimly. Mifroid was not going to find that so easy to do. Nor was he going to find this particular quarry so easy to capture, even in his lair. He had been preparing for this since the Opera opened. Since before then, since the days when he had made quiet alterations to Garnier's plans, always knowing that some day it would come to this. They were never, never going to capture him.

Kill him, perhaps. But not capture him.

For three days I walked around half-holding my breath, waiting to see what the managers were going to do. What did it really mean, Ricard refusing to put up with the Phantom anymore? Maybe it was as meaningless and unimportant as Erik said. But I didn't like the feeling around the Opera.

I found Carlotta equal parts annoying and amusing, but I'd always known she wielded power at the Opera. I listened to the stories circulating and realized it all again in a new way. Carlotta's particular circle of devotees were the most visible, but they had friends and connections, and when Carlotta started a story, it spread. I was sure the Phantom stories circling the Opera now had started with Carlotta, but they were everywhere and endless.

There was the Phantom's supposed attempt to poison the diva, an event that had grown all out of proportion to what had actually happened, despite (or maybe because of) the number of witnesses. The story was linked up with that long ago croaking incident, which brought everyone back around to Christine's disappearance. They had been telling that story for months, but something in the balance of stories had shifted.

The Company had always told stories of ghostly figures and dripping blood, but they had usually seemed to realize how dramatic they were being. These stories felt…different. More edge, more darkness. Less delight in the hysteria. Much more about people who had mysteriously died or disappeared. Buquet, Christine, Philippe, and a vague multitude of "other people," friends of friends, no one any storyteller actually knew but always someone they'd heard about from someone else.

And the police commissaire was back, having long conversations with the managers and interviewing Company members. I kept expecting him to ask to speak with me. Every time I had to pass him in the halls, and I couldn't always avoid that even though I tried, it seemed to me that he always watched me go by. Every time I thought he would say something, to stop me, but he never did.

I was both grateful and surprised by that. Maybe he didn't feel anymore that 'Christine's friend' had useful information to offer. I wished he felt that way about everyone. Instead, he had to keep poking, keep pushing, and the people he talked to seemed all the more eager to go Phantom hunting afterwards.

It had never come to much months ago, when Commissaire Mifroid had vowed on his own to hunt the Phantom. He was an outsider, and even people who didn't feel about the Phantom as I did seemed to feel the police were meddling. It was different now, when it was Ricard starting the whole business. He was one of us. Sort of. This time, people seemed more and more eager to help, as the police commissaire returned day after day and the stories kept growing uglier.

Maybe Erik had been right this entire time, that he was walking a knife's-edge with his fearsome reputation. Something as small as the usually cowed Monsieur Ricard deciding not to be afraid of the Phantom anymore made too many other people think that the Ghost might not be so unassailable after all.

Maybe I didn't really notice everything in those first days after Ricard's declaration, as Mifroid began prodding around again with a new energy. Maybe it only seemed clear afterwards. After I arrived at the Opera one morning two weeks after Easter, to see everyone hurrying off in the same direction. Everyone always hurried, but usually it was every way at once, not this steady tide. So I fell into step, because I'm as curious as the next person. Maybe more.

As I moved through the halls, following the general trend, I spotted Adalisa and Francesca farther ahead and quickened my pace to catch up with them. "What's going on?" I asked.

"Haven't you heard?" Adalisa said, cheeks pink with excitement. "Everyone's talking about it—no one's sure who heard first, but somehow the word got out and—"

"The police are going after the Phantom!" Francesca burst in.

It was a miracle my feet kept walking forward without stumbling. I stared at Francesca's shining eyes, mind already scrambling to make her sentence not as bad as it sounded. "Of course, Monsieur Ricard already said…"

Francesca shook her head, stray curls flying. "Yes, but now they're actually *doing* something! That's what everyone says. That somehow the managers and the police commissaire know how to find him, and they're going to go catch him."

My mind conjured up a ridiculous image of Moncharmin and Ricard running about with butterfly nets. I wanted the amusing picture to counter the sudden sick fear in my stomach, but it didn't work. I couldn't make Mifroid amusing. "But…" I struggled for a coherent question. "…but how do they know how to find him? No one's ever been able to find the Phantom."

No one. Ever. No one knew how to find him. That was as sure as—as anything, anything you could name, so this had to be wrong. A silly rumor the Company had run away with that wasn't true.

Adalisa and Francesca didn't have an explanation, and we didn't have time to talk about it as we turned a corner and found where everyone else had been going to. The crowd filled the wide hallway outside the managers' office, and I could only see Moncharmin, Ricard and Commissaire Mifroid at the front by rising onto my toes.

Ricard was raising his arms in a placating gesture. "Now, everyone, please, just stay very calm…"

From the rumbles and grumbles of the crowd, 'calm' was a long way off. I wished that Mother was here. *She* would be calm, and practical, and probably disdainful of the whole business. But she wasn't scheduled to work until later, and I had come alone this morning.

A burly man I recognized as a scenechanger called out, "We just want to know if it's true. Do you really know the way to the Phantom's lair?"

Only at the Opera would someone use the word 'lair' with a straight face. I tried to smile, tried again to be amused by the whole business—but meanwhile I was straining to hear the answer over the muttering of the crowd and the pounding of my own heart.

Ricard was hardly worth hearing. "Well, you see, that is, we, ah…" Whatever confidence he had found was limited. But I began to hope anyway. They didn't know anything, not really.

But then Moncharmin spoke up, thumbs hooked into his vest, chest expanding with pride. "The rumors are *entirely* true. We have the exact route to the Phantom's hidden lair."

My heart beat harder as more exclamations arose, though of course he was wrong, he had to be wrong. Only, 'lair' didn't sound funny anymore. It sounded different when Moncharmin said it. It didn't describe the room I'd spent so much time in, it wasn't right at all, but it was how they'd think of it. Men have apartments. Monsters have lairs. And they were going to hunt a monster.

"I must ask for calm," Mifroid said, voice loud and authoritative over the general rumble, much more imposing than Ricard's. "This was not intended to be public knowledge, and this kind of display is inappropriate. I am seeking a dozen men as volunteers to support our capture of the Phantom, but the rest of you should go about your normal business."

In another, less charged moment, I could have laughed at that. Mifroid didn't really understand the Opera Company after all, if he thought this sort of news could stay secret, if he thought everyone would quietly disperse. No one at all moved away.

Although—I didn't understand enough about the police commissaire. Why was he seeking volunteers at all? Why were only two of his men standing with him? And why, I suddenly noticed, was he out of uniform? He was still wearing dark clothes, still standing as though he was on duty, but he wasn't in uniform. A new prickle of worry joined all the other fears assailing me. If Mifroid was acting unofficially, why? And what rules changed for the policeman, if he wasn't here acting as the police?

Questions were still being called, demands and comments flying. "But where did this route you know come from?" someone else in the crowd shouted, a little louder than the rest. A male voice, but I didn't see who.

"A civic-minded citizen chose to share it with us," Moncharmin said firmly, "but the individual prefers to remain anonymous."

Who would know directions to the Phantom's apartment? I had directions, of course, but—I felt suddenly sick. They couldn't have—

no. My directions were hidden away at the back of my drawer in the ballet's changing room. My locked drawer. I hadn't needed them for weeks and I had put them away in what seemed like a perfectly safe location until right at this moment. Maybe I should have taken them home, but I had tucked them away when I still needed them, wanted to have them ready to hand, but now—no, no one knew the directions existed, they couldn't have—

The Persian. There was the Persian too. I had forgotten him, but he knew the way. My head snapped around, searching the crowd. I didn't see him, and he was usually easy to spot, with his red fez and the space that always opened around him. But he wouldn't do this. Would he? I didn't *think* so. Erik had still never entirely explained him, but the Persian had seemed concerned about Erik, they had seemed friendly at the Mardi Gras and…

"Why are we wasting any more time?" This new voice was unmistakable, and my gaze easily found its source. Signora Carlotta, her devotees surrounding her and keeping the crass crowd back. She was wearing some ridiculous headdress with peacock feathers in it, and had her nose up in the air. "We know how to find the Phantom, so—let us go! We have suffered under his persecution long enough."

I held my breath, not because I really thought anyone would contradict her, but…it was *possible*. Instead the rumble of the crowd just grew darker.

"I agree we must move forward and quickly," Mifroid said, and there was a shock merely in hearing him agree with La Carlotta, of all people. "But we must do so in an orderly fashion."

"Why should the police decide how we handle this?" Carlotta sneered. "This is *Opera* business!"

Too many voices rang out to agree with her.

Slowly, carefully, I began to edge backwards, away from Adalisa and Francesca, out of the crowd. I looked upwards, of course seeing a ceiling empty of anything but gold decorations. Maybe he was here, though. Hidden behind any of these walls, listening to the whole thing, laughing at the management—well, not laughing, he never laughed, but that idea. Maybe.

Or maybe he wasn't. Maybe he was sitting at his pipe organ several floors below me, completely oblivious. Maybe he didn't know at all what was going on.

I got out beyond the fringe of the crowd, hurried down the corridor against the cross-traffic of people still rushing towards the excitement. I walked as fast as I dared, aching to run but it would attract too much attention.

I was still moving fast enough to collide right into someone when I turned a corner away from the crowd. I had a confused impression of dark clothing as my nose connected with a black-coated shoulder before I stumbled backwards and would have tipped over if not for hands on my arms steadying me.

"Oh—sorry," I gasped, mostly still intent on getting around this obstacle, getting below, getting to Erik. Then my gaze lifted to see the face of the Persian, still impassive in the face of angry mobs and a careening ballet girl. "It's you!"

"Yes," he agreed, inclined his head slightly in a gesture that reminded me of Erik, and released my arms now that I had my balance back. His tone was calm, his face was calm, and yet his gaze moved faster than usual, looking over my head, back towards the rumbling crowd.

I hadn't talked to him since Mardi Gras, if that brief exchange even counted, and we'd done little more than nod to each other for months. That didn't stop me from speaking now as though we were old friends who understood each other perfectly. "What are you going to do? Do you have a plan? A way to help him?" No need to specify who, too dangerous to name names here, and yet even with that consciousness I felt newly hopeful. Because here was an ally, someone who could do something, someone with mysterious abilities of his own, so much more likely to be effective than me.

His gaze remained turned towards the crowd, out of sight around the corner. "He will take care of himself. He always has. I am leaving, and I recommend you do the same."

I gaped at him, all my brief hopes meeting a sudden death. "What? No, you have to—you must be able to help! You can't just—*abandon* him!"

"He will take care of himself," the Persian repeated, with emphasis. "That mob is looking for someone different to attack. Do not imagine that I do not fit that description, or that it could not fit you as well." His gaze fixed on me, hard and piercing. "Leave now, do not involve yourself, do not let them realize that you are different too. He would tell you the same."

Yes, of course he would. "Just because someone doesn't ask for help," I said icily, "that doesn't mean they don't need it. Or that they shouldn't be given it."

"Do not be foolish," he said harshly, "there is nothing you can do."

"No," I retorted, "not if I stand here talking to you. Go run away while I *do* something."

I stepped around him, evaded his hand as he reached for my arm again with an agitated, "Mademoiselle Giry, you cannot—"

"You wouldn't let me come last time," I said without slowing my pace or turning around. "It's not up to you anymore."

He didn't speak again, and I didn't look back. I just quickened my pace down the corridor and took the first stairs down into the cellars.

I reached the prop room without anyone else stopping me or paying me much mind, and found it blessedly, thankfully empty. I cut through the racks of fake swords over to the wall of masks. I had to tap the pegs three times before I got the sequence right. I had thought I could do it in my sleep, but today my mind raced and my hands shook and it took three tries but finally I got it open.

I stepped into the darkness beyond, closed the wall behind me. For just a moment I waited. Because if he had been watching, he would have seen me leave, would have guessed where I was going, could step out of the deeper darkness *right now*...

Nothing. The darkness stayed quiet, silent, empty.

It took four matches to get the lantern lit. And then I ran. No one to see me here.

I ran until I had a stitch in my side and my lungs burned, then walked with one hand pressing against the pain until the need to move overpowered the struggle to catch my breath, and then ran again. The fear of taking a wrong turn barely crossed my mind. I was too full of the fear of what I had left behind me, of what might be happening up there this very moment.

I'd be in a lot of trouble if they caught up to me down here, if they found me in the Phantom's rooms. But what else could I do?

At last I reached the final corridor, passed the gargoyles without stopping to say hello and all but ran into Erik's door. I pounded one fist against the wood, waited a heartbeat or two, pounded again. My nerves were jangling and my heart was beating fast and I only hesitated one very brief, gasping breath before I tried the handle. Locked, of course.

But I had seen Erik open this door many times, and he never used a key. Now I didn't even hesitate, pressed several leaves in the carving around the handle. The last one descended a fraction, gave a faint click, and when I tried the handle again, it turned.

I was sort of breaking and entering, but I couldn't stop to think of that. I shoved the door open, burst into Erik's parlor. His dark, empty parlor. The light of my lantern was enough to show that.

I ran out of momentum a dozen paces in, stopped within arm's length of the nearer maroon couch. "Erik!" I called, turning in place as though somehow I could have missed him in the room. "*Erik*! You have to be here because I have to talk to you, and—and *please* be here, I—"

"All right, all right, I'm here!" The side door near the couch swung open and Erik entered the room almost as quickly as I had, *his* momentum bringing him within just a few steps of me.

And my driving, focused thoughts of getting here, warning him, suddenly scattered in a thousand directions and I froze where I was.

Because his white half mask was in place but his hair and pants were both rumpled, and he was still pulling a shirt on.

It was hardly as though I had never seen a man's bare chest before. Some of the Opera's costumes showed much more than what was revealed by an unbuttoned shirt.

But this was *Erik*. Erik who I was struggling not to think about too much anyway, and besides, Erik of the collared dress shirts, the silk vests, the black suit jackets and the voluminous cloaks, everything always buttoned and tucked and perfectly in place, immaculate as armor and no more inviting. Apparently he had been hiding a nice physique under there, not bulky but with a hint of muscles not entirely hidden by the dark hair across the upper part of his chest. I wondered if it would feel soft or coarse, and in this light I couldn't tell if it was long enough to curl or not...

My cheeks burned. This was *not* the time. It was *never* going to be the time for this kind of thinking.

"Sorry," Erik muttered, half-turning away as he hastily buttoned his shirt, hiding all revelations from view. "I was asleep."

Unbidden, the image of Erik asleep in bed, with no shirt at all, appeared in my mind. Not *now*. I firmly seized my self-control and temporarily banished the image.

Erik cleared his throat, and it might have been awkward or irritated or both. "Would you like to tell me what on earth this is all about?" He snapped his fingers and all the candles in the room lit themselves, returning some degree of normalcy to the scene. "How did you even get in the door?"

Right. Right, I had a reason for being here, and it was *not* to stare at Erik's chest under a slightly translucent white shirt. "Upstairs. The managers. Mifroid." I dragged in a breath, assured myself that I was out of breath from *running*. "They know how to find you. Here. I mean." I waved my hand, more or less indicating the space around us. "How to find here."

All he did was raise his eyebrow. "That seems highly unlikely."

"I don't care if it's *unlikely*, it's *happening!*" My heart was still pounding but I didn't even try to tell myself that was from running. "I came from upstairs—they just told an entire crowd they know how to find you, Mifroid is recruiting men to help—they wouldn't do that if they weren't sure. Even Moncharmin and Ricard aren't that stupid, and you know Mifroid isn't."

Erik's lips tightened a little. "True." The corners of his eyes crinkled and for just an instant I read some emotion—pain, fear, regret, I couldn't tell—and then he blinked and it was gone. "Well, it was bound to happen eventually," he said, tone brisk. "Eight years is actually a very good run, considering."

"Sure. All right," I said at random, sagging back against the couch beside me. I wasn't sure what I had expected. Alarm, maybe. I didn't know what to do now that I wasn't seeing that.

He turned away then, strode over to the door and hit his palm against one stone that didn't look any different from any other. A click, and the edge of a beam of wood emerged from the doorframe. The door had always been thinner than the stone wall, framing it in a kind of stone archway. Now I saw why, as Erik slid the beam across the door, sinking it into a hollow on the opposite side, forming a defensive crossbar.

I might have felt more reassured by the security of that if he hadn't next moved to the side wall, hit another stone so that the section of the wall with his bookshelves pivoted, hiding the books away to be replaced by a blank expanse. Then he strode over to the painting next to the bookcase, a view of Rome, and pulled it down from the wall.

I shook my head. "What are you doing?"

"Preparing," he said without looking at me. "How long do you think it'll be?"

Preparing? "I—don't know. Carlotta sounded ready to light the torches when I left and—now, Erik, it could be *now*. What do you mean, preparing?"

He set the painting down, leaning it against the wall, and moved towards me again, worry finally in creases on his face. "If it's now, you can't be here. They can't find you here. You need to leave."

I gaped at him. "*I* need to—Erik, they can't find *you* here! That crowd is fast turning into a mob and it's one that wants to kill you. Mifroid probably wants to arrest you, but everyone else, they want to kill you!" I wished I was exaggerating, but I remembered the rumble of the crowd and knew I wasn't.

"It wouldn't be the first time," he said, moving past me to the large painting of angels, lifting that down from the wall too. "You should leave, before it's too late."

"Fine, good, come with me!" I circled around to the other side of the couch, closer to him. "We'll both go. Stop messing about with silly paintings—"

"They're not silly," he interjected, resting the bottom edge of the painting against his table. "Do you know how valuable a Bouguereau is?"

"I don't *care*. Let's just go and—"

"I can't. If they're actually marching, this isn't going to go away. And this is the best place to make a stand."

"You don't have to make a stand!" What was this, some kind of absurd male bravado? "This is not an opera, you don't have to have a dramatic fifth act finale! There's an entire opera house up there and you know it better than anyone. Don't stay in the one place they're looking, just *leave*."

He stared at me, into me. "No." No arguments, no reasoning, just no.

I stared back and he looked away first, lifting the painting again.

"All right," I said, and sat down on the couch, arms folded. "Then I'm staying too."

He swung around, narrowly avoiding hitting the table with one edge of the frame. "That's not the same thing at all! You can't just— why would you possibly—"

"Maybe I can help." I wanted the words to come out firm, unyielding, as definitive as his flat no. Unfortunately, my voice wavered. I rushed on to add, "Maybe I can reason with them."

"You can't reason with a *mob*," Erik protested, hoisting the painting a few inches higher. "That's practically the definition of a mob, a crowd you can't reason with."

"I know, but…" My voice trailed off and I swallowed. "But still." I didn't see how I could just walk away and leave him here. I had known he'd tell me to. The Persian had said he would, and I had known it anyway. Knowing didn't reconcile me to the idea.

Erik grimaced, hauled the painting several steps over to stand it up against the side door. Then he came back around the couch and sat down at the far corner, leaning forward towards me. "Listen to me, this is not—you can't..." He stopped, closed his eyes for a moment, long enough for me to notice that he hadn't fastened the top button of his shirt—or maybe it had come undone when he was moving paintings. When he opened his eyes and spoke again, his voice had gone softer. "Thank you for warning me about this. Thank you for wanting to help. That—means a lot to me. More than I can say. But you can't do anything here. I can handle this. I will handle it. I need you to let me do that. And to leave, now, so that you don't get caught up in this too."

I stared into his green eyes, his brilliant, jade green eyes looking back into mine. If he had argued I could have fought back, but this was—different. "All right," I said finally. I still hated the idea—but maybe he was right, maybe it was better that I wasn't here, that I left him free to deal with this. And besides, discussing it was only taking up time he didn't have.

I watched his face relax, worry receding—somewhat. "Thank you," he said, and anyone else might have hugged me then, or squeezed my hand. Erik just got up from the couch, crossed past me to the other side of the room to pick up the violin resting on top of the pipe organ.

I rose to my feet, slowly, picking up the still-lit lantern I'd carried in with me. I felt like there ought to be more to say, something important. I didn't know what, though, and what I said wasn't it. "You didn't have to be nice like that; you could have been angry and tried to scare me into leaving."

"That wouldn't have worked." He said the words without turning away from the hidden compartment in the wall where he was now stowing his violin. I thought I saw his shoulders tense, but at the moment, that could have been in response to anything. He glanced over one shoulder and added, "I assume?"

It took me a second to realize he was asking if he was right, that it wouldn't have worked. "No. I suppose it wouldn't have."

He just nodded, returned his attention to the wall long enough to close the compartment. Then he turned back around, gaze darting around the room, checking, assessing, making decisions he didn't voice. I should be going. I should leave. I took a step, then two, gladly halted again when he said, "One other thing—if something does happen to me—"

"Nothing will," I protested in an immediate jolt of renewed fear. "You just said you could handle this."

"And I don't intend to let anything happen," he said, voice patient. "But *if* something happens—"

"Erik!"

This time he went on as though I hadn't spoken. "—most of the money is in the hidden drawer above the mantle. You remember how to open it?"

Money? He was talking about dying and now he was talking about money? I shook my head. "That's not important right now."

His gaze was locked on my face, and somehow I hadn't noticed him moving near me again. "Do you remember how to open it?"

"*Yes*, it's the pale gray stone with the crack in it, tap twice. But why does—"

"Good." He nodded again, more decisively this time. "If something happens, today or in the future, remember that. I can't make a will because I don't legally exist and neither does the money, but if anything happens, remember how to get into that drawer and remember that I wanted you to have it. Understand?"

Some other time, I might have been surprised or touched or grateful. But at *this* time, when his death seemed not only possible but potentially imminent, I could only feel horrified. I dropped my gaze to the patterned rug beneath my feet. "We can't talk about this, this is—"

His hands closed around my shoulders. Startled, I looked up to find his face inches from mine. "*Do you understand?*"

I stared into his eyes. I still wasn't scared, not of him, but I felt breathless, shaky. "Yes," I whispered.

Maybe it was a minute longer that he looked into my face. Maybe it was only a heartbeat. It felt as though time stretched and held suspended, frozen and infinite, and I couldn't read his expression and I couldn't breathe through my own tumult of emotions, a hundred butterflies were doing pirouettes in my stomach, and for just a moment I thought that maybe he…

He released me and turned away, eyes going distant before his gaze even left my face. "That's all right then."

I reached a hand out to grasp the arm of the couch. If I had been standing by the seat, I would have sat down.

Erik had gone back to the side door he'd first entered from, opened it and started moving paintings through. "Maybe I should be more careful," he remarked, voice light and almost strangely at odds with the intensity of a moment before. "If I'm too generous, you might change allegiance."

My spine straightened and my head snapped up. "Don't ever say that again."

I don't know what was on my face, but he stopped with the Bouguereau painting halfway through the doorway, looked at me and then ducked his head, shoulders hunching slightly. "I only meant—it was just—"

"Just don't say it again," I said flatly.

He stared at the frame under his hands. "Sorry."

I wanted to tell him I would never, ever do that to him. That I would never betray him, that I would always, always be on his side, I didn't care who I had to fight or how much I could lose in the process. I wanted to say that I had never felt about anyone the way I felt about him.

Maybe I even wanted to say that I loved him.

But as sure as I was that I wasn't afraid of him, I *was* afraid of telling him anything like that. So though it sounded loudly in my head, none of it made it into the air.

After a moment, he resumed sliding the painting through the doorway, and when he came back into the room he said, "You should go." He snapped his fingers, and the bar across the door slid back.

Another trick of the Phantom. I hoped he had enough of them. "I know. I'm going."

I got most of the way to the door before I looked back over my shoulder. Erik wasn't watching me. His expression was distant, eyes fixed on nothing in particular, obviously wrapped in his own thoughts.

Only two minutes ago he had been looking into me as though he couldn't see anything else, and in that short a time he had already receded so far. I could almost *see* the wall around him now, the one he radiated to keep everyone away. I was lucky he let me within three feet. For most people, the walls were too big and thick and high to even let them into the same room with him.

Obeying an impulse I didn't try to define, I turned around, re-crossed the space between us in a few quick steps, and walked right through his wall. I had a brief glimpse of his surprised expression. Then I put my hands on his shoulders, lifted up onto my toes, and brushed a kiss onto his unmasked cheek, his skin warm beneath my lips.

In that moment, I knew that if he died, so would I. I'd go on breathing, but the person I was now would never be the same, and the person I would go on to be if he was in my life…she was never going to exist.

"Be careful," I whispered. "Be safe."

I wanted to wrap my arms around him, hug him tight and never let him go. But instead I stepped back, turned away to hurry towards the door. I didn't dare look at him again until I was already on the threshold, and only peeked then.

He was watching me, one hand covering his cheek.

Chapter Thirty-Three

T he door clicked shut behind Meg. Erik blinked, shook his head, and tried to regain his focus. A mob. There was a mob coming. Yes. That was what he needed to think about.

It wasn't as though he hadn't expected this. He had been expecting this for eight years, the final inevitable result of being the Phantom of the Opera. Or perhaps the Phantom had actually kept this at bay, and this was simply the inevitable result of being himself. Rejection was his *leitmotif*, the theme that kept repeating again and again in his life. Even if it faded out of the melody for a few stanzas, it always returned.

And it was back now, the tempo picking up, and he was running out of time. He had done what he could down here and he had got Meg to leave. That second was the most important point, the most vital thing.

It meant more than he could say that she had offered to stay, but he could never ask that of her. Whatever was coming, he would face it alone, as he faced everything. He had played a solitary melody for so long, he didn't even know how to play with accompaniment, with someone else's music joining his own.

He had only minutes left now, if that, and he had one more thing he had to do. He desperately needed a different mask.

He replaced the bar over the main door then ran for his side door, started up the spiral stairs beyond. If his front door held, he'd have just enough time—if Meg hadn't come to warn him, he wouldn't have had time for anything at all. They would have found him asleep in bed, utterly vulnerable and—he paused for just an instant on the top step, as the thought suddenly occurred to him that, a year ago, he wouldn't have cared about a warning. He would have welcomed a mob, pikes, torches and all, and if he'd fought back he wouldn't have been trying to survive. But now… Well, he had told Meg he would handle this. So that was that.

417 days, nine hours. That's how long he had lived since *she* had gone. And if he didn't figure out how to survive this, that would be the final total.

He needed black. It might not have been appropriate for the masquerade, but it was today. Upstairs at his wardrobe, he yanked off the white shirt and reached for a black one. He winced a little, remembering. Why he couldn't have buttoned the shirt *before* he opened the door—but she'd sounded so upset, and…

Besides, apart from that first moment, he thought he had mostly appeared quite calm and collected while Meg was here. She didn't need to know that his heart was beating faster and there'd been a sick weight in the pit of his stomach ever since he'd understood her news.

This was inevitable. He had expected it. He was prepared. That's what he wanted her to believe, what he wanted to believe himself. Hopefully he had convinced her more than he had convinced himself. He perhaps had been a little too intense about the money…but it was important. If he did die today, he wanted to have done *something* worthwhile. If the best he could do was leave Meg enough money to take care of her for the rest of her life, well, that wasn't meaningless.

His hand strayed up to touch his cheek, to the spot where she…

A mask. He still needed a different mask. This white one was all wrong, not nearly forbidding enough, showing far too much of his face. He picked up his skull mask instead, fit it into place, just as a new sound filtered in through the walls: the thudding of too many footsteps, here in his silent world where no one ever came. His heart seemed to increase tempo in time with the sound.

He took a deep breath, moved to the far wall of his bedroom and used the peephole to look down on the last hallway. Bobbing torchlight and half-shadowed, half-illuminated figures. Standing at the wall he could hear them more clearly, the steady rhythm of feet, the accompanying rumble of voices. Hard to count, but a few dozen people jostling together at the front, a bigger crowd following farther behind. All of them, coming for him. How had they got past all of his traps? How had Mifroid finally found the way?

That was a question for later, if he had a later to ask it in.

For now he straightened his black jacket, and forced himself to look over the crowd, to look through the shadows for anything of use. He tried not to dwell on the faces twisted with fury and hate. Many just looked excited, which wasn't much better. Commissaire Mifroid was right at the front, walking with steady strides, face set in an expression that was not angry or excited, but disturbingly intense. Moncharmin and Ricard were farther back though still in the first group, Carlotta near them—she was not dressed appropriately for the occasion, a clump of feathers sticking out of her hair.

Mifroid was nearly to the door now; he had no more time for observation. He let his gaze rove once more over the crowd at large, glancing towards the back group as they came closer. It wasn't all scenechangers and armed men there; the second crowd seemed to be a cross-section of all the different parts of the Opera Company, as if they had all come to participate in a grand performance. Musicians, chorus members, even ballet girls—he froze suddenly, palms pressing harder against the wall as though he could somehow look closer.

Of course. How stupid of him not to realize, of course she would do this. There, in the midst of a few other ballet girls, was Meg. He'd convinced her to leave, but she'd contrived to come back the only possible way, by joining the mob.

He did not want her here. He *did not* want her seeing this. He did not want her to see him being the monster. He didn't even know if he could put that mask on while she was watching.

But he had to. Because the monster was the only one with a chance of surviving a mob.

I really meant to leave. I still didn't like the idea, but I could see the reasonableness of it. I let Erik's door shut behind me, paused just long enough to pat the head of each gargoyle and try not to wonder if I'd see them again—if I'd see *him* again—then started back up towards the Opera.

I didn't get far before I heard a noise that didn't fit the usually silent lower levels. An indistinct rumble at first, it quickly resolved into footsteps and voices, many of both. They were coming. And I couldn't afford to be found here.

I was at the base of the "magical" staircase, currently recessed into the wall. I stepped quickly past the point of its bottom step, pressed back against the wall, and blew out my lantern.

Immediately the darkness rushed in around me, wrapping me up in shadows. I forced myself to take a slow, careful breath against the sudden tightening of my throat. The darkness was a refuge, a protection, a shelter. And with a mob on the march, shadows were the last thing I should be afraid of.

Probably they were going a different way. Probably they didn't know about the stairs. I'd just wait until the sound faded, until they passed on to a different area. I always carried matches now; I'd re-light the lamp, continue on my way.

But the noise was getting louder and the darkness was growing less black. I looked up, just in time to see the topmost step slide out, its darker shadow falling across my face. Above its black silhouette, torchlight glowed. A second step slid out, and a third. The mob was coming this way after all, and I pressed back harder against the wall, biting my lower lip, hoping the suddenly tattered darkness would be enough to conceal me.

They moved onto the stairs, a thunder of indistinguishable footfalls and voices above me. It was too many people, at least double the dozen Mifroid had said he wanted to recruit. I could hear the low tones of male voices, imagined the commissaire and his policemen and an assortment of the biggest, strongest of the men who worked around the Opera.

However many of them there were, however big they were, they should continue on the way they were facing. There was no reason at all for them to look back in my direction, I'd just stay hidden until they had gone and—

And then what? Slink back up to the surface? Pace around the halls, wondering and praying and worrying?

I hated that idea, but could see no way around it. I waited until the footsteps and the voices and the glow of torchlight had continued along the path beside the underground lake. I was just about to step out, to ascend the stairs myself, when a faint noise made me pause just in time. I could still hear the noise of Mifroid's group, but this sound was from above. More footsteps, more voices, a second group coming behind the first.

By the time they were on the stairs I could tell from the voices that this was a more mixed group, and knowing the Opera Company I could guess what was happening. Mifroid had probably selected the men he wanted to bring and ordered everyone else to disperse. The Company had proceeded to ignore that order, and to follow along anyway. Perhaps they had already been into the tunnels before Mifroid even knew they were there. He had to know by now, but he probably didn't have the men to spare to force them back.

I could hear women's voices among this second crowd…and that gave me an idea. Maybe I didn't *have* to go upstairs right now after all. There was another option. It was risky, probably stupid, and I knew Erik wouldn't like it. But I had sat passively by the last time an enemy had descended on the Phantom. Then it had only been one stupid vicomte, but still I'd done nothing. At least, I assumed Raoul had somehow got below the Opera to find Christine—since I had done nothing, since I hadn't been there, I still didn't really know. Maybe there was nothing I could do this time either. But at least this time I could know what happened. At least I could be Erik's witness.

So I waited until this second crowd had reached the bottom of the stairs, until the last person was continuing along the walkway beside the lake. Then I set my lantern down in the deepest shadow, slipped out from below the stairs, and fell into step at the back of the mob.

At first I held my breath for fear someone would ask where I had suddenly come from. But the crowd was rough and chaotic, and no one gave me a glance in the shifting torchlight.

Soon I was feeling fear for other reasons. As ugly as the mood of the crowd had been when I left it upstairs, it had grown worse. Whatever the managers, or more likely Carlotta, had been saying, it had fanned the flames of anger and hate and vengeance.

Vengeance. There were many mutterings about that. For what, though? For a lot of ghostly tricks and even more excellent musical advice? For Philippe? I couldn't believe anyone here really cared about the nobleman, except perhaps Mifroid.

For Christine? All these people who had so happily told tales about the terrible things the Phantom must have done to Christine—I could well imagine they might claim they were coming in her name. Even though none of them had truly known her, not like I did. And even I had no idea if she would want this. Surely not, not if she had known Erik even a fraction as well as I did.

Almost unthinkingly I began pushing my way farther forward into the crowd, trying to find someone less alarming to walk beside. I fetched up among a few ballet girls, Francesca and Adalisa among them. I paced along behind them for a minute before Adalisa glanced over her shoulder and saw me.

Her forehead wrinkled. "Meg? I thought you stayed upstairs."

"No," I said, made myself smile a little. "Of course I'm here. It's just hard to see anyone in these shadows."

"I just thought…" She shook her head. "I suppose."

I moved up alongside the ballet girls then, but it wasn't much more comfortable. Their faces shone with an excitement and glee that was almost more frightening than the anger on other faces around us.

Erik wasn't the only one to forget this wasn't an opera. It's all well and good to applaud the crowd who defeats the villain at the end, usually to rousing choruses, but it feels very different when you're in the middle of it. And when you're in love with the villain. When he's charming and awkward and not so villainous at all, just tangled up in the trappings of villainy and…

And he was going to handle this. He *told* me, he would handle this. But my gaze still darted to the faces around me, and I shivered. I knew these people, this crowd of dancers and singers and musicians, of people who sold tickets or managed scenery or worked among the costumes. They weren't police or fighters or even scenechangers who were mostly distinguished for their strength. These were artists, my community, people I liked. And I didn't recognize them right now.

My gaze lingered on Pierre Morel, a baritone. Every winter he brought extra coal to the ballet's practice room, and always tried to slip out without being thanked. Now his brow was low, his hands clenched into fists, and his broad shoulders and thick arms seemed threatening for the first time. I looked past him to Marcelle, a chorus girl who talked endlessly about her fiancé Emile, which might have annoyed people except she was so happy whenever she talked about him that it was hard to object. Her forehead was puckered into a glower and I doubted she was thinking of Emile right now.

All around me, everyone I could see had undergone a similar transformation.

I wasn't paying attention to our surroundings, only realized we'd come to the last hall when the people in front of me stopped walking. I rose up onto my toes, trying to see what was going on farther up. It looked like Mifroid and his group were right up to the door, while this second group was hanging a little farther back. I couldn't see much, with the number of people in front of me, though I could spot Carlotta's stupid feathers sticking up. She apparently had enough clout to be right at the front.

By unspoken agreement, everyone around me was going quiet, trying to hear what was happening. There seemed to be some dissension at the front.

Carlotta's imperious voice rang against the stone walls. "Well, go on then, get the door open."

"The door is locked," Mifroid said coldly.

"*Of course* it's locked," Carlotta snapped. "Break it down!"

"Thank you, Signora, that was my intention," Mifroid said, voice hard, and a moment later a gunshot rang out.

Everyone jumped and a few people screamed. I flinched backwards, dropping back onto my heels, not before I caught the glint of the gun in Mifroid's hand.

This was the first time I'd ever seen him fire it—at a door, yes, but that didn't make me feel any better. He probably had six shots in that gun, and where were the other five going to go?

"The door appears to be barred," Mifroid said, and I couldn't see clearly enough to know what he was looking at to know that. "Someone help me break it down."

Movement at the front, and three of the burliest scenechangers worked together to throw their strength against the door. Erik built solidly and it took several tries. But they got the door down, the wood splintering and falling with a crash.

I stared at that gaping doorway, only darkness beyond, and I think everyone else was doing the same. No one seemed eager to be the first one across the threshold.

And while everyone stared silently, a low voice echoed through the hall, soft and silky and coming from every direction at once. "So you've found your way through the Phantom's domain at last, Commissaire. Surely you didn't need all this frightened rabble to come along with you."

Everyone around me jumped, at least three girls shrieked, and even my breath caught. Because it was Erik's voice, I knew that well enough, and yet…it sounded so very, very different.

"I am here to arrest you, Phantom," the commissaire said, voice ringing out, and though the words were appropriate enough, the level of intensity in them scared me. "Arrest you or kill you. The choice is up to you."

"So let's get inside!" one of the men who'd shoved the door growled, and plunged in through the doorway, torch held high. Mifroid was barely a step behind him, the others who'd battered the door followed and then everyone was pushing forward. The managers and Carlotta went too, though not in the front. I hurried to pick up my step and follow.

Almost unconsciously I had been moving towards the front of this second group, trying to see what was happening, so I was near Erik's doorway when Mifroid snapped out, "Keep that throng back," and two tall men stepped into position to block the entrance.

I grimaced but didn't try to shove through, trying to be content with looking past them. Erik's parlor looked very different in the dancing torchlight, with the angry crowd pressing around me, shadows shifting across their faces. The pipe organ gleamed on the far wall, but the other walls felt stark with every painting removed and the books hidden out of sight. I understood why he'd hidden the Bouguereau painting, but maybe it would have given them pause, to see the Madonna and Child on the Phantom's wall. In the orange torchlight, with the walls blank and the maroon couches and thick rugs shining red, a room I'd grown to think of as cozy seemed strangely not unlike a lair after all.

My gaze, roving the room to search for and not find a cloaked figure, passed over the side door and then tracked back—because the door wasn't there where it should be, only an empty stone wall. That explained why it had been enough to merely move everything valuable beyond the doorway.

Mifroid and the men with him were spreading out through the room, growing quiet as they moved their torches to light the shadowed corners. Carlotta was looking at Erik's piano, the managers were in conference with each other close to the doorway, and Mifroid was holding his torch up high, not too high to still see the tension on his face even from where I was standing.

"I see I have guests." Erik's voice broke in on the silence, still rolling from everywhere and nowhere, too soft to be thunder, and somehow that made it even more sinister. No doubt he knew that. "I don't recall inviting you. You aren't welcome."

With no more warning than that, a net fell down from the ceiling, entangling two of the men standing near the couch. They shouted and thrashed about, and when another man moved to help them a trapdoor opened beneath him and he disappeared with a sharp cry.

"Everyone, stay still!" Mifroid swung his gun about, but there was no one to point it at.

Carlotta and the managers were ignoring the order and bacvking up towards the door again, perhaps rethinking taking this matter into their own hands. They hadn't moved far before a knife came shooting out of one wall, spinning through the air and slicing off Carlotta's feathers before striking the opposite wall. Carlotta shrieked and ducked down beside the piano.

My heart was pounding in my chest because it felt so *strange* to think that Erik must have had these traps all along, here in this place where I had come to feel so at home.

Though it occurred to me, if possibly not to anyone else, that he *could* have aimed that knife lower, could have dropped something more deadly than nets from the ceiling. He was trying to scare them, not kill them. I doubted that would give any of them pause.

"Enough tricks!" Mifroid shouted. "Show yourself!"

I prayed he wouldn't, that he'd stay hidden, stay safe.

An edge of humor joined the ominous silk in his voice. "But wouldn't I be a rather dull specter with no tricks? Haven't you enjoyed my little games all these years?"

Although she didn't stand up, Carlotta wasn't too afraid to shout, "There has been nothing amusing about your continual persecution!"

A pause of a breath, and then there was even more humor in Erik's voice. "Oh, I disagree, Signora. And if they were being honest, everyone but you thought the spider in your drink was hilarious. Even Monsieur Moncharmin."

Moncharmin launched an immediate protest, while my throat grew tighter. It was even worse, hearing Erik take the blame for something stupid *I* had done. We might not be here right now if I had just exercised a little common sense and self-control and not deliberately poked the vindictive diva.

"We are not here because of silly tricks," Mifroid said loudly over Moncharmin's nonsense. "We are here because of the death of Philippe de Chagny, the death of Joseph Buquet, and the crashed chandelier. Now show yourself and face justice!"

More of the crowd added shouts to Mifroid's voice, the men in the room and the people behind me. I imagined Erik had intended to frighten them with his traps, and he had—but he had also made them angrier, and the balance between the two feelings was still shifting back and forth. But the trend was growing towards one message, a demand that he stop hiding and face them. Because one man facing down a hundred people was obviously a reasonable and sensible idea.

I prayed he wouldn't, prayed with increasing intensity right up until candles flamed to life in stands on either side of the pipe organ at the far end of the room. Between them, on the wooden upperboard above the keys, stood the Phantom of the Opera, as though he had been there in the shadows all along.

No one had gone quite that far into the room, and most fell back a pace at his sudden appearance.

He didn't look like the man who had come tumbling into the room with his shirt half off. Back to all black clothes, beneath a dark cloak swept out to either side like wings, with a wide-brimmed hat pulled low above a grinning skull mask.

I heard more than one invocation of saints around me, and more than one equally fervent curse. And still other people, farther back, demanding to know what was happening, as though this was somehow still a show.

"Well?" Erik said, tone mocking and biting. "So you've cornered the Opera Ghost in his lair. Did you have a plan for what to do next?"

My mind spun crazily towards a long ago childhood memory, a dog I knew who madly loved to chase chickens but was at an utter loss the one time he actually cornered one. Things had turned out all right for the chicken, but there had been a farmer to intervene.

"You are under arrest," Mifroid growled.

Erik spread his arms wide. "Brave words. But you still have to actually *capture* me."

"You can't kill all of us," someone called out, braver or more foolhardy than the rest.

"No," Erik agreed, "I can't kill *all* of you."

He let the words hang there and I felt a shiver crawl down my spine. He didn't mean it. I knew he didn't mean it. But I was the only one.

I had wanted desperately for him to just keep hiding. And in one way, he still was. No one in this room *really* saw him, not the man behind what I was nearly sure was a carefully crafted monster mask, no one except me—and even I was struggling to see the Erik I knew.

"So," the Phantom said, after a no doubt strategically silent moment, "who wants to be first?"

I don't think anyone expected it to be Monsieur Ricard. Mifroid took a step, but Ricard moved faster, lifted a hand that only shook a little, and pointed a gun toward Erik. This was even more shocking, more horrifying, than a weapon in the police commissaire's hand. "We are putting an end to your terrorizing of the Opera Company. Surrender, and we'll see that you receive a fair trial."

Erik sighed loudly. "Oh really, Ricard, who let you have a gun?"

The manager kept doggedly on. "If you resist apprehension, we will not be responsible for the—"

"Why do you imagine that a trial would be an incentive anyway?" Erik asked in near rhetorical tones—and before anyone had time to answer he jumped from the pipe organ.

More shrieks, more recoiling backwards, and Ricard, probably by instinct, fired his weapon. Shrieks and recoils redoubled as the sound echoed in the room and I had to struggle to keep my gaze on the black cloaked figure who was *not* falling or visibly bleeding, who hadn't jumped forward anyway but off to the side and now was launching straight into the curtains covering that wall—and disappeared through them.

I'd had no idea there was a door in that corner. But why not? It was so Erik. A hidden door inside a secret apartment that could only be reached through a labyrinth of passages including a secret stair, a labyrinth that could only be reached by, again, a hidden door. It was so very Erik that a possibly hysterical bubble of laughter tried to rise up out of my throat and I had to swallow hard to keep it down.

Because this wasn't over yet. It took only a moment for others to realize what must have happened. Mifroid cursed and plunged after him. And that shifted the balance—the mob had been hesitating between fear and anger, and now that they had a prey to chase, anger was winning out. The men already in the room were quick to pursue, and the crowd behind me surged and shoved forward. The two men blocking the door gave way at once, more interested in following the Phantom, and the lot of us spilled into the room like a wave.

Few seemed to give thought to the possibility of more traps, and though the thought crossed my own mind, it didn't stop me from following either. This wasn't over and I had to see what was going to happen. Maybe he had a secret door, maybe he was going to disappear into the labyrinth after all.

He had to know what he was doing. Had to.

I had never seen this hidden corridor, a narrow space of stone walls and no decoration or any evidence of living going on inside it. But why would there be, it was only an escape tunnel. From the coolness and a slight damp in the air, I thought we were alongside the underground lake. Sure enough, after a minute or two, the corridor opened up onto the edge of the lake. Not right on the edge—there was plenty of room for everyone who had followed to stand, without getting too close to the low wall bordering the lake. Or to Erik, standing on that wall.

If he had looked ominous in his own parlor, the effect was even greater here, in the stone cavern with the high archways, the thick shadows, and the dark water behind him. It was enough that the mob had stopped again, a little distant, but closer than they had been before. Sheer force of atmosphere wasn't going to hold them back for long.

I could just see Mifroid through the crowd, pacing two steps closer to Erik than anyone else, his gun still drawn. "You have no choice now but to surrender."

"Surrender?" Erik repeated, tone mocking. "You want the Phantom of the Opera to *surrender*?" He spread his arms to either side, black cloak rippling. "And then what? Then you toss me into some cage somewhere? To be exhibited? Everyone line up to see the monster! Also the composer, the architect, the scholar, but no one's going to care about that, no, the sign will read *come see the monster.*" He shook his head, very slowly, gaze moving over the mob. "Not today. Not ever. No one is ever going to cage me."

"Stop making *speeches*," Mifroid growled. "I'm not here to watch an opera, I'm here to arrest you. You have nowhere to run and no more tricks, now get your hands above your head and get off that wall." His gun was raised high now, sighted and aimed. One press of the trigger and it would all be over, but Mifroid didn't seem to want to do that—he seemed to want to take Erik alive, and surely that would be better...wouldn't it?

Slowly, Erik's arms spread farther out to either side, slowly his hands started to rise, and I shivered, his words about never being caged came back to me. This wasn't handling the situation, this wasn't a solution—this was just allowing something to happen, something that I suspected Erik felt was even worse than dying.

"Maybe," Erik said softly, "I have one more trick. One last, greatest escape."

"No more—" And however Mifroid meant to finish that sentence, no one heard it, because a single gunshot sounded, cutting off the words.

Erik jerked, wavered, balanced for just an instant, then plummeted backward, off the wall, into the dark lake below.

Chapter Thirty-Four

F or just a second, the whole world went still. I felt cold and I couldn't breathe and I couldn't make sense of what I'd just seen.

"*No!*" The cry split the stunned silence. Not me, my voice wasn't that deep—Commissaire Mifroid, sprinting to the edge, hands landing on the wall bordering the water, tensed as though—Moncharmin caught him by the arm, dragged him back a step.

It was only Mifroid's reaction that made me realize it wasn't him who had shot Erik, and while the crowd surged forward around me, an audience rushing to see the next scene of the show, I looked frantically around for some kind of explanation.

And I saw the Persian, standing on a chunk of masonry at the very back of the crowd, positioned to fire above everyone's heads, gun still in his hand. For a moment, his gaze met mine, his expression still that same, impassive, unreadable blank it always was. Then he looked away again.

I wanted to push through the crowd back towards the Persian, to demand an explanation, to find out if I had been completely wrong about him all this time. And I wanted to push the other way, through to the wall, to shove through the throng crowding there to get a glimpse at the lake where Erik had disappeared, to see if—to see…

I turned towards the lake, because answers were more important, more urgent than explanations, and I had to—to see whatever I could see.

I pushed and wriggled and ducked between and around people and it felt excruciatingly slow—but the crowd had fanned out and it was really only a few people deep now, not so great a distance to get through before I bumped up against the wall. I curled my fingers around the rough stone, feeling it scratch against my skin, and stared into the shadows.

The water stretched on and on into the darkness, the ripple where Erik had gone in already dissipating and fading and the water going smooth.

"Let go of me, you fool," I heard Mifroid growl somewhere to my left. "And someone restrain that man!" I knew without looking that he could only mean the Persian. Out of the corner of my eye I could see Mifroid himself step up to the wall again and stay there, torchlight glinting on his gun.

My mind's eye was supplying the image of red blood in water that was too dark to actually show blood, adding in the picture of Erik floundering and drowning and—involuntarily my eyes squeezed shut. Then I opened them again, quick, but nothing had happened, nothing had changed.

He hadn't surfaced. And he didn't surface. He never surfaced. We watched and the water grew completely still and I managed to drag in breath after painful breath and Erik never came up out of the water.

Somehow this had to be a trick, one of his tricks. He had told me he would handle this, and drowning was *not handling it.*

But had he planned on the Persian? Had he expected to be shot? Had he lost control at the very end, run out of tricks, met something he hadn't anticipated?

Carlotta's voice pierced through my thoughts again. "No one could survive underwater this long. He must be dead."

Ricard sounded doubtful. "Shouldn't the body bob up then?"

"So the cloak was heavy," Carlotta said in tones of dismissal and disinterest. "He did not come up. That is what matters."

My fingers clutched the stone wall so hard they hurt. They were wrong. *Wrong.* But they were supposed to think this, to think that he was dead. That was the trick, that was what made it clever.

The water had nothing more to show. Whatever had happened in its depths, the surface could tell us nothing. I turned away, looked back again towards the Persian, now being held on either side by Mifroid's two policemen. No one else was getting anywhere close, still giving the Persian the wide berth they always did, many hands making signs against the Evil Eye. The commissaire had also given up on staring at the lake, was stepping now into the empty space around the Persian.

"Why?" Mifroid demanded, voice almost a snarl. It wasn't the calm, restrained tone I was used to hearing from him. "I was going to take him alive—I was going to get *answers*!"

The Persian merely stared back at him, unruffled even in this situation. "You were not going to take him alive," he said with calm assurance. "Did you not hear what he said about a last trick? I know the madman from many years ago in Persia. I led the police's efforts there to capture him. He is very skilled with explosives. If I had hesitated now, none of us would be here. He undoubtedly has the area outfitted with gunpowder."

The words at least made Mifroid pause, whether it was the explanation or the Persian's allusion to being a member of the police.

My mind, meanwhile, was still spinning furiously, because this wasn't an explanation that made sense to *me*. If the Persian wanted to capture or kill Erik, he could have done it long ago. So what else wasn't true? I didn't believe Erik would have blown us all up—but maybe the Persian did believe that, had done what he thought he had too. Or maybe he had only meant to spare Erik from the capture that he knew would be worse than death.

Or maybe it was somehow a trick, one they had planned together. I wanted to believe that last possibility so much that I didn't trust my own opinion about how true it could be.

Mifroid, meanwhile, seemed to have control of himself again. "Hold him for further questioning," he directed his two men, "and we should all return to the surface." His voice was again the formal, restrained voice of a man who was doing a job, who was far above the dramatics of opera people. Somehow that, more than anything, made me feel that all this, whatever this was, was done. "We'll need to have the lake dragged for the body."

The body. Not Erik anymore, not even the Phantom. *The body.* But maybe, maybe they were wrong.

I hadn't been paying much attention to the people around me, had stopped thinking about the ballet girls much earlier, only thought of them now when Francesca reappeared at my side. She piped up with, "Do you think the Phantom has dead bodies hidden in his room? Do you think we should go find out?"

"I haven't the slightest idea," I said through barely moving lips, watching the policemen pull the unresisting Persian along, fighting the urge to look back towards the water again. I had to pull myself together, I had to go back to pretending I was part of all this, that I didn't care any more than anyone else what happened to the man who'd gone into the lake and not come out.

My job depended on that. If I still cared about it.

But maybe it was a trick, maybe he wasn't dead, and that meant I couldn't get myself thrown out of the Opera, because then what? I had to be at the Opera Garnier because that's where Erik was. Where he *still* was. I hoped.

I wasn't reacting quickly enough. Francesca was only interested in going to look for skeletons and blood stains and just needed someone to agree and go along with her. But Adalisa was here too, and I realized after a moment that she was looking at me too closely.

"Meg, are you all right?" she asked, moving a little nearer and putting a hand on my shoulder.

"Yes," I said automatically, though it was possible I had never been less all right. "Of course. I just—it was all rather horrible, wasn't it?" Suddenly I desperately wanted her to agree with me. She didn't have to like the Phantom, I didn't expect that, but just to agree that a mob descending on one man, that man being shot in front of us all, was a hideous thing. "So sudden and violent and the way everyone—I mean, it was just really…"

I could see concern in her eyes—and confusion. Not agreement.

I gave up, changed direction. "...and it made me think of Christine, you know? And everything last year, and it's all just—it's so—and I don't know what she—and I just feel—it's all so overwhelming and..."

She pulled me into a hug and said, "Of course, I understand exactly how you feel," which was convenient since I was sure I hadn't made the slightest bit of sense.

"Come *on*," Francesca said, positively bouncing from foot to foot. "Everyone's going back to the Phantom's lair. Let's go see what we can find!"

There wasn't any real point to staying here by the lake. I knew that. So I let myself be swept along by Francesca and Adalisa, back through the tunnel, back to Erik's parlor.

It looked worse now, with the Opera Company scattered throughout, tearing and prodding and digging into everything. They had just watched the Phantom die, and they weren't afraid anymore. Every piece of furniture that could be knocked over had been, several people were involved in rolling up the rugs to carry them away, and the managers were hunting through papers, tossing stray pieces aside as they went.

I was surprised Mifroid didn't stop them. Wouldn't he want to do a proper investigation? But though he had come into the parlor too, he was still staring back towards the secret door, towards where Erik had—possibly died. He didn't seem to be noticing the chaos around him.

As horrible as the chaos was, that was easier to pay attention to than to remember what had just happened. Or just appeared to happen. I looked for familiar faces in the madness.

Ricard was back to trailing a step or two behind Moncharmin. "Do you really think he'd leave money sitting around?"

"It has to be somewhere," Moncharmin snapped. "20,000 francs a month doesn't disappear. What could he have spent it all on?"

Automatically, involuntarily, my gaze went to the mantle, to the stone above it hiding the secret drawer with Erik's piles of money. I quickly looked away again, even though no one would attach any significance to where I happened to be looking.

My glance landed on the papers scattered around—maybe from Moncharmin and Ricard's search, though many were probably there to begin with. Erik never put his musical scores away once he got them out. I automatically reached down, picked up the nearest crumpled paper and began smoothing it out. Lines of music, of course, and without thinking I turned it right side up to see if I recognized it.

"Did you find something interesting?" Adalisa asked, near enough that I jumped.

"Uh, no, not really," I said hastily. "Although—I guess he really is a musician." Or should I have said *was* a musician? No. I couldn't say that.

Luckily Adalisa was intent on looking at the paper, not questioning my grammar. "I suppose so." She half-hummed the first line. "Does it sound familiar?"

Suddenly I thought of the danger of anyone connecting Erik Rouen's music with the musical scores in the Phantom's room. That would be the end of Erik's just begun music career, the end of anyone hearing that magical music. But that wouldn't happen, they had hardly any of Erik's music really… I crumpled the sheet anyway, managing not to wince as I did. "Oh, he probably writes terribly dark music in minor key. You know."

I tossed the crumpled paper aside. He should have organized all this *months* ago. Now the Opera Company was tearing through it—already I could see sheets crumpled and torn and stepped on all over the room. So much gorgeous music destroyed. It made my heart hurt.

But it wasn't *lost*. He had it all memorized. It could all still be there, in his head.

"You must be pleased, Meg," a new voice purred. Jammes. How had I missed her in the crowd earlier? But it had been dark, the bobbing torchlight making even familiar faces strange. "I should think you would be, as Christine's friend." She was staring at me, and her eyes were hard in the torchlight. "Or are you not pleased after all." Somehow, it wasn't a question, sounding closer to an accusation.

I felt as though I was playing a part and had lost the script. What was I meant to say? Did she suspect—but she couldn't. And if she did, how did I allay it? What was the response I was meant to give? "I'm—glad that there's finally been justice," I said at last. "For Christine. For whatever may have happened."

"Really," Jammes said, and this time the skepticism was obvious. "Or aren't you a bit sad, for your Phantom?"

"He's not my Phantom," I snapped, instantly, automatically, because he wasn't, he never had been, never would be, no matter what happened. Only after I'd spoken did I think to question her words. It wouldn't be the first time Jammes had spoken to me about my Phantom, but this felt different. It felt…confident. Even triumphant. But what did she have to take as a triumph?

How had the Opera Company found their way here? Ruling out the Persian, I was the only one with directions. If someone had found them—if someone had suspected I might know something about the Phantom and had gone searching—if Jammes had snooped the way I knew she did—

No. That couldn't be it. They must have learned a route some other way. It *couldn't* have been my directions, never mind that they came by my route, avoided every trap, even used the secret staircase. It *must* have been something else, because if it was my directions, this was too much my fault, and if Erik was really—but he couldn't be. He had told me he would handle this. So he wasn't. And they must not have. And Jammes must not have either. And it wasn't—it all wasn't—

My head was beginning to pound and for the first time I could feel all that earth and stone above my head and the room felt dark and close and crowded and I needed air and sunlight and—

"Enough of this," Mifroid's voice suddenly snapped out, as though he had woken up just as I was losing my focus. "There must be a proper investigation of these rooms—everyone out, now!"

They wouldn't leave quickly, and he didn't have enough men to enforce that order. But it gave me the excuse I needed, to step away from Jammes, to make for the door. To *leave* this horrible nightmare.

Chapter Thirty-Five

I walked back through the tunnels with all the rest, back to the light up above. We came out through the prop room, through the same hidden door I had always used. I tried not to think about that, what that meant. We were back into the air, still belowground in the prop room but this was a comparatively normal landscape. And I still felt trapped in the same nightmare.

"Do you suppose Madame Thibault is holding ballet practice?" Adalisa asked, as we ascended the last stair up to ground level, to the sunlight of the upper portions of the Opera. It seemed strange that it was still day, after the twilight darkness below.

Ballet practice had never even entered my mind. "I don't know. Maybe." It would be like her. Mobs, murders, revolutions, it didn't matter; ballet practice would go on.

"We should go see," Francesca said quickly. "Maybe we haven't missed all of it."

I was sure that had nothing to do with dedication to her craft and *everything* to do with the opportunity to crow over the story with all the girls who hadn't managed to come along.

I could not think of anything I less wanted to do right now. "I'm not—feeling very well," I said, because it was true and I couldn't come up with a better excuse. "I think I'd—better go rest."

Adalisa gave me a sympathetic smile, a sympathetic squeeze of my shoulder, and then she was running off with Francesca. I had only the vaguest idea what exactly Adalisa thought I was distraught over—

something about Christine, probably—but it hardly mattered, as long as she didn't guess the truth.

I had something else I had to do, something I desperately didn't want to do but knew I needed to. I had to go see if my directions were still in my drawer. If they weren't there, if it was clear someone had been into my belongings...

I took a deep breath, and walked through the halls of the Opera to the ballet's changing room. With practice going on, it was a rare time when the room was empty, making it a rare opportunity. I went straight over to my table.

Quickly, before I could lose my resolution, I unlocked the drawer and pulled it open, to look for the folded sheet of directions I had hidden away in the very back.

I didn't see them.

My heart beat harder.

With increasing desperation, I sorted through the old playbills, cheap jewelry and handkerchiefs that filled the drawer. I needed the directions to be here, I *needed* to know that they weren't somewhere else.

But they weren't here. They weren't where they belonged, and the mob had used my route to find Erik, and Jammes had looked at me with too much knowledge, too much *smugness* on her face.

Jammes had stolen my directions and given them to Mifroid or the managers or Carlotta, and the mob had found Erik and now he was—not dead. He couldn't be dead. I wouldn't believe he was dead, because that was simply too horrible to face.

I couldn't face the Opera Company right now either, and yet I also couldn't imagine just walking out the door, going on with my day and my life in the world outside the Opera.

So there was really only one place I could go. The roof, of course. I climbed up all ten flights of stairs and came out onto the rooftop in the sunshine, the extreme opposite end from the dark cavern far, far below. I sat down near the edge, looked out over the vista, played with my small gold necklace and tried to just breathe.

When I heard footsteps behind me, I knew it wasn't him. He always walked silently. But my breath caught anyway and my fingers tightened where they curled in my lap.

"I thought you might be up here."

I exhaled. "Hello, Mother," I said without turning around.

She sat down next to me, back to the view I hadn't been seeing anyway, and looked into my face with a worried crease on her forehead. "The stories around the Opera are saying—"

"I don't want to talk about it. Because he's fine."

The crease deepened. "I know rumors exaggerate, but according to the reports—"

"Yes, of course, because that's what he *wants* them to think." It seemed very important that Mother understand this, that she agree that it all made sense and everything was all right. "You see, I went to warn him, so he was prepared."

"You went to—"

"And he promised me, he said he was going to handle it. And he did."

"By getting shot and drowning."

"No, by *pretending* that was what happened!"

She stared at me for a moment, blinked, and her voice was too calm when she spoke again. "So he told you he was going to fake his own death? That he had a plan with the Persian?"

"Well—no. But they know each other, they could have planned something—and it's so like him, it's exactly what he'd do!"

Mother reached out to clasp my hand. "Meg…"

"You don't *know*!" I protested, fingers clamping tight around hers. "You weren't there and you don't know him and—and—" I exhaled in a gasp. "And I swear if he let himself die like that, I'm going to kill him!"

Mother, bless her for it, did not point out the wild illogic of that, or comment on the tears on my face. She just put her arms around me and neither of us said anything.

For the rest of the day I refused to talk about the Phantom with Mother, and when I had to come back that evening for a performance (and a scolding from Madame Thibault for missing practice which had, of course, gone on), I told everyone I had a headache and mostly they didn't try to talk to me. Though I still had to listen to them talk to each other.

I did not sleep well that night, and I really did have a headache when I came in the next morning. I dragged my way into the ballet's changing room and over to my dressing table.

A dozen daffodils were lying on the table.

I sank down onto my seat, staring at the golden blossoms against the white painted surface. My favorite flowers, left for me. Left overnight at the Opera.

"Ooh, is that from Léon?" Adalisa asked, leaning over my shoulder and reaching for the flowers.

Automatically I put my hand out, covered the stems and held the bouquet in place. "There isn't a note. So maybe," I said, and knew she'd take it as a yes.

It *could* be from Léon. I'd probably mentioned liking daffodils to him some time, and he could have arranged its delivery easily enough. But it wasn't his style. Léon was given to extravagance more than to elegance. He wouldn't have this neat, ribboned cluster delivered, he would have covered the table with flowers to make a statement.

Erik, on the other hand, had given Christine a single, perfect orchid.

Not that this was exactly the same as that, and not that I thought this had any of the same significance, of course. But simply as an indication of style, surely this was more like Erik than Léon.

"I didn't think daffodils were even in season anymore," Adalisa remarked.

"They're not," I said, and couldn't stop the smile tugging at the corners of my mouth. "It must be magic."

Excerpt from the Private Notebook of Jean Mifroid, Commissaire of Police

30 Apr, 1882

So it is finished at last. The Phantom of the Opera is dead. The man I know murdered Phillipe de Chagny is dead.

And yet something feels. . .wrong. It did not happen the way I intended. I wanted to capture him. I wanted answers. I wanted to know who he was, why he did all this. I wanted remorse, regret, justice. Failing that, I wanted to end him myself.

Even at the last, he still mocked me.

Would it have been different with the right support? The Opera Company mob turned the whole business into a farce, unprofessional, absurd. I had none of the support I needed, could not prevent the Opera Company's involvement. Still I had no control.

Why can I not <u>feel</u> that this is over? Why is there no satisfaction in his death?

For the next two days, the favorite subject at the Opera was the Phantom's death. There was nothing new to tell, which didn't stop the story from growing and distorting and expanding. I was glad I had been there; I could spot the obvious fabrications as the story kept being retold.

The other favorite subject was a rumor that the management was making plans for another special performance—and since the rumor included the detail that Moncharmin only felt comfortable holding one because the Phantom was dead, that was really still part of the same subject.

The only person who could have told me more, the Persian, had vanished as completely as Erik had. I didn't know if Mifroid had arrested him, or given him a medal for saving us all from the Phantom's deadly explosions. I didn't know if the Persian had really shot him, or if it had all been a clever trick. And I didn't know how to find him, to learn any of that.

At the Opera, no one seemed quite sure whether to hail the Persian as a hero who had killed the Phantom, or to decide that this was proof of his own villainy after all. But mostly people liked discussing the details of how the Phantom had died, endlessly adding embellishments. Everything new was clearly false. At least, until Monday, when I was sitting on the marble steps with some of the girls after the morning's ballet practice, talking idly about what we might do that afternoon.

Nanette, a girl from the chorus I only knew slightly, came rushing over from the direction of the Grand Foyer and dropped onto the lowest step. "Have you *heard*?" she asked, eyes bright with excitement.

"No, what is it?" Isabelle demanded, as all around me girls leaned in towards the newsbringer—and all right, maybe I did too.

Nanette beamed, pleased by her news or by her status as the first one to get it told. The smile was hideously jarring beside the message she announced. "They found the Phantom's drowned body!"

A collective "Oh!" went up and I felt chilled to my core.

It wasn't true. Of course it wasn't true. I tightened my fingers on the edge of the step beneath me, trying not to sway where I sat. It wasn't *true*.

Nanette was chattering on, I wasn't taking in a word of it, and I spoke right over her to ask, "Who says they found the Phantom's body? Where did you hear it?"

She blinked at me. Maybe she had just said that. I didn't care. She shrugged. "Oh, it's all over the Opera. Everyone's saying it."

My next breath came a little easier. If 'everyone' said it that didn't mean much, that was just another rumor gone wild...

She scrunched her nose and said, "I think the word came from the managers first. Mifroid found the body in the Seine, like the comte's, and reported to them about it."

She kept talking, and my head was spinning worse again. The managers, Mifroid, that was worse than 'everyone,' that was people who might actually know—but they didn't, they couldn't—there had been the daffodils, and he *said* he would *handle it…*

I clutched at my necklace, got unsteadily to my feet, only realizing I'd have to explain what I was doing when heads turned to stare at me. "I—don't feel very well," I said, and probably looked white enough to make it a very plausible lie. It barely was a lie. "It's all—drowned bodies and—I think I'll just…" I managed to thread my way through most of the group seated around me, out off the stairs.

Adalisa started to rise too. "You do look ill; maybe I should come with—"

"No!" I put out a hand, as though to physically ward her off. She meant well, but she *couldn't* come, not now. "Thank you, but I—I just need to go—sit. Alone."

I had no idea if I was making any sense, if they believed me or were suspicious, but I couldn't make myself care and I couldn't wait around to find out. I had to get to the prop room, to the secret door.

I had to see him.

It had made sense that I hadn't seen him—I couldn't be seen going through the secret door, he couldn't be seen up here, it was all right, it was logical and sensible and now I didn't care anymore about all of that. Now the police thought they had the Phantom's body, Erik's body, and it wasn't enough to tell myself he had employed a clever trick, to hope or even to believe that he was fine. I had to *know*.

I had just presence of mind enough to make sure no one saw me slipping through the door in the prop room. In the cool darkness beyond, the light and the noise and the chattering, happy, uncaring people closed away behind me, I got just a little more sense back. Just enough to stop, and press my forehead against the cold stone, and breathe deeply until—well, not until my nerves stopped jangling or my heart stopped hammering or my hands stopped shaking, but until I felt like my galloping fear was slowed enough, contained enough, that I wouldn't get lost down here in the twists and turns and secret spaces. And then I shoved away from the wall and headed down below the Opera.

I didn't stop again until I was in the last passage, until the light of my lantern showed the gargoyles and Erik's door. Someone had knocked the right-hand gargoyle over. He was lying face down, wings pointing up towards the ceiling. I stared at him, walked over, wrapped my fingers around the curve of one wing and gave a tug. The heavy stone barely rocked. But just because *I* couldn't move the gargoyle, that didn't mean he…

I blocked that thought before it could finish, hurried forward to the door—still hanging off one hinge—and pushed through it.

Nothing my lantern showed had changed. Crumpled papers still scattered everywhere. The furniture tipped over, just as far askew as the gargoyle. No paintings back on the walls. Still blank stone instead of books, instead of the side door.

No sign that anyone had been here. No sign of life.

"Erik?" The name came out as barely a whisper. I coughed, as though that would help the tightness in my throat, wrapped my fingers around my necklace so that the gold disk dug into my skin. "Erik!" A little louder that time. "*Erik!*" Please, please, answer, please be here, please be all right, please don't be dead.

Please, God, don't let him be dead.

The saga continues in

𝒟𝒶𝓌𝓃 𝒜𝑒𝓁𝑜𝒹𝓎

The Guardian of the Opera, Book Three

Also by the Author

The Wanderers
A wandering adventurer, a witch's daughter, and a talking cat – what could go wrong? With damsels to rescue, monsters to fight and Good Fairies to avoid at all costs, you'll recognize elements of a number of fairy tales as Jasper, Julie and Tom set off down the road.

The Storyteller and Her Sisters
A retelling of the Brothers Grimm story, "The Shoes That Were Danced to Pieces," the twelve princesses tell their own story here–about defying their father, who hopes to marry them off to successful champions or behead the ones who fail, in order to rescue twelve cursed princes.

The People the Fairies Forget
Let Tarragon, an unusual fairy, lead you through some familiar fairy tales–and introduce you to some characters you may not have noticed. Like the servants who fall asleep in the castle when Sleeping Beauty pricks her finger, or the young woman who fits into Cinderella's slipper but doesn't want to marry the prince.

The Lioness and the Spellspinners
A brooding heroine with a dark past finds herself trapped on an island where she finds the locals suspiciously friendly–and their talk of magical knitting doesn't reassure her.

Find out more on Cheryl's blog, Tales of the Marvelous.
http://marveloustales.com/NovelNews

Acknowledgements

My love affair with this story began when I was eighteen years old –
thank you, Cate and Panda, for introducing me to the madman in a
mask. And thank you, Meaghan, who has been waiting ever since then
for this book to finally be published.

Thank you to all the people who let me wax on about the Phantom and
this story over the…six? seven? years I've been writing this trilogy—if
you remember any conversations like that, I mean you! Thank you to
the Stonehenge Writing Group for all the scenes you read and the
encouragement you gave that, yes, even for some of you who had never
met the Phantom, you liked this story and this character. Erik and I are
grateful—Meg too, but she'd be less surprised.

Thank you especially to Karen, Ruth, Kelly, Jackie, Dennis, and
Meaghan, for your beta-reading and invaluable feedback.

I am indebted, of course, to Gaston Leroux, who began it all, and to
Andrew Lloyd Webber and Susan Kay, who carried it forward so
beautifully. I am grateful to all the men who have portrayed this
complicated character in so many ways: first and particularly, Michael
Crawford, who will always be the voice of my Phantom; Lon Chaney,
Claude Rains, David Staller, Charles Dance, Earl Carpenter, and too
many more Webber Phantoms to name. I am grateful too to Terry
Pratchett, whose *Maskerade* is the funniest book I have ever read, and
whose Christine is surprisingly closer to mine than any other I've seen.

And thank you to Charlies Garnier, for all the inspiration of your
gorgeous opera house, and apologies for making you share the credit
with a masked Phantom. Erik and I both recognize your genius.

About the Author

Cheryl Mahoney lives in California and dreams of other worlds. She has been blogging since 2010 at Tales of the Marvelous (http://marveloustales.com). Her weekly Writing Wednesday posts provide updates about her current writing, including excerpts and updates on books that are coming soon. She also posts regularly with book and movie reviews, and reflections on reading. She has been a member of Stonehenge Writers since 2012, and has completed NaNoWriMo seven times.

Cheryl has looked for faeries in Kensington Gardens in London and for the Phantom at the Opera Garnier in Paris. She considers Tamora Pierce's Song of the Lioness Quartet to be life-changing and Terry Pratchett books to be the best cure for gloomy days.

A Note on Research

This trilogy has been the undertaking of many years, and has involved extensive research into the Phantom of the Opera, classical music, ballet, the Opera Garnier, and France of the late 1800s, as well as two trips to the Opera Garnier itself. For those wanting to seek out more information for themselves, here are some of the sources that were most useful in this adventure.

Burrows, John, editor. *The Complete Classical Music Guide*

Fenby, Jonathan. *France: A Modern History from the Revolution to the War with Terror*

Gill, Miranda. *Eccentricity and the Cultural Imagination in 19th-Century Paris*

Guest, Ivor Forbes. *The Paris Opera Ballet*

Hall, Ann C. *The Adaptations of Gaston Leroux's* Phantom of the Opera, *1925 to the Present*

Hart, Charles, Richard Stilgoe and Andrew Lloyd Webber. *The Phantom of the Opera.* Really Useful Group, 1986.

Kay, Susan. *Phantom*

Leroux, Gaston. *The Phantom of the Opera.* Leonard Wolf, Editor

Lofts, Norah and Margery Weiner. *Eternal France*

Meyer, Carolyn. *Marie, Dancing*

Meyer, Nicholas. *The Canary Trainer*

Moatti, Jacques. *The Paris Opera, photos*

Perry, George. *The Complete Phantom of the Opera*

The Phantom of the Opera. Directed by Rupert Julian. Performance by Lon Chaney. Universal Studios, 1925.

Phantom of the Opera. Directed by Arthur Lubin. Performance by Claude Rains. Universal Studios, 1943.

The Phantom of the Opera. Directed by Tony Richardson. Performance
by Charles Dance. Hexatel, 1990.

The Phantom of the Opera. Directed by Darwin Knight. Performance
by David Staller. Hirschfield Films, 1991.

Siciliano, Sam. *The Angel of the Opera*

Schlor, Joachim. *Nights in the Big City: Paris, Berlin, London, 1840-
1930*